KT-365-540

TRISHA ASHLEY

Twelve Days of Christmas

AVON

AVON

A division of HarperCollins*Publishers*
77–85 Fulham Palace Road,
London W6 8JB

www.harpercollins.co.uk

A Paperback Original 2010

5

First published in Great Britain by
HarperCollins*Publishers* 2010

Copyright © Trisha Ashley 2010

Trisha Ashley asserts the moral right to
be identified as the author of this work

A catalogue record for this book is
available from the British Library

ISBN-13: 978-1-84756-115-2

Set in Minion by Palimpsest Book Production Limited,
Falkirk, Stirlingshire

Printed and bound in Great Britain by
Clays Ltd, St Ives plc

Mixed Sources
Product group from well-managed
forests and other controlled sources
www.fsc.org   Cert no. SW-COC-001806
© 1996 Forest Stewardship Council

FSC is a non-profit international organisation established to promote the
responsible management of the world's forests. Products carrying the FSC
label are independently certified to assure consumers that they come
from forests that are managed to meet the social, economic and
ecological needs of present and future generations.
Find out more about HarperCollins and the environment at
www.harpercollins.co.uk/green

TWELVE DAYS OF CHRISTMAS

Trisha Ashley was born in St Helens, Lancashire, and gave up her fascinating but time-consuming hobbies of house-moving and divorce a few years ago in order to settle in North Wales.

For more information about Trisha please visit www.trishaashley.com

By the same author:

Sowing Secrets
A Winter's Tale
Wedding Tiers
Chocolate Wishes

Acknowledgements

I would like to thank Pauline Sheridan for both her expert advice on Arab horses and the excellent recipe for warm horse mash; and also Carol Weatherill for a little light goat husbandry, especially the toast and treacle!

For my good friends and fellow 500 Club members, Leah Fleming and Elizabeth Gill, with love.

Prologue: The Ghost of Christmas Past

Even though it was barely December, the hospital ward had been decked out with a tiny tree and moulded plastic wall decorations depicting a fat Santa, with bunchy bright scarlet cheeks and dark, almond-shaped eyes. He was offering what looked like a stick of dynamite to Rudolf the very red-nosed reindeer, but I expect you need explosive power to deliver all those presents in one single night.

My defence strategy for the last few years has been to ignore Christmas, shutting the door on memories too painful to deal with; but now, sitting day after day by the bed in which Gran dwindled like snow in summer, there seemed to be no escape.

Gran, who brought me up, would not have approved of all these festive trappings. Not only was she born a Strange Baptist, but had also married a minister in that particularly austere (and now almost extinct) offshoot of the faith. They didn't do Christmas in the way everyone else did – with gifts, gluttony and excess, so as a child, I was always secretly envious of my schoolfriends.

But then I got married and went overboard on the whole idea. Alan egged me on – he never lost touch with his inner child, which is probably why he was such a brilliant primary school teacher. Anyway, he loved the whole thing, excess, gluttony and all.

So I baked and iced spiced gingerbread stars to hang on the

tree, which was always the biggest one we could drag home from the garden centre, together with gay red and white striped candy canes, tiny foil crackers and twinkling fairy lights. Together we constructed miles of paper chains to festoon the ceilings, hung mistletoe (though we never needed an excuse to kiss) and made each other stockings full of odd surprises.

After the first year we decided to forgo a full traditional turkey dinner with all the trimmings in favour of roast duck with home-made bottled Morello cherry sauce, which was to become my signature dish. (I was sous-chef in a local restaurant at the time.) We made our own traditions, blending the old with the new, as I suppose most families do . . .

And we were so *nearly* a family: about to move to a tiny hamlet just outside Merchester, a perfect country setting for the two children (or maybe three, if Alan got his way) that would arrive at neatly-spaced intervals . . .

At this juncture in my thoughts, a trolley rattled sharply somewhere behind the flowered curtains that enclosed the bed, jerking me back to the here and now: I could even hear a faint, tinny rendering of 'The Twelve Days of Christmas' seeming to seep like a seasonal miasma from the walls.

Perhaps Gran could too, for suddenly her clear, light grey eyes, so like my own, opened wide with an expression of delighted surprise that had nothing to do with either my presence or the home-made pot custard I'd brought to tempt her appetite, the nutmeg-sprinkled top browned just the way she liked it.

'*Ned? Ned Martland?*' she whispered, staring at someone only she could see.

I'd never seen her look so lit-up and alive as she did at that moment, which was ironic considering those were her last words – and the words themselves were a bit of a puzzle, since my grandfather's name had been Joseph Bowman!

So who the hell was Ned Martland? If it *had* been Martland, of course, and not Cartland, Hartland, or something similar. But no, I was pretty sure it was Martland – and he'd obviously meant a lot to her at some time. This was fairly amazing: had my grave and deeply reserved grandmother, who had been not so much buttoned up as zipped tightly shut and with a padlock thrust through the fastener for good measure, been keeping a romantic secret all these years? Had she lived her life without the man she truly loved by her side, just as I was living mine?

Perhaps there's a family curse, which would account for why, after Alan's death, she kept going on about the sins of the fathers being visited on the next generations – though actually, as I pointed out to her, that would have meant me rather than my husband. But if there *is* a family curse it looks set to end with me, because I'm the end of the line, the wrong side of thirty-five, and with my fruit in imminent danger of withering on the vine.

I've had too much time to think about that lately, too.

I've no idea what Alan's last words were, if any, because I was still asleep when he went for his early morning jog round the local park before work. When I woke up and went downstairs there was no sign of him and it was all worryingly Marie Celeste. The radio was spilling out some inane Christmas pop song to the empty kitchen and his bag, with its burden of marked exercise books, was on the floor by the door. A used mug and plate and a Tupperware box of sandwiches lay on the table and the kettle was barely warm.

As I stood there, puzzled and feeling the first stirring of unease, the police arrived to break the news that there had been an accident and Alan would never be coming home.

'Don't be silly,' I heard my voice telling them crisply, 'I'm doing duck with some of my bottled Morello cherry sauce for Christmas dinner – it's his favourite.'

Then, for the first and only time in my life, I fainted.

* * *

Alan had been trying to rescue a dog that had fallen through the ice on the boating lake. How stupid was that? I mean, if a *dog* fell through, then even a slightly built man like Alan would, too. The dog was evidently *not* a retriever, for it swam through the broken ice created by Alan's fall, scrambled out and ran off.

I was so furious with Alan that at the funeral I positively *hurled* the single red rose someone had handed me into the grave, screaming, '*What were you thinking of, dimwit?*'

And then I slipped on the snowy brink and nearly followed it in, though that was entirely due to the large shot of brandy my friend Laura, who was also Alan's sister, insisted we both drink before we set out. Luckily her husband, Dan, was on my other side and yanked me back at the last minute and then Gran walked around the grave from where she had been standing among a small cluster of elderly Strange Baptist friends and took a firm grip of my other arm, like a wardress.

But by then I was a spent force: grief, fury and guilt (the guilt because I had refused to take up jogging with him) seemed to blend so seamlessly that I didn't know where one ended and another began.

He'd left me on my own, closing the door on the future we had all planned out. How *could* he? I always thought we were yin and yang, two halves of the same person, soulmates destined to stay together forever throughout eternity – if so, I'd have a few choice things to say when I finally caught up with him.

My coping strategy had been to close the door on Alan in return, only allowing my grief full rein on the anniversary of his death in late December and shutting myself away from all reminders of the joyous seasonal festivities he had taught me to love during the all-too-brief years of our marriage.

There's even less reason to celebrate Christmas now . . .

Christmas? Bah, humbug!

Chapter 1: Pregnant Pause

Since Gran had been slipping quietly away from me for years, her death wasn't that much of a shock, to be honest. That was just as well, because I had to dash straight off to one of my house-sitting jobs right after her austere Strange Baptist funeral, though finding her journals in the small tin trunk in which she kept her treasures just before I left was a *very* poignant moment . . .

When I'd locked up her little sliver of a terraced house in Merchester (not that there was anything in it worth stealing) I'd taken the trunk home with me: the key was on her keyring with the rest. I already had some idea of what was in it from glimpses caught over the years – postcards of Blackpool, where my grandparents spent their Wakes Week holiday every year, my annual school photographs, certificates and that kind of thing – layers going back in time.

I'd only opened it meaning to add her narrow gold wedding band, but then had lifted up a few of the layers to see what was underneath – and right at the bottom was a thin bundle of small, cheap, school exercise books marked 'Esther Rowan', bound together with withered elastic bands. Opening the first, I found a kind of spasmodic journal about her nursing experiences starting towards the end of the war, since the first entry was dated October 1944, though it began by looking back at earlier experiences:

*I'd started working as a nursing auxiliary at fifteen, which
meant that when war broke out at least I wasn't sent to do
hard, dirty work in the munitions factory, like many
Merchester girls.*

I thought how young they started work back then – and, reading
the following entry, how stoical she was:

*Tom, my childhood sweetheart, enlisted in the navy straight
away, though I begged him to wait until he was called up.
Sure enough, he was killed almost immediately, to the great
grief of myself and his poor, widowed father. After this, I
resolved to put all girlish thoughts of love and marriage
behind me and threw myself into my nursing duties . . .*

That last line struck me as being much like the way I'd moved
house and thrown myself into a new job right after Alan died:
only somehow in my case it didn't seem stoical, more a denial
of those wonderful years we had together.

I knew Gran had eventually gone on to marry the father of
her childhood sweetheart – she had said to me once that they
had felt they could be a comfort and support to one another
– so where this Ned Martland came in was anyone's guess! I was
starting to think I must have imagined the whole thing . . .

Gran seemed to have filled the ensuing pages with a moralising
mini-sermon on the evils of war, so I put the journals back in
the trunk again, to read on my return.

I spent a week in Devon, looking after a cottage for one of my
regular clients, along with two budgerigars called Marilyn and
Monroe, Yoda the Yorkshire terrier and six nameless hens.

It was very soothing and allowed me the space to get a lot of
things straight in my mind – and also to make one large and
potentially life-changing decision – before coming back home

braced and ready to sort out Gran's house, which belonged to a church charity. They were pressing me to clear it out and hand back the keys, so I expect they had a huge waiting list of homeless and desperate clergy widows.

I had a week before my next Homebodies assignment, which I was sure would be more than adequate. And I was quite right, because I'd almost finished and was starting to look forward to escaping to the remote Highland house-sit which would safely take me over Christmas and into New Year, when it was suddenly cancelled.

Ellen, the old schoolfriend (or so she calls herself – Laura and I remember things a little differently) who runs the Homebodies agency, tried to persuade me to cook for a Christmas house-party instead, but she did it with little hope.

'I don't know why she even bothered asking,' I said to Laura, who had popped in to help me sort out the last of Gran's belongings. Well, I say *help*, but since she was heavily pregnant with her fourth baby she was mostly making tea and talking a ┊ She's blonde, pretty and petite (my exact opposite), and carri┊ the baby in a small, neat bump under a long, clingy tunic to the same shade of blue as her eyes.

'She asked because you're a brilliant cook and it pays so much better than the house-sitting,' she replied, putting two fresh mugs of tea down on the coffee table. 'Plus, she has all the tact of a bulldozer.'

'But she knows I need a rest from the cooking in winter and I don't do Christmas. I like to get away somewhere remote where no-one knows me and pretend it isn't happening.'

Laura sank down next to me on Gran's hideously uncomfortable cottage sofa. 'She probably hoped you'd got over it a bit and changed your mind – you've been widowed as long as you were married, now. We all still miss Alan dreadfully, especially at this time of year,' she added gently. 'He was the best brother anyone could ever have. But he wouldn't want us to grieve forever, Holly.'

'I know, and you can't say I haven't picked up the pieces and got on with my life,' I said, though I didn't add that even after eight years the grief was still mixed fairly equally with anger. 'But Christmas and the anniversary of the accident always bring things back and I'd much rather spend it quietly on my own.'

'I expect Ellen's forgotten that you weren't brought up to celebrate Christmas in the same way as everyone else, too.'

Laura and I go way back to infant school, so she understands my slightly strange upbringing, but Ellen only came on the scene later, at the comprehensive (and though she denies it now, she tagged on to the group of girls who bullied me because of my height).

'No, the Strange Baptists think the trappings of the season are all pagan manifestations of man's fall from spiritual grace – though Gran could play a mean Christmas hymn on the harmonium.'

aura looked at the space opposite, where the instrument stood against the magnolia blown-vinyl wallpaper. now how you managed to fit that harmonium into cottage, I bet it weighed a ton even though it wasn't

id, but I was determined to have it because it was Gran's and joy – the only time she seemed happy was when she playing it. It *just* fitted into the space under the stairs.'

I hadn't kept a lot, otherwise: the pink satin eiderdown that had covered my narrow bed as a child and two austere cross-stitch samplers sewn by my great-grandmother. One said, 'Strange are the ways of the Lord' and the other, 'That He may do His work, His strange work'. That was about it.

What was left was a motley collection of cheap utility furniture, battered enamel and aluminium saucepans and the like, which were being collected by a house clearance firm.

The house had been immaculate, apart from a little dust, and Gran had never been a hoarder, so there hadn't been that much to sort out. Her clothes had already been packed and collected by a local charity and all that was left now to put in my car was a cardboard box of neatly filed household papers.

'I think I'm just about finished here,' I said, taking a biscuit from the packet Laura had brought, though Garibaldi are not actually my favourite – a bit too crushed-fly looking. 'So, are you going to call this baby Garibaldi, then?'

Now, this was not such a daft question as you might suppose, since during her last pregnancy Laura had been addicted to Mars bars and she had called her baby boy Mars. He should thank his lucky stars it hadn't been Twix or Flake.

She giggled. 'No way! But if it's a girl we might call it Holly after you, even though it will be a very early spring, rather than a Christmas, baby.'

I hated my name (my late mother's choice), but I was quite touched. 'I suppose it *would* be better than Garibaldi,' I conceded, 'especially for a girl.'

I took a sip of the pale, fragrant tea, which was the Earl Grey that Laura had brought with her, rather than the Yorkshire tea that Gran had always made strong enough to stand a spoon in. 'The van will be here any minute, so we've just got the box of papers to stick in my car and we're done. The meter reader came while you were in the kitchen, so I expect the electricity will be turned off any minute now, too.'

As if on cue, the dim bulb in its mottled glass shade went out and left us in the gathering shadows of a December afternoon.

'"*Lead kindly light, amid the encircling gloom*,"' I sang sepulchrally.

'You know a hymn for every occasion.'

'So would you, if you'd been brought up by a Strange Baptist.'

'Still, it's just as well you'd finished sorting out,' Laura said. 'She wasn't a great hoarder, your gran, was she?'

'No, apart from the few mementoes in that tin trunk I took home – and I've been reading a bit more in that sort of diary I told you I'd found. Some of it is fascinating, but you have to wade through lots of Victorian-sounding moralising in between.'

'You could skip those bits?' she suggested.

'I thought about it, then decided I wanted to read it all, because I never felt I really knew her and it might give me some insight into what made her tick.'

'She was certainly very reserved and austere,' Laura agreed, looking round the sparsely furnished room, '*and* frugal: but that was probably her upbringing.'

'Yes, if ever I wanted to buy her a present, she always said she had everything she needed. She could never resist Yardley's lavender soap, though, but that was about as tempted by the lures of the flesh as she ever got.'

'She was very proud of you, having your own house and career.'

'I suppose she was, though she would have preferred me to train to be a teacher, like you and Alan – she didn't consider cooking much above skivvying. And when I left the restaurant and signed up to Homebodies instead, she thought cooking for large house-parties in the summer and looking after people's properties and pets in the winter was just like going into service.'

'It's worked very well though, hasn't it? You get paid so much for the summer jobs that you can take the poorly paid home-sitting ones in the winter.'

'They're more for a change of scene and a rest, so staying rent free in someone else's house suits me fine: I get to see a different bit of the country and they get their house and pets taken care of, so they can enjoy their hols without any worries.'

'But now your next home-sitting job has fallen through, you could spend Christmas Day with us, couldn't you?' she suggested. 'We're going over to Mum and Dad's for dinner and Mum is always saying she hardly sees you any more.'

'Oh no, I *couldn't*!' I said with more haste than tact.

'It would be better than staying home alone – *and* I've just invited my cousin Sam to stay. His divorce has been finalised and he's at a loose end. You got on so well when you met in the summer and went on that date.'

'Laura, that wasn't a date, we just both wanted to see the same film. And he's at least a foot shorter than me.'

'That's a gross exaggeration – a couple of inches, at most! Anyway, he said he liked a woman who knew her own mind and the way you wore your hair made him think of Nefertiti.'

'Did he?' I said doubtfully. My hair is black, thick and straight and I keep it in a sort of long, smooth bob that curves forwards at the sides like wings. 'I expect he was just being kind. Not many men want to go out with someone taller than themselves.'

'They might if you ever gave them the chance, Holly!'

'There's no point: I met my Mr Right and I don't believe in second-best.' Alan had found me beautiful, too, though I had found it hard to believe him at first after all that school bullying about my height and my very untrendy clothes . . .

'It doesn't have to be second-best – I know you and Alan loved each other, but no-one would blame you, least of all me, if you fell in love with someone else now. Alan would be the last man to want you to mourn him forever.'

'I'm not still mourning, I've moved on. It's just . . .' I paused, trying to sum up how I felt. 'It's just that what we had was so perfect that I know I'm not going to find that again.'

'But *was* it so perfect? Is any marriage ever that?' she asked. 'And have you ever thought that you weren't actually married for long enough for the gilt to wear off the gingerbread?'

I looked at her, startled. 'What do you mean?'

'Well, you *were* very happy, but even the best relationships change over time: their little ways start to irritate you and you have to learn a bit of give and take. Alan wasn't perfect and neither are you: none of us are. Look at me and Dan, for instance. *He* can't understand why I need forty-six pairs of shoes and *I*

11

hate coming second in his life to rugby – but we still love each other.'

'Apart from our work, the only thing Alan and I didn't do together was the running – we shared everything else.'

'But one or both of you might have felt that was a bit claustrophobic eventually. Alan was a dreamer too – and he dreamed of writing. You couldn't do that together.'

'Well, I didn't stop him,' I said defensively. 'In fact, I encouraged him, though the teaching took up a lot of his time and energy. And I was going to write a house-party cookbook, so we *did* share that interest too, in a way.'

'Oh yes – I'd forgotten about the cookbook. You haven't mentioned it for ages.'

'It's nearly finished, just one more section to go.'

That was the one dealing with catering for a Christmas house-party, which I had been putting off.

'I do realise the dynamics of the relationship would have changed when we had children, Laura, but we had it all planned. I wish now we hadn't waited so long, though.'

'There you are, then,' she said triumphantly, 'if you find someone else, it's not too late to start a family – look at me!'

'Funnily enough I was thinking about that in Devon, and I decided that although I don't want another man, I *do* want a baby before it's too late. So I thought I'd try artificial insemination. What do you think?'

She stared at me from startled, long-lashed blue eyes. 'Really? Well, I suppose you *could*,' she conceded reluctantly after a minute. 'But wouldn't you prefer to try the natural way first?'

'No,' I said simply. 'I want the baby to be just mine.'

'How would you manage financially? Have you thought it through?'

'I own the cottage,' I pointed out, because I'd paid off the mortgage on our terraced house with the insurance money after Alan died, then moved out to an even smaller cottage in the countryside between Ormskirk and Merchester. 'And I thought I could finish off the cookery book and maybe start doing party catering from home.'

'I'm not sure you've seen all the pitfalls of going it alone with a small child, but I know what you're like when you've made your mind up,' she said resignedly. Then she brightened and added, 'But I could help you and it would be lovely to be able to see more of you.'

'Yes, that would be great and I'll be counting on you for advice if I get pregnant.'

'I must say, you've really surprised me, though.'

'I surprised myself, but something Gran said right at the end made me realise I ought to go out there and get what I want, before it's too late.'

'You mean when she said some man's name you'd never heard of?'

I nodded. 'It was the way she said it – and she could see him, too. I'd never seen her smile like that, so she must have loved and lost him, whoever he was – and perhaps her journal will tell me that eventually. Her face went all soft, and I could see how beautiful she must have been when she was young.'

'Just like you, with the same black hair and light grey eyes.'

'Laura, you can't say *I'm* beautiful! I mean, apart from being the size of a maypole, I've got a big, beaky nose.'

'You're striking, and your nose isn't beaky, it's only got the tiniest hint of a curve in it,' she said loyally. 'Sam's right, you do look like that bust of Nefertiti you see in photographs . . . though your hair is a bit more Cleopatra.'

I was flattered but unconvinced. Gran's skin had been peaches and cream and mine was heading towards a warm olive so that I look Mediterranean apart from my light eyes. Gran's mother's family came from Liverpool originally, so I daresay I have some foreign sailor in my ancestry to thank for my colouring – and maybe my height, which has been the bane of my existence.

'I quite liked Sam, because at least he didn't talk to my boobs, like a lot of men do,' I conceded and then immediately regretted it, because she said eagerly, 'So you *will* come to us, if only for Christmas dinner? I promise not to push you together, but it would give you a chance to get to know him a bit and—'

My phone emitted a strangled snatch of Mozart and I grabbed it. Saved by the muzak.

Chapter 2: Little Mumming

At my last hospital I was frequently left in sole command of a children's ward in a separate building, night after night. When the air raid sirens went I took all the children down to a dark and damp cellar, where I had to beat hundreds of cockroaches off the cots and beds before they could be used. Finally, earlier this year, weakened by too many night shifts, lack of sleep (for I found it impossible to sleep during the day), too much responsibility and poor food, my health broke down and I was sent home to recover.

October 1944

I hoped the call wasn't the man from Chris's Clearance saying he'd decided against collecting Gran's fairly worthless sticks of furniture and bric-a-brac, but no, it was Ellen from the Homebodies agency.

'Holly, you know I said there was nothing else on the books over Christmas?' she said in her slightly harsh voice, without any preamble. Ellen doesn't do polite, except to the customers. 'Well, now something's come up and I'm going to ask you to do it for me as a *big, big* favour!'

'A favour?' My spirits lifted. 'You mean a *house-sitting* big favour?'

Laura caught my eye and grimaced, shaking her head and mouthing, 'Don't you dare!'

15

'Yes, a major crisis has just blown up,' Ellen explained. 'You remember Mo and Jim Chirk?'

'You've mentioned them several times, but I haven't met them. They're one of your longest-serving and most dependable house-sitting couples, aren't they?'

'They *were*,' she said darkly. 'And they were supposed to be house-sitting up on the East Lancashire moors over Christmas – they'd been two or three times and the owner asked for them again – but no sooner had they got there than their daughter had her baby prematurely and they're flying out to Dubai to be with her.'

'You mean, they've already *gone*?'

'They're on their way home to repack and get their passports, then they're booked onto the first flight out. They phoned me just before they left – and so they should, too, because they've dropped me right in it!'

'It doesn't sound as if they could help it, Ellen – it's just one of those things. I hope the baby is all right.'

'Which baby?'

'Their daughter's baby.'

'I have no idea,' she said dismissively, which wasn't any surprise, since where business is concerned she's totally single-minded.

'Look, could you help me out by taking the job on? It should be two people really, because it's a large manor house in its own grounds, and a bit remote and there are a couple of pets to look after, too. Only there's no-one else free on the books apart from you. Could you possibly go? Tomorrow? I'll make sure you get double pay,' she wheedled.

'If there are pets, who's looking after them at the moment?'

'The owner's elderly aunt and uncle live in the lodge and say they will keep an eye on things until you get there, but I don't think they can really be up to it, or presumably Mr Martland wouldn't have needed Homebodies in the first place.'

16

'*Martland?*' I interrupted.

'Yes, Jude Martland. Have you heard of him? He's quite a well-known sculptor – he did the Iron Horse next to the motorway near Manchester, all welded strips of metal – very modern.'

'Oh yes, I think I have. But actually, I heard that surname recently in another context and it's unusual, that's why I was surprised.'

'Just a coincidence, then – truth is stranger than fiction,' she said, disinterestedly rustling some papers.

'That's true,' I agreed, and of course these Martlands could have no relationship to the Ned Martland Gran had mentioned (assuming I'd even heard the name right): she was a working-class girl and wouldn't have mixed in the same circles as minor gentry from moorland manor houses.

'Anyway, he inherited the pile, which is called Old Place, about a year ago and he's abroad somewhere, but so far we haven't managed to get hold of him to tell him what's happening. He isn't coming back until Twelfth Night.'

I'd turned away from Laura's disappointed face, though I could feel her eyes boring accusingly into my back. I was starting to suspect she'd hastily invited her cousin Sam for Christmas as soon as I'd told her my Christmas job had fallen through – the idea had probably never crossed her mind until then.

'It doesn't sound too arduous,' I said to Ellen. 'I've looked after quite big houses before single-handedly. What are the pets you mentioned?'

'One dog and . . . a horse.'

'*A horse*? You call a horse a *pet*? Ellen, I don't do horses!'

'It's very elderly and you do know a bit about horses, because you went to that riding school with Laura, remember.'

'I only watched her, that hardly qualifies me to look after someone's horse, does it?'

'I expect you picked up more information than you think you

did. Mo said she was very easy to look after and all the instructions were written down.'

'Yes, but—'

'I expect the elderly couple in the lodge can advise you if there's any difficulty. And there's a cleaner and a small village nearby with a shop, so it isn't *totally* isolated. What do you say?'

'Well . . . I suppose I could. But I'm a bit worried about the horse. I—'

'Oh, that's *wonderful*!' she broke in quickly. 'I'm sure the horse won't be a problem, it's probably in a field and you only have to look at it once a day, or something. And the good news is, Mo and Jim felt so awful at landing the job on someone else at such short notice that they left all their supplies for Christmas behind for whoever took it on. Though actually, I suppose they could hardly take a turkey and all the trimmings out to Dubai with them!'

'No, but it was a kind thought. Where exactly *is* this place, did you say?'

'I didn't, but I'll email you directions and all the details now. It's a bit off the beaten track, but you usually *like* that.'

'Yes, especially over Christmas. That aspect of it is perfect.'

'I don't know what you'll do up there, because apparently the TV reception is lousy and there's no broadband.'

'I'll be fine – I'll take my radio and lots of books.'

Clicking off the connection, I turned to find Laura looking at me reproachfully. 'Oh, Holly, it would have been such fun to have you here for Christmas!'

'Believe me, it wouldn't: it would have been like having the Grinch. And I'll enjoy myself in my own way. There are only two animals to look after, so I'll have lots of time to experiment with recipes and write that last section of the book. If I'm going to go ahead with the baby idea, I need to get it finished and find a publisher!'

Laura sighed and cast her eyes up in mock resignation, but she knew me too well to try and persuade me out of it.

'Now, what can you remember about horse management?' I asked hopefully.

I printed out Ellen's instructions as soon as I got home and she was right – it was in a remote, upland spot, near a small village I'd never even heard of.

Getting ready that night was all a bit of a scramble, though I couldn't resist continuing my nightly reading of a page or two of Gran's journal, which was getting more interesting again now she wasn't talking about the past, but engrossed by the present. By November of 1944, she was evidently well enough to go back to work:

> Now I have recovered I have been sent to Ormskirk hospital, which pleases me because it is nearer home and also Tom's widowed father, a sweet, kindly man, is the minister at the Strange Baptist chapel here. But my lodgings are very poor, in a nearby house run by a dour, disagreeable woman. The food is scanty and bad and we sleep dormitory-style, so there is little privacy. The treat of a fresh egg, which was a parting gift from my mother, I gave to my landlady to boil for my breakfast – but it never appeared and my enquiries about it met only with surly grunts.

I read on a little further as she made new friends and settled in, but really I was way too tired to keep my eyes open and there would be lots of time to read the journals over Christmas – in fact, I would take the whole trunk of papers with me to sort out.

Early next morning I loaded the tin trunk into my car along with everything else I usually take with me on assignments – boxes of herbs, spices and other basic ingredients, general food supplies, a cool box of perishable stuff, vital utensils, cookery books, laptop, house-party recipe book notes and my portable

19

radio . . . It was pretty full even before I added a suitcase, holdall and my wellies.

Laura, resigned now to my decision, had driven over to give me my Christmas present (she's the only person who ever gives me one). In return I gave her a bag of little gifts for the family, some of them home-made and edible.

She also gave me strict instructions to call her daily, too. 'Tell me all about it. Old Place sounds terribly posh, somehow, and I've never even heard of the village – what did you call it again?'

'Little Mumming. It's near Great Mumming, apparently. I'd never heard of it either, but I've found it on the map.'

'It's all been such a rush – are you sure you've got everything you need?'

'Yes, I think so – most of it was still packed up ready to go. And I've put in my wellies, jeans, dog-walking anorak . . .'

'A smart dress, in case the local squire's lady leaves calling cards and you have to return the visit?'

'You need to stop reading Jane Austen,' I said severely. 'And I think this Mr Martland might *be* the Little Mumming equivalent of the local squire, in which case, if there is a lady, he will have taken her away with him, won't he?'

'Unless she's upstairs in Bluebeard's chamber?'

'Thank you for sharing that unnerving thought.'

'You're welcome. But the house can't be that big, can it? Otherwise there would be some live-in help.'

'Not necessarily, these days,' I said, drawing on my long experience of house-party cooking, where sometimes the only live-in staff had been myself and the family nanny. 'Ellen mentioned a daily cleaner. It's big enough to have a lodge though, because the owner's elderly uncle and his wife live there and I'm to call in for the keys on my way up to the house.'

'I can see you're dying to go, but I still don't like to think of you marooned in a remote house all on your own over Christmas,' Laura said. 'Have you got your phone and charger, and enough food and drink in case you're miles from the nearest shop? I mean, the weather report said we were in for a cold snap next week and the odds on a white Christmas are shortening.'

'Oh, come on, Laura, when do they ever get the long-term forecasts right? And come to that, how often does it snow here, especially at Christmas?'

'But it's probably different in East Lancashire, up on the moors.'

'It might be a bit bleaker, but I'll believe in this snow when I see it. And Ellen said Jim and Mo have left me all their food, since they won't need it – they were only stopping at home long enough to fling some clothes in a suitcase and get their passports before they flew out to Dubai. I'm hardly likely to eat my way through a whole turkey and all the trimmings over Christmas, even if I do get snowed in.'

I gave her a hug – but cautiously, because of the very prominent bump. 'I'll be fine, you know me. Give my love to your parents and have a great time and I'll see you on Twelfth Night!'

I climbed into the heavily-laden car and drove off, Laura's small figure waving at me in the rear-view mirror until I turned the corner, realising just how fond of my best friend I was.

Now Gran had gone, was there anyone else in the whole world who *really* cared about me? Or who *I* really cared about? I couldn't think of anyone . . . and it suddenly seemed so terribly sad. I'd had other friends, but mostly they'd been Alan's too, and I'd pushed them out of my life after the accident.

But soon, if my plans for a baby came to fruition, I would have someone else to love, who would love me in return . . .

My spirits lifted as I drove further away from home, just as they always did, for the joy of each assignment was that no-one knew me or my past, or was interested enough to find out: I was just brisk, capable Holly Brown from Homebodies, there to do a job: the Mary Poppins of Merchester.

Chapter 3: Weasel Pot

I have made friends with Hilda and Pearl, who have the beds either side of me at the lodging house, and they are showing me the ropes at the new hospital. Like many of the other nurses their chief desire seems to be to marry, preferably to one of the young doctors, and they teased me until I explained that I had lost my sweetheart in the first months of war, so that I now saw nursing as my life's work.

November, 1944

Little Mumming lay in a small valley below one of the beacon hills that run down East Lancashire, where a long chain of fires was once lit as a sort of ancient early warning system.

On the map it hadn't looked far from the motorway, but the poor excuse for a B road endlessly wound up and down, offering me the occasional distant, tantalising glimpse of Snowehill, topped with a squat tower, but never seeming to get any closer.

Finally I arrived at a T-junction that pointed me to Little Mumming and Great Mumming up a precipitous, single-track lane – though rather confusingly, it also pointed to Great Mumming straight ahead, too. All roads must lead to Great Mumming.

I took the sharp left uphill turn, sincerely hoping that I wouldn't meet anything coming in the opposite direction, because although there were occasional passing places, there were also high dry-stone walls on either side, so I wouldn't be able to see them coming round the series of hairpin bends.

I passed a boulder painted with the words 'Weasel Pot Farm' next to a rutted track and shifted down a gear. Was there *ever* going to be any sign of a village?

Then I crossed an old stone humpbacked bridge, turned a last bend past a pair of wrought-iron gates and came to a stop – for ahead of me the road levelled and opened out, revealing Little Mumming in all its wintry glory.

It was a huddled hamlet of grey stone cottages, a pub, and a small church set around an open green on which sheep were wrenching at the grass as if their lives depended on it. Perhaps they did. Winters were presumably a lot bleaker up here.

High above on the hillside a Celtic-looking figure of a horse had been carved out from the dull red earth or sandstone, using just a few flowing lines. It could be an ancient hill marking, or maybe some more recent addition to the landscape.

After a minute I carried on and pulled in by the green, turning off the engine. I needed a moment to unclench my hands from the steering wheel after that ascent.

The village looked as if it had grown organically from the earth, the walls and roofs all lichen-spotted and mossy. There was a raw wind blowing and it was midmorning, so I suppose it wasn't surprising that it was deserted, though I did have the sensation that I was being watched from behind the Nottingham lace curtains . . .

But the only movement was the sign swinging in the wind outside the pub, the Auld Christmas, which depicted a bearded old man in a blue robe, holding a small fir tree and wearing a wreath of greenery round his head. Very odd. The pub advertised morning coffee and ploughman's lunches, which would have been tempting had the journey not taken so much longer than I expected.

The shop Ellen had mentioned was nearby, fronted by sacks

of potatoes and boxes of vegetables, with the Merry Kettle Tearoom next to it, though that looked as if it had closed for the winter. It was probably just seasonal, for walkers.

I consulted my map, started the engine, then continued on past a terraced trio of tiny Gothic cottages and over a second, smaller bridge to yet *another* signpost pointing to Great Mumming up an improbably steep and narrow strip of tarmac.

No wonder all the vehicles parked outside the pub were four-wheel-drive!

After half a mile I turned off through a pair of large stone pillars and came to rest on a stretch of gravel next to a lodge house that had been extended at the back into a sizeable bungalow.

It was very quiet apart from the rushing of water somewhere nearby and the rooks cawing in a stand of tall pine trees that must hide the house itself, for I couldn't see even a chimney stack.

As I got out a little stiffly (I hadn't realised quite how tense that drive up had made me), the lodge door opened a few inches and a tall, stooping, elderly man beckoned me in.

'There you are! Come in quickly, before all the warm air gets out,' he commanded urgently, as if I was a wayward family pet.

I sidled carefully past a large and spiky holly wreath into a long hallway. Once the door was safely shut behind me he turned and came towards me with an odd, slightly crablike gait, holding out his hand.

'Noël Martland. And you must be Holly Brown – lovely name, by the way, very suitable.'

'Oh? For what?'

'Christmas,' he replied, looking vaguely surprised that I needed to be told. He wore a drooping, ex-Air Force style moustache, partially covering the extensive, puckered shiny scars of an old burn.

He caught my eye: 'Plane shot down in the war. Got a bit singed, landed badly.'

24

'Right,' I said, admiring the economy of description of a scene that would have occupied half a film and had you biting your knuckles on the edge of your cinema seat.

'Best to say straight off: people always wonder, but they don't like to ask.'

He took my coat and hung it carefully on a mahogany stand, then ushered me into a small, square, chintzy sitting room that would have been very pleasant had it not been rendered into a hideous Christmas grotto. Festoons of paper chains and Chinese lanterns hung from the ceiling, swags of fake greenery lined the mantelpiece and the tops of all the pictures, and there were snowglobes and porcelain-faced Santas on every flat surface.

In the bow window, fairy lights twinkled among so many baubles on the small fake fir tree that the balding branches drooped wearily under the strain.

Observing my stunned expression with some satisfaction he said, 'Jolly good, isn't it? We like to do things properly in Little Mumming.' Then he suddenly bellowed, 'Tilda! She's here!'

'Coming!' answered a high, brittle voice and with a loud rattling noise a tiny woman pushed a large hostess trolley through a swinging door from what was presumably the kitchen.

'My wife, Tilda,' Noël Martland said. 'This is Holly Brown, m'dear.'

'So I should suppose, unless you've taken to entertaining strange young women,' she said tartly, eyeing me from faded but still sharp blue eyes. Though age had withered her, it had not prevented her from applying a bold coating of turquoise eye shadow to her lids and a generous slick of foundation, powder and glossy scarlet lipstick. Under the white frilly apron she was wearing a peach satin blouse with huge dolman sleeves that finished in tight cuffs at the wrists, and a matching Crimplene pinafore dress. Her matchstick-thin legs in filmy loose stockings ended in pointed shoes with *very* high stiletto heels. I felt glad she had the trolley to hang onto.

'The agency said you were coming on your own, though really a couple would have been better. But I suppose we're lucky to get *anyone* at such short notice, over Christmas,' she said, eyeing me critically.

'I am sure you will cope splendidly!' declared her husband.

'That remains to be seen, Noël,' she snapped back. 'Miss or Mrs?' she suddenly demanded, with a glance at my naked left hand.

'Mrs,' I said, 'I'm a widow. I do a lot of cooking, so I've never been much of a one for rings.'

'A widow? Tough luck,' she said, taking the covers off a couple of dishes to reveal plates of pinwheel sandwiches and butterfly sponge cakes.

'You shouldn't have gone to so much trouble,' I protested. 'I really wasn't expecting to be fed, just to pick up the keys!'

'I didn't – we always have an early lunch anyway, so I made extra. My housekeeper has gone home for Christmas as usual, but I do most of the cooking in any case – it's nothing to me. I was a TV chef, you know, in the early days. If I'd known the exact time of your arrival, I could have whipped up a soufflé.'

'This looks lovely,' I said, taking a sandwich. 'Were you a TV cook like Fanny Craddock, then?'

Her face darkened alarmingly and it didn't need Noël's appalled expression and shake of the head to inform me that I had made a faux pas.

'Don't mention That Woman to me,' she snapped. 'She was nothing but a brass-faced amateur!'

'Sorry,' I said quickly.

'I was Tilda Thompson in those days – and much more photogenic than *she* ever was, all slap and false eyelashes.'

This seemed to me to be a case of the pot calling the kettle black, but I made a vague noise of agreement.

'Coffee?' Noël chipped in brightly, pouring me a cup with a slightly trembling hand.

'Thank you.' Having tasted the sandwich I was eager to accept anything that might wash the flavour away ... whatever it was.

'Did you call Jessica?' Tilda Martland asked her husband.

'On my way to the door, m'dear. But perhaps I had better call again.'

Upstairs a door slammed and footsteps thundered down the stairs like a herd of inebriated rhinos.

'No need,' she said dryly.

Jess was a tall, skinny, dark-haired girl of about twelve or thirteen (not quite as tall as I had been at that age, but even skinnier), dressed entirely in black, from glasses frame to shoes. Anyone less like a Jessica I never saw. She certainly stood out against the chintzy, ornament-laden and over-bedecked sitting room.

'This is our granddaughter, Jessica,' Noël Martland said.

'Jess, Grandpa,' she corrected, in a long-suffering way.

He smiled at her affectionately. '*Jess*, this is Mrs Brown who is going to look after Old Place until your Uncle Jude gets back.'

'Please do all call me Holly,' I suggested.

'Then you must call us Tilda and Noël.'

Jess eyed me curiously, in that slightly-shifty adolescent way that generally denotes nothing much except acute self-consciousness. 'I'm only here on my own because my parents are in Antarctica. But now my great-uncle's dead and Jude's gone off somewhere, we can't stay at Old Place over Christmas and New Year like we usually do. It's a drag.'

'Jess's parents are studying pelicans,' Tilda said, unveiling another plate of tiny sandwiches, this time cut into teddy bear shapes.

'Penguins,' corrected Jess. 'Emperor penguins. And how old do you think I am, Granny?'

'Going by your manners, six.'

'Ha, ha,' said Jess, but she took a teddy bear sandwich and, after lifting up the top to examine the innocuous-looking ham filling, ate it.

'It's such a pity that Mo and Jim had to go off suddenly like that, isn't it?' Noël said. 'But it couldn't be helped. I only hope you don't find it too lonely up there – there is a cleaner twice a week, but the couple who used to look after my brother, the Jacksons, retired and my nephew looks after himself when he's home.'

'That cleaning girl is a slut: I don't think she ever does more than whisk a duster about for half an hour and then drink tea and read magazines,' Tilda said. 'But I expect you will soon have everything shipshape again, Holly.'

'I'll certainly make sure the areas of the house I *use* are kept neat and tidy,' I said pointedly, because it was a common misconception that home-sitters would also spring-clean and do all kinds of other little jobs around the house and garden and I often found it as well to make the real position clear from the outset. 'I'm here simply to make sure the house is safe and to look after the animals. I believe there are a dog and a horse?'

'Lady – she was my great-aunt's horse, so she's ancient,' Jess said. 'Me and Grandpa went up in the golf buggy yesterday afternoon and again this morning and I filled her water bucket and haynet, but I couldn't get too close because I'm allergic to horses. I sneeze.'

'That's a pity,' I said sincerely, because I could have done with a knowledgeable, horse-mad child.

'Yes, but I'm all right with dogs as long as I don't brush them, so I took Merlin out for a run.'

'That's something,' I agreed, assuming Merlin to be the dog I'd been told about.

'We left Lady in for the day, with the top of the stable door open, in case you were late arriving – it goes dark so early at this time of year,' Noël said, 'and you wouldn't want to be bringing her in from the paddock in the dark, before you've got your bearings.'

'No indeed,' I said gratefully.

'Jude sets great store by her, because she was his mother's horse,' Noël said, eating one of the strange pinwheel sandwiches with apparent relish. I had tried to swallow the rest of mine without chewing.

'He was happy enough to leave her in the Chirks' care again, but I'm not sure what he will think about someone he has never met taking over,' Tilda said.

'Ellen, who runs Homebodies, has been trying to contact Mr Martland to inform him of what has been happening. Will you please explain, if he calls you?'

'Yes, of course,' said Noël, 'and he is bound to, in the next day or two. He may then call you up, too.'

'I admit, I'll feel happier when he knows there has been a change of house-sitter.'

'Well, it's his own fault for staying away so long,' Tilda said. 'We didn't think he meant it when he suddenly said he didn't intend coming back from his trip to America until after Christmas, did we, Noël?'

'No, m'dear, because normally, as Jess said, we move into Old Place for Christmas and New Year. My sister Becca also stays from Christmas Eve until Boxing Day, too – you probably passed her house on the way here, New Place? Big wrought-iron gates, just the other end of the village.'

'Of course she passed the damned house,' snapped Tilda, 'did you think she was parachuted in?'

'Turn of speech,' he said apologetically, but twinkled at me.

I suddenly wondered if Alan and I would have ended up like this, with me bossing him about and him good-naturedly suffering it? There was no denying that I *was* bossy and organising. But then, *he* had had a stubborn streak, too . . .

'Still, it would have been a bit difficult this year, what with my poor brother passing away last January and then Jude falling out with Guy,' Noël sighed.

'It wasn't Guy's fault, really,' Tilda said dispassionately, 'that girl just got her hooks into him.'

I didn't ask who Guy was because, to be honest, I wasn't terribly interested in people I was never going to meet. I finished my coffee and put down my cup and plate. 'Well, that was unexpected but delicious: thank you so much! And now I'd better get up to the house and settle in.'

'Sharon, the cleaner, should still be there, so get her to show you round before she goes. It might be the most useful thing she's done all year,' Tilda suggested.

'I expect she does her best: it is a large house for one person to clean,' Noël said mildly. 'Not that Jude can make much of a mess, because when he is home he seems to spend most of his time down at the mill, working on his sculptures, or in his little study next to the library.'

'Oh yes, I heard he was a sculptor.'

'He's *very* famous,' Jess said, '*and* very bad tempered. He only cancelled Christmas because he saw that engagement announcement and I think he's *mean*. I bet he didn't even remember that Mum and Dad wouldn't be able to be here this year and I'd be coming on my own.'

'Jess, that will *do*!' commanded Tilda, and she lapsed into sulky silence.

I got up. 'Well, I think I'd better go up to the house while it's still light and settle in.'

Noël also got up and found me a vast bunch of keys, pointing out the largest. 'That's the front door. I expect you will work the rest out for yourself.'

'I could come and show you,' Jess offered quickly.

'Now, Jess, you know you've promised Old Nan you will visit her this afternoon: you'd better go and get ready, you can't disappoint her,' Tilda said. 'She'll have made you a special tea.'

'*More* nursery food!' Jess said disgustedly.

'And change into something that isn't black.'

Jess groaned and stomped off upstairs.

'She's so disappointed not to have Christmas at Old Place,' confided Noël in a whisper, as though he thought we could be overheard from above, 'and whatever she says, she adores Jude. It will be very quiet here for her, I'm afraid. Mo and Jim kindly invited us to share their Christmas dinner and that would have been *something*.' He sighed again. 'I am an expert on Christmas, you know – I've written a book on its history and traditions, so I do like to celebrate *properly*.'

'And so we will! I have a plump little chicken that will do very well for the three of us,' Tilda said stoically.

I suddenly wondered if they were expecting me to offer to cook Christmas dinner instead of the Chirks, even though I hadn't even arrived at Old Place yet, so I said quickly, '*I* don't celebrate Christmas.'

'Not celebrate Christmas?' Noël looked as stunned as if I had admitted to some abhorrent crime.

'No, I was brought up as a Strange Baptist.'

'Oh – right,' he said uncertainly. 'I think I've heard of those . . . And the lady who runs the Homebodies agency – Ellen, is it? – mentioned that you have not long since lost your grandmother, so I don't expect you feel particularly festive this year?'

'No, not at all . . . or any year, in fact.'

'My dear, I am *so* sorry,' Tilda said and added, graciously, 'We quite understand – and if you feel at all in need of company at any time, you are always welcome to call on us.'

'But surely – with a name like Holly – you must have a *birthday* to celebrate during Christmas?' Noël asked suddenly.

'It's Christmas Day, actually, but I don't celebrate that, either.'

'So is mine and I feel *just* the same,' he said understandingly. 'It would simply be too presumptuous to share the Lord's birthday, wouldn't it?'

Chapter 4: Rose of Sharon

I was brought up to consider the tawdry trappings of Christmas and the practice of avarice and extreme gluttony to be far removed from the way we should celebrate Christ's birth. And yet, the gaiety of my fellow nurses was heart-warming as they decorated the hospital wards and endeavoured to bring some seasonal cheer to the patients.

December, 1944

Safely back in the car I tried to decide what had been in the pinwheel sandwiches. Whatever it was had tasted like decayed fish paste, but *looked* like black olive pâté. It was a complete mystery to me and I might have to ask Tilda for the recipe, out of sheer curiosity.

The drive went up one side of a steeply-banked stream through the pine wood and then turned away, opening up onto a vista of sheep-nibbled grass across which, beyond a ha-ha, I could see a long, low, Jacobean building. It was rather larger than I had expected, though I suppose the size of the lodge should have given me some idea. The low-slung wintry sun sparkled off the mullioned windows, but there was no sign of life: not even a wisp of smoke from one of the line of four tall chimneys.

I drove over a cattle grid and pulled up on the gravel next to a battered red Ford Fiesta, noting as I did so that the flowerbeds that flanked the substantial front door inside an open porch looked neglected and the doorknocker, in the shape of a Green Man with frondy foliage forming his hair and beard, had not been cleaned for months.

I longed to have a go at it with Brasso. It's not that I love cleaning, because I don't, just that I like things neat, clean and orderly. I really have to fight the urge sometimes in other people's houses; you'd be surprised what a mess they can leave them in.

As I got out of the car, a youngish woman came out, a half-smoked cigarette in one hand. Her magenta hair was scraped back into a ponytail, apart from one long, limp strand that hung over her face like wet seaweed, and she was wearing a salmon-pink velour tracksuit that left a goose-pimpled muffin top of flesh exposed.

'Hello,' I said, holding out my hand. 'You must be the cleaner, Sharon? I'm glad you're still here, I'm late and I thought you might have gone by now.'

'I was just about to when I heard your car,' she said, taking my hand as if she wasn't quite sure what to do with it and then letting it go immediately. 'Call me Shar – and I'm not really a cleaner, I've just been helping Jude out for a bit of extra cash since my Kevin's been laid off. Not that he pays me the going rate, he's too mean.'

'Isn't that illegal?'

'Cash in hand, innit? He's got me over a barrel. You'd better watch out you get your money.'

'Oh, that's okay, the agency pays me.'

'You won't see me no more after today, because I'm starting behind the bar in the pub in Great Mumming after Christmas, a regular job. So Jude Martland can stick his miserly money and his smart-arse comments where the sun don't shine.'

'Right,' I said noncommittally, reeling slightly under this information overload. 'So ... Mr Martland knows you're leaving?'

'I told him I wasn't doing Christmas and no-one works over New Year,' she said sulkily, 'especially if they don't get a bonus.

Then he said since he could never tell whether I'd been in to clean or not, I didn't even deserve what he paid me, let alone any extra. He's such a sarky bugger!'

'I see.'

'So if I've took another job, it's his own fault, innit? I'm not bothered.'

'I expect it is.'

'If he rings, you can tell him I've had a better offer.'

'If he should ring, I'll certainly tell him you've resigned from your job,' I agreed. 'Now, before you go, do you have time to quickly show me over the house and where everything is?'

'I don't *know* where everything is, do I? I only vacuum and dust, and that's too much for one person. An old couple used to do the cooking and see to the house and generator, but they retired after the old gent, Jude's dad, died. January, that was.'

'So I've heard . . . and did you say there was a *generator*? I thought the house had mains services.'

'It does, but the electric's always cutting out *and* the phone line is forever coming down between here and the village because the poles need replacing. The TV doesn't work very well either, because there's no Sky dish, though they've got one at the lodge. It's a complete hole, I don't know what you're going to do with yourself.'

'That's all right, I'm not bothered about TV. I've brought my radio with me and lots to read.'

Sharon looked at me as if I was a strange and alien species with three heads. 'There's no mobile phone reception either, unless you walk halfway up Snowehill, or down past the lodge,' she informed me as a clincher.

'Well then, if the phone line goes dead, the exercise will do me good,' I said pleasantly. I have worked in remote places before – the house I should have been minding in Scotland was much more isolated than this – though I had not, admittedly, previously had to cope with a generator. I only hoped the electricity didn't cut out before I found the instructions on how to operate the thing!

I smiled encouragingly at her. 'Now, I'd *really* appreciate it if you could quickly show me round? Normally we try and visit a property beforehand to meet the owners and get the lay of the land, as it were, but obviously in this case it wasn't possible.'

Sharon sullenly and reluctantly agreed and stood back to let me past her into a long stone entrance chamber. It had a row of heavily-burdened coat hooks, a brass stand full of walking sticks and umbrellas, and a battered wooden bench, under which was a miscellaneous collection of wellingtons and walking boots.

'Go through the door at the end,' she directed and I found myself standing in a huge, high-ceilinged sitting room the size of a small barn with an open fireplace practically big enough to roast an ox in. A worn carpet in mellow, warm colours covered most of the stone floor and an assortment of occasional tables, velvet-covered sofas and chairs was grouped on it. A dogleg staircase rose from one corner to a balustraded gallery above, that ran around three sides.

'What a lovely room! It looks as if it started out as a great hall in a much older building?'

'They say this is the really old bit in the middle, the rest was added on later,' she said indifferently. 'There's two wings – the kitchen one is set back, you go through a door behind that wooden screen over there. This other side is bigger, with the family rooms and another staircase. Come on, I'll show you.'

She ushered me briskly through a series of dark-oak-panelled rooms with polished wooden floors. Some had elaborate white-stuccoed ceilings, but they all looked dusty, dull and neglected. There was a small morning room with a TV, a long dining room sporting a spectacular, if incongruous, Venetian mirror over the hearth, and a well-stocked library with a snooker table in the middle of it.

She paused at the door next to it. 'Jude uses this room to work in and he locks it when he's away.' She sniffed. 'You'd think he didn't trust me.'

He probably didn't, though actually I'd found that there were quite often one or two mysterious locked rooms in houses I was looking after: Bluebeard's chambers, as Laura had suggested, though their secrets were probably only of the mundane kind.

But this room revealed its secrets, for the top of the door was glazed – perhaps it had been the land agent's office, or something like that. It held a tilting draughtsman's table, a large wooden easel and several tables bearing a silting of objects, including jars of pencils, brushes and lots of small models, presumably of sculptures. It was hard to make out what they were from that distance. There was also what looked like one of those hideaway computer workstations – but if so, then it must be dial-up, because there was no broadband here and, given the apparent unreliability of the phone lines, being able to connect with the internet must be a matter of luck. But that was okay – Ellen was the only person who ever emailed me much, with details of jobs.

'There's never been anything of value to lock away in Old Place anyway,' Sharon was saying scathingly, though I noticed a wistful look on her face like a child at a sweetshop window. 'Though Jude's that famous now, they're saying that even his little drawings of horses for those weird sculptures of his can fetch hundreds of pounds.' She nodded through the glass door. 'And he just crumples them up and tosses them in that waste-paper basket!'

'Well, that's up to him, isn't it? Presumably he wasn't happy with them.'

'You'd think he'd leave the basket for me to empty, but no, he takes them outside and puts them in the garden incinerator!' She obviously bitterly regretted this potential source of income going up in flames.

'That *does* seem a little excessive,' I agreed, amused.

Apart from a couple of china and linen cupboards, the only

other door from the passage was to a little garden hall with French doors leading outside. The trug of garden tools on the bench looked as if they hadn't been touched for half a century and were waiting for Sleeping Beauty to wake up, don the worn leather gauntlets, and start briskly hacking back the brambles.

'Is that a walled garden out there?' I asked, peering through the gathering gloom.

'Yes, though no-one bothers with most of it since Mrs Martland died . . .' She screwed up her face in recollection. 'That would be ten years ago now, thereabouts.'

'Is there a gardener?'

'An old bloke called Henry comes and grows vegetables in part of it, though he's supposed to have retired. He lives down in Little Mumming, in the almshouses – those three funny little cottages near the bridge.'

'Oh yes, I noticed those. Victorian Gothic.'

'I wouldn't know, I hate old houses,' she said, which I could tell by the state of this one.

There was a little cloakroom off the hall, with a splendid Victorian blue and white porcelain toilet depicting Windsor Castle inside the bowl, and I was just thinking that peeing on one of the Queen's residences must always have seemed a little lese-majesty when Sharon said impatiently, 'Come on: I need to get off home,' and gave me a dig in the back.

We went upstairs by a grander flight of stairs than that in the sitting room, with a stairlift folded back against the wall.

'That was put in for Jude's dad,' she said, hurrying me past a lot of not very good family portraits of fair, soulful women and dark, watchful men, when I would have lingered. 'Six bedrooms if you count the old nursery and the little room off it, plus there's two more in the staff wing.'

She opened and closed doors, allowing me tantalising glimpses of faded grandeur, including one four-poster bed. The nursery, up a further stair, was lovely, with a white-painted wooden bed with a heart cut out in the headboard, a scrap-screen and a big rocking horse.

'There are more rooms on this floor, but they're shut up and not used any more. The heating doesn't go up that far.'

'Oh yes, I noticed there were radiators – all mod cons! I'm impressed.'

'I wouldn't get excited, it never gets hot enough to do more than keep the chill off the place.' She clattered back down the stairs and hared off along the landing. 'Two bathrooms, though Jude's had an en suite shower put into his bedroom since he inherited.'

'That isn't bad for a house of this size,' I said. 'There's the downstairs cloakroom, too.'

'And a little bathroom in the staff wing, where you're sleeping. This is the family wing, of course – your room's in the other, where the old couple who used to look after the place lived.'

Evidently house-sitters ranked with servants in Jude Martland's eyes – but so long as I was warm and comfortable, I didn't mind where my room was.

The bedrooms either opened off the corridor, or the oak-floored balcony, where I stopped to gaze down at the huge sitting room, which looked like a stage set awaiting the entrance of the actors for an Agatha Christie dénouement, until Sharon began to rattle her turquoise nails against the banister in an impatient tattoo.

Once through the door into the other wing the décor turned utilitarian and the bathroom was very basic and ancient, though with an electric shower above the clawfooted bath. The bedroom that was to be mine was plain, comfortable – *and* clean. I expect Mo and Jim did that as soon as they arrived.

As if she could read my thoughts, Sharon said, 'Mo and Jim changed the bed ready for you, but they hadn't time to wash the sheets, so you'll find them in the utility room, I expect. I don't do washing.'

I was tempted to ask her exactly what she *did* do, but managed to repress it: it was none of my business.

We went down the backstairs to the kitchen, a very large room with an electric cooker as well as a huge Aga, a big scrubbed pine table in the middle, a couple of easy chairs and a wicker dog basket. This looked like the place where the owner did most of his living – it was certainly warmer than the rest of the house.

'The Aga's oil-fired – the tank's in one of the outhouses – and it runs the central heating, but you don't have to cook with it because there's a perfectly good stove over there.'

'Oh, I like using an Aga,' I said, and she gave me another of her 'you're barking mad' looks, then glanced at her watch.

'Come on. Through here there's the utility, larder, cloakroom, scullery, cellar . . .'

She flung open a door to reveal two enormous white chest freezers. 'The nearest one's full of Mo and Jim's food and so are the cupboards, fridge and larder.'

'Yes, they said they were leaving it for me, which was kind of them.'

She closed it again and led me on. 'That's the cellar door and there's firewood down there as well as the boiler. This by the back door is sort of a tackroom, it's got feed and harness and stuff in it for the horse.'

Something had been puzzling me. 'Right – but where's the dog?'

'In the yard, I don't want him under my feet when I'm cleaning, do I?'

'Isn't it a bit cold out there?' I asked and she gave me a look before wrenching the back door open. A large and venerable grey lurcher, who had been huddled on the step, got up and walked in stiffly, sniffed at me politely, and then plodded past in the direction of the kitchen.

'That's Merlin. He's past it, should be put down.'

I said nothing and she added, leading the way across to a

small barn on the other side of the cobbled yard, 'Like the horse – it was Jude's mother's and it's way past its three score years and ten, if you ask me. But he won't hear of it.'

There was something familiar but very spiteful about her tone when she mentioned Jude Martland's name that made me suspect a touch of the woman scorned. Maybe she had taken the job hoping for a bit more from him than a weekly pay-packet?

Now she looked at me sideways, slyly. 'You single?'

'Well, yes – widowed.'

'Don't get your hopes up, then – he goes for skinny blondes, does our Jude – though his brother stole his last one.'

'I'm not remotely interested in what he goes for and anyway, I won't meet him: he'll return after I've left, on Twelfth Night.'

'Oh – Twelfth Night! You want to watch yourself in Little Mumming if you're still here on Twelfth Night! Did you ever see that old film, *The Wicker Man*?' And she laughed unpleasantly.

'Well, I'll just have to take my chance, won't I?' I said cheerfully, since she was obviously trying to put the wind up me. Sure enough, she was talking about ghosts and haunting a minute later as she slid back the bolt and opened a barn door.

I've cooked in some of the most haunted houses in the country and all I can say is, the kitchen and the servants' bedrooms are *not* where they generally hang out.

Failing to get a rise out of me, she said, 'Your instructions for looking after the horse are on the kitchen table in that big folder thing. He's a great one for instructions, is Jude Martland.' She gestured inside the barn. 'The horse is down the other end.'

I could see a couple of looseboxes and a pale equine shape in one of them, but I didn't disturb it: time enough when I had read the instructions!

'Well, that's it then,' Sharon said, bolting the door again and leading the way back into the kitchen, where she pulled on a red coat that clashed with the magenta streaks in her hair and picked up her bag. 'I'm off. I expect the old people at the lodge will tell you anything I've forgot and you won't starve, at any rate, because there was enough food here to withstand a siege even before Mo and Jim brought all their stuff.'

When she drove off I was more than glad to see the last of her. I think the old dog was, too, because when I went back into the kitchen carrying the first load of stuff from my car, he wagged his tail and grinned in that engaging way that lurchers have, with a very knowing look in his amber eyes.

'Well, Merlin, it's just you and me, kid,' I told him, in my best Humphrey Bogart voice.

Chapter 5: Hot Mash

Hilda gave me a bar of good soap, which I was very glad of,
and Pearl a lovely purple felt pansy she had made to pin to
my coat. Luckily Mr Bowman – Tom's father and the minister
at the chapel here – had recently presented me with several
very pretty old bookmarks with Biblical texts and silk tassels,
so that I had something by me to give them in return.

Christmas 1944

By the time I had brought all my stuff in, put the perishable
food in the fridge and taken my bags up to the bedroom allocated
to me, I was more than ready to sit down at the kitchen table
with a cup of coffee and the Homebodies file, which Ellen gives
to all the clients to fill in with essential information and emergency phone numbers. Jude Martland's was crammed with
printed pages, mostly relating to the care of the dog and horse.

First I read the note that Mo and Jim had left tucked inside
it, for a bit of inside information, and learned that the owner
was more than happy for the house-sitters to help themselves to
any of the food in the house, including the fish and game in the
larger of the two freezers. '*But not the alcohol, since the wine
cellar is locked*' had been added, which was okay by me, because
I wasn't much of a drinker. Other than that, the TV reception
was lousy and mobile phones worked best if you stood in the
ear of the horse on the hill, or ten paces down the lane from

the lodge and two steps right. (I expect finding that out kept Jim occupied for *hours*.)

I glanced at the generator instructions and discovered it was in an outbuilding and was automatic, so should in theory look after itself, and then made sure I knew where the main water stopcock was and the fuse box. The latter I found in the tackroom, with a working torch next to it on a shelf, together with a couple of candle lanterns and a wind-up storm lamp.

I was starting to form a picture of Jude Martland, who was clearly quite practical and obviously cared about the animals . . . And yet, he paid his cleaner a pittance and neglected his lovely house, so he was either broke or mean – maybe both. Or perhaps those with an artistic temperament simply don't notice muck?

I went back in the kitchen, poured another cup of coffee, and checked out the animal care instructions. Merlin, who was now leaning heavily against my leg with his head on my knee, was easy: two meals a day, with a pill for his arthritis crushed into the breakfast one, and he needed daily walks to help prevent him stiffening up.

Well, didn't we all?

I'd already spotted his brush, food, biscuits and a supply of rawhide chews in a cupboard in the scullery, next to a hook with a dog lead and a large brown pawprint-patterned towel helpfully marked 'DOG', in case I had found it a struggle to make the connection.

The horse was an Arab mare called Lady, which I would have thought a delicate breed for an exposed, upland place like this. She was twenty-five years old and that sounded quite an age for a horse too. But then, what do *I* know?

She had a paddock with a field shelter behind the house, where she spent the day unless the weather was extremely bad, though he had omitted to define what 'really bad' entailed. I should ensure the water in the trough was not frozen over and that a filled haynet was hung on the paddock fence. Billy would go out with her.

Who, I wondered, was Billy? I puzzled over that for a moment and then read on.

She was brought into the stables at night and this would need mucking out and the water replenishing every day, a process I vaguely remembered from Laura's brief horse-mad phase. She was to keep her rug on all the time, except when it was removed daily for grooming and to check for rubbing.

In the evening she had a warm mash cooked up from ingredients to be found in metal bins in the tackroom and liberally spiced with a medication called Equiflex . . .

Good heavens! I was starting to think that Lady was going to take up most of my time and be a lot trickier to care for than I'd hoped, and I admit I was getting slight cold feet about it. So I thought I'd better take a proper look at her before the light totally vanished and Merlin, seeing me put my coat on, was determined to accompany me, even though I thought he ought to stay in the warm.

Along one side of the cobbled yard were the outbuildings that I knew contained the woodshed, generator and the extremely large oil tank that supplied both that and the central heating – but exploring those would have to wait for the next day.

Merlin and I went into the barn and I found a light switch by the door. Lady put her head over curiously and I saw that she was not much bigger than the ponies Laura had ridden and had a gentle expression and big, liquid dark eyes. Emboldened, I opened the door of the loosebox and slipped in to check her water and hay, and the fastenings of her rug . . . and I was just stooping over the bucket when the straw rustled and then something butted me hard in the legs: it was a small, black goat.

Billy? Obviously. But someone might have mentioned it! Luckily it had no horns, but it was now staring at me with light, slightly-mad-looking eyes.

I topped up the water bucket from the tap just outside the loosebox, foiling Billy's attempt to get out, because I wasn't sure how easy he would be to get back in again.

There was plenty of hay, both up in a net out of Billy's reach and in a hayrack lower down. Lady's warmly-lined rug was secure and she looked comfortable, so I left them to it for the moment.

I'd taken Merlin's lead out with me and now attached it to his collar: I wasn't sure if he was likely to run away, but I have learned through long experience that it's better to be safe than sorry. We went out of the side gate and followed the track alongside the paddock towards the hill. We didn't go far, though, just enough to stretch Merlin's poor old legs and mine. By the time we turned back I needed the torch I'd put in my pocket, and the lights in the courtyard looked bright and beckoning.

The wind was biting, so the threatened cold spell might actually be coming and I think we were both glad to get back into the warmth of the kitchen. I was feeling really weary by now, but there was one last task to be performed before I could settle down there: Lady must have her hot mash.

I followed the recipe to the letter: one scoop of quick-soak dried beet, steeped in boiling water for ten minutes, one scoop of chopped alfalfa, two scoops of pony nuts and a handful of linseed cake. Then I left it to cool a bit before stirring in the Equiflex.

It smelled quite nice, considering.

Merlin would have come out to the stables again with me, except that I thought he had had enough of the cold for one day and so shut him in, despite his reproachful expression.

Lady was eager to get her head in the bucket, though I had to hold off Billy, who wanted to share. Even little goats, I found, were surprisingly strong. I'd taken a handful of biscuit-shaped things from a container marked with his name that I'd spotted in the tackroom, but he was more interested in the mash.

Horses give off a surprising amount of heat, don't they?

* * *

Merlin greeted my return with huge relief, as if I'd been gone a week, so I expect the poor old thing was feeling terribly confused.

When I'd thawed out I phoned Laura, but only for long enough to give her the number here to ring me back: clients don't appreciate you running up huge phone bills, but obviously using my mobile was going to be tricky. I only hoped Sharon was exaggerating the frequency of the phone lines going down . . .

'How are you getting on?' Laura asked. 'What are the animals like?'

'The dog's an old lurcher, a sweetie called Merlin – he's a bit lost and lonely, I think, because he keeps following me around. The horse is a white Arab.'

'Grey, horses are never white.'

'You can call it grey, but Lady's as white as snow, with huge, dark eyes. She's very old, quiet and gentle, so I don't think looking after her is going to be a problem – except she's living with this little goat no-one mentioned.'

'A *goat*?'

'It was in the loosebox with her, so I suppose it's keeping her company. It's got a bit of the evil eye and it kept trying to eat her hot mash. I had to hold it off, and it was surprisingly strong.'

'Hot mash? You had to cook *dinner* for the horse?'

I described the cordon bleu horse mash and confessed my worry about looking after the elderly, delicate-looking mare, and she made reassuring noises.

'I'll tackle mucking out and grooming tomorrow. I only wish I'd been interested in that sort of thing while you were having riding lessons, though I expect it's just a matter of common sense.'

'You wheelbarrow the old bedding to the manure heap, and then spread a layer of new straw – simple. Mucking out will be good exercise, too.'

'Yes, I expect it will.'

'So, what's the house like?'

'Lovely. I've only had a quick tour around so far but I can see it's mostly Jacobean, though part of it looks much older. The central heating isn't very efficient so I'll probably light a fire in the big inglenook fireplace in the sitting room tomorrow and that should warm the house through. My bedroom isn't too bad, because it's right over the kitchen with the Aga.'

'How big *is* this place?'

'Bigger than I expected, but I've cooked for house-parties in much larger and grander houses. The sitting room is huge and looks like it might have started life as a medieval hall, but then two new wings have been added and lots of dark panelling and moulded ceilings.'

'That sounds pretty grand to me!'

'You could fit the floor space of my entire house in the kitchen wing with room to spare,' I admitted.

'That's a stately home as far as I'm concerned – and you are in sole possession, the lady of the manor.'

'Yes, but I know my place: the hired help's bedroom is in the service wing, though there's a bathroom opposite with a decent electric shower. I expect I'll spend most of my time in the kitchen and just take a quick daily walk round the rest of the house to check everything is all right.'

'Sooner you than me, rattling around alone in a spooky old house in the middle of nowhere.'

I laughed. 'You know I don't believe in ghosts or the supernatural! No, I'll be fine. The cleaner showed me round when I arrived, but she isn't coming back because she's got another job. She won't be any loss, though, because the place is totally filthy and neglected, she can't have been doing anything. Then again, Jude Martland was paying her a pittance, so you can't really blame her for that.'

'So – you'll be entirely alone all the time? It isn't *really* haunted, is it?'

'Sharon – that's the cleaner – tried to put the wind up me,

telling me about ghosts and an annual local ceremony on Twelfth Night. She seemed to be implying that the villagers would want to use me as some kind of ceremonial sacrifice, but I wasn't really listening because it was all entirely daft!'

'You won't be there that night anyway, will you?'

'No, I'm leaving that morning, before the client gets back – that was the arrangement Mo and Jim had.'

'Is it very isolated? I can't imagine what you'll do with yourself.'

'Apart from trying to finish off my cookbook, I've brought that tin trunk of Gran's papers to sort and I'm going to carry on reading her journal at bedtime, too. She's been sent to a new hospital and made friends, so it's getting more interesting.'

'Perhaps that Ned Martland she mentioned was one of the doctors and she had a crush on him?' she suggested.

'Maybe,' I agreed. 'I'll tell you if I find out. And I'm not totally isolated here, because the village is only about half a mile away and, if I feel like company, the old couple at the lodge have invited me to drop in any time. But you know me – I like being alone.'

'Sam was really disappointed when I told him you weren't coming for Christmas Day after all,' she hinted, but I just laughed.

By now, it seemed like a week since I had set out for Little Mumming and I decided on an early night.

Merlin and I had our dinner, and then he accompanied me around the ground floor while I checked the doors and windows. We'd returned to the kitchen and I was just about to fill my trusty hot water bottle, when suddenly the phone on the large dresser rang loudly, nearly giving me a heart attack.

'Is that Holly Brown?' demanded a deep voice that seemed to vibrate right down to my feet and back again in a very novel, if slightly disturbing, way.

'Yes, speaking.'

'Jude Martland: I just caught up with my emails and found one from Homebodies saying the Chirks had had to leave and *you* were taking over.'

'That's right, and I'm so glad you've rung, because—'

'No, it's damned-well *not* all right!' he rudely interrupted. 'I've just called my uncle, and apparently you're not only alone in the house, but you've also no experience with horses whatsoever!'

'Look, Mr Martland,' I said soothingly. 'I always house-sit alone and your instructions were very comprehensive – *exhaustive*, even. Well, apart from the goat,' I qualified.

'What?'

'Billy. There was no mention of him.'

'Of course there was – you just didn't bother looking for it! But what really matters is that I left Old Place, Lady and Merlin in safe hands, with people I knew and trusted – then suddenly I hear that someone totally unsuitable has been drafted in, without a by-your-leave!'

'Actually, I'm repeatedly rebooked by the same clients, year after year,' I said evenly. 'You were lucky that my Christmas placement had also fallen through, so that I was free to step into the breach! And thank you, Holly Brown, for coping with the emergency,' I found myself adding acerbically.

There was a pause, then he growled, grudgingly, 'I suppose there was no alternative, but I'm not happy with the arrangement – or that Homebodies went ahead and did this without asking me.'

'Ellen did her best to contact you and, in any case, she knows I'm completely trustworthy and capable.'

'Sending a young woman to look after an isolated house alone, especially over Christmas, can hardly be ideal.'

'Thank you, but I don't celebrate Christmas, I'm not actually that young and I *prefer* isolation.'

'Noël mentioned you didn't celebrate Christmas – and that's another problem, because my aunt and uncle were looking

49

forward to having Christmas dinner with the Chirks and *I* felt better knowing Tilda wouldn't have to cook it. I know she still does most of their cooking, but she's looking quite frail these days.'

'Yes, so she said, but I don't think she's going to attempt the full monty – they're having a roast chicken instead,' I said. 'And I expect her granddaughter will help her.'

'Oh God, I'd entirely forgotten about Jess being there on her own this year!'

'Mmm . . . I'm afraid you don't seem to be her favourite person at the moment, Mr Martland.'

There was a pause, and then he suggested, 'Perhaps you could cook the Christmas dinner instead of the Chirks? You *can* cook?'

'I'm a professional chef, that's what I do during the summer,' I said icily, 'and my charges are *very* high. In winter I prefer to house-sit for a rest. Catering for family dinner parties doesn't come into my current plans and besides, as I've said, I don't celebrate Christmas in any way.'

'But—'

'Mr Martland,' I interrupted firmly, 'while I'm sorry your arrangements have been put out, you can rest assured that I'll keep an eye on your property and look after the animals until your return on Twelfth Night.'

'But how can I be sure of that when I know nothing about you, except that you have no knowledge of horses and—'

'Look,' I said, 'you don't have any alternative! If you think I'm going to drink your gin and fall into a drunken coma over Christmas, neglecting the animals and burning the house down, I suggest you email Ellen for my CV and references. Good *night*, Mr Martland.'

And I slammed down the receiver.

I regretted my lapse into rudeness almost immediately. It must have been tiredness, but also there was something about his manner that rubbed me up the wrong way. While a bit of snappishness might be allowable in a cook of my calibre, provided I produced delicious meals, which I always did, it's not such a good idea with house-sitting clients.

The phone rang again almost immediately. Sighing, I picked it up.

'You hung up on me!' he said incredulously.

'I'm sorry, but the conversation seemed to have run its natural course. Now, it's been a long day and I was just on my way to bed . . . Oh, and by the way,' I added as an afterthought, 'your cleaner has resigned, with effect from today. But going by the filthy state of the house, I daresay you'll hardly notice.'

This time when I put the phone down, he didn't ring back. I filled my hot water bottle, patted Merlin, and took myself off up to bed where, despite my exhaustion, I found myself going over and over the conversation with the irritating and unreasonable Jude Martland. I would be sure to leave *long* before he came home on Twelfth Night!

In the end I switched on the bedside lamp and read a few more entries in Gran's journal until, soothed by the small dramas of the hospital ward and her battles with her awful landlady, I finally fell asleep.

Chapter 6: Horse Sense

A new case has arrived on Pearl's ward – a bad leg wound and they are trying penicillin on it, which seems to be doing the trick. The patient is a young man and apparently a member of a local gentry family. Pearl and the others were whispering and giggling about him and how good looking he was, though I told them it was what was on the inside that mattered, not the outside. But I am ashamed to say that, stirred by curiosity, I peeped in later to see what all the fuss was about and Sister nearly caught me!

January, 1945

After breakfast next morning I checked on Lady and her smelly little companion, fed them a few chunks of carrot, then clipped back the top of the stable door to the courtyard.

They both looked fine, but I thought I would leave them where they were until it was fully light and took Merlin for a walk up Snowehill. He seemed to be moving a little easier this morning and I suspected he'd missed a couple of his pills and regular exercise in the last few days.

The closer we got to the red horse hill figure, the harder it was to make out what it was. It had been cut out of the turf and the earth banked on either side to make a raised edge. The natural red sandstone lay revealed, though it didn't stand out like the white horse ones I'd seen elsewhere and was on a much smaller scale. I wondered if it was ancient, perhaps Celtic? I seemed to recall that Celts were keen on horses. Or perhaps it was a more modern addition to the local scenery?

A track up to the beacon ran right by it and, looking down, I could see that it met the road above Old Place, where there was another farm. It was well trodden, so I expect lots of walkers come here to climb up to the folly. I'd do it myself one day, too, only not this particular one: I had too much to do.

I was just about to go back down when there was a quick spatter of Mozart from my pocket. The ringtone somehow didn't seem quite right for a windswept Lancashire hillside, but I'm not sure what would. Ride of the Valkyries?

'Caught you!' Ellen said triumphantly. 'I tried the house but there was no reply.'

'No, I'm up on the hill behind the house. In fact, the only mobile reception is up here, or down near the village, so you're lucky to have caught me at all.'

'What are you doing on the hill?'

'Walking the dog – and he's old and arthritic so I can't keep him standing about here very long.'

'I only wanted to warn you that I found a flood of emails from Jude Martland in my inbox this morning and he isn't happy about the change of home-sitter, though he should be grateful I could find *anyone* at such short notice!'

'Yes, that's what *I* told him.'

'You mean, you've spoken to him? He didn't mention that . . . or maybe I just haven't got as far as that email yet.'

'He rang last night and he struck me as a very autocratic and disagreeable person – and totally unreasonable! I told him I was perfectly capable and competent, but I'm not sure he believed me.'

'*I* told him much the same, but he still wanted to see your CV and references, so I faxed them. They're all glowing so they'll put his mind at rest.'

'I doubt it, because he seemed more worried about the horse than anything and you have to agree that I've no experience with them at all. But still, the instructions he left were clear enough and I'm sure I can manage. I made her hot mash last night and I'm going to put her in the paddock shortly and have a go at mucking out.'

'Oh, you'll be fine,' she said comfortably, which was easy for her since she wouldn't be the one coping! 'Well, I just wanted to warn you in case you got a phone call, but obviously you've dealt with him. And once he's read your CV I expect he will feel much happier. I told him he was lucky that one of my best house-sitters was free to step into the breach.'

'I hope so, though he may want regular bulletins on the horse and dog. Some pet owners do.'

She agreed and rang off, and Merlin and I went home again. I was dying to have another look around the house, but thought I'd better tackle Lady's stable first. From what I recalled, it was simply a matter of removing the old straw and replacing it with new: how hard could *that* be?

I changed into old jeans, a warm fleece and wellies, girded my loins and went to do the Augean stable bit. Merlin heaved himself up out of his basket with a resigned expression, but I gave him one of the rawhide chews out of the cupboard and left him in the kitchen with it: I needed my full attention on what I was doing.

At least by the New Year I would be able to add looking after horses and goats to my CV if I wanted to, though I wasn't entirely convinced I would ever want to see a goat again.

It was still very cold, though there was a wintry sun shining, and I had no idea whether I should put Lady in the paddock or not. Or perhaps just the cobbled yard, while I tried to sort out her bedding?

The shovel and wheelbarrow were easy to find – and so was the manure heap over the wall in the paddock. There were bales of straw and one or two of hay at the opposite end of the barn to Lady's box, and more in a sort of half-loft overhead, with a rickety wooden ladder. Luckily I can tell straw from hay because guinea pigs, rabbits and chickens have all been previous charges of mine.

I was still debating what to do with Lady and her companion – *especially* her companion – when help arrived unexpectedly in the form of a large, elderly woman on a stocky brown cob. She hailed me from the other side of the gate, then dismounted and led her horse through, shutting it behind her. She was wearing a Burberry check headscarf tied pirate-fashion instead of a riding hat and a hugely-caped wax jacket, so she looked like a slightly eccentric highwayman.

'Hello,' she said in a deep, hearty voice, holding out her hand. 'I'm Becca – Becca Martland, Noël's sister. He told me you'd arrived, so I thought I'd ride this way and see how you were doing.'

We shook hands. She was by no means as tall as me (at six foot, not many women are!) but she made up for it in girth.

'I'm very glad to meet you – especially since I was just about to muck out Lady and I wasn't sure what to do with her while I did it,' I confessed, seeing knowledgeable help was at hand. 'Is it too cold to put her in the paddock, do you think?'

'Not at all, Arabs are tough as old boots and she'll go in the field shelter if it rains, or to get out of the wind. Have you taken her rug off and brushed her?'

'No, though I did check that it was secure last night.'

'We'll do that first, then, because I don't suppose anyone has for a couple of days. You go and open the gate to the paddock, while I tie Nutkin up in the barn out of this cold wind and fetch the brushes from the tackroom.'

We let Billy out while we groomed Lady – Becca assured me he never went far from her side. Indeed, he dithered in the open door until I gave him a quick shove and closed it behind him and then he hung about outside, bleating.

'Lovely creature, Lady,' Becca said, stripping off the rug and then handing me one of the two oval brushes with the concise instruction, 'Firm strokes in the direction of the hair.'

'But she's terribly old, isn't she? I was a bit worried about that when I read Mr Martland's notes.'

'Oh, twenty-five is nothing for an Arab! I'd look after her myself when Jude's away, but it takes me all my time to look after one horse these days. And I'm not taking on the bleeding goat,' she added. 'Noël said you hadn't had much experience with horses?'

'No, to be honest, going to the riding school with my best friend when she had her pony phase was about it,' I explained. 'Mr Martland's instructions are very detailed and I'm sure I can manage perfectly well, but it would be wonderful if I could call on you for anything that puzzled me? It might make Mr Martland feel better too – he rang last night and was fretting about whether I could cope.'

'Oh, did he phone? I don't suppose he said he was coming back for Christmas after all, did he?' she asked hopefully, stopping her brisk brushing and staring at me across Lady's snowy back.

'No, I'm afraid not. Did you think he might change his mind?'

Her face fell. 'Not really, it's just that the Martlands have always celebrated Christmas together, here at Old Place. It doesn't seem right to have the head of the household on the opposite side of the world.'

She put her brush down and showed me how to put the rug back on securely, which was simple enough with Lady, but I should imagine very difficult with a less cooperative horse!

'Jude loves horses and he's particularly attached to Lady,' she said. 'She was his mother's horse, you know, so he's bound to worry about her. But of course you can call me if you're concerned about anything, I'll leave you my phone number. Not that you can always get through, because the lines are hanging loose from the poles like limp spaghetti and a good wind can cut the connection to Old Place for a week or more.'

She said this as if it was the most normal thing in the world.

'Couldn't the lines be repaired?' I would certainly have had it sorted out in no time, if I lived here!

'Apparently all the poles need replacing and they'll get round to it eventually, but there's only Old Place and Hill Farm up this road until you get to Great Mumming, so it's not exactly high on their priority list when it comes to allocating resources.'

'Oh yes, I saw the farm when I walked Merlin up to the red horse earlier and I noticed the sign on the main road pointed two ways to Great Mumming, so presumably it carries on past Hill Farm?'

'That's right, but the road beyond the farm isn't much more than a track with tarmac over it that goes round the side of Snowehill – a bit of ice and you don't even want to *think* about trying it,' she said, then gave a deep laugh. 'One of those SatNav things keeps sending motorists up here as a short cut to the motorway – and it might be, as the crow flies, but not by car!'

Billy's plaintively protesting bleats rose to a crescendo. We let Lady out into the paddock and he followed her, butting against her legs.

Becca picked up a fork. 'Come on – now I'll help you muck out. You bring the barrow.'

She must have been in her seventies, at least, but she could still wield a fork with the best of them and gave me what was essentially a very useful masterclass. Under her direction I trundled the used bedding over to the manure heap, then spread a thick layer of clean straw in the loosebox, padded out at the sides and round the washed and filled bucket.

'You don't need to do this every single day – just pick up the manure and put down a bit of fresh straw if it isn't too bad.'

'How cold does it have to get before I keep her inside during the day?'

'Oh, she can go out even if it snows, but you might need to double-rug her,' she said breezily.

'Right . . .' Jude Martland and his aunt seemed to have two different views on just how fragile Lady was!

I was glowing by the time we'd finished mucking out, and probably steaming gently in the chilly air, just like the replenished manure heap.

'There – that's fine, all ready for bringing her in before it goes dark. Did you manage her warm mash all right last night?'

'Oh yes, it was just a matter of following the recipe. And thank you very much for showing me what to do, it's been invaluable,' I said gratefully.

'I'd better pop back in a day or two and give you a few more pointers,' she suggested.

'That would be great, if you can spare the time.'

'Noël says you're from West Lancs, near Ormskirk? What do you shoot over there?'

'Shoot? I don't shoot anything!'

'Pity – there's not an awful lot up here either, bar the odd rabbit and pigeon,' she commiserated, 'but you'll find some of those, and a few pheasants and the like, in one of the freezers.'

While I've cooked an awful lot of game over the years for house-parties, I think killing something simply for pleasure is a bad thing – but when working I just cook, I don't give opinions!

'I'm a town girl, really, brought up in Merchester,' I admitted, 'though my work usually takes me into the country from late spring to early autumn when I cook for large house-parties. The rest of the year I take home-sitting assignments, like this one.'

'Oh, you cook? It's a pity we can't have a house-party at Old Place over Christmas, then,' Becca said wistfully. 'I call it a bit selfish of Jude to go off like this, even if he has been crossed in love. His brother Guy ran off with his fiancée last Christmas, you know.'

'Your brother did mention something about it,' I admitted. 'He and his wife told me you all usually spend Christmas together and their granddaughter had been looking forward to it, but actually, in winter I like a rest from all the cooking and, besides, I don't celebrate Christmas.'

'Against your religion, I expect,' she said vaguely, with a glance at my black hair and pale olive skin. People are always asking me where I am from and seem surprised when I say Merchester.

'And the old people really look forward to having their Christmas dinner here too,' she went on. 'I don't think they've quite taken in that it isn't going to happen this year.'

'You mean Noël and Tilda?' I ventured. Clearly she wasn't numbering herself among the ranks of the elderly!

'Well, yes, but actually I meant Old Nan and Richard Sampson, who was the vicar here until he retired. They live in the almshouses in Little Mumming. Of course, there's Henry too, but he always goes to his daughter's for his dinner, including Christmas Day. Did you notice the almshouses as you came through the village?'

'The row of three tiny Gothic-looking cottages?'

'Yes, that's where the family stash away the last of the retainers. Old Nan is in her nineties, but bright as a button, and Richard's about eighty, fit as a flea and walks for miles. By the way, Henry still comes up here when the fancy takes him and hangs out in the greenhouse and walled garden – you might suddenly stumble across him.'

She nodded at a small gate set in an arch. 'Through there – small walled garden, Jude's mother loved it, but it's pretty overgrown now apart from the vegetable patch. The greenhouse backs on to the stables and barn and Henry has a little den up at one end with a primus stove to make tea.'

'Right – I'll keep an eye out for him! But I do hope the other two have understood the situation and made other arrangements for Christmas Day?'

'I don't know, old habits are hard to break.' Becca shook her head. 'Like Tilda – she talks as if she still does all the cooking, but really that Edwina of hers does most of it now, with Tilda getting in her way and bossing her about. So it's always been very convenient that they can come here for a week at Christmas while Edwina has a break.'

'Mr Martland's absence does seem to have created quite a lot of disappointment and difficulty,' I said, thinking that since he must have known how all these elderly people relied on him, it was very selfish indeed of him to flounce off abroad like this, even if he *had* been crossed in love.

'Well, it's not *your* fault,' she said briskly.

'Do you have time to come in and have a cup of tea?' I asked. 'I brought a fruit cake with me.'

'Lovely, lead the way!'

She didn't take her scarf off, but removed the wax jacket, revealing a quilted gilet and cord riding breeches of generous and forgiving cut. Merlin hauled himself out of his basket to greet her.

'Hello, old fellow,' she said fondly, stroking his head with a large hand. 'Stayed here in the warm, did you?'

'He's already had a run, I thought he'd be better in,' I said, making tea and taking the cake out of the tin. 'The house seems a little chilly despite the central heating, so I thought I'd light the big fire in the sitting room later.'

'Jolly good idea. There's always been a fire lit there in winter, it's the heart of the house, but Jude's been neglecting the place since the Jacksons retired, though they were getting a bit past it and glad to go once my brother died. Noël told me you'd just lost your grandmother, too – sorry,' she added abruptly, but with sincerity.

'Thank you, yes, it *was* quite recent. She brought me up because my own mother died soon after I was born.'

'Sad,' she said. 'Jude's mother died several years ago now, but he adored her. I think that must have been where he got his arty ways, because there was never anything like *that* in the family before. And I expect that's why he dotes on Lady too – but then, he loves all horses, even if they do sometimes look a bit tortured in those sculptures he makes!'

'I don't think the one I've seen near Manchester looked tortured, just . . . modern. You could still tell what it was.'

'He has a studio in the woods just above the lodge – the old mill house. You'll see a path going off the drive to it, but it'll be locked up, of course.'

There was nothing in the instructions about looking after that as well, thank goodness, though I expected I'd walk down that way with Merlin one day.

Even though the family's disappointment over Christmas was none of my doing, my conscience had been niggling away at me slightly, so when she got up to go I said impulsively, 'You wouldn't like the enormous frozen turkey and giant Christmas pudding the Chirks left, I suppose? Then you, your brother and sister-in-law and Jess could have a proper Christmas dinner together.'

'Oh, *I* can't cook anything more complicated than a boiled egg! So it looks like I'll be eating Tilda's roast chicken dinner at the lodge on Christmas Day and then going home to cheese, cold cuts and pickles.'

That made me feel even more guilty, though why I should when none of these broken arrangements were my fault, I can't imagine! It is all entirely down to the selfishness of Jude Martland!

Chapter 7: The Whole Hog

Sister is a great lump of a woman, big and cold enough to sink the Titanic, though she moves silently enough for all that and caught Pearl sitting on the edge of the new patient's bed, a heinous crime. Now Pearl has been moved to the children's ward and I have taken her place, Sister saying she trusts me not to flirt with the patients! This does not, of course, stop them trying to flirt with me . . .

January, 1945

When Becca had gone (with a big wedge of foil-wrapped cake in her coat pocket), I finally had time to take another look around the house, Merlin at my heels. He had taken to following me about so closely now that if I stopped suddenly, his nose ran into the back of my leg. It felt quite cold and damp even through my jeans; generally a healthy sign in a dog, if not a human.

I wanted to familiarise myself with the layout and especially with the position of anything that might be valuable, and make sure that I hadn't missed any windows last night when locking up. I would mainly be living in the kitchen wing, unless the urge suddenly came upon me to watch the TV in the little morning room . . . Though actually, I'd really taken to the sitting room, vast though it was, so I might spend some time there once I'd lit a fire.

I can't say I found any valuables, apart from a pair of tarnished silver candlesticks and an engraved tray on the sideboard in the dining room, and a row of silver-framed photographs on the upright piano at the further end of the room.

When I lifted the lid of the piano I was surprised to find it was only slightly out of tune and I wondered who still played it. I picked out the first bit of 'Lead Kindly Light' (a hymn Gran taught me to play on her harmonium), which echoed hollowly around the room. It was a lovely instrument, but in the event of a fire I'd be more inclined to snatch up the silver than heave the piano out of the window.

Closing it, I examined the photographs, most quite old and of family groupings – weddings, picnics, expeditions in huge open-topped cars – all the prewar pleasures of the moneyed classes.

At the end of the row was a more recent colour picture of two tall, dark-haired young men, one much bigger, more thick-set and not as handsome as the other, though there was an obvious resemblance. The handsome one was smiling at whoever held the camera, while the other scowled – and if this was Jude Martland and his brother, then I could guess which was which, even after speaking to the man once!

The library held a very mixed selection of books, including a lot of old crime novels of the cosy variety, my favourite. I promised myself a lovely, relaxing time over Christmas, sitting beside a roaring fire with coffee, chocolates and cake to hand, and Merlin and the radio to keep me company.

The one wall free of bookshelves was covered with more old photographs of family and friends – the Martlands were easy to pick out, being mostly tall and dark – but also of men strangely garbed and taking part in some kind of open-air performance. It might have been the Twelfth Night ceremony Sharon mentioned, in which case it looked to me like some innocuous kind of Morris dancing event.

The key to the French doors in the garden hall was on my bunch and I let myself out into the small walled garden, after pulling on an over-large anorak. If this belonged to Jude Martland, then he was a *lot* bigger than me – about the size of a grizzly bear, in fact!

The garden had a schizophrenic personality: half being over-grown and neglected, with roses that had rambled a little too far and encroaching ivy; while the other was a neat array of vegetable and fruit beds. The large, lean-to greenhouse against the back of the barn could have done with a coat of paint, but inside all was neat and tidy, with tools and pots stowed away under benches or hung up on racks, and a little hidey-hole at the end behind a sacking curtain where Henry hung out, though it was currently vacant. He had a little primus stove, kettle, mug and a tin box containing half a packet of slightly limp digestive biscuits and some Yorkshire Tea bags.

I went back indoors, shivering. It was definitely getting colder and if we did get ice and snow, as the forecast for next week had hinted we might, I was sure that the steep road down from the village would quickly become impassable and we'd be cut off. This was a situation that had often befallen me in Scotland, so I wasn't particularly bothered by the idea, though I made a note to check that I had all the supplies in the house that I needed, just in case. I could call in at the lodge and make sure *they* were well prepared too.

Upstairs I wanted to check on the attic, but the door to that was locked and I didn't have the key – which would be unfortunate if the pipes or water tank leaked or froze! But perhaps it had been entrusted to Noël for emergencies and I made a mental note to ask.

I stopped by my bedroom to hang up the rest of my clothes and stack the books I'd brought and my laptop and cookery notes on a marble-topped washstand, ready to take downstairs later. Gran's little tin trunk looked right up here, the sort of thing a servant might once have had . . . I sat on the edge of the bed and flicked through the first journal until I found where I had left off reading last night: the next few entries seemed to increasingly mention the new patient . . .

Firmly resisting the urge to skim, I closed the book: I was enjoying slowly discovering my gran through her journals every evening, a couple of pages at a time, and didn't want to rush that.

'Come on, Merlin,' I said, gathering up my books and stuff for downstairs, and he uncoiled himself from the little braided rug at the end of the bed and followed me.

I dumped everything in the kitchen then checked out the cellar, where I was happy to see a whole wall of dry logs and kindling for the sitting-room fire and the boiler burbling quietly away. The wine cellar door was locked of course, but funnily enough, Jude Martland seemed to have overlooked the drinks cabinet with its decanters of spirits and bottles of liqueur in the dining room, so if the urge *did* uncharacteristically take me to render myself drunk and disorderly, the means were freely to hand.

But this was unlikely: I like to be in control way too much!

By the time we emerged back up into the kitchen, Merlin had begun to heave long-suffering sighs, so I put some dog biscuits from an open packet into his bowl and had a lunch of bread, cheese and rich, chunky apricot chutney from a jar I'd brought with me, before checking up on the provisions.

The kitchen cupboards were well stocked, though some of the food looked as if it hadn't been touched for months. The tall fridge contained butter, eggs, bacon and an awful lot of cheese left by Mo and Jim, plus the few perishable items I'd brought with me. Mo and Jim obviously liked to go the whole hog at Christmas, because as well as the gigantic turkey and a ham joint in the freezer, there was a pudding the size of a small planet, jars and jars of mincemeat and even some of those expensive Chocolate Wishes (like a delicious fortune cookie) that are made in Sticklepond, a village near where I live.

The biggest freezer was packed with game, meat and fish, and the other contained an array of bread, pizza, chilli and a whole stack of instant meals of a sustaining nature: these probably formed the owner's staple diet, in which case gourmet he was *not*. What with those and a very plentiful supply of tea bags, coffee, longlife milk and orange juice, I was starting to get the hang of what Jude Martland lived on when he was home!

I noted down anything I thought I might run out of, which the village shop could probably supply, but I was unlikely to starve to death any time soon.

Merlin, bored, was now fast asleep in his basket by the Aga – sweet!

I chopped up a carrot and took it out to Lady, dropping a bit down for Billy, who was scrabbling at the fence with frantic greed. Lady has lips like softest velvet and, although her coat is snowy white, oddly enough the skin under it is black.

When the carrot had all gone, she and her odoriferous little friend wandered back up the paddock and I went to check the level of oil in the huge tank in the outbuilding (satisfyingly full), and had a look at the generator. This was a dauntingly large piece of machinery but apparently should switch itself on if the mains electricity fails, then back off again when it returns. The Homebodies folder did mention that if it didn't turn on automatically, you had to come out here and do it manually . . .

I was just leaning over it, examining the switches, when a voice suddenly rasped behind me, 'You don't want to mess with that there bit of machinery, gurl!'

I whipped round, startled, to find I had company in the shape of an elderly man, small and thin, with long limp wisps of snuff-coloured hair on either side of his cadaverous face. He was holding a bulging sack in one hand and a slightly threateningly raised stick in the other. I have seen more prepossessing old men.

'Women shouldn't meddle with what they don't understand.'

'You wouldn't be Henry, would you?'

He nodded. 'My daughter ran me up to fetch a few taters and carrots. And you're the gurl has come to look after the place, instead of Jim and Mo?'

The tone of his voice left me in no doubt that this was not, in his opinion, a good exchange. In fact, I was beginning to find Jim and Mo Chirk a hard act to follow: they seemed to have made themselves very popular with everyone in previous visits!

'I haven't been described as a girl for years,' I said pleasantly, 'and I'm actually one of Homebodies' most experienced house-sitters.'

'You're a grand, strapping lass, I'll allow that,' he conceded, 'but all the same, you shouldn't meddle with the generator. I showed Jim the way of it, but I'm not having it messed about by any Tom, Dick or Harry.'

'Thomasina, Richenda or Harriet?' I suggested and he looked at me blankly. 'If the electricity goes off and it doesn't switch itself on, then I'll have to know how to do it, won't I?'

'Nay, you leave it to them as knows what they're doing.'

'Meaning you?'

'That's right.'

'But you might not be around when I need to switch it on – perhaps we'll get snowed in, and then what would I do? But don't worry, Mr Martland left instructions and it looks *perfectly* simple.'

'You don't want to tinker with it,' he insisted obstinately.

We seemed to have reached an impasse. I said calmly and perfectly politely, 'I'm sorry, but it's part of my job to keep the place in good running order, so if I have to run the generator, I will: after all, I can't be expected to sit in the dark in a cold house over the Christmas holidays, can I?'

He gave me a look of deep disfavour, but seemed eventually, after much rumination, to accept the logic of my argument. 'I can see you're a stubborn, determined creature, just like Jude, who always thinks he knows best . . . Well, I suppose I'd better show you the way of it, then, but you're not to touch it unless you can't get hold of me, mind?'

'Certainly,' I agreed, and we shook hands on it, though since he spat into his palm first, it was possibly the most disgusting thing I have ever had to do while maintaining a polite expression.

I couldn't see what all the fuss was about really with the generator, it was quite simple. Then Henry said his daughter was waiting and hobbled off with his sack of booty and I went indoors and washed my hands with bacteria-busting hand gel.

I fully intended raiding his vegetable plot myself, but I would be scrubbing everything well before cooking it, because I wouldn't put it past him to pee on the compost heap like a lot of old gardeners – if not worse.

Once I'd thawed out, I cleaned out the hearth in the sitting room and laid a fire, fetching up kindling and logs from the cellar in an ancient-looking wicker basket. I only hoped the chimney had been recently swept, because setting the place on fire would probably be the end of my home-sitting career. But luckily the smoke drew upwards, rather than billowed out, and no clouds of soot descended.

Once it was going well I set the brass fireguard in front of it, then opened all the unlocked doors in the house to let the warm air circulate through – old houses could quickly get musty if you didn't keep them aired.

I settled down for a nice rest in front of the sitting-room fire once I'd done that, with a good, strong pot of tea and another slice of my slightly depleted fruit cake to hand.

I felt I deserved a break: there was quite a bit to do at Old Place compared to some other house-sits, though I was sure I'd soon fall into a routine with the animals now I'd got the hang of it. Then the rest of the time would be my own . . . except that

I really would have to clean this lovely room if I intended spending much time in here!

I'd been half-expecting Jude Martland to ring again much later in the day, but it was typical of the man I was beginning to know that he should instead call just as I'd finally sat down for a rest! The phone in here was on a round table by the window, too, with only a hard chair next to it.

This time he was fractionally more conciliatory, presumably because he'd read my glowing references from satisfied clients, and I was determined to keep my cool.

'Miss Brown, I don't think I thanked you yesterday for stepping into the breach at such short notice,' he began stiffly.

'Mrs – and of course I understood that you were concerned that your house and animals were being taken care of by a total stranger. But you can rest easy: everything is *perfectly* under control and your Aunt Becca came here and gave me some excellent advice about Lady, as well as her phone number, should anything crop up.'

'Oh good!' He sounded relieved. 'You did put Lady's medicine in her warm mash last night, didn't you?'

'Of course.'

'And kept Billy away from it until she'd eaten it?'

'Naturally,' I said, though it had been quite a tussle to stop Billy diving into the bucket before Lady was finished. 'Lady's fine. And your gardener, Henry, helpfully showed me what to do if the electricity goes off and the generator doesn't come on automatically.'

'*Henry* told you?' he repeated incredulously.

'Of course! He could see the necessity, in case he wasn't available to come to Old Place and deal with it himself. And I mean to walk into Little Mumming tomorrow, so I'll call in to see your aunt and uncle at the lodge to ask them if they need any shopping. So you see, you've nothing to worry about and can enjoy your holiday,' I finished kindly.

'It's not entirely a holiday: there was a ceremony to unveil one of my sculptures yesterday.'

'Oh yes, I've seen that horse you did up on a hill near Manchester and it's very nice.'

'*Nice?* Do try not to sound *too* impressed,' he said, seeming a bit miffed. 'I'm supposed to be off to the Hamptons to stay with friends for Christmas tomorrow, but I don't see how I can possibly relax and enjoy it when I know you're alone at Old Place looking after everything – the weather can be bad up there, you know, Little Mumming is often cut off in winter.'

'So I've already been told – and really, the dimmest person would be able to appreciate that if the steep hill down from the village was icy, it would be impassable. But don't worry, I've often been snowed in up Scotland and it's not a problem.'

'You don't mind isolation then?'

'No. In fact, I enjoy it. I have some work I want to finish off too – a book of house-party recipes I'm compiling.'

'Yes, you said you were a cook,' he said thoughtfully. 'Look, I know you said you didn't celebrate Christmas, but I really think you might reconsider—'

I could see he was about to ask me to cook the family Christmas dinner all over again, probably due to a suddenly guilty conscience, so I interrupted him quite firmly before he got going.

'Mr Martland, I try to ignore Christmas as much as I can and also I recently lost the grandmother who brought me up. She was a Strange Baptist, so I wasn't raised to think the worldly trappings of the season of importance in any case.'

'What was strange about her being a Baptist?' he asked, diverted.

'Nothing. Strange Baptists were a breakaway sect at the turn of the century, though there aren't that many of them left.' I glanced out of the window. 'Now, if you'll excuse me, your uncle and niece have just arrived in a golf buggy, so I'd better go and let them in, there's a biting wind out there.'

'No, wait,' he ordered, 'go and fetch him to the phone, so I can speak to him. I—'

'Call him yourself later, if you want to,' I interrupted and put the receiver down. Cut off in his prime again. This was getting to be a habit – but he was proving to be a most *irritating* man, especially that deep, rumbling voice: it was as disturbing as distant thunder!

Chapter 8: Deep Freeze

The new patient's leg is answering well to the penicillin but he teases me when I am changing his dressings and tries to make me laugh . . . and sometimes succeeds, despite my best attempts to keep a straight face.

January, 1945

'We thought we would call in and see how you were getting on,' Noël explained, 'though Becca stopped briefly on her way home and said you were doing fine. But I wanted to return some books to the library in any case. Jude doesn't mind my popping in and out, I've always had the run of the place. And Mo and Jim said they didn't mind in the least, either.'

'Of course, it's your family home, so you must come and go as you please,' I assured him.

'Thank you, m'dear,' he said, with his attractively lopsided smile, 'only of course, now I have had to give up driving the car, the golf buggy is very chilly and really not up to winter weather conditions.'

'I drove Grandpa up,' Jess said. 'I was bored and I like driving the buggy; only I'm not allowed to do it on my own.'

Seeing she was looking wistfully at my slice of fruit cake I said, 'Can I get you both some tea and perhaps a slice of cake? Mine has gone cold because your nephew just rang again, so I was going to make a fresh pot anyway.'

'Oh, Jude got through?' he asked. 'What a pity we were not here in time to speak to him.'

'I'm afraid he simply *had* to go. But I expect he'll phone you back later.'

'Very likely . . . but we don't want to disturb you if you are busy,' he said, with a look at the pile of papers next to the easy chair.

'Not at all, I was only going to look at some notes for a recipe book I'm compiling – *Cooking for House-Parties*. I've been collecting recipes and tips for years, but now I'm finally hoping to get it ready to send out to publishers in the New Year.'

'Do people have large house-parties any more? I remember them as a young man, and jolly good fun they were, too!' said Noël a little wistfully.

'Oh yes, you'd be surprised – but probably they're very different from the ones you knew.'

'I know Becca still gets invited to shooting and fishing ones,' he said. 'And the family have always gathered here at Old Place between Christmas and Twelfth Night, so *that* is a house-party too, I suppose.'

'I think your book needs a less boring title than *Cooking for House-Parties*, Jess said frankly.

'That's just the working title, but if you can think of a better one, let me know.'

'I'm writing a vampire book, with lots of blood,' she confided.

'I expect there would be in a vampire book.'

'There wasn't a great deal, as I recall, in Bram Stoker's *Dracula*,' her grandfather said doubtfully.

'There will be in mine. I'm going to kill off all the girls at school I don't like – *horribly*.'

'Good idea – that sounds immensely satisfying,' I said.

Noël settled comfortably on the sofa in front of the fire. Jess came through to the kitchen with me and, while I brewed a fresh pot of tea and laid the tray with cups and saucers and the remains of my fast-vanishing fruit cake, fetched a carton of long-life orange juice from the lavish supply in the larder and opened it.

'Jude likes this with his breakfast.'

'Going by the ready meals in the freezer, he doesn't do much cooking, does he? There's lots of other food in there, but most of it looks as if it's been there for ages, especially the game.'

'I think he forgets to cook half the time, apart from breakfast. It's Aunt Becca who puts all the game and trout and stuff in the freezers – she's forever visiting friends and coming back with more than she knows what to do with. She gives it to Granny, too. Do you *like* rabbit?'

'When it's cooked properly.'

'I don't. I can't help thinking about how harmless and nice rabbits are.'

'Well, no-one's going to force you to eat one, are they?' I said with a smile. 'I could make you a rabbit you *would* like one day though – a chocolate blancmange one! There's a lovely Victorian glass mould in one of the cupboards and I'm dying to try it. You could come to tea, if your grandparents say it's all right.'

'Oh, they won't mind. What's blancmange?'

'A kind of flavoured milk jelly.'

'Is it like Angel Delight? Granny has some of that in the cupboard.'

'Sort of. You know, someone ought to eat up the game in the freezer, it's such a waste otherwise.'

'As long as it isn't me. Though actually, your cooking might be better than Granny's – her food is all a bit weird.'

'I expect she just cooks like she did early in her career and tastes have changed,' I said tactfully. 'By the way, the black stuff in those pinwheel sandwiches she gave me for lunch . . . I don't suppose you know what that was?'

'It's a heavily guarded secret. I call it minced rancid car tyre.'

'That's a pretty fair description,' I admitted.

'I know Granny carries on as if she does all the cooking herself,

74

but actually Edwina does most of it really,' Jess confided. 'That's the *real* reason why they always move into Old Place when she goes off to her relatives for Christmas and New Year. Goodness knows what Christmas dinner will be like this time!'

I felt another inconvenient pang of conscience, though why I should I can't imagine, since it's Jude Martland who ought to be having them, not me!

'You can help her with the cooking,' I suggested. 'I used to help my gran, that's what started me off thinking I wanted to become a chef.'

'She's very bossy and says she doesn't want little girls in the kitchen under her feet when she's busy, even though I'm nearly thirteen and way taller than she is! I help Grandpa with the washing up, instead.'

The tea was ready and I carried the tray into the sitting room, finding Noël half-asleep before the fire, though he woke up the instant the crockery rattled.

'Lovely to see the fire lit in here again,' he said, 'it seemed so cold and unwelcoming without it.'

'I thought it would air the house out – old houses seem to get dank and musty very quickly, don't they?'

'Yes, indeed. Of course, with only a week to go until Christmas Eve, this room would usually be decorated for Christmas by now, with the tree in the corner by the stairs and a kissing bough . . .' he said regretfully. 'All the decorations are in the attic, though Jude's mother used to make swags of greenery from the garden, she was very good at that sort of thing.'

'The attic is locked, as are one or two other rooms,' I said. 'That's fine, but do you have the keys in case there's an emergency, like a burst water pipe?'

'The attic isn't locked, it's just the door that's very stiff,' Jess said. 'I remember that from playing hide and seek last Christmas. When I went up there, no-one found me for ages.'

'That was because it was supposed to be out of bounds,' Noël reminded her. 'But yes, I do have all the rest of the keys, including the one for the mill studio, just in case.'

'Oh good. I don't suppose for a minute I'll need them, I just like to know. I expect I'll only really use this room, apart from the kitchen wing – it has a lovely warm, homely feel to it, despite being so big.'

'Yes, it was always the heart of the house.' He sighed and his gaze rested on a black and white family group photograph that stood on one of the occasional tables. 'There were five of us children, you know, and now only Becca and I are left. Jacob was the eldest, but he was killed at Dunkirk, poor chap, and another brother, Edward, was badly wounded later. Alex – Jude's father – inherited, though he didn't marry until late in life. But they're all gone now, all gone . . .' He shook his head sadly. 'Alex passed away last January, after a long illness.'

'I noticed the house had some adaptations for an invalid, like the stairlift . . . and excuse me, but did you say one of your brothers was called Edward?' I asked.

'Yes, though we always called him Ned.'

I was startled by the revelation that there had indeed been a Ned Martland, a contemporary of Gran's – but surely this was just one more of those strange coincidences that life throws at you? I couldn't see how their paths could ever have crossed . . .

'He was a bit of a rip, but full of fun and mischief – Jude's younger brother, Guy, reminds me of him.' Noël shook his head with a rueful smile. 'There was no real harm in him, but he *was* the black sheep of the family, I suppose, whereas Guy has settled down very well lately – he's an international banker in London, you know.'

'He's settling down with Uncle Jude's ex-fiancée,' Jess pointed out. 'And *I* don't think Uncle Guy is very nice at all.'

'He is very naughty to tease you,' Noël said, 'but he doesn't mean any harm by it.'

Since Jess was at the age where your main wish in life is to be totally invisible and anyone even *glancing* at you could be an agony, I thought Guy Martland sounded very insensitive and mean indeed! Just as objectionable, in his own way, as his brother Jude, in fact.

'I'm sure it was all for the best that Jude's fiancée broke the engagement, because she can't have been in love with him,' Noël said, 'and I am a firm believer in marriage being for life.'

'Yes, me too – and beyond,' I murmured absently, my mind still on Ned Martland.

'Guy and Coco – that's her silly name – just got engaged,' Jess said. 'It was in the paper and I think that's why Uncle Jude said he wasn't coming back from America until after Christmas.'

'Oh, but he already had the invitation to spend the holidays with friends after the event to mark the installation of his sculpture … Though perhaps you are partly right, Jess,' her grandfather conceded. 'I expect Guy would have thought nothing of turning up for a family Christmas despite everything, had Jude stayed at home.'

'They haven't spoken since last Christmas,' Jess explained. 'Jude invited Coco here to meet the family and she and Guy got *very* friendly. Uncle Jude was pretty grim.'

'I expect he would be!' I agreed, though going by the photographs I'd seen, and my brief conversations with him, he was *always* pretty grim.

'Then she and Jude had a big argument and Guy drove her home and that was it.'

'I don't feel that Guy behaved very well in the circumstances, even if there was a mutual attraction between him and Coco,' Noël said, looking troubled. 'It upset my brother, too, that there was a breach between his two sons and Jude thought it hastened his last illness.' He shook his head sadly. 'Not that Alex liked her very much – it was her first visit to Old Place and she made it clear she was expecting a much larger and grander house.'

'It seems pretty large and grand to me,' I said, surprised.

'Still, she won't have to live here if she marries Guy – and Jude will just have to forgive and forget.'

'I don't suppose she'll come here much anyway,' Jess said. 'She didn't seem to like being in the country at all and wouldn't go out except in the car, because she hadn't brought any shoes except stiletto heels, though she could have borrowed some wellies. *And* she's scared of horses and dogs. Granny says she's all fur coat and no knickers, and Guy could do better.'

I swallowed a sip of tea the wrong way and coughed, my eyes watering.

'I don't think you should repeat that phrase, really,' Noël said mildly.

'How on earth did she meet Jude in the first place?' I asked. 'It doesn't sound as if they had a lot in common.'

'She is a model and also, I believe, aspires to be an actress. Someone brought her to Jude's last big retrospective exhibition and introduced her. She's very, very pretty indeed, if your taste runs to fair women.'

'Uncle Jude's must, mustn't it?' Jess said.

'I suppose we do tend to be attracted to our opposites,' I suggested.

'You're very dark, so was *your* husband fair?'

'Jess, you really shouldn't ask people personal questions!'

'I don't mind – and yes, my husband had blond hair and blue eyes. His younger sister is my best friend and has the same colouring – she's *very* pretty too.'

How I'd longed to be small, blonde and cute when I was at school, rather than towering above everyone, even the boys! I'd been thin as a stick too, which had made me even more self-conscious – though actually I wasn't sure it was any better later when I filled out and men started to talk to my boobs instead of me . . . except Alan, of course.

'Well, I think we ought to be going!' Noël said, getting up.

'I'm walking down to the village tomorrow, to explore,' I told him. 'I'll call in at the lodge to see if there's anything you'd like me to bring back from the shop.'

'I'll ask Tilda,' he promised. 'You are very kind!'

It seemed to me that, far from being isolated and alone at Old Place, I was going to be inundated with visitors!

The day had gone by in a flash, so I went to put the dried beet to soak in a bucket for Lady's bedtime mash and then went out with it and some of Billy's goat munchies to lure them back into the stable.

Thanks to a bit of timely advice from Becca, I knew that if I was carrying the bucket then Lady would simply follow me into her loosebox and Billy would come with her, and so it was. Then I shut them both up all cosily for the night.

After my conversation with Noël, I abandoned my cookbook notes and brought down Gran's journal and read on steadily into the evening. I was again tempted to flick forward and see if I could spot any mention of Ned Martland, but I'd been enjoying all the details of Gran's life as she slowly came out of her shell under Hilda and Pearl's influence and I didn't want to rush it: this was a girl whose idea of a night of dissipation was a trip to the cinema!

I finished that journal and read the first page or two of the next in bed before I went to sleep. By then Gran had started referring to the new patient as 'N.M'! It occurred to me that there was a very natural way her path might have crossed with the Old Place Ned Martland – and after what Noël had said about his brother being a black sheep, I'll be really worried for her if it turns out to be him.

But I suppose even if it is, then given Gran's upbringing and nature, it could only have been some kind of *Brief Encounter*!

Chapter 9: Daggers

Hilda and Pearl kindly warned me that N.M. was a flirt and not to take anything he said seriously, but he was very sincere and sweet when I told him about Tom and my intention to devote my life to nursing. He is kind when he is being serious and easy to talk to.

February, 1945

Next morning the wind had died down a bit, but everything was thickly furred with frost. But then, it's been growing steadily colder since I got here and, according to the radio, the odds on it being a white Christmas were getting shorter and shorter by the minute.

The house was already starting to warm through now I'd lit the fire, though, and I was keeping it going by a lavish application of logs from the cellar. The place will soon feel cosy, despite its size.

After breakfast (which I ate with the latest of Gran's journals propped in front of me) I let Lady and Billy out. Billy ignored the open gate and jumped straight over the fence like a . . . well, I was going to say *goat*!

I hung a filled haynet on the rail, high enough so that Lady wouldn't catch her feet in it when it was empty (another bit of advice from the invaluable Becca!) and broke a thin skin of ice on the trough, before tidying up the loosebox.

Merlin had wandered off up the paddock, which I thought was probably exercise enough for the morning, so I went back in and prepared to give the sitting room the sort of cleaning my Gran always referred to as 'a good bottoming', something it clearly hadn't had for quite some time.

It's part of the Homebodies remit that we keep the rooms of the house that we actually use neat and clean, it's just that the houses aren't usually quite on this scale!

I don't enjoy the process of cleaning, but I *do* love a nice clean room, so I suppose you could call that job satisfaction. Although it's not in the same league as providing an excellent dinner for twenty-five people with mixed dietary requirements every day for a fortnight with effortless expertise. Now *that's* satisfying on a creative level, too – I sometimes think cooking is a kind of ephemeral art form.

Anyway, by the time I'd vacuumed the pattern back into existence on the lovely old carpet, mopped the bit of stone floor around the edges, removed spider's webs from every corner and polished the brass fender, fireguard and furniture (and even the front door knocker, while I was about it), it all looked wonderful – and *I* looked a grubby mess and had to go and shower again.

By this time it was late morning, so I put on my warm, down-filled jacket and set out for the village with Merlin, since he was desperate to come with me. The poor old thing seems to have attached himself to me already, but life must have been very confusing for him lately.

As well as exploring, I wanted to see if the shop had the extra supplies I had on my list and anything Tilda might want, so I hoped there would be something to tie Merlin to outside it. I suppose I should have taken the car really, only I like to walk and my rucksack is very roomy.

Noël insisted I went into the lodge for a moment, even though

Merlin seemed to take up a lot of space in the small, cluttered room, and when he wagged his tail he nearly took out the Christmas tree and a snowglobe. I felt a bit like Alice in Wonderland when she'd drunk the get-bigger potion, myself.

Tilda was reclining on the sofa, resplendent today in an orange satin blouse and a long black skirt, though I thought she looked a little tired under the lavish makeup. Jess was sitting on the floor doing a vampire jigsaw on the coffee table, the lid with its gory picture propped up in front of her.

'There aren't enough corners,' she said by way of greeting.

'Life's like that sometimes,' I commiserated. 'Or sometimes there are too many.'

She gave me a look from under her fringe.

'Have you tried the phone up at the house today? Only you'll find it keeps going dead, because of the wind,' Tilda said.

'The wind?'

'Blows the wires about, but it's much worse than usual,' Noël said. 'We hadn't noticed until George Froggat – he owns Hill Farm further up the lane – told us. One of the poles is leaning at an angle between here and the village, so the wire is practically down. He called BT and they say it'll be after Christmas before they can get someone up here to look at it, but those poles have wanted replacing the last two years and more.'

'That's a nuisance,' I said, but thinking that at least it might spare me one or two of Jude Martland's irritating calls!

'It will be if it falls right down and cuts us off completely,' he agreed. 'Jess's mobile works, but not terribly well.'

'And only if I walk down the lane towards the village,' Jess said. 'Uncle Jude phoned when we got back yesterday and the phone was a bit dodgy even then, wasn't it, Grandpa?'

'Very, I could only hear what he was saying intermittently.'

'I suppose he was fretting about Lady again?'

'Her name *did* crop up,' he admitted. 'But then he said something about you coping, so I expect he has realised that everything will be absolutely fine. The line went dead after that and he didn't try and ring back again.'

'Anyone would think we would all fall apart without his lordship home,' Tilda scoffed. 'But even when he is here, he spends most of his time shut up in his studio.'

'Did you want me to get you anything from the village?' I offered.

'George brings us the paper every morning, that's why he stopped by, but you could fetch us a bottle of sherry from the pub,' Tilda said. 'In fact, you should have lunch there; they do a good ploughman's or a pot pie.'

'Do they? That would be nice,' I said, remembering that I hadn't had lunch yet and breakfast seemed an awfully long time ago, 'but I'll have to do it another day because I wouldn't be able to take Merlin in.'

'Oh, the Daggers won't mind.'

'The *who*?'

'Daggers. The Dagger family have always had the Auld Christmas. In fact, Nicholas Dagger plays the part of Auld Man Christmas in the Revels on Twelfth Night,' Noël said. 'Jude is Saint George and I used to be the Dragon, only I've had to hand the part on to a younger man.'

'I'm sure Holly isn't interested in our local customs, you old fool,' Tilda said.

'I think they sound fascinating,' I said politely, though I've never been a great one for Morris dancing and the like, and if this one was all Christmassy too, then that took the icing and the cherry off what was already a quite uninteresting cake.

'It's a pity you will miss it,' Noël said.

'Yes, I'll be leaving that morning, because your nephew will be on his way home from the airport. Now, I'd better get going.'

'Can I come down to the village with you?' asked Jess. 'In fact, can I come to lunch at the pub with you, too?'

'Well, I—' I began, hesitantly, glancing at her grandparents.

'Not if you don't want her to,' Noël told me.

'I'm afraid she is having a very boring holiday here in the lodge this year,' Tilda said, 'but that is no reason why she should impose herself on you if you don't feel like company.'

I didn't really mind and, even if I had, it would have been impossible to say so. I just hoped they were right about the pub letting in dogs. Jess went off to get her coat, which was of course black, and Tilda made her put on a beanie hat and gloves. Then, to her complete disgust, she handed her a wicker basket shaped like a coracle in which reposed three greaseproof-wrapped parcels.

'Cheese straws,' confided Jess once we were walking down the lane. 'Granny keeps making them because they're dead easy, but they don't taste of anything much, especially cheese. They're for the oldies in the almshouses.'

'Oh yes, that's the old Nanny—'

'*Everyone* calls her Old Nan – she's ninety something.'

'And the retired vicar?'

'Richard, Richard Sampson. He's pretty old too, but he walks miles, though he's a bit absent-minded and sometimes forgets to turn around and come back. People phone up Uncle Jude from miles away and he has to go and collect him in the car.'

'Then let's hope the weather keeps him at home until your uncle gets back! The other house is Henry the gardener's isn't it?'

'Yes, but he's pretty active too and although he's retired he's always up at Old Place.'

'Yes, the walled garden and the generator do seem to be his chosen stamping grounds. He sounded a bit territorial about them.'

'His daughter lives in the village and keeps an eye on him – she works in the Weasel Pot farm shop in summer. But Old Nan and Richard haven't got any relatives left, they're *way* too old, so they're used to coming up to the house for Christmas Day dinner. I'm not sure what they're going to do this year – I'm not even sure I've got it into their heads yet that it isn't going to happen.'

I had another of those inconvenient pangs of conscience – which are so unfair, since none of this was my fault in the least!

'Now Jude has gone away I wish Edwina, Granny and Grandpa's housekeeper, were still here, because I think Granny's Christmas lunch will be a major disaster,' Jess said frankly. '*And* she's overdoing things. I don't really think she's up to it.'

'Mr Martland's absence does seem to have made it very difficult: selfishly flouncing off when he must know that everyone depended on him!'

'Yes, he's a selfish pig,' she agreed and sighed. 'Even having Christmas dinner with Mo and Jim was something to look forward to, but now everything is *so* boring I was even glad to see Aunt Becca yesterday.'

'Don't you like her?' I asked, surprised. 'I thought she was very nice.'

'I like her, but all she ever talks about is horses, fishing and shooting things and she didn't even stop more than a couple of minutes because the wind was too cold to leave Nutkin tied up outside.'

'She was a great help telling me what to do with Lady. A horse is quite a responsibility when you're not used to looking after them.'

'She said you were competent and capable and she didn't see why there should be any problems.'

'No, I don't either, though it's good to know I can get hold of someone who knows a lot more about horses than I do if a problem comes up.'

'Aunt Becca said Mo and Jim left you the huge turkey and everything for the Christmas dinner we were having,' Jess remarked with a sideways look at me from under her fringe. 'Couldn't you cook it instead, Holly?'

I was taken aback by her directness. 'You haven't been talking to your Uncle Jude, have you?'

'No, it just seemed like a good idea.'

'Well, it might do to you, but it's not what I bargained for when I agreed to take this job! I do house-sitting so I can have a rest from cooking the rest of the year,' I told her firmly, and her face fell. 'And remember I said that I don't celebrate Christmas anyway? In fact, I do my best to ignore it.'

'Oh, that's right, it's against your religion.'

'Strictly speaking, I don't actually have a religion any more,' I admitted, 'but the grandparents who brought me up only celebrated the religious aspects of it – extra chapel services and readings from the gospels – so it's not something I really miss.'

'You mean when you were little there were no presents, or a Christmas stocking or anything?' she demanded, turning stunned brown eyes up towards me.

'No, there was nothing like that, and no big blow-out special dinner either, though Gran was a good plain cook. Her raised pork pie was *legendary*.'

Jess was unimpressed by pork pies in the face of my other childhood deprivations. 'No tree, or decorations, or Father Christmas . . . ?'

'No, though I secretly used to exchange presents with my best friend, Laura – I did a paper round, so I had some money of my own. But when I got married my husband loved all that side of Christmas, so we celebrated it just like everyone else. We'd buy the biggest tree we could tie on top of the car and load it down with lights and baubles; hang garlands and Chinese lanterns and make each other surprise stockings full of silly bits and pieces . . . it was fun.'

But then, everything I'd done with Alan had been fun . . .

'Then why did you stop?'

'Because he died,' I said shortly. 'It was just before Christmas and there didn't seem any point in celebrating it at all after that.'

'What did he die of?' she asked with the directness of the young. 'And was it ages ago?'

'It was an accident . . . eight years ago on Monday.'

This was an anniversary I usually marked quietly and alone, though the way things were going, that would not be an option here unless I stopped answering the door and took the phone off the hook.

'What sort of accident?'

'He fell through the ice on a frozen lake.'

'I keep thinking my parents are going to fall through the ice in Antarctica and a killer whale or something will eat them,' she confessed.

'Oh, I shouldn't think so, I'm sure they know what they're doing.'

'Yes, but Mum tends to keep walking backwards with the camera.'

That *did* sound a bit dodgy.

'A lion nearly got her once – I saw it. If they're not home during the holidays I usually fly out to wherever they're working, only I couldn't really do that this time.'

'No, I don't think it would be very easy to get to Antarctica,' I agreed. 'By the time you got there it would probably be time to turn around and come back, too. You go to boarding school, don't you?'

'Yes and I quite like it really – I've got lots of friends.'

'I used to get bullied because I never fitted in and I was always taller than my classmates, even the boys. There was a group of girls who made my life a misery – I was really self-conscious about my height.'

'I get that a bit sometimes, but we all have a sixth-form mentor we can talk to and they sort it out for us.'

'Sounds like a good idea. I wish we'd had something like that.'

We'd arrived at the village by now and Jess decided to offload the cheese straws first, starting with Old Nan, who when she answered the door was the size of a gnome and wrapped in a crocheted Afghan shawl. On her feet were fuzzy tartan slippers with pompoms and a turn-over collar that fitted snugly round her ankles.

Jess introduced us and said, 'We're not stopping, Nan, because we're going to the shop and then the pub for lunch, but Granny sent you some more cheese straws.'

Old Nan took the parcel without much enthusiasm. 'A body could do with something a bit tastier from time to time,' she grumbled.

'Well, you should try living at the lodge – it's all lumpy mashed potato, tinned rice pudding and not much else at the moment,' Jess said. 'At least you all get to go over to Great Mumming tomorrow in a minibus for the WI Senior Citizens Christmas dinner so that will be a change, won't it?'

'If the weather holds, because there's snow on the way. Not that it's like dinner up at Old Place anyway. They use those gravy granules and tinned peas, you know.'

'So does Granny. But I hope you're right about the snow, because I've never seen *really* deep snow.'

'Be careful what you wish for. And be off with you, if you won't come in, I'm letting all the warm air out standing here like this.' And she shuffled backwards and closed the door firmly.

'She gets a bit grumpy when her rheumatism is playing up,' Jess explained, stepping over a low dividing wall and knocking on the next door.

The retired vicar, Richard Sampson, was a small, wiry, white-haired man with vague cloud-soft grey eyes and an absent expression. He came to the door with his finger in his book to mark the page, and seemed to struggle to place Jess for a minute, let alone take in her introduction to me. Then a smile of great charm transformed him and he shook hands. Unlike Old Nan, he seemed genuinely pleased about the cheese straws.

'He forgets to eat and I'm sure he hardly ever cooks,' Jess

explained, leading the way to the third and final door. 'He does have something hot in the pub occasionally, though, if Henry calls for him on the way there.'

'Speak of the devil,' I muttered, because the old gardener had presumably heard the knocking next door and come out from curiosity already.

'Afternoon,' he said to me and then added to Jess, 'if those are more of Tilda's blasted burnt offerings, then you can keep them!'

'These aren't burnt,' Jess said. 'And if you don't want them, just give them to Richard, he seems keen on them. Oh, and remind him about the Senior Citizens lunch tomorrow and don't let the minibus go without him.' She thrust the package at him. 'Right, now we've got other things to do. Bye, Henry.'

'Women!' Henry muttered, closing the door.

We passed the little church in its neat graveyard. Next to it was a dark-green painted corrugated iron building, little more than a shed, that according to a sign was the parish hall, but the rest of the village was across a small stone bridge over the stream, where we were nearly flattened by a big, glossy four-wheel-drive vehicle taking it too fast.

It stopped and reversed, nearly getting us again, and the side window slid down to reveal a pair of annoyed, puzzled faces.

'Where's the Great Mumming road?' demanded the driver, who was shaven-headed and seemed to have been designed without a neck, since his chin just ran away into his chest. 'The SatNav says we can turn down to the motorway from there.'

'This little lane can't be it, can it?' said the woman next to him, resting a handful of blue talons along the window. 'We must have missed the turn.'

'No, this is the road to Great Mumming – but only if you're a sheep,' Jess said. 'That's why people keep following their SatNavs.'

'Are you being cheeky?' the man said belligerently.

'No, she's simply being truthful,' I said quickly. 'Apparently it

89

isn't much more than a track so the SatNav has an error. You'd be better off turning round and going back down the way you came.'

'Left at the bottom of the hill and you'll get to Great Mumming,' Jess put in.

'Oh, bollocks, what a total waste of time!' he said.

Without a word of thanks the window slid up, the car shot forward, turned noisily in front of the church, and then streaked past us going the other way again. But we were ready for it and had run across the bridge and onto the pavement.

'Charming,' I said.

'People following the SatNavs *are* just like sheep,' Jess said. 'At least most of the lorry drivers take one look at the lane down by the junction and realise there's a mistake, though once one did turn into it and got stuck on the first bend. They had an awful job getting it out, Grandpa says, and had to rebuild a bit of the dry-stone wall.'

The small shop next to the shuttered Merry Kettle café had overflowed onto the pavement with a stand of fruit and vegetables, bags of potatoes and carrots and netting bags of firewood.

'I love this shop! Mrs Comfort's got everything.'

'It certainly looks like it,' I agreed. 'What shall I do with Merlin?'

'There's a hook in the wall to tie him to and a bowl of water,' she pointed out. 'There, under the table.'

There was, too, and Merlin, tethered, sat down on a piece of flattened cardboard with a look of patient resignation. I think he'd been there before.

Inside, the shop proved to be a Tardis, since it went back quite a way into what had probably originally been the second room of the cottage. In America I think they call this sort of shop a Variety Store and there was certainly an infinite variety of stuff crammed into this one.

Mrs Comfort was plump, with a round face and high

cheekbones that turned her eyes to slits when she smiled – rather attractive, in a Persian cat sort of way. Her straight mouse-brown hair was pulled back tightly and clamped to her head with a large, crystal-studded plastic comb.

'Hi, Mrs Comfort, this is Holly, who's minding Old Place for Uncle Jude over Christmas.'

'I thought that couple were back again, that have been before?' she said, looking at me curiously as I ducked my head to avoid the wellingtons hanging by strings from the beams.

'They had to leave because their daughter had her baby much too early,' I explained.

'Shame – hope the poor little mite is all right?'

'I don't know, they haven't told us.'

'Well now, what can I get you?' she asked, a hopeful glint in her eye.

'Do you have newspapers?'

'There's a *Mail* left, but that's the last. I've had three lots of lost drivers in already, and they've all bought one. That SatNav's good for trade!'

'We just saw another one,' Jess told her, 'but they didn't hang about after we told them they'd gone wrong.'

'I expect there's more of them in the pub – I sometimes think the Daggers must have paid the SatNav people to send cars up here, they do a much better winter trade in coffees and lunches now than they used to.'

'It's an ill wind that blows nobody any good,' I said and she agreed fervently.

She had most of the things on my list, including dried fruit so I could bake another cake to replace the one that had vanished. I bought more flour too, because if I was getting daily visitors, I might as well offer them a seasonal mince pie or two, and the Chirks had left several enormous jars of mincemeat.

While I was buying all this Jess had expended much time and thought over the line of sweet jars and now purchased a supply of Fairy Satins, triangular humbug-shaped sweets in alarmingly bright colours, and a large bag of wine gums.

'And can I see proof that you're over twenty-one, young lady?' asked Mrs Comfort.

'Ha, ha, very funny,' said Jess. 'You know there isn't a drop of alcohol in them.'

'How's the book coming along, dear?' asked Mrs Comfort, weighing out Satins on the scales and tipping them into a paper bag, which she twisted at the corners.

'I'm on Chapter Six now and the vampires are having a midnight feast.'

'That sounds like fun.'

'Not for the girls they're feasting on – but they deserve it,' Jess said.

'Mrs Comfort is a poet,' she confided to me as we left the shop and collected Merlin. 'There are lots of writers here: me, Mrs Comfort, Grandpa with his Christmas book and Granny's cookery books. Richard has written a couple of pamphlets too, on the Revels and the red horse.'

'Little Mumming is clearly a hive of literary activity!' I said, impressed.

Chapter 10: Wrung

I find myself looking forward to seeing N every day now, which makes me feel disloyal to Tom's memory, so that I was hardly able to meet his father's eye when I went to the chapel. But soon he will be well enough to leave and things will be as they were.

February, 1945

The Auld Christmas was a smallish hostelry with a large barn behind it and a cobbled forecourt on which a few vehicles were parked. Now I was closer I could see that the old man on the sign seemed to be wearing a mistletoe and oak-leaf crown and carrying a club, but it was hard to tell, because the coats of varnish protecting it had turned it the colour of Brown Windsor soup.

'Are you sure about the dog?' I asked as we went in.

'Yes, come on,' Jess urged me, pushing open an inner door to the left of the passage.

We stepped down into a dark cavern, lit at one end by a roaring open fire and at the other by the dull glow of a fruit machine. Behind the counter was a buxom, red-haired woman of about forty-five and a couple of obvious locals were sitting near the fire, eating bread and cheese. An even more obvious pair of strangers were eating at a table nearby and they looked at Merlin with acute disapproval.

'Do you mind the dog?' I asked the woman behind the bar. 'Only Mr Martland said—'

'Oh, we know Merlin, Jude brings him down here all the time and he's better behaved than most of our customers,' she said, then shot a look at the muttering strangers and added loudly, 'and them that don't like it can go in the public bar next door or take themselves off.'

The complaining voices abruptly ceased.

The woman wiped her hand on a pink-spotted, duck-egg blue apron and held it out to me: 'Nancy Dagger. My husband Will's down the cellar, changing kegs and that's his old dad over there near the fire.'

A tiny man with a long, snowy beard suddenly leaned forward out of a hooded chair, the like of which I had never seen before, and said in a high, piping voice, 'That's right – I'm Auld Man Christmas, I am!' Then he laughed wheezily, like a pair of small musical bellows. 'Heh, heh, heh!'

'Take no notice,' Nancy said. 'We know you're looking after Old Place instead of those Chirks what have been here before, Henry told us all about it last night. But I've never known Martlands to be away from Old Place at Christmas before!' And she shook her head. Then she gave me a sharp look and added, 'But then, I suppose you're family?'

'Not at all, I just work for the same agency as Jim and Mo.'

'I thought you had the look of a Martland, being tall and dark and all,' she insisted, eyeing me closely – but then, it *was* gloomy in there.

'No, I'm not related to them – and Mr Martland will definitely be back for Twelfth Night, because I'm due to leave that morning.'

'He should be here now, that's how it's always been,' she said. 'People round here don't much like change.'

'It's because he argued with Guy and didn't want to see him,' Jess told her. 'But I think it's mean of him not to think of the rest of us.'

'Well, talking won't mend matters,' Nancy said. 'What can I get you ladies? Are you having lunch?'

I ordered a hot pot pie and, after much deliberation, so did Jess. 'Pies aren't my favourite thing,' she explained, 'but I'm getting a lot of cold food from Granny, so I might as well have something hot while I can.'

'I expect the old folk will have a bit of a struggle to cope this year, poor things,' Nancy said. 'I can make you a nice cup of drinking chocolate, how about that? Squirty cream on top.'

'Oh yes, that would be lovely, thank you!' Jess said. 'Oh, and Grandpa gave me some money to pay for Holly's lunch, too.'

'That was a kind thought,' I said, touched – and also still feeling uneasily and illogically guilty again after Nancy's remarks.

I did have all the food for Christmas dinner and cooking it wouldn't be a problem . . . so was I now obstinately punishing Noël, Tilda and Jess, simply because Jude had got my back up? Was I being as selfish as he was?

How much of a hardship would it really be, to put my personal inclinations on one side and invite them for one meal?

It was no use, I was simply going to *have* to do it!

I could look on it as research and write that Christmas chapter for my book, after all!

When we got back to the lodge I handed over the sherry, then said, 'I've been thinking things over and you know, it seems such a pity to waste all that lovely Christmas food that the Chirks left behind, because I won't be able to eat it all. So, even though it's very short notice, I wondered if you could possibly all come for dinner on Christmas Day with me anyway?'

'Oh *yes*!' exclaimed Jess, bouncing up and down in her large, black lace-up boots.

'But you don't celebrate Christmas, m'dear, so surely that would be an imposition?' Noël asked doubtfully.

'I don't have to *celebrate* it, just *cook* it,' I said brightly. 'Anyway, I'm sure it will make a nice change.'

'Well, in that case . . .' he said, glancing at his wife.

'It's very kind of you,' Tilda said. 'Of course, I *was* fully prepared to do a festive lunch, but I do see your point about not wasting the Chirks' food.'

'Lovely – then that's settled,' I said. 'If Mr Martland gets through to you again on the phone, will you assure him that Lady and Merlin are both fine, if he is still fussing about them, and tell him of the change of plan? He did suggest yesterday that I carried on with the Chirks' invitation, so he can't have any objection.'

'Oh, did he? How kind and thoughtful of the dear boy,' Noël said.

'Yes, wasn't it just?' I replied, slightly sourly.

'Of course it will be a lot more work for you than you bargained for originally,' he said. 'I expect you usually charge quite a lot for cooking, don't you?'

'Yes, but actually you'll be doing me a favour, because I still have to write the chapter on Christmas house-party catering for my book, so it'll be good research.'

'I may well be able to give you some useful tips for your book, too,' Tilda said graciously, and I thanked her.

'I think you *should* be paid a little more – I'll speak to Jude about it,' Noël insisted.

'No, please don't – I'm sure I'll love doing it and of course I'll bill him for any extra food I have to buy.'

Noël rubbed his gnarled hands together gleefully. 'Well, well – a Martland family Christmas celebration after all – how splendid! And I include *you* in the family now, m'dear, because you already feel like one of us.'

'Nancy Dagger thought she was a Martland,' Jess said.

'Only because I'm tall and dark,' I said with a smile. 'It's quite gloomy in the pub, isn't it?'

'I expect that is it,' he agreed, 'and by the way, do call Jude by his first name. There is no need to be formal when we are going to be seeing such a lot of each other.'

'But I'm not going to be seeing anything at all of Jude,' I pointed out. 'Though if the telephone works, I suppose I'll *hear* a lot more.'

'Do call him Jude – he isn't one to stand on formality,' Tilda said. 'The artistic type, you know.'

'Not really, the most artistic I ever get is cake decorating . . . and that's a point, because the Chirks didn't leave a Christmas cake. I'd better get back and start one. Thank goodness I just bought more dried fruit and candied peel!'

'It is too late in the day and it won't taste right,' Tilda objected. 'But I have a Dundee cake in a tin that Old Nan gave us, so I could bring that.'

'No, it's fine, I have a last-minute recipe where you steep the fruit in spirits for a couple of days before making it and it really tastes rather good. If I do that today, it can have a good long soak.'

'Oh great,' said Jess. 'And you were going to make mince pies anyway, you said.'

'Yes, those too. Would you mind if I borrowed this basket, Tilda? Only I bought much more than I expected. Jess was a huge help carrying everything back, though – she had the heavy rucksack.'

'Good girl,' Noël said.

'*And* I'll come and help you put the decorations up,' Jess offered.

'Decorations?' I echoed, not having thought any further than food, drink and the chore of cleaning the dining room for Christmas Day lunch.

'Yes, all the decorations are in the attic, and there's holly and ivy in the woods for the taking.'

'I – hadn't thought that far yet,' I hedged. 'Let me make a start on the baking first.'

97

'Okay, and then we'll do it,' she persisted. 'There's a couple of trunks of amazing old clothes in the attic you might like to see, too . . . though I'm too old for dressing up now, really.'

'Oh . . . well, we'll see.'

Tilda, suddenly looking much more alert and bright-eyed, swung her legs off the sofa and slid her feet into a pair of improbably tiny black velvet high-heeled slippers, edged with waving fronds of pink marabou. 'Now, what would you like us to bring? We have a lovely big box of luxury crackers – and Noël has the keys to the cellar, of course, so he can find us something decent to drink.'

'If you're sure Mr – I mean *Jude* – won't mind?'

'Not at all, he's the most generous of souls.'

I hadn't seen much sign of anything except selfishness yet, but perhaps, as well as hidden cellars, the unknown Jude had hidden depths too?

But as far as I was concerned, they could stay hidden: I'd never before liked a man less just on the sound of his voice! And now, because of him, instead of spending the anniversary of Alan's death in quiet contemplation, I would be gearing up for a feast.

I got up. 'Well, if you'll excuse me, I'd better get back. I have a lot to do.'

Merlin retired to his basket by the Aga, exhausted, and watched me with his bright amber eyes while I listed all the things I needed to do before Christmas Day.

I'd been working on it all the way up the drive – not only deciding on the menu (traditional), starting a cake and getting the large ham I had spotted out of the freezer to slowly defrost so I could cook it, but also finding the formal cutlery and crockery . . . *and* cleaning the dining room and downstairs cloakroom, too.

At least I'd already done the sitting room!

I would ignore the bit about decorations. Jess could come and put them up, if she really wanted to, though it hardly seemed worth it for one day.

I found a huge mixing bowl in one of the cupboards and into it went the dried fruit and chopped peel I'd bought that day, bulked out with some sultanas and a packet of slivered almonds (only a month out of date) from the store cupboard.

Into the mix went the drained and chopped contents of a jar of cocktail cherries (these, tiny silverskin onions and olives seemed to be well stocked in the larder, among the pickles and preserves), and the brandy from the decanter in the dining room, eked out with a bit of rum.

Then I covered the bowl with cling film and put it on a shelf in the larder, before ticking that task off my increasingly extensive to-do list.

Advance organisation is the absolute *key* to successful catering for large parties – I make that plain on the very first page of my book!

It wasn't a huge surprise to me when Jude rang just after I got in from giving Lady her warm mash and Billy a distracting handful of goat biscuits, and shutting the two of them in for the night. The wind had dropped, letting a few flakes of snow float idly down like feathers, so presumably the floppy phone lines weren't blowing about.

'Jude Martland,' he announced brusquely, as if I hadn't already guessed who it would be.

'Lady's fine – she's just had her mash and she's snugly bolted in for the night with Billy,' I assured him, before he could ask. This time I was determined I wouldn't let his autocratic manner annoy me, but remain my usual calm, professional self. 'And Merlin had his arthritis tablet with his breakfast and I've just given him a good brushing – which he badly needed, by the way.'

'Oh . . . right.' He sounded slightly disconcerted. 'That wasn't actually what I was going to say. I've just spoken to Noël and Tilda – the line was too bad to hear a word earlier.'

'I know, it was a bit windy.'

'I understand you've agreed to do what I asked and cook Christmas lunch for the family?'

'Yes, but only because I was in an impossible situation and there was nothing else I could do. But it was *your* responsibility to look after everyone, not mine to try and pick up the pieces after you'd swanned off in a huff.'

'I did *not* swan off in a huff! And anyway, it's no business of yours why I decided to spend Christmas over here – nor can I see why you're making such a fuss about laying on Christmas dinner, when everything has been provided for you by the Chirks and you're a cook anyway!'

'Chef,' I said icily, though normally I don't mind being called by either title. 'And you obviously have *no* conception of the amount of work involved – not just preparing, cooking and clearing up dinner, but cleaning your filthy dining room and the downstairs cloakroom, which looks as if mud wrestlers have had a bout in there.'

'Then get what's-her-name – Sharon – to help,' he said shortly.

'You've forgotten – she's resigned.'

'Oh yes . . . Well, it's not *that* bad, is it? You're exaggerating! A quick run-over with a duster and the Hoover . . .'

'Look, I'm used to keeping the parts of the house I'm using clean and tidy – though even then they don't usually need a total deep-clean – but that's *all* I'm contracted to do, other than look after the animals! Conversely, when I'm doing house-party cooking, my clients don't expect me to do anything except produce delicious meals – and my charges for that are *extremely* high!'

'Oh, I see! I suppose that's what this is really all about, trying to get a lot more money out of me?'

'No, it isn't – and you couldn't *afford* my prices,' I snapped.

'According to that boss of yours at Homebodies, I'm going to be paying you double house-sitting rates anyway, so at this rate it would probably be cheaper to send them out to a good restaurant in a taxi,' he mused gloomily, 'except that they wouldn't go. They seem to think that you invited them out of the kindness of your heart – they've no idea how very cold and mercenary you are, Mrs Brown.'

'I'm not in the least cold and mercenary, I simply resent being put in the position of picking up the pieces of the mess you left after you walked away from your responsibilities. And what about the elderly people in the almshouses who usually spend the day here, too?'

'I sent them a Christmas hamper each,' he said indignantly. '*And* Henry.'

'Big of you, Mr Martland!'

'You know, I think you could start calling me Jude, now we're on insulting terms,' he suggested. 'Holly certainly suits *you*: spiky!'

'And you're objectionable and overbearing. And don't you think you're making a lot of unfounded assumptions about someone you've never met?'

'Well, aren't you?'

'No, I'm basing my opinion of you on hard evidence. But believe it or not, my only reason for agreeing to do the cooking was that I like your aunt and uncle and Jess and felt sorry for them – Tilda's really too frail to cope alone. But think what you want to. Meanwhile I don't think we've anything further to say to each other. Good night – *Jude*.'

'Don't you *dare* put the phone down on me again—' he growled, just as I did exactly that thing.

It rang again almost instantly, but I ignored it and then later, when I was going to ring Laura, it was dead as a dodo.

101

Chapter 11: Slightly Tarnished

*Today I asked N what his home was like and he said it was
an old house up in the hills – in fact, just below one of the
beacons. So I said, was it Rivington Pike, because I remember
a Sunday school day trip there as a girl but he laughed and
said no, much smaller than that and the little stone tower on
the hill – nothing much to look at.*

February, 1945

Last night I lay in bed reading Gran's journals late into the night
again, more and more convinced that N.M. would turn out to
be the Ned Martland she had loved and lost – and one and the
same as the black sheep of Old Place and therefore closely related
to the obnoxious Jude. The description of his home was the
clincher.

By some amazing coincidence Fate had directed me here – but
then, they say truth is always stranger than fiction.

I could tell she was increasingly fascinated by him (and he had
quickly become simply 'N', so presumably they were now on first-
name terms), but he sounded like a hardened flirt to me. Poor,
innocent, chapel-bred Gran wouldn't have stood a chance . . .

However, since she then spent two sleep-inducing pages on
pious reflections about the state of the world before the next
entries, maybe she would prove entirely unassailable.

There was a light sprinkling of snow when I went out to the

stables, but, remembering what Becca had said, I put Lady and her smelly little friend out in the paddock anyway, where she immediately started to paw the snow from the grass as she grazed.

I am quite getting into a routine now, and soon had the loosebox mucked out and freshly laid with new straw ready for the evening. The exercise made me glow, so I expect it did me good. After that Merlin and I took a little walk up to the red horse, which was actually now white like everything else, though you could still see the bumps and hollows of its outline.

I found a sheltered spot behind some gorse bushes and rang Laura on my mobile. She'd just got back from dropping the children at her mother's house for the day, to give her a rest.

I asked her how she was and she seemed to be blooming, as she always was during pregnancy.

'I hope mine goes as well, when I follow plan A in spring,' I said. 'I thought I could cook all summer to get some money in, and then retire until the baby has arrived. Assuming it works, of course – there's no guarantee it will at my age.'

'Haven't you met any nice men up there? I was hoping you might, and give up the whole mad AI thing,' she asked hopefully.

'Yes – Noël Martland's lovely, but he's ancient and married. And I suppose you could say I've met Jude Martland via the phone, but I'm *so* glad I'll have left before he gets back, because he's selfish, overbearing, autocratic . . . quite horrible! I think all he really cares about are his horse and dog.'

'You seem to have gathered a lot about him from a couple of phone calls,' she said, amused.

'We argue every time – he's quite insufferable. He's got a really deep voice, too, and sort of *rumbles* at me down the phone.'

'What, one of those knicker-quiveringly deep voices?' she asked with interest. 'The kind that vibrate down your spine and back up again?'

'Laura!' I exclaimed, then laughed. 'But, yes, it does and I suppose it *would* be quite sexy if he wasn't being so rude to me. And unfortunately I just can't seem to stop saying horrid things back, which isn't like me at all: normally I manage to keep a professional relationship going, whatever the provocation. But it isn't just his calls that make me dislike him, it's also seeing how his actions have affected everyone here.'

And I told her how he'd abandoned his duty to look after his family and the elderly people in the village and taken himself off in a fit of pique, after he saw the engagement announcement between his brother and his former fiancée.

'I expect he was so upset he didn't think it through,' she suggested.

'Perhaps not, but once he'd had time to think he could have come back, couldn't he? And then he seemed to assume that because the Chirks had invited his aunt and uncle to Christmas dinner, I should be happy to do the same . . . and actually,' I added, 'I am.'

'What, cooking Christmas dinner for his family?'

'Yes, the Chirks left an enormous turkey and Christmas pudding anyway. And then Tilda Martland is so frail I don't think she should even be *trying* to cope with the cooking, especially since she has her granddaughter to stay. Once I realised that, there wasn't anything else to do but invite them.'

'You *are* kind, Holly!'

'I'm not, really – I didn't want to do it. Only then I started to feel that I was being as mean and selfish as Jude.' I sighed. 'So now I'm committed to hosting a family Christmas dinner in a house that doesn't belong to me and which is in need of a damned good clean, using food left by someone else!'

'You'll cope, you always do.'

'We've had some snow too, and I can see that we're likely to get cut off if it carries on – you've never seen such a steep, narrow, bendy road as the one up to the village! Luckily, there's an amazingly well-stocked shop and enough food in the house to last a year, I should think, if you don't mind eating a lot of fish and game.'

'Jude shoots, then?'

'No, it's his Aunt Becca who does that, the horsy one. And she fishes, so she's probably responsible for the trout and salmon – *and* the whole frozen pike.'

'A *pike*? How do you know it's a pike?'

'Everything is labelled. I've never cooked pike before, but they're supposed to be good eating . . . I have a recipe for stuffed pike in my book of old English cookery,' I added thoughtfully.

I always took my favourite recipe books away with me, along with my giant notebook, and it was just as well. It's amazing what I'm asked to cook sometimes!

'Are you serious?'

'Yes, of course. I couldn't eat a whole one myself, it's pretty big, so I would have to ask the Martlands back another time to help me eat it. On Christmas Day it will be turkey and all the trimmings, of course, because that's what they're expecting.'

'It's quite funny, when you think about it, that you ran away from the idea of spending a family Christmas with me, but ended up having to host one yourself!'

'Yes, I know, I can see the irony of it,' I agreed. 'Still, after Christmas Day, things will go quieter and I can relax and get on with my book again. Meanwhile, Jude accused me of trying to squeeze a whole lot of money out of him for cooking for the family, when I don't intend charging for it at all! So I'm going to phone Ellen and tell her that if he calls, she isn't to tell him what I charge for house-party cooking. I told him he couldn't afford me.'

'Isn't he rich? The house sounds very grand!'

'Grand but neglected, with just that useless cleaner coming in, and she told me he paid her half the going rate so he has to be either poor or stingy – or maybe both. But artists don't usually have loads of money, do they?'

'I think he's doing all right, he's quite well known.' She paused.

'It's the weekend – Ellen hates being called then unless it's an emergency, doesn't she?'

'Tough.'

'*And* she's going to be really mad if you go ahead and get pregnant and then hand your notice in! You're her best and most reliable cook, she told me so.'

'Double tough. Laura, you know those wartime journals of Gran's?'

'Yes, they sound fascinating.'

'They're getting even more fascinating,' I said, and described how there seemed to be a romance forming between her and one of the patients – and my growing conviction that the Ned Martland she had once loved was Noël Martland's younger brother.

'It does sound likely, doesn't it?' she agreed. 'It's such a coincidence that you should be there. Really, it's just like a novel!'

'That's what I thought, though I hope it's not a tragedy, because Noël's brother sounds like a bit of a bad lot. I'll have even more reason to dislike Jude Martland if his uncle broke Gran's heart!'

'They say everyone has got a novel in them, don't they? Only I'd have thought your grandmother's would have been a fairly sedate Mrs Gaskell sort of affair.'

'Yes, that's what I'm hoping. And I don't think I've got a novel in *me* but I might just have a recipe book – if I ever have the time to finish it,' I added bitterly.

'How's it going?'

'Not very fast so far, because there's simply been too much to do and a constant stream of visitors. And when I've had a spare minute, Gran's journals have been a bit too fascinating to resist.'

'Well, ring me if you find out anything else interesting!'

I was getting chilly by then and only got Ellen's answering machine when I tried her number, so I left a message on that, before heading for home.

* * *

I gave the fruit soaking in brandy a stir and it was already starting to smell delicious: you really can't fail with that recipe.

Looking at my by now extensive to-do list, I thought I had better gird my loins and start on the rest of the cleaning, on the principle of getting done first what you least want to do.

It was already evident to me that the Jacksons, the elderly couple who had since retired, had really cared for the house. The linen cupboard, where tablecloths, runners and napkins were kept, smelt of lavender sachets and a plentiful supply of cleaning materials lined the utility-room shelves.

I filled a cream enamel housekeeper's bucket with everything I thought I would need and carried it through to the dining room, along with the old upright vacuum cleaner and a long-handled, slightly-moulting brown feather duster.

Always start at the top of a room and work downwards: that was the lesson Gran had taught me. I dealt with the cobwebs and worked my way down the panelling, then vacuumed some of the dust out of the curtains using the extension hosepipe, set on low. I'd polished the furniture and was well into cleaning the floor when Jess suddenly appeared.

I nearly had a heart attack when I caught sight of her dark figure with its pale face standing silently in the doorway. I gave a yelp and she said, 'Did I make you jump? I did knock, but I had Grandpa's key, so when there was no answer, I came in. Granny sent me to see if you needed any help. Not that I *like* housework,' she added mutinously.

'Neither do I, actually, but I *do* like the look and smell of a fresh, clean room. It would be wonderful if you could give me a hand. I've nearly finished in here and I was going to do the garden hall and cloakroom next, so if you could take the feather duster and get rid of all the cobwebs in the corners first, that would be great.'

'Oh – okay,' she said, brightening slightly, presumably because I hadn't immediately handed her the vacuum cleaner.

Merlin followed her out – he didn't seem to like the noise.

I finished off the floor, then took the silver candlesticks and tray through to the utility room to clean later, before going to see how Jess was getting on.

'Merlin eats spiders,' Jess told me. 'I suppose he thinks they're snacks on legs.'

'Good, I hate them.'

Jess's main contribution to the cleaning after that was to entertain me while I worked by telling me the details of the plot of her vampire novel, until finally I straightened my aching back and declared, 'Lunch time, I think.'

'You look very hot and grubby!'

'That's because your uncle has let his house get filthy – he should be ashamed of himself.'

'I don't suppose he even noticed,' Jess said. 'When he's working he doesn't, and he's working most of the time. Even when he isn't you can tell he's still *thinking* about it. What are you having for lunch?'

'Nothing exciting – an omelette probably. What are you having?'

'God knows,' she said gloomily. 'Probably tinned soup – and I'll be the one in charge of heating that up, because Granny's tired today and Grandpa is hopeless.'

She got up. 'I suppose I'd better come back tomorrow and help you make beds. That's why Granny sent me, really, to tell you to make sure the bedrooms are aired.'

'Beds?'

'Granny said it would be much more convenient if we all stayed on Christmas night.'

'Convenient for who?' I said, startled. I was sure they'd only been coming for lunch when Mo and Jim were doing the catering and I don't remember any previous mention of staying over . . .

'For you, of course, so you won't have to drive us back to the lodge. And they've told Auntie Becca that Christmas lunch was on again, so she's coming too.'

'What – to *stay*?'

'Yes.' She counted up on her fingers. 'So that's three bedrooms, isn't it?'

'I suppose it is,' I said faintly. 'Oh, joy! And yes, you'd better come back tomorrow and help, because I expect I'll now have to clean the bedrooms before I can make the beds up.'

I'd have to revise my menu plan, too, if I was catering for rather more than just Christmas lunch! It was just as well the warmth from the big log fire in the hall was permeating all the rooms upstairs and airing them – except for the owner's Bluebeard's chamber, of course. If that was damp and dank and chilly when he got back, that would be his own fault.

'Your Uncle Jude called last night, so I assume the phone is working again.'

'Did he? I think he must like you!'

'No, I think it's the opposite, actually.'

'Auntie Becca called back later to say that since Christmas was on as usual, she'd popped down to the village to tell Old Nan and Richard.'

'Oh my God!'

'Is that a problem?'

'Oh no,' I said faintly, 'I mean, after looking forward to a quiet and restful few weeks on my own, I should be delighted that I'm now going to be cook, cleaner and general factotum for a large house-party, where everyone bar you is so elderly they're obviously not going to be a lot of help, shouldn't I? *Whatever* gave you that idea?'

She grinned. 'I know you're joking – and it's going to be much more fun than last year, when Great Uncle Alex was so ill and Guy and Jude fell out over Guy and Coco flirting, though Guy flirts with *everyone*. Aunt Becca said she was surprised when she saw the announcement of his engagement to Coco, because although he always wanted whatever Jude had, he lost interest once he'd got it.'

That seemed very acute of Becca. 'A bit of a Cain and Abel syndrome?' I asked, interested, but she looked blank.

'I hate Guy, he's always winding me up and he never buys me a present either, just gives me money.'

'That *is* a present, it just means he has no idea what you want.'

'Jude usually gives me a present even if sometimes it's a bit weird. But I don't suppose he even thought of it this time, dropping everything and rushing off like that.'

'He said he sent hampers to Old Nan and Richard, so I'm sure he will have remembered.'

'You know,' she said with an air of one making a major discovery, 'I like Jude much better than Guy, even if he is grumpier! If he says he'll do something, he does. And when he's home, he lets me go and mess about in the studio with modelling clay sometimes and he's going to teach me to weld, too.'

'Well, that's certainly a life skill that not a lot of girls your age have.'

She jumped up. 'Look at the time! I'd better go, or Granny will be trying to open that tin herself.'

'I'll bring you some homemade soup down tomorrow,' I promised. 'I usually have a big pot of it permanently on the go and top it up every day, but I just don't seem to have had a minute since I arrived, so there isn't enough at the moment.'

Making more soup and having a good turn-out of the kitchen cupboards occupied most of the rest of the day, and no call from Jude Martland marred my peace . . . until he rang really late, just as I was thinking about bed.

'I emailed your boss at Homebodies and asked her how much you charged for your cooking,' he said without any preamble. 'My God, I don't know who can afford those wages!'

'I expect she gave you the weekly rate, but I told you I was expensive.' Trust Ellen to try and get more money out of a client without even consulting me, too!

'If you add that on top of double house-sitting rates, it's extortionate,' he said. 'And you won't be doing anything millions of women won't be doing for their families for nothing over Christmas.'

'They will be doing it for love – and it makes you think, doesn't it? Christmas is always hard work for women.'

'That's not what I meant . . . though I suppose you have a point,' he agreed grudgingly.

I was about to tell him that I had no intention of charging him for anything other than the house-sitting, and would have a word with Ellen about it, but something seemed to hold me back. He probably wouldn't have believed me anyway.

'Did you want anything else, or did you just ring me to complain about the Homebodies charges?'

'I phoned for the sheer pleasure of hearing your voice,' he said sarcastically and then I was listening to the empty air: he'd gone.

I fell into bed, exhausted and irritated in equal measures and wasn't much soothed by the next few pages of Gran's journal, since I could see ominous signs of where things were heading:

> *Sister caught me laughing with N this morning and hauled*
> *me over the coals for it. I was very upset by this, and was*
> *lucky not to be moved from that ward. N was sweet and*
> *said he would make it up to me once he is well again,*
> *though he didn't say how . . .*

Still, at least I might get the chance to find out more about Ned Martland from Noël over Christmas, so every cloud has a silver lining, even if it is slightly tarnished.

Chapter 12: Deeply Fruited

N was discharged from hospital today and sent home to convalesce, but before he left he caught my hand and pleaded with me to meet him on my next half-day. Against my better judgement I eventually agreed, though I stipulated that it must be somewhere out of the way, since I do not wish to be the target of idle gossip among the other nurses.

February, 1945

Yesterday's snow had half-melted by evening, but it froze overnight and then a fresh covering over the top made things pretty treacherous outside. I was worried about Lady on the cobbles and rang Becca to ask if I should still let her out.

'Of course,' she said, and she was quite right, because Lady walked across to the paddock with small, cautious steps as if she'd been doing it all her life – which actually, I expect she had.

Becca had also said she was looking forward to Christmas Day. I seemed to be the only one who wasn't. I'd caught her on the way to church, because apparently the vicar comes over from Great Mumming once a fortnight to hold a service here and today was the day: in fact, I could hear the distant peal of the bell as she rang off.

The brandy-soaked fruit for the Christmas cake smelt intoxicatingly delicious when I fetched the bowl into the kitchen and then began assembling and weighing the rest of the ingredients, which is the most time-consuming bit, along with greasing and lining a cake tin. Luckily there was a good selection of those in all shapes and sizes and I had found a suitably large one in the cupboard yesterday.

Once the cake was safely baking, as well as some mince pies to offer what I now foresaw would be a permanent flow of famished visitors, I had a sit-down with a cup of coffee to brace myself for another bout of the hated cleaning, this time of the bedrooms.

I was getting heartily sick of it – not to mention of Jude Martland, the cause of all this extra work! So when Jess turned up again, this time I was much more remorseless in making her help me.

She told me which rooms her grandparents and Becca usually had and said she herself always slept in the old nursery. The rooms didn't seem to have been used since the previous Christmas, so that apart from a coating of dust and needing the beds made up with lavender-scented linen from the big cupboard at the end of the passage by the stairs, they didn't actually take a huge amount of time to do – much less than I expected.

Jess showed me the cupboard full of old toys in the nursery, though some of them were more recent, mainly miniature instruments of mass destruction that had probably belonged to Guy and Jude. The room was at the back of the house and, like mine and Jude's, afforded an excellent view of the horse figure on the side of the folly-topped Snowehill, which was certainly living up to its name today. The red horse was now white and practically indistinguishable, much like Lady in the paddock below, though Billy was a small dark blob.

By the time we'd finished upstairs, the scent of fruit cake from the slow oven had wafted gently through the house to tantalise our nostrils and I took the cake out and tested it with a skewer while Jess wolfed down the first batch of mince pies I'd made earlier.

She watched me curiously. 'Why are you poking holes in it?'

'One hole, just to see if it's done. If it isn't, the cake mix will stick to the skewer.'

'Oh, right. These mince pies are much nicer than shop ones,' Jess added, with an air of discovery.

'I've made them the way I like them best, with lots of filling and thin pastry, but the shop ones tend to go the other way. There's a box of them in the larder that the Chirks left, but I don't like the look of them.'

'I could take them back with me,' offered Jess. 'Grandpa would probably be glad of them, because they have to be better than anything Granny whips up, even though he always says he enjoys everything she cooks.'

'How is she today?'

'Quite lively – she said she was going to make a batch of rock cakes, though I don't suppose they'll be any nicer than the cheese straws.'

'I'll give you some soup to take back for lunch, I've made a lot more.'

I'd found one of those giant Thermos flasks earlier with a wide mouth for soups and stews, so I scalded it out and ladled the soup into that.

'There, thick enough to stand a spoon in, as my Gran would have said.'

'It smells lovely. I'd better take it back now, because they've probably decided to have rock cakes for lunch and that's not enough to keep them going. Meals at the lodge are getting weirder and weirder by the minute.'

When she'd gone I had a bowl of the soup myself, with a warm, buttered roll (luckily there was a good supply of bread in the freezer too, and also several of those long-life part-baked baguettes in the larder), then I covered the end of the kitchen table with newspaper and sat there with a pot of tea to hand, polishing up the tarnished silver from the dining room.

When I was coming back from replacing them on the sideboard, I glanced out of the sitting-room window and spotted a tractor coming up the drive with a snowplough contraption on the front. It swept gratingly around the turning circle in front of the house, narrowly missing my car, then vanished up the side, but not before I'd caught sight of Henry in the passenger seat next to the fair-haired driver.

I presumed he was being dropped off at the back gate and, sure enough, by the time I got to the kitchen he was stumping across the courtyard to the door and I could hear the roar of the tractor departing again.

'Hi, Henry,' I said, 'was that George Froggat, the farmer from up the lane?'

'That's right, Hill Farm. Gave me a lift, he did.'

'That was kind.'

'Nay, he was coming up anyway, seeing the council pays him and his son to plough the lane to the village, and Jude pays him to do this drive and Becca's. He makes a good thing out of it.'

'Oh yes, I think Tilda and Noël mentioned something about that.'

'Saw you at the window, did George. Said you looked a likely lass. I said you were none too bad,' he conceded grudgingly.

'Well . . . thank you,' I said, digesting this unlikely pair of compliments.

'I told him you were a widow, too. He's a widower himself.'

I glanced at him sharply, wondering if he was about to try a spot of rural matchmaking and saw that he looked frozen, despite wearing numerous woolly layers under a tweed jacket obviously built for someone of twice his girth.

'Look, come in and get warm,' I ordered and, despite his protests, I thawed him out in the kitchen with tea and warm mince pies. The first batch had almost gone already, so it was just as well I had loads more baking, which I intended to put in the freezer.

'The weather's turning worse and I might not get back up over Christmas, so I've come to show you where the potatoes are stored, and the beetroot clamp and suchlike, in case you need to fetch any more in,' he said, when he'd drunk his tea and regained a less deathly complexion.

I was touched by this kind thought and we went out to the walled garden, once I'd donned my down-filled parka and gloves.

I returned half an hour later with a basket of potatoes and carrots and a string of onions, leaving Henry to retire to his little den in the greenhouse, though I told him to tell me later when he was leaving. His daughter couldn't fetch him today, so he'd intended walking home, but I would insist on driving him back, however icy the road down was.

The drive *was* slippery, but someone (presumably George) had sprinkled grit over the steepest bit of the lane below the lodge, so we got down that all right.

Going by the leaden sky I thought we might be in for another snow fall, and it was a pity the shop was closed because I would have bought yet more emergency supplies while I had the car with me, especially now I was having lots more visitors!

I pulled up outside the almshouses and Henry clambered out, clutching his usual bulging sack of booty.

'Her at the end's wanting you,' he said with a jerk of his thumb and I saw Old Nan was waving at me from her window with surprising enthusiasm. But this was soon explained when Jess shot out of her cottage, still fastening her coat, and climbed into the passenger seat next to me.

'Great, I thought I was going to have to walk back,' she said, turning round to pat Merlin, who was on the back seat.

'We both might, if the car won't go up the lane – it's pretty icy. What were you doing down here?'

'Granny made about three million rock cakes and they weren't very nice, so I volunteered to bring some for Old Nan and

Richard, just to try and get rid of them quicker. Your soup was good, though.'

I got back up the hill by the skin of my teeth and dropped her at the lodge, but I didn't go in because it was quickly getting dark and even colder by then, and I wanted to bring Lady and Billy in.

I should have left a light on in the porch: it was slightly eerie and silent when I got out of the car, just the scrunch of my boots on the drive and the sudden high-pitched yelp of a fox not far away, which Merlin took with matter-of-fact disinterestedness.

It's odd, growing up in Merchester, I'd had this idea of the countryside as a quiet place, but in its way it's usually just as noisy as the city: foxes scream, hedgehogs grunt, sheep baa, cows moo, birds sing, rooks caw, tractors roar . . . it's a cacophony! A cacophony interspersed with moments of deep silence. This was one of them.

I was glad to get inside and switch on the lights in the sitting room, where the embers of the fire only needed a log or two to spring back into life.

When I checked the phone, I seemed to have missed a call from Jude. What a pity!

I spoke too soon, because when I came back in from the stables he rang again before I could even get my freezing hands around a hot mug. (I'd been tempted to plunge them into Lady's warm mash!)

'You weren't in earlier,' he said accusingly. 'I tried to ring you two or three times.'

'No, I am actually allowed to leave the premises occasionally for a couple of hours under the terms of the Homebodies contract,' I said. 'I'm sure I told you that I was going to the village to do some shopping – and I called in on your aunt and uncle and everything seemed fine. I got them a couple of things they needed from the village, too.'

'Oh? Is that little service going on the bill, too?' he said nastily. 'And I rang *much* earlier too and you weren't there then, either, so—'

'This *was* much earlier. I came back ages ago and then went straight out to bring Billy and Lady in and do her warm mash. *They* are both absolutely fine too – I rang Becca this morning to ask her if it was too cold to put them in the paddock and she said it wasn't. So in fact, the only creature around here that *isn't* fine is me, because I'm tired, freezing cold and hungry,' I added pointedly.

'Well, sorry for disturbing you!'

'That's all right, I have had one or two previous clients who were so neurotic about their pets they called every day. Did you have any particular reason for ringing this time?'

'No, it's simply that the novelty of having my employees insult me hasn't worn off yet.'

'I am not actually your employee,' I pointed out. 'I work for Homebodies. And I return the compliment: my clients tend to praise me rather than insult my integrity.'

I think we might have been neck-and-neck with slamming the phone down that time.

Chapter 13: Christmas Spirits

On my half-day I cycled out to meet N at a teashop. One of his brothers dropped him off there, though he did not come in, and was to pick him up later. It was good to see him again and though at first I felt very shy, we were soon as at ease with one another as we had been at the hospital.

February, 1945

I read a bit more of Gran's journal over breakfast. Now that she seemed to be embarking on a clandestine romance with Ned Martland, I was even more tempted to skip forward and discover what went wrong, but restrained myself.

I did wish she wouldn't keep going off into long-winded soliloquies about the state of her conscience and what she thought God's purpose for her was between entries, though.

I kept thinking about her while I did my chores and then took Merlin for a little run, so I called Laura to talk it over when I had gone far enough up the hill to get a good signal.

'How are you feeling?' she asked me.

'Me?' I said, surprised. 'Oh, *I'm* fine, except there is so much to do here. Laura, you know those old journals of Granny's?'

'Mmm, you said you were reading a bit every night and were beginning to suspect that one of the Martlands might have been your Gran's lost love – see, I'm keeping up with the plot,' she said encouragingly.

'Yes, that's Edward – Ned – Noël Martland's younger brother and I'm positive he's the N.M. she's nursing back to health in her journal. She seems to be slowly falling for him and they're having clandestine meetings!'

'Well, you already knew she loved him. I wonder what went wrong?'

'I don't know, I just hope he didn't break her heart, because he sounds a bit of a rake. I expect I'll find out a bit more about him over Christmas . . .' I began, but then there was a crash and a wailing noise at her end as one of the children had some minor disaster and she had to ring off quickly.

At least everything is now more or less in hand for Christmas Day. I've taken the fine ham the Chirks left behind out of the freezer and put it in the fridge to defrost slowly, the menu is planned, the cake awaits its marzipan and icing and I have the wherewithal to bake endless mince pies.

But I went quite mad and cleaned through the rest of the house, too – or at least everything that wasn't locked up. Having set my course, there seemed no point in being half-hearted about things just because Jude Martland was so objectionable, and anyway, the clean bits made the rest of it look so much worse . . .

The slightly musty, dusty scent of neglect has given way to the homelier ones of wood fires, beeswax and lavender polish, baking and fresh coffee.

While I was working away I'd been keeping an eye on the weather, for outside large slow flakes of snow were stealthily falling. I saw George snowplough up the drive and turn down again, but this time he was alone. If he gets paid by the council for every trip, I suspect I'll see a lot of him!

By early afternoon the snow was even thicker and showed no sign of letting up, so I decided to bring Lady and Billy in early, then took off Lady's rug and rather inexpertly groomed her. She seemed to enjoy this, though Billy was a nuisance as always, forever butting me in the legs and nibbling the hems of my jeans.

I'd almost finished and was just putting Lady's rug back on, when Jess made one of her silent appearances: I think she must practise them.

'Don't stand there in the snow, come in,' I invited, so she did, with a cautious eye on Lady and then sidled gingerly past Billy.

I think actually she's afraid of horses and has invented an allergy to conceal it, because she never sneezes or shows any other symptoms.

'To what do I owe the honour of this visit?' I asked, but then looked up and saw her pale, anxious face. 'What is it? Is something wrong?'

'Grandpa asked me to walk up and tell you that Granny had a little fall in the kitchen last night.'

I stopped fastening the strap of the rug and turned to stare at her. 'Is she hurt?'

Her lower lip wobbled slightly. 'She bumped her head and knocked herself out, and we weren't sure if she'd broken anything, so we didn't like to move her. I had to ring for an ambulance.'

'Oh, poor Tilda – and poor Jess, too,' I said, giving her a hug. 'But why didn't you ring me?'

'It all happened so fast! Granny had come round a bit by the time the ambulance arrived, but they insisted on taking her to hospital for X-rays and a checkup, so Grandpa and I went too.'

'So, is she still there?'

'No, she refused to stay even though they wanted to keep her in overnight for observation and we came back in a taxi about two this morning. It only just managed to get up the hill!'

'Wow, you *have* been having a time of it! I only wish I'd known.'

'Grandpa didn't want to bother you, but if they had kept her in hospital he was going to ring and ask you if I could move up here for a bit.'

'Of course you could, that wouldn't have been a problem. How is your granny this morning?'

'Still in bed and Grandpa's trying to persuade her to stay there. I think she's a bit shaken up and bruised and she's probably going to have a black eye, too. I made us all some toast for breakfast . . . and we don't seem to have got round to lunch,' she said, and then added hopefully, 'I washed the soup Thermos out and brought it back.'

'Good thinking – some nice, hot soup will do them both good.' I gave her another hug and then finished fastening Lady's rug. 'You know, they're really not up to looking after themselves any more, are they? It's a pity their housekeeper had to go away just now, though I'm sure the poor woman is entitled to take Christmas off.'

'She always has the same two weeks, while Granny and Grandpa are happy to move up here for Christmas and New Year and me and Mum and Dad are usually here, too.' She paused and swallowed hard, tears not far away again. 'Grandpa said, just think how awful it would have been if Granny'd been cooking and holding something hot when she fell.'

'God, yes, he's right – it could have been so much worse!'

Jude Martland, you've got a lot to answer for! I thought – swanning off and leaving everyone to cope alone, when he must have seen how frail his elderly relatives were getting.

'Come on,' I said, leading the way out of the loosebox, 'we'll go and phone your Grandpa.'

'You can't, that's why I had to come and tell you. The phone line was a bit iffy this morning when Grandpa called the mobile number Uncle Jude gave him, and just after he'd told him about Granny's accident and her going to hospital, it all went totally dead. I walked down the lane to have a look and one of the poles was right down, so that's it and we're cut off.'

'Oh – then at least your Uncle Jude knows what's happening,' I said, relieved, 'though I don't suppose he said anything remotely useful?'

'I don't think he got the chance,' she said doubtfully.

'He might try and call you back on your mobile?'

'He doesn't know the number . . . and that's not working now either, because I dropped it down the toilet at the hospital.'

'Oh, yuk! I don't even want to know how you managed that,' I said. '*Or* what you did with it afterwards.'

'It's in a plastic bag one of the nurses gave me.' She looked at her watch. 'I'll have to get back soon – Grandpa's very tired and he must be hungry, because *I'm* ravenous and I don't want him to get ill, too.'

She sounded as if the cares of the world were on her small shoulders, poor child.

'Of course, and I'll come with you,' I said, and we set out as soon as I'd put more hot soup in the flask and quickly made cheese and tomato sandwiches.

A worried Noël was obviously deeply relieved to see me. 'It's very kind of you to come, m'dear. I really didn't want to be any more of a nuisance.'

'You're not a nuisance at all. How is Tilda now?'

'Furious with me for getting Jess to call the ambulance but she's still in bed,' he said, lowering his voice. 'Very unlike her, so it must have shaken her up. She says she has a headache too, but insists she will get up later and cook lunch.'

'It's nearly teatime, Noël! But I've brought hot soup, sandwiches and mince pies that you can all have now. And then do you think you ought to call the doctor about Tilda's headache?'

'She won't hear of it – only takes homeopathic remedies, you know. Never lets illness get the better of her!' he added proudly.

But there was no homeopathic cure for the encroaching infirmities of old age, which must overtake us all in the end . . . There seemed to be only one way of preventing Tilda from trying to carry on as usual and hurting herself even more in the process . . .

'You know, I really think it would be best if you all moved up to Old Place this afternoon and stayed, at least until Tilda is better,' I said with resignation.

'Oh *yes!*' said Jess eagerly.

'I had thought of asking, but I really didn't want to burden you with extra work,' Noël said anxiously.

'Not at all: Jess has helped me clean and make the beds already, so it'll be no trouble at all,' I lied.

A huge expression of relief crossed his face. 'If you are sure . . . and perhaps you will like the company?' he suggested, brightening. 'Jess and I will help you as much as we can, too.'

'Will Tilda be happy to move up to Old Place?'

'Oh yes, I'm *sure* she will.'

'Then shall I come down in the car in a couple of hours and collect you, when you've packed a few things?'

'No, that's all right, George will call in later with the newspaper, if it has got through to Little Mumming, and I'm sure he won't mind bringing us up in his Land Rover.'

'He seems very obliging and he certainly keeps the drive free of snow!'

'He's a very nice chap, is George. He and his son Liam do a good job of keeping the lane clear, and then the folks at Weasel Pot Farm below the village keep the lane on that side ploughed too, though sometimes they have to give up on the last steep bit down to the main road if the snow is too heavy.' He glanced through the window. 'If this keeps up, we might well be snowed in for a couple of days.'

'Then up at the house will be the best place for you – there's lots of food, it's warm and if the electricity fails, there's the generator.'

'Very true!' Noël was cheering up by the minute, as was Jess. 'Well, this will be fun, won't it? A proper family Christmas at the old home after all!'

'Yes, won't that be great?' I said slightly hollowly.

'Oh, but I was forgetting – you don't celebrate it, m'dear?'

'Not at all, I'm sure it's going to make a *lovely* change,' I said valiantly, and left them to their sandwiches, soup and packing.

As soon as I got home, I started to prepare for my visitors and then George drove them up when it was practically dark in a long-wheelbase Land Rover, together with all their baggage, a carton of perishable foodstuffs, and a huge plastic Santa sack full of wrapped presents.

George Froggat was a tall, well-built, middle-aged man with a mop of pale flaxen hair, a healthily pink face, sky-blue eyes, and an engaging grin. It was just as well that he was built on sturdy lines, because he had to lift Noël down and then he simply scooped Tilda up, carried her in and deposited her on the sofa by the fire in the sitting room.

He came back and shook hands and said he was very pleased to meet me, then helped carry everything else in. He wouldn't stay for a hot drink, but just as he was going, he said, 'Nearly forgot, here's something from me and my family.' Then he hauled out a Christmas tree bound with sacking from the back of the Land Rover and propped it in the porch.

'Gosh, that's almost as tall as I am!' I exclaimed.

'Aye, you're a grand, strapping lass,' he said approvingly, looking me up and down, then got back into the driving seat. 'I'll call in to see how things are going in the morning, or my boy Liam will, when we clear the drive.'

Tilda and Noël were still in the sitting room in front of the fire while Jess, looking martyred, was ferrying luggage upstairs in relays. I could hear the whine of the stairlift, so she wasn't carrying all of it herself.

'Would you like tea?' I asked. 'Or – maybe something stronger?'

'Good idea! There's whisky, gin and brandy in that little cabinet in the dining room, and glasses,' Noël said.

'I'm afraid I've finished off the brandy,' I confessed, 'and the cellar's locked.'

'Not surprised you needed it in this weather,' Noël said. 'And I've got the keys, all right. Jude leaves them with me when he's away and there's plenty more down there.'

'Actually, the brandy was for the Christmas cake, I didn't drink it.'

'*That* should have been made months ago, I told you,' Tilda piped up disapprovingly in her cut-crystal accent, from the depths of a sofa. Shaken up and bruised or not, she was wearing stiletto-heeled shoes and full makeup, despite being dressed only in a warm coat over her nightdress. I expect they made her feel more herself.

'It smelled delicious when Holly took it out of the oven,' Jess said. 'And we hadn't got one at all!'

'I kept thinking Jude wouldn't be away for Christmas, after all,' Tilda said, 'so I put off buying one. But there's the Dundee cake in a tin that Old Nan always gives us at Christmas, I've brought that. Where did you put it, Jess darling?'

'In the kitchen, with the other food and stuff.'

'Really, this quick Christmas cake recipe comes out surprisingly well and I thought Jess might help me ice it later,' I said.

'Wonderful,' Noël said, rubbing his hands together. 'And we can go up into the attic and look out the decorations tomorrow.' Then his face fell. 'But I have forgotten, there is no tree. We put up a little artificial one for Jess, but we didn't think to bring it.'

'It's all right, George left one as a gift in the porch,' I said. 'I thought it would be better left out there for the moment.'

'Oh, jolly good! Is it a big one? That always goes in the corner over there by the stairs.'

'It's *huge*,' I said with resignation. It looked as if I was in for a traditional Christmas whether I wanted one or not, so I might as well just give in right now and go with the flow!

* * *

After tea and mince pies – or whisky and mince pies in Noël's case – Tilda went upstairs to lie down, using the stairlift under protest, though she was obviously still shaky. When I took her a hot water bottle presently, I found her half-asleep already under the flowered satin eiderdown, though that was probably the exhaustion of directing Jess with the unpacking of the suitcases.

Noël stretched out on the sofa for a nap while Jess and I went into the kitchen and had a fun, if messy, time marzipanning and icing the cake and sticking a lot of old decorations on it that we found in a Bluebird Toffee tin in one of the cupboards. There was a complete set of little plaster Eskimos, sledging, skiing or throwing snowballs, and an igloo.

'Didn't you even have a Christmas cake when you were little?' asked Jess, positioning a polar bear menacingly near one of the Eskimos.

'No. My gran often made lovely fruit cakes, but she didn't set out to make a Christmas cake as such.'

'I think it's really sad that you never had a tree, or presents or crackers or anything, until you were grown up.'

'I thought so too, when I was at school,' I said ruefully. 'I so envied all my friends! I expect that's why I went overboard with the whole seasonal gifts, food and decorations thing when I got married. But that isn't really what Christmas should be about, is it?'

'But it's *fun!*' she protested. 'I love everything about Christmas – but not as much as Grandpa. He's an expert, you know, he's written a book about it.'

'Oh yes, I think he mentioned that.'

'It's called *Auld Christmas*, like the pub name, and it's about ancient traditions being absorbed into new ones and stuff like that, and how the Twelfth Night Revels celebrate the rebirth of the new year and goes back way before Christianity.'

'Does it? It sounds like *you're* an expert too,' I said, impressed.

'Oh, Grandpa's forever going on about it, and my parents have always brought me to Old Place for Christmas, so it's just sort of seeped in.' She looked a bit forlorn suddenly. 'I wish they could be here this time, too, but I do understand. They could hardly fly back from Antarctica just for the Christmas holidays, could they?'

'No, but they must be missing you an awful lot.'

'Oh, they'll be so into what they're doing they won't even remember I exist until they get back!' She sounded tolerant rather than aggrieved by this. 'But they did record a DVD wishing me Happy Christmas before they went, a bit like the Queen's message, though Granny says I can't have it until Christmas Day.'

'That's something to look forward to.'

'Yes, and I don't mind them not being here so much now we're staying with you. Christmas is going to be much more fun! You don't really mind if we have a proper one, do you?'

'I suppose not, and it's starting to sound as if I'll have enough of Christmas this year to make up for all the ones I've missed.'

'And presents, too. I make all mine and I've got a wonky one I practised on you can have,' she said generously.

I couldn't imagine what she'd made, but I thanked her anyway. 'I wasn't expecting anything – I wasn't even expecting *Christmas*, come to that! Mind you, I do have one present already, from my best friend.'

'What's she like?'

'She's my husband's younger sister and my opposite in every way: tiny, fair and blue-eyed like he was . . . but she doesn't look like him otherwise.'

'Was your husband short, then? Uncle Jude is a *giant*.'

'He was exactly the same height as me – six foot.'

'That's tall enough to be a model, except they're all skinny.'

'Well, you know what they say: never trust a skinny cook.'

'Do they?' She frowned. 'Oh, I see: it means you don't love food.'

'And won't eat your own cooking!'

When we'd finished and I'd fixed a paper frill (also from the toffee tin) around the cake, I covered it with a large glass dome I'd spotted in one of the old glazed-fronted cupboards that lined one wall of the huge kitchen, then put it in the larder.

'Now, perhaps we'd better make some more tea and you could take it through while I start dinner. Could you pop up and see if your Granny's awake and would like some?'

I'd taken some beef mince out of the freezer as soon as I'd got back earlier and now quickly made a large cottage pie and put it in the oven, then cored baking apples to stuff with dried fruit, brown sugar and cinnamon. There was long-life cream, ice cream and a half-used aerosol can of squirty cream that had come from the lodge with the other perishable food . . . and when I counted, there were a total of four and a half aerosol tins of sweetened cream, so it must play a large part in their diet!

Tilda had a tray in bed and the rest of us ate around the big pine table in the kitchen. By the time I'd cleared this away and then gone out for one last check on Lady and to give Merlin a run, I was exhausted.

But I still felt on edge, as if waiting for something – and I realised it was Jude's daily call! In a peculiar way, I sort of missed the adrenaline rush of crossing swords with him, even if he had managed to provoke me into losing my temper on more than one occasion.

Noël had gone to bed and Jess was in the morning room watching something fuzzy and probably highly unsuitable on the TV, half-glazed with sleep. I sent her upstairs, but she made me promise to come and put her light out on my way up in a few minutes. The child in her was only just beneath the surface: I ended up reading her a bit of *The Water Babies* from a book we found on one of the shelves, before tucking her up with her teddy bear and saying good night.

*   *   *

Tonight I could only focus on the journal entries for long enough to discover that Gran's first meeting outside the hospital with N seemed set to become the first of many.

Then my eyes started to close as if weighted with lead and I switched out the light and sank back on the pillows – only to start awake again a moment later, my heart racing, filled with shocked guilt because for the first time in eight years, I had forgotten the anniversary of Alan's death!

I climbed out of bed and fetched his photograph in its travelling frame from the top of the washstand: and that's how I fell asleep, holding onto my lost love, my face wet with tears.

Chapter 14: Toast and Treacle

I met N again and this time he had borrowed his brother's car, though I am sure he should not yet be using his injured leg so much. When I told him so he laughed and said that he was fine, and would soon be getting his motorbike out of storage, though he needn't think I will get on it!

February, 1945

I was up much earlier than everyone else, seeing to Merlin and double-rugging Lady, as Becca had suggested doing if it got really cold, before letting her and Billy out into the snowy paddock.

It was bitterly icy out there and the wind felt as if it was coming straight off the tundra so, after hanging the haynet on the fence and breaking the ice in the water trough, I was glad to go back in and thaw out. Mucking out would have to wait for later.

By now I'd found a note about the care of Billy, which had come adrift from its place in the file and been pushed into the pocket at the back. However, apart from feeding him some of the goat biscuit things every day, which I had been doing anyway, he seemed to eat much the same as Lady. At the bottom of the typed page, Jude had written: *If Billy gets ill and goes off his food, tempt him with toast and treacle.*

Was he serious?

I got the defrosted ham out of the larder and boiled it, pouring away the water. Then I smeared it with honey and mustard, stuck it with cloves, and put it in to bake.

By the time I'd followed this up by making a blancmange and a quick chocolate cake from a favourite recipe, Noël and Jess had appeared. Tilda was, as I expected, still shaken, bruised and stiff, though she'd apparently announced her intention of coming down later.

When I asked them what they would like for breakfast, Jess said, 'A bacon and egg McMuffin, if you *really* want to know.'

'There are muffins in the freezer, you could have a Holly Muffin instead, if that would do?'

In fact, we all had bacon and egg-filled muffins, including Tilda, though Jess took hers up on a tray along with toast, marmalade, butter and a little fat pot of tea.

Apparently she usually eats a hearty breakfast, though if she got through that lot, then she must eat her own body weight every day, since she's the size of a sparrow!

Fortified by that, Noël and Jess were all set for an expedition to the attic to fetch down the Christmas decorations.

'There are only two days to go before Christmas, so there's no time to waste,' Noël said. They wanted me to go with them, which in my new spirit of drifting with the seasonal flow I agreed to do, just as soon as I'd cleared the breakfast things.

Jess was dispatched to collect her granny's breakfast tray and tell her where we were going to be, in case she thought we'd deserted her. I was just checking the ham when there was a hammering at the back door.

George must have snowploughed up the drive again, for the tractor with the heavy blade on the front was on the other side of the gate and, to judge from the footsteps across the snowy cobbles, he'd already made a couple of trips to and fro. There was a large holdall and a suitcase at his feet, and he was holding an assortment of other stuff, including a lot of greenery.

He gave me his attractive grin over the top of it, his healthy pink face glowing under its shock of white-gold hair and his sky-blue eyes bright.

'Morning! Met the postie in the village and thought I'd save him the trouble of bringing your mail up, seeing I was coming anyway. I've brought the old folks', too, though theirs mostly looks like Christmas cards.'

'That's kind of you.'

'If you take that?' he suggested and I relieved him of a large bundle held together with red elastic bands, two parcels, a hyacinth in a pot and the bunch of holly and mistletoe.

'Henry sent you the hyacinth, and the holly and bit of mistletoe are from me. I'll cut some more and drop it off in the porch later.'

'Oh – how kind of you both,' I said, gingerly holding the prickly bouquet and trying not to drop anything. 'And the bags . . . ?'

He picked them up and heaved them over the threshold.

'Becca's. I cleared as far as New Place and she called to me and asked if I'd drop them off.'

'She did?'

I supposed it made sense, when I came to think about it, since if it carried on snowing she might have to walk up through the snow on Christmas Day. She did seem to need an awful lot of stuff for one night, though!

'We've just finished breakfast – why don't you come in and have a cup of tea?'

'Nay, I haven't time, but I'll carry Becca's bags through for you if you like, one of them's heavy.' He stamped the snow off his boots and came in, shutting the door behind him.

'Is that George?' called Noël from the kitchen. 'Tell him to come through!'

'I can't stop,' George called back, but walked up the passage anyway, while I lingered to put the holly and mistletoe in the utility room together with the hyacinth, until I could find it a saucer to stand on.

133

Despite what he'd said, he was sitting at the kitchen table when I went in and Noël was pouring him a mug of slightly stewed tea.

I put a plate of mince pies in front of him and, sniffing the air as appreciatively as a truffle hound, he said, 'Something smells good in here!'

'That's the ham cooking . . . and maybe the cake I made earlier.'

While he consumed a succession of mince pies he told us what the lane down to the main road was like, which was pretty bad for anything except four-wheel-drive vehicles, especially the last steep, bendy stretch from Weasel Pot Farm.

'Their lad Ben's doing a roaring trade, pulling the SatNav people out of the ditch on the first corner. They get partway up it, then slide down again.'

'You'd think they would take one look and realise the SatNav was wrong,' Noël said.

'More money than sense, buying those things in the first place,' George said.

'But the postman got up it all right?' I asked.

'He's got a Post Office Land Rover and he's used to it,' he explained. 'Did you make these mince pies yourself, flower?'

They were quite small, but even so, I'd never seen anyone put a whole one in their mouth before. I nodded, fascinated.

'They're champion – you're a grand cook as well as a strapping lass,' he said with approval.

Jess giggled and he grinned at her. 'And you'll be another strapping lass too, when you've finished growing.'

Jess blushed, but actually I think she was quite pleased.

'The forecast says more snow is likely on higher ground,' Noël said, 'so I suppose we might get cut off.'

'Maybe, though we usually manage to keep the lane to the village open, don't we? But you couldn't get even the tractor over the Snowehill road to Great Mumming, now.' George consumed the last mince pie on the plate as though he was popping Smarties,

134

then got up. 'Well, I'll be going: the dog's on the tractor and it's bitter out there. I'll drop you more greenery off later, Holly, you'll want it for the decorations – this first lot's more of a token gesture. And maybe you'll have hung the mistletoe up in the porch when I come back,' he added with unmistakable intent, and it was my turn to blush.

'Oh yes, we *must* hang up the mistletoe later,' Noël agreed, 'and have lots of green stuff in the sitting room. We were just about to go up into the attic and bring down the decorations when you arrived.'

'Then I'll leave you to it.'

Noël showed him out, while Jess got the giggles. 'George *fancies* you!'

I carried on sedately stacking the mince pie plate and the mugs in the dishwasher. 'He fancies my cooking, Jess, that's all.'

'Do you think he's nice-looking?'

'Yes, he's very handsome, in a rugged, outdoor kind of way.'

Noël came back in. 'It's bitter out there, isn't it? And what are these two bags he's brought?'

'They're your sister's – I suppose she thought she might as well send her overnight things up with George while she had the chance, in case the weather worsens. Jess, you could help me carry them up to her room while we're going in that direction. Take the overnight bag and I'll have the case.'

'I'll look through our mail later,' Noël said.

'There's already a whole stack for Jude. It's piled on that table in the front hallway,' I told him.

'I'll bring it all in later and sort it out,' he promised. 'A lot of it is probably junk.'

We dumped the bags in the room that had been assigned to Becca and then Noël checked again on Tilda, who was fast asleep, before we carried on up past the nursery.

Jess gave the attic door a good shove and it opened reluctantly with a protesting screech.

'Jude ought to get that fixed, it's always sticking,' Noël said, pressing down a light switch and illuminating a large space, well filled with the abandoned clutter and tat of centuries.

'There's another, smaller attic over the kitchen wing, but there's nothing much in it, as I recall. In the days when there were several servants, I think some of them slept there.'

'I hadn't even noticed a way into it,' I confessed.

'It's in a dark corner of the landing and looks like a cupboard door.'

'That would account for it.'

Noël led the way to a dust-sheeted pile between a large trunk and a miscellany of broken chairs. 'Here we are,' he announced and Jess tore off the sheet eagerly.

'We need all these boxes marked with a large C, and that red metal stand for the Christmas tree,' he began, then noticed he'd lost my attention. 'I see you are admiring the Spanish chest, m'dear?'

'Yes, it looks ancient?'

'Parts of the house are extremely old and the chest has always been here. We think it might be Elizabethan and came into the family when an ancestor married a Spanish bride, or perhaps a few years later. Did I mention that family legend has it that Shakespeare once visited Old Place, too?'

'No,' I said, 'though it doesn't surprise me, since they found those Shakespeare documents over at Sticklepond recently. He seems to have got about a bit, doesn't he? You'd probably be hard-pressed to find any large house in West Lancashire that he wasn't alleged to have visited!'

'Very true!' he acknowledged. 'You know, until recently we used to act out *Twelfth Night* on New Year's Eve: "If music be the food of love, play on . . ."' He sighed wistfully. 'Oh well . . .'

'I'm not allowed to go in that chest for dressing-up things,' Jess said.

136

'No, the mumming costumes for the Revels are in it, though the heads are stored in the hayloft behind the Auld Christmas.'

'The *heads*?' I repeated.

'The Dragon and Red Hoss and the Man-Woman's hat and mask,' he explained, though that didn't make things much clearer: the opposite, if anything.

'You know,' he added, looking at me with a puzzled air, 'you already feel so much like one of the family that I keep forgetting that you are not, and don't know all our little ways and customs. But I *have* mentioned the Revels on Twelfth Night, haven't I?'

I was glad to be thought of as one of the family, even though I was doubling as cook and general factotum, because I was in a strange position: it's easier when I'm on cooking assignments, because then I'm *definitely* staff.

'Is it Morris dancing? I've noticed the photographs, especially in the library.'

'That's right, dancing and a little play-acting – just a simple ceremony . . .' he said vaguely. 'It takes place on the green in front of the Auld Christmas and has been performed for centuries, though of course there have been changes over the years. I'll show you some more photographs after dinner, if you like?'

'Thank you, that would be really interesting,' I agreed, thinking that this might be a way of getting him to tell me more about his brother Ned.

'Oh look – sledges!' Jess said, spotting them leaning against the wall behind the boxes. 'Two of them and they're plastic, so they must have belonged to Uncle Jude and Guy.'

'That's right,' Noël said. 'There are a couple of old wooden ones around somewhere too, that we oldies had when we were children – or maybe they fell apart, I can't remember.'

There was so much clutter; *anything* could be up there, including Santa and all his reindeer. It could do with a jolly good clear-out.

'I think the blue one was Jude's and the red one Guy's, though

I expect they fell out over *that*, too – Guy always wanted what his older brother had and they were forever squabbling.'

'I suppose that's natural,' I said.

'In a child, but perhaps not so allowable in an adult ... though now Guy's getting married and settling down, I expect he will see things differently. There's nothing like having children of your own to give you a new perspective on life.'

'*I* was a mistake,' Jess announced.

'More of a very welcome surprise,' amended her grandfather.

'Would it be all right if I used one of the sledges, Grandpa?'

'Take them both down, m'dear: perfect weather for sledging and perhaps Holly will join you. I wish *my* poor old bones were up to it,' he added wistfully.

Jess carried the sledges downstairs first, then came back up and started ferrying down boxes of decorations to the sitting room. I took the tree stand and a carton marked 'swags and door wreath' while Noël clutched the box containing a precious antique hand-carved wooden Nativity scene. By the time we'd stacked everything in a corner of the sitting room, I had to go and start making lunch.

Tilda stubbornly insisted on coming downstairs and joining us for soup, egg sandwiches and chocolate cake. Apart from a slightly black eye, she looked a little better, though moving very stiffly. Afterwards she established herself on the sofa in the sitting room and exhibited a slight tendency to issue orders to all of us, but especially me, wanting to know exactly how I would be coping with the catering over Christmas. But I didn't really mind that, because when I cook for house-parties I'm used to consulting over the menus, so I sat down with her for a good discussion.

'Luckily the house is extremely well stocked and I always bring my cookery books, recipe notebook and favourite store cupboard ingredients with me, so there should be no problem. There's a shelf of cookery books in the kitchen, too.'

When I'd leafed through one or two well-thumbed-looking ones, I'd found additions pencilled next to the recipes, so someone had been a keen cook: either the last housekeeper or perhaps Jude's mother.

'We might run out of fresh salad, fruit and perishable things if the village is snowed in, but we can get by without them,' I added. 'There's loads of bread in the freezer, and butter, eggs, cheese, long-life juice, milk and cream. We certainly won't starve.'

'And you have everything you need for the traditional Christmas dinner?' she asked.

'Yes, there's no problem there. I cooked the ham this morning and I've taken the turkey out of the freezer and put it in the larder to defrost slowly. What time do you usually have it? Are you a lunch or evening family?'

'About two in the afternoon, then we only need a late supper of sandwiches and cake instead of dinner. We do the same on Boxing Day.'

'Right . . . though perhaps we might like a change from turkey on Boxing Day? I noticed a whole salmon in one of the freezers and thought we could have that instead, then a second roast turkey dinner the next day, before I use up the remains in dishes like curry for the freezer.'

Tilda gave her gracious approval to all my plans, which was just as well, since I would have carried on regardless. I don't let any of my clients interfere with my cooking, with the exception of dietary requirements; although since I smile and nod while listening to them issuing orders, I'm sure they think the resulting wonderful food is all their own idea.

'We have champagne with Christmas dinner,' Noël said, 'but I'll see to the drinks so you needn't worry about that.'

'I'll need some more brandy for the pudding too,' I told him, 'because I used up what was in the decanter.'

'I'll go down and get some now and scout out what else Jude's got in the wine cellar,' he promised.

'There's no rush – let your lunch settle first,' I suggested. 'You've had a busy morning.'

'And now that the main menus have been sorted, I think I'd like cake or scones for afternoon tea, today,' Tilda said autocratically, before going back upstairs to rest.

'Sorry, m'dear, she's a bit bossy and she keeps forgetting you aren't staff,' apologised Noël.

'Well, I suppose I *am* really, since I'm being paid to be here.'

'Edwina doesn't stand any nonsense, she just says to her, "You'll get what you're given, my lady, and like it!"'

I grinned. 'You just can't get the serfs to behave themselves these days, can you?'

'I think of you more and more as one of the family,' he said kindly, 'though since we've made so much more work for you over Christmas, you deserve to be paid for it – and if Jude doesn't do something about it, then we will make it up to you.'

'Oh no, really – I'm enjoying the company and I love cooking,' I insisted, because he is such a sweetie. 'I'm *perfectly* happy with my house-sitting fee!'

Chapter 15: Advent

I meet N whenever I can slip away – I can't help myself. He says we were meant to be together, he knew it from the moment he saw me and I feel the same way, though horribly guilty when I think of poor Tom. I did sincerely love him, just not in the way I now love N . . .

February 1945

The sky, which had earlier been almost as blue as George's eyes, had turned leaden again. Jess took one of the sledges up to the top of the paddock where it sloped quite steeply, while I finally got round to mucking out the loosebox. I'd only just started when the side gate clanged and I looked out to see Becca leading Nutkin through it.

'Hell of a journey!' she greeted me, closing the gate behind her. 'I had to bribe George to bring my bags earlier – have they come? He's making a mint out of the bad weather, the rascal.'

'Yes, he dropped them off after breakfast and we've put them in your room. But I'm surprised to see you, since it isn't very good weather for riding, is it?'

'I led Nutkin on the worst bits, but I couldn't leave him alone at home if there was a chance I'd get snowed in here, could I?' she asked reasonably. 'Weather's closing in again, so I thought I'd better take the chance and come up now, especially with Tilda, Noël and Jess being here already.'

'You mean – you've come to stay, too?'

'That's it,' she agreed. 'One more can't make any difference to you, can it? In fact, it'll be easier, because I can give you a hand with the horses.'

'Great,' I said faintly, though I suppose having an equine expert on hand *would* be a relief if we were snowed in. She put Nutkin in Lady's loosebox and rubbed him down briskly with wisps of hay, then we went in to tell Noël she had arrived. Jess came too, since she said her fingers were freezing and so was her bottom.

Noël, who was snoozing on one of the sofas in the sitting room, woke up and blinked as we all trooped in. 'Becca! This *is* a surprise!'

'Weather's getting worse, so I thought I'd send my bags up and come to stay now. I've brought Nutkin,' she explained succinctly.

'Well, how nice, a jolly family party!' Noël rubbed his hands together. 'It's a pity the boys can't be here too, but there you are.'

'Stopped at the Auld Christmas on the way, to bring a little cheer.' Becca reached into two deep pockets inside her waxed, caped coat and produced a bottle of sherry from each. 'We're all partial to a drop of good sherry . . . which reminds me, where's Tilda?'

'Resting, but she'll be down again later. She says she isn't quite so stiff now the bruises have come out – though she's black and blue, poor old girl!'

'I brought some horse liniment – always does the trick for me.'

'Yes, but it smells disgusting, Becca,' he objected dubiously.

'Nicholas Dagger said to tell you they were all set for Twelfth Night and rehearsed for the dancing.'

'Good, good!' he said. 'Aren't you going to take your coat off?'

'No, I'm going straight back out to see to the horses,' Becca said. 'Lady's loosebox still needs mucking out and I'll have to make the other up for Nutkin.'

'But you must be frozen, and I can do that,' I offered.

'Not at all – you've got enough on your plate already. But I'll need Jess to wheel the barrow to the manure heap and fill the buckets.'

'I'm allergic to horses and I'm cold and wet,' Jess said sulkily. 'I'd rather just help Grandpa get the decorations up.'

'You mean you're allergic to hard work,' Becca said severely. 'You don't have to come near Lady or Nutkin. Now, run up to my bedroom and fetch the holdall – it's got Nutkin's rug and headcollar in it.'

Jess gave in, though *not* graciously.

I put on a large casserole to slow-cook for dinner, using some very nice beef from the freezer, home-grown carrots and a good splash of beer from a stash of large bottles I'd discovered on the stone floor of the larder, pushed well back under the bottom shelf. I drank what was left – it was best bitter and I probably needed the iron.

Jess came back in looking limp, so I suggested she go and start putting up the decorations with Noël when she had warmed up a bit.

But Becca, who was still full of energy, borrowed my radio and took it into the tackroom, where she was sitting cleaning Nutkin's saddle when I followed her with a substantial slice of chocolate cake and a cup of tea to keep her energy levels up.

Later she made the hot mash and went out again to get Lady and Billy in, since it was starting to get dark, so she was proving to be worth her weight in pony nuts already.

Jess and I carried in the Christmas tree and managed to angle it into its red metal holder, though the top of it almost brushed the gallery above. Then she and Noël steadied the stepladder while I draped the garlands as they directed, from each corner of the room to the middle of the ceiling, and hung Chinese lanterns and baubles from the wall light fittings.

Then I left them unpacking the Nativity scene and went back to the kitchen, where even sober Radio 4 was intoxicated with the spirit of Christmas.

Luckily, no-one seemed to have any objection to eating meals off the kitchen table, which made life much easier than traipsing to and from the dining room with plates and platters, though we would use it on Christmas Day and Boxing Day, of course.

There was a chocolate blancmange rabbit for dessert, quivering on a bed of chopped green jelly, which proved surprisingly popular with everyone, not just Jess. It vanished right down to its tail and, what with that and the chocolate cake, I was starting to wish I had brought more than one tin of cocoa powder with me!

Tilda hadn't got any at the lodge when I asked her, only Ovaltine, which was not at all the same thing, but she thought the village shop stocked it, so another trip was clearly needed.

After dinner was cleared away (and thank goodness there was a dishwasher! If the electricity did go off, I only hoped the generator was up to running it), we retired to the half-decorated sitting room and Noël, as he had promised earlier, fetched the photograph albums that charted the Revels from the library.

They all seemed to feature the same strangely-dressed and masked figures and, as I had suspected, Morris dancing, though they carried swords. I don't suppose they were *real* ones, though.

One picture of four tall, dark young men standing with a young version of Becca particularly interested me.

'That's me,' Noël said, pointing to a handsome man, little more than a boy, 'and that's Jacob, my eldest brother, but he was killed at Dunkirk, poor chap. Ned was injured too, but later – that's him next to Jacob and then Alexander, Jude's father, who inherited Old Place.'

'And then me,' said Becca.

144

'I recognised you instantly, you haven't changed much,' I told her, and she looked pleased.

'Keep pretty fit, considering,' she said. 'Of course, I'm the youngest.'

I looked again at the photograph. 'So . . . what happened to Edward? You said he was injured?'

'He had a bad leg injury, but they tried penicillin on it and he made a speedy recovery. It seemed he was going to settle down after that, but it wasn't to be . . . and he never played Red Hoss in the Revels again.'

Noël seemed about to drift away into old, and perhaps unhappy, memories so I said, 'Red Hoss? I think you mentioned that character before.'

Noël thumbed forward until he found a photograph of a man wearing a rather scary and fierce horse mask. 'That one – I forget you know little about it,' he said apologetically, 'as I said earlier, I feel we have known you for ever – and you look so like one of the Martlands that you would fit into the family album quite easily. It's a strange coincidence, isn't it?'

'Yes, it certainly is,' I said absently, staring at another photograph of Ned Martland, without the mask, next to it. It was neither large nor clear, but something about his expression reminded me of a framed photograph of my mother that had always had pride of place on top of Gran's harmonium . . . and still did, though it was now in my cottage. But then, when I leaned forward for a better look, I realised it was just a trick of the light.

'And I don't suppose you had ever heard of the Twelfth Night Revels in Little Mumming before, had you?'

'Or about the red horse hill figure,' I agreed.

'We try not to publicise either of them – and actually, these days the Revels are more of a Twelfth Afternoon ceremony. Since the war, you know. But traditionally, a fire was lit on the beacon, as well, and then there was a procession back down from it.'

'I don't suppose you could light fires at night during the war, it'd be way too dangerous.'

'No, it was the blackout, you see. And with most of the young men off at war, some of the older ones who took their places were not really up to climbing the hill. But my father kept the Revels going as well as he could.'

'Wouldn't publicising the Revels bring lots of tourists here?'

'That's the whole point, m'dear. We have plenty of walkers, cyclists and stray drivers from spring to autumn: the pub, the shop and the Merry Kettle do well, the farm shop at Weasel's Pot thrives, and George gives trailer rides behind his tractor up to the beacon: that is enough for us. We don't want the Revels to be taken over by a lot of arty crafty folk who will want the whole thing preserved like a fly in amber, instead of letting it gently evolve as it has done over the centuries.'

'I see what you mean,' I agreed.

'Richard Sampson wrote a short pamphlet about the Revels and the red horse, for private circulation only, and I can look you out the library copy if you are interested?'

'Yes, I'd love to read it. Won't the Revels be snowed off this year if the weather carries on like this? Unless a thaw sets in soon, of course.'

'Oh, we've had heavy snow in January before and it has gone ahead. We all live locally, you see, and it's only half a mile down to the village from here. If the snow hasn't gone by then, Jess can pull me there on the sledge!'

'I might, Grandpa, but I'm not pulling you back up the hill again!' she protested.

'I wasn't serious, m'dear. Your Uncle Jude will be back by then and he will manage something.'

I had been drawn back to studying the prewar photograph of the young Martlands. 'So, Ned recovered from his leg wound? What happened to him after that?'

'It was ironic, really – he was killed in a motorbike accident only a couple of months after the war ended.'

'That's . . . quite tragic,' I said slowly and, since Noël was looking troubled, I didn't press him for more details.

But maybe that's why nothing ever came of Granny's big romance? And if so, it was terribly sad! Noël had implied that his brother Ned was a bit of a black sheep and he *had* sounded like a flirt at first, only now he really appeared to have fallen for Gran, just as she'd fallen head over heels in love with him.

Poor Gran – now I knew that her happiness would be cut short by Ned's accident, it made reading about it that night even more poignant!

> *When I confided in Hilda and Pearl, they said if N really*
> *loved me, why did it have to stay a secret that we were*
> *seeing each other? So then I asked N when we were going*
> *to tell our families that we were courting, and he said there*
> *was no hurry, because he didn't want to share the few*
> *precious hours we could spend together with anyone else at*
> *present.*

He must have had a lot of charm to persuade a girl with her strict upbringing to meet him clandestinely! It seems very odd at this remove in time that they should have felt the need to keep their romance secret, but class differences and the social divide were more important then, I suppose.

Then my eye fell on the next, short entry and I had a total 'Oh, my God!' moment: I think I *seriously* underestimated Ned Martland's charm!

Chapter 16: Comfort

I am too ashamed to go to chapel and look Tom's father in the eye. I am a sinner, a grievous sinner.

March, 1945

I woke up later than usual, heavy-eyed after a night full of strange, uneasy dreams, and lay there thinking about Gran. I still couldn't see any other interpretation for what I'd read but the one I'd originally thought of, and all sorts of possibilities and implications kept going through my head.

Eventually I resolved to try to put it to the back of my mind until I could talk it over with Laura, though that was easier said than done. In the end I decided I'd take the current volume down with me to dip into if I got a quiet moment alone. I could put it on the cookery book shelf in the kitchen, because no-one else ever looked there.

When I drew the curtains it was still almost dark but I could see that there had been a further fall of snow. Becca was obviously an early bird too, because I could see her below me, turning Nutkin into the paddock to join Billy and a well-rugged-up Lady. Her presence here is obviously going to be a huge asset while I am so busy with everything else, though I suppose if Jude knew she'd taken over most of my horse-minding duties, he would want to dock my house-sitting fee!

I still had the care of Merlin, though, and carefully stirred his medicine into his food every morning, though actually he was such a soft, biddable creature he would probably have eaten it straight from my hand. I was getting very attached to him – he was such a lovely, affectionate dog, always pleased to see me.

Becca and I had breakfast together and then she sat on with a mug of tea, listening to the radio and watching me as I soaked trifle sponges I'd found in the cupboard (which were indeed more than a trifle out of date, but well sealed up) in a little sherry purloined from the drinks cabinet in the dining room and then made a pheasant terrine, having defrosted the birds overnight.

'You're very organised!' she commented.

'It's just my job – thinking ahead and knowing what to prepare for the dishes I intend making is second nature. Forward planning.'

'Well, I wish you could stay here and cook permanently.'

I smiled. 'I don't think your nephew would be too pleased about that – we don't seem to get on very well when he rings,' I told her, though oddly enough I had sort of missed our slightly acerbic exchanges ever since the phone had gone dead . . .

When Noël and Jess appeared, Becca had a second breakfast with them but Tilda had hers in bed again, though that seems to be a habit rather than a sign that she's still feeling under the weather.

While they were eating they discussed their plans for the day. Jess and Noël proposed to finish putting up the decorations and then do the Christmas tree, but before they could put that plan into action, Becca dragged Jess out to help with mucking out, buckets and haynets.

Noël fetched Tilda's tray down while I cleared up and checked on the terrine, which was both looking and smelling good. I've always found it a popular dish.

Becca and Jess were not outside long and returned with pink

noses and chilly hands just as Noël was making a fresh pot of tea, which seems to be about the extent of his culinary skills.

'George has been up and he says he's left you some more holly and stuff in the porch. I'll help you put it up, once I've thawed out,' Becca promised, 'but one of my favourite old films is on later and I thought I might watch that – *Winter Holiday*. If Tilda is down, she might want to see it, too.'

'She has come down. I just came to get her a cup of tea.'

'Then you can pour me one too, it's bloody nithering out there.'

'I've never heard of *Winter Holiday*,' Jess said, 'and the reception is so bad here you can hardly see anything anyway. I don't know why Uncle Jude hasn't got Sky like Granny and Grandpa. At least at the lodge I could watch something *good*!'

'There's a video and DVD player,' Noël pointed out. 'You brought some DVDs up with you, didn't you?'

'Yes, but I've seen them all a million times. And I can't play computer games because Jude keeps it locked away in the study – and anyway, it's really, really ancient so it's too slow for any of the games I've got. If he wasn't so mean he would have got a new one by now.'

'You shouldn't call him mean,' chided Noël. 'I expect Father Christmas is bringing you a lovely present from him.'

'Oh, *Grandpa*!' She rolled her eyes. 'I'm much too old to believe in Father Christmas *and* I saw that big parcel with American stamps that George brought yesterday. I suppose there are some from Mum and Dad in that big sack of presents you brought up with you?'

Noël tapped the side of his nose and tried to look mysterious, while I suddenly realised that I would be the only one who wasn't giving or receiving presents on Christmas Day . . . like Granny's first Christmas at the new hospital in Ormskirk, when she had nothing to give to her friends in return for their gifts, until she'd thought of the bookmarks . . .

I didn't even have bookmarks – and, come to think of it, Jess had said she was going to give me something she had made herself, so presumably I would have one present at least.

As if she could read my mind, Jess piped up just then and said, 'We can put all the presents under the tree when we've finished decorating it. I've nearly finished making all mine, but I've still got to wrap them.'

'Jess is an expert in origami,' Noël said proudly.

'I make origami jewellery and sell it at school,' Jess explained. 'Tiny, fiddly origami.'

'That's very clever,' I said, 'I'd love to see some of it.'

I'd been wondering whether to take a last trek down to the village to stock up on odds and ends that seemed likely to run out, like cocoa powder, and now I thought I ought to get in a supply of small emergency Christmas gifts too, just in case!

'Are you going to help us decorate?' asked Noël. 'You seem to have been very busy already, so perhaps you would rather put your feet up for a bit, m'dear?'

'No, I'm fine. I'll help you for half an hour and then I think I'll walk down to the village. I need a few last things from the shop and to stretch my legs, but I won't take Merlin – it's a bit freezing out there for his arthritis and I'd have to tie him up outside.'

I could see Jess was torn between coming with me and decorating the tree, and added quickly, 'I'd be grateful if you could keep an eye on him while I'm out, Jess? The poor old thing is missing his master and has latched on to me as a substitute, so he isn't going to like my going off without him.'

'Yes, and I'll need you to climb the stepladder while I hold it,' Noël pointed out. 'I can't do it alone and our old Father Christmas needs to go on top of the tree.' He held aloft a brownish figure of moulded paper. 'My brother Jacob bought this with his pocket money when he was about five, so that makes it well over eighty years old,' he said sentimentally.

'He's a venerable Santa,' I said, touched, 'and he's earned his place. And actually, I think if I leaned over the balcony I could put him on top of the tree from there.'

I managed to put quite a lot of small baubles on the top of the tree that way and helped drape the long string of fairy lights around it, so at least when I went out I knew Jess wouldn't be teetering about too high up on the ladder.

'You will be careful while I'm out, won't you?'

'Of course – we're a team, aren't we, Jess?' Noël said. 'The sitting room will be a picture by the time you get back!'

'I'm sure it will,' I said and left them to it while I made a few preparations in the kitchen and then got wrapped up for the walk. (I didn't fancy my chances of getting the car back up the hill this time.)

Merlin was beginning to look anxious, but when I went back into the sitting room Jess stopped unravelling a garland and made a fuss of him.

'I'm just off, but I've left soup in the pan on the back of the stove and sandwiches in the fridge for lunch. There's carrot cake or mince pies for after. You don't need to save anything for me, because I'll have bread and cheese in the pub.'

'I'll sort that out and from the sound of it, I don't think we'll starve while you're gone,' Becca said cheerfully. 'And if you *don't* come back, we'll send out search parties!'

'If I gave you the keys, could you possibly pop into the lodge and just make sure everything is all right?' asked Noël. 'No burst pipes – always a worry at this time of the year.'

'Yes, of course.'

'And if you need anything from the kitchen, just help yourself,' Tilda said graciously from the easy chair where she had placed herself to direct the decorating proceedings.

'Thanks – that would be very useful, especially if you have almond and vanilla essences?'

'I'm sure there are. Bring back what you need.'

'I don't like to ask for yet another favour,' Noël said, 'but if I gave you Jude's mobile phone number, could you try calling him while you are down there, and tell him where we are?'

'I'll give it a go,' I said dubiously, since I'm not in the habit of making transatlantic calls.

'And go and make sure Old Nan and Richard are all right while you are down in the village, too,' ordered Tilda autocratically, though it did show a caring and thoughtful side to her.

'Actually, I've wrapped up half a dozen mince pies each for them already.'

'Good idea.'

'Wine gums,' said Jess suddenly. 'Can you bring me back a big bag?'

'You'll rot your teeth,' said Tilda.

I left Jess hanging onto Merlin's collar and set out, feeling just like one of those tiny figures in a vast snowy Breughel landscape painting. I followed the ploughed track down the driveway (I *thought* I'd heard the roar of the tractor earlier), slipping and sliding a bit on the fresh snow that had half-filled it. It was easier going under the pine trees by the river, where the ground was free of snow, and on impulse I turned up the wide path off it to where I knew Jude's mill studio was.

It was only a few yards until the trees opened out to reveal a tall, narrow building with the remains of a mill race and dark, deep-looking pool below it. I peered through the window and saw that it was open right up to the rafters and full of all kinds of mysterious shapes, most vaguely equine.

It was pretty freezing so I didn't linger, but went on to the lodge, where everything looked fine. The kitchen cupboards didn't reveal much that I hadn't got already, apart from a few flavourings, spices and ground almonds, which I put in my rucksack in case I forgot them on the way back.

The lane down to Little Mumming had been cleared and grit spread on the worst part of the slope, but it was still slippery, so I was grateful when George stopped his long-wheelbase Land Rover and offered me a lift. I had to share the front seat with his slightly smelly sheepdog, but to be honest, by then I was just glad of the warmth.

'You must have been out really early, George! How is the road down beyond the village?'

'Liam was the one out first thing and he said you could still get a four-wheel drive up and down to the main road, but anything else would be in trouble,' he said. 'My lad and Ben from Weasel's Pot are friends, so one ploughs up and the other down and it gives them a chance to meet in the middle and waste time, like.'

I smiled. 'You all seem to work really hard already – you must have plenty to do without all this road clearing.'

'Ah, but farmers have to diversify to make the money these days, and the council pays well for road clearing. Then Jude and one or two others pay me for clearing their drives too, so it all helps.'

'Yes, I suppose it must.'

'And in the summer I hitch up this dinky little trailer with bench seats behind the tractor and take the tourists up the track to the beacon and back. Pays better than the sheep, that does.'

'That's very enterprising,' I said and, as we came down past the church, added, 'you know, I hadn't thought to ask if the shop would even be open today!'

'Oh, Orrie will only close Christmas and Boxing Day and she'll always open in an emergency – she lives above the shop. Yes . . . very obliging, is Orrie,' he added thoughtfully – I could see I had an established love rival!

'She certainly seems to have a wide-ranging stock, doesn't she?'

'Yes, well, she's a general store and gift shop rolled into one, you see – caters for the tourist trade in summer and opens that café of hers for cream teas. Were you wanting anything in particular?'

'Not really, just a few bits and pieces I thought we might run out of, and Tilda wanted me to check up on Old Nan and the Vicar – do you think you could drop me by the almshouses? I've been wondering how they'll get up to Old Place for Christmas dinner. At a push, I expect I could drive them home again in my car, but I'm sure it won't go up this hill. I'd have to leave it down there.'

'Nay, that little car of yours won't be much good on ice! It's a pity Jude took his old Land Rover with him, or you could've used that.'

'But I couldn't use someone else's car and I've never driven a Land Rover before.'

'Well, don't you fret about Christmas Day: our Liam can plough the road to the village and your drive first thing and then one of us will go down and fetch the old folks up for you.'

'Surely you won't be out on the roads on Christmas morning?'

'We're farmers: we'll be out tending the livestock anyway, Christmas morning or not.'

'You're very kind,' I said gratefully.

'My pleasure,' he said, with a quick sideways glance accompanied by his engaging grin.

Some children were making a snowman near the church and it all looked picturebook with its coating of snow . . . until I saw where the children had chosen to stick the carrot.

'Little bleeders,' George said amiably, glancing at them as we passed and circled the green.

'Noël's told me a bit about the Revels. He said there would be a ring of twelve fire braziers as well as the bonfire.'

'That's right. Originally there were twelve small bonfires and one big one, but Jude made some wrought-iron basketwork braziers that spike into the ground, so we use those instead now. It's the same idea, just easier and safer.'

He gave me another sideways look from his sky-blue eyes as he pulled up outside the almshouses. 'Noël doesn't usually say much to strangers about the Revels: none of us do. He must have taken an uncommon shine to you.'

'I think it's because he keeps forgetting I'm not one of the family, since I'm tall and dark, which seems to be usual with Martlands.'

'Yes, the dark side does seem to win out, and you do have a Martland look – I thought so from the first.'

I wasn't sure if that was a compliment or not!

'I'm starting to be sorry I'll miss the Revels. Do you take part in them?'

'Oh yes, there've always been Rappers from Hill Farm,' he said mysteriously as I got out, and added that he was going to see his sister, who lived on the far side of the village, but would look out for me on the way back.

Although Henry was out (I left his foil-wrapped package on a little shelf inside the porch and hoped it would be all right), the other two both seemed pleased to see me and accepted as a matter of course the news that someone from Hill Farm would pick them up and bring them to Old Place on Christmas Day. In fact, Old Nan told me that George wouldn't need to bother, since Jude would come himself, he always did. Clearly she had lost the plot again.

Richard had also lost it, since he addressed me as Miss Martland and told me to inform the family that he would take a midnight carol service on Christmas Eve, since the vicar from Great Mumming was unlikely to make it. 'He usually does an early service here, then goes on to the church in Great Mumming.'

'Won't you be exhausted taking a late service – and in the cold?' I asked.

'I don't sleep much these days, anyway. And there are paraffin heaters in the church, you know – we have to keep the damp out.'

I didn't go in either cottage, or keep them lingering in the cold: I wanted to get on and get my errands done so I could have a quiet lunch . . . and I had Gran's latest journal in the pocket of my rucksack. I had a feeling I was going to be too busy after this to spend much time relaxing.

There was a call box in the village, but it was out of order and goodness knows how much change I would have needed to call a mobile phone in the USA, anyway! I stayed in there out of the cold while I tried the number Noël had given me on my phone, but a disembodied voice told me it was unavailable.

Well, at least I had tried . . . and, since I'd been braced to deal with Jude's brusqueness (especially when I told him I'd be billing him for the call), I now felt strangely deflated!

Mrs Comfort, who was sitting behind the shop counter knitting, perked up and greeted me with enthusiasm, especially when I said I needed a few last-minute presents.

'Gifts are mostly through in the Merry Kettle,' she said, pointing through the open door into the café where the overflow of her goods was displayed, probably to tempt the visitors in summer while they consumed their cream teas.

I could feel her eager, beady eyes boring into my back as I looked around at the limited selection of toys, games and novelties. There was also a large wooden display stand of everything from mugs to dishcloths printed with inspirational thoughts and labelled 'The Words of Comfort Range from Oriel Comfort'.

I was curious more than anything, because I'd already decided to make my emergency gifts myself: I'd noticed a cache of old, clean jam jars, wax discs, labels and cellophane lids in the scullery at Old Place and I intended filling them with sweets.

So I bought lots of the brightly coloured shiny ones that Jess liked, along with wine gums, humbugs, Liquorice Allsorts, mint imperials and coconut mushrooms, then added Sellotape, Christmas tags and a big roll of flimsy, cheerfully garish gift-wrap. I even found some red gingham paper napkins that could be cut into circles to make covers for the jars, too, and a bag of elastic bands to secure them.

As my pile of purchases mounted up on the counter, Mrs Comfort looked cheerier and cheerier and began to make helpful suggestions.

'Noël likes Turkish Delight,' she confided, 'and his missis likes Milk Tray chocolates – he often buys her some. This is the last of the Turkish Delight, you're in luck. And what about these chocolate tree decorations?'

Unbidden, she added them to the heap and then cast her eyes over her stock, obviously wondering what else she could offload onto me.

I whisked out my shopping list. 'There are a few things I need, if you have them, like cocoa powder, icing sugar, jelly . . .'

In fact, there weren't many things she *didn't* have. It felt a bit like watching a magician producing endless doves from a top hat.

'And you'll want the last tins of squirty cream,' she urged me.

'We've already got tons of the stuff!'

'Love it, they do, at the lodge,' she assured me. 'Can't get enough of it.'

I ticked the last thing off (more matches) with a sigh: I was wondering how I would get everything up the hill again, unless George spotted me.

Oriel took a new tack: 'Old Nan, she likes chocolate mints and the vicar is partial to humbugs. Henry's more of an Uncle Joe's Mint Ball man.'

Surely, I thought, I wouldn't need presents for people I'd barely met, who were only coming for dinner? But then, it might be better to be sure than sorry.

'All right,' I capitulated, 'but I ought to leave Henry's now, in case I don't see him again before Christmas.'

'I'll slap a bit of gift-wrap on it for free and take it across later, shall I?' she suggested obligingly.

'If you wouldn't mind, that would be great.'

'Not at all.'

'Well, that *must* be everything!'

But she wasn't about to let me go without a struggle. 'What about Jess's Christmas stocking? Got everything you need for that?'

I stared at her, startled. A stocking on Christmas morning like all my friends had had was the thing I'd most desperately longed for when I was a little girl: but surely Jess was now too old?

'She's nearly thirteen, so I would have thought she was too grown up for one this year? But if she isn't then I suppose her mother or Tilda will have seen to it.'

'Perhaps – perhaps not. And in my experience, you're never too old for a stocking. Perhaps you should take a couple of bits and pieces, just in case they've forgotten about it?'

'Like what? *I've* no idea what she would like!'

'Let me see,' she mused. 'It's a funny age: they're a child one minute, quite grownup the next.'

She took down a jar containing sugar mice with string tails in white, lurid yellow, or pink and prepared to give me a master class in Christmas stocking preparation.

'You need one of these at the bottom, with a tangerine or something like that to start with. When I was a little girl there used to be a handful of nuts, though I never knew why, since you could hardly crack Brazil nuts in bed with your teeth, could you?'

'We've got fruit and nuts, but I don't think Jess would be very excited by finding them in her stocking, since she can help herself any time she likes.'

'It helps to fill it up, but we can put in a packet of Love Hearts instead. Most of my toys are too young for her, but there's a pack of Happy Family cards and a couple of jokes, like the whoopee cushion and the ink blot, that I expect she'd like. And maybe a fluffy toy sheepdog? I keep them for the summer visitors, with the postcards and stuff.'

'Do you think she's a fluffy toy sort of girl?' I asked doubtfully, but she was already delving deep into a large wicker basket and came up with a black, wolfish-looking creature with yellow eyes that had been lurking at the bottom.

'I just remembered – this came in mixed with the last lot of collies, and I never got round to sending it back.'

'Right,' I said, and then on impulse added an elasticated bracelet of polished dark grey stones.

'How about a jigsaw puzzle? I always think a big puzzle is something the whole family can do together on Christmas Day.'

'I'm sure I saw a whole stack of them in the old nursery,' I said quickly.

'This one's got a lovely Christmas scene on the front – and if you return it afterwards with all the pieces, I'll buy it back for half price,' she added enticingly and, my willpower totally sapped by now, I nodded dumbly.

Paying for that lot pretty well cleaned me out of cash, since Mrs Comfort didn't take cards of any kind, and once I'd filled the rucksack I had to buy a big jute bag with one of Oriel's inspirational thoughts on it: *A Loving Heart Keeps You Warm on Winter's Nights.*

It had been a choice between that or *Love Circles – Pass It On.*

You know, when I looked closer, the things on that stand were irresistibly awful!

Chapter 17: Rapping

N says nothing can be wrong when two people truly love each other, as we do, but I know what we did should only happen within the bounds of marriage . . .

March, 1945

I hauled my purchases over to the church and sat on a stone bench in the porch out of the wind, to phone Laura on my mobile. (I did dutifully try Jude's number again, but got the same message.)

'Oh, good,' she said when she answered, sounding relieved, 'I've been trying to get through to the house and it kept saying there was a fault on the line.'

'There is – one of the poles holding the phone wires up has fallen down and taken the next one with it. Is everything okay? How are you?'

'Oh, *I'm* all right and the baby's kicking like mad. The other three are so excited about Christmas they're hysterical and Dan's just helpfully vanished, presumably to buy my present. He's always so last minute! But how are *you* doing? I'm worried about you, taking so much on and being so isolated.'

'Isolated is the last way I'd describe Old Place, actually, Laura!'

'You sound a bit worried – which is not like you at all. What is it, are you finding it too much?'

'Of course not – you know me, I *thrive* on a challenge,' I

assured her, though she didn't yet know quite how *much* of a challenge my current post had become! 'But there's something on my mind I'd like to run past you, to see if you think I'm imagining things.'

'Go on, then, tell me.'

'It's Gran's diaries. Things between her and Ned Martland have hotted up quite a bit and . . . well, I think they had *sex*.'

'Good heavens,' she said mildly, 'I didn't think that was invented until the sixties.'

'It certainly wasn't for good Strange Baptist girls like Gran, that's for sure, especially in 1945! She must have been sure they were going to marry, but obviously that didn't happen – and since I just found out that Ned was killed in an accident I'm hoping that was the reason, not because he abandoned her!'

'Didn't you skip forward and try to find out? I would have!'

'No, because to be honest, so much is happening that I'm exhausted by bedtime and I hardly have a minute to myself during the day, though I did have another quick look while I drank my first cup of coffee this morning.'

'And did you find out what happened?'

'No, she's been wrestling with her conscience for pages and pages, but I'm keeping the current journal in the kitchen and dipping into it whenever I have a minute on my own. But the thing that's worrying me is that Noël implied that Ned was a bad lot as far as women were concerned: charming and lovable, but unreliable. I keep thinking: what if Gran got *pregnant* and relied on him to make an honest woman of her?'

'Aren't you jumping the gun a bit? She hasn't said so, has she?'

'Not so far, but I can't help wondering . . .' I paused. 'Laura, you know I'm not fanciful, but I've felt at home here from the minute I arrived and that I sort of . . . fit in. And the other thing is, I'm constantly being mistaken for one of the family – even Noël forgets that I'm not. The Martlands are all tall and dark, though they don't have light grey eyes like me and Gran.'

'Your Gran wasn't tall, but didn't she have dark hair when she was young?

'Yes, and she told me my colouring came from her side of the family – her ancestors came from Liverpool, a seafaring port and I've always assumed there was a good dose of foreign blood. So I might just be imagining any resemblance to the Martlands . . . My mother was quite tall and had black hair too,' I added, though that proved nothing one way or the other. Unfortunately, I have no idea what my father looked like, because after my mother died soon after giving birth to me, he emigrated to Australia and vanished out of our lives. Gran neatly cut him out of all the wedding photographs.

There were rumours that he'd started a new family over there, so I might have half-siblings somewhere, but although I'd had one try at tracing him (without Gran's knowledge!) I didn't get anywhere.

'I can see where you're going with all this, Holly, but it could still be just a coincidence that you're tall and dark. And with your grandfather being a Strange Baptist minister, I don't suppose he would have married your gran if he knew she was pregnant by another man, would he?'

'It doesn't sound very likely when you put it like that,' I admitted.

'He was much older than she was, wasn't he?'

'Yes, she told me once he was the father of her childhood sweetheart, who was killed in the war, and it seemed natural that they should marry and console each other. I barely remember him, though everyone says he was the nicest, kindest of men.'

'Perhaps you should just carry on reading the journal and not try to join up the dots yet,' Laura suggested.

'I suppose you're right – and besides, I'm way too busy to worry about it, really. But I might just try and discover when Ned's accident was and then check that against the dates Gran got married and my mother was born – I've brought the whole trunk of her papers with me. If it doesn't all match up, then I'll know for sure.'

'That's true,' she said. 'And there's no point in worrying over it, when it's all in the past. I mean, it's not like you're going to claim a stake in the family fortune or anything, is it?'

I laughed. 'I don't think there is one! The house is pretty shabby and Jude Martland didn't hire any live-in staff when the last ones left, plus he seems obsessed with how much money I'm costing him – or he *thinks* I'm costing him. I really should charge him for all the extra work I'll be doing, because things are escalating!'

'So what's happening? I thought you were just having the family from the lodge up for Christmas dinner?'

'I was, only they've moved in already and so has Becca, Noël's sister, so I'm hosting a Christmas family house-party at Old Place. I'm cook, groom, maid and cleaner – though to be fair, Becca seems to have taken over looking after the horses.'

And I told her all about Tilda's accident and how inviting them to move into Old Place immediately was the only possible solution, and then Becca turning up on Nutkin and the discovery that there would also be two more guests for Christmas dinner – the retired vicar and the family's old nanny.

'If Jude Martland doesn't like any of this, it's tough, and he'll have to sort it out with his relatives when he gets back, because I could hardly stop them, could I? And we couldn't consult him first, because of the lines being down.'

'You could call him on your mobile, or from the village?' she suggested.

'I just tried and it said his number was unavailable. It's a relief not having him calling me every day and harassing me, really, because none of my clients have ever done that before!'

'It'll be okay, Holly – I mean, what else could you do? It was really taken out of your hands,' she said, laughing.

'You're right, I couldn't do anything else, even though it means

164

a lot more work – *and* being part of a big family Christmas celebration.'

'You might even find yourself enjoying it,' she suggested.

'At least there's enough food and drink in the house for a twelve-month siege, and Noël has the keys to the cellar, so that's his responsibility.'

'So, even if you are totally snowed in, you can manage?'

'Oh yes, and I've just bought up the village shop, too! There were a few things I was running out of and I suddenly wondered if I needed some presents.'

When I explained about the sweets and then Oriel Comfort's suggestion of a Christmas stocking for Jess, Laura thought *that* was funny too.

'If Jess isn't too old for one, surely her granny or mum will have it in hand?' I said.

'Perhaps, but you can never have too many things in your stocking.'

'I bought a huge jigsaw puzzle of a Christmas scene too, because I thought it would keep everyone occupied if the weather was bad. Oriel says if I take it back afterwards with all the pieces, she'll give me back half the price.'

'She sounds a hoot.'

'She is – and I think she's also my love rival. George, the farmer who gave me a lift down today, is an admirer.'

'Oh? What's *he* like?' she asked, interested. 'Hunky?'

'He's well-built, with white-blond hair, bright blue eyes and a very attractive smile.'

'Sounds lovely!'

'But on the downside, well the wrong side of forty and a widower with an adult son. He said I was a strapping lass and he liked my mince pies, which may constitute an offer of marriage round here, for all I know. Only I think, from something he said, that Oriel was favourite before my mince pies stole his heart.'

'Are you going to fight her for him?'

'No, I think I'll probably retire gracefully from the field . . . though he is nice. I've bought you one of Oriel's pamphlets of inspirational verse for your birthday present, with matching shopping bag.'

'I can't wait! Ring me on Christmas Day if you get a chance, but I know it'll be difficult to get away so I won't worry if you go quiet for a couple of days at some point.'

'I'll do my best. And could you ring Ellen and just update her with the situation for me?' I asked, to cover my back in case the objectionable Jude was miffed at my arrangements. 'And tell her not to bill Jude extra for the cooking and cleaning, because she's sent the list of charges to him and he thinks she is.'

She promised to do that and then she had to go. My bottom had practically frozen to the bench while talking, but I left my bags there while I had a quick look into the unlocked church, which was chilly, but quiet and lovely, with an old stained-glass window at one end showing Noah's ark and all the little animals going in two by two, including a pair that looked like giant slugs. I think Noah should have given those a miss, together with spiders and a few other unlovely things.

Collecting my shopping I trudged through the snow to the Auld Christmas, where I ate delicious crumbly Lancashire cheese, bread and pickles in a snug empty of anyone except old Nicholas Dagger, who was in the same hooded chair by the fire.

I chatted with Nancy a bit and then, perhaps awoken by our voices, Nicholas poked his head around the side of the chair like a strange species of tortoise.

'I'm Auld Man Christmas,' he piped. 'My father was Auld Man Christmas and his father before him, and—'

'Yes, we know, Father,' Nancy said soothingly, adding to me in whispered explanation, 'he gets excited at this time of year.'

'That's all right, Noël Martland told me a little bit about the Revels and then George Froggat did too, on the way down when he kindly gave me a lift.'

'They told you, did they, then?' She looked at me thoughtfully.

'Only a bit – I know it's a fairly private ceremony, just for the village. Do you play a part in it, too?'

'Oh no, I only watch. Women have never taken part in it.'

'Isn't that a bit sexist?'

She looked doubtful. 'No, because we don't want to be in it. There's a man dressed up half as a woman, though. I like the Rapping best.'

'You know, George said he joined in the Rapping, but I thought I'd misheard him – it seemed a bit unlikely. They don't breakdance too, do they?'

She giggled. 'No, the Rapping's just dancing with swords.'

'What, on the ground, like Scottish dancing? Rapiers?'

'Rapper dancing is different to that – they weave their swords together to make a sort of knot pattern. Then after the Dragon kills St George, it puts its head in the middle of the knot and they chop it off.'

'It *kills* St George?'

'Yes, but it's only pretend and the Doctor makes him better. Old vicar says it's all deeply symbolic – rebirth and suchlike. It's in his little pamphlet.'

'Noël said he would look for that in the library later, I must read it. So is that the end of the Revels, after the Dragon's head is chopped off?'

'Pretty much. St George gets up and they all dance again and that's it. We open up the pub afterwards, but everyone's usually still full of wassail.'

'Sounds fun.'

'Mrs Jackson, that used to be the cook-housekeeper at Old Place, she used to bring the Revel Cakes, but of course they retired after Jude's father died.'

'Oh? What were they like?'

'Spicy little buns with candied peel on top and lots of saffron to make them yellow. Sort of coiled round like a Cumberland sausage.'

'They sound interesting – I'll look for the recipe. It may be up there somewhere, she left a lot of recipe books. If I find it, and I've got the ingredients, I'll make some before I go and Jude can bring them down with him on the day.'

'Or you could stay for the Revels and bring them yourself?'

'I think Jude is expecting me to have gone by the time he gets back. I'll probably be exhausted by then anyway and ready for a rest! I'm used to cooking for very large house-parties, it's my summer job, but then the food preparation and cooking are all I do. Now I'm cleaning and doing all the rest of it, too.'

'It's a hard time for women anyway, Christmas: nothing but cooking and washing up, cooking and washing up . . .' She sighed heavily.

'Yes, and you're working in here as well.'

'Well, that's the way of it,' she said with resignation and then she was called into the public bar on the other side, which was getting busier, and I was left to the roaring fire, the snoring Auld Nicholas and the rest of my bread and cheese.

I sat there quietly reading the next few entries in Gran's journal, though without making any further major discoveries other than her desire to get their romance on to an official footing.

As I was about to leave, I remembered that I wanted to buy a half-bottle of brandy for the flaming Christmas pudding, because the stuff Noël had brought up from the cellar looked much too good to use for the purpose. Nancy was just giving me my change when the outer door slammed heavily and a thin, tall blonde staggered into the snug, dragging behind her an enormous glittery pink suitcase on wheels with a vanity case strapped to the top of it.

'It must be one of them SatNavvers,' Nancy whispered. 'Barking mad if she tried to get a car up the lane in this weather!'

Chapter 18: Ice Maiden

Today I accused N of putting off telling his parents about us,
because he feared they would not be pleased and think me
not good enough, being the daughter of mill workers. He said
neither would mine approve of him, since he was not a Strange
Baptist or, indeed, any other kind of Baptist.

March, 1945

'Hello?' she said, looking from one to the other of us while
pushing back a large, white fur hat that had slipped drunkenly
over a face that was still extremely pretty, despite being pink and
shiny with cold, exertion and temper. 'Thank *God* there's some
sign of life in this hole. I was starting to think everyone had
been wiped out by the plague, or something!'

'Did you turn off the main road to get to Great Mumming?'
I asked her. 'Only those SatNav things send you the wrong way.'

'No, I *intended* coming here, but my car slid on the ice on the
first bend and now it's in the ditch. I need someone to drive me
to Old Place.'

Nancy had been eyeing her narrowly. 'Aren't you that model
that was engaged to Jude and came here last Christmas, the one
that took up with his brother, instead? Arrived with one, and
left with the other?'

'I suppose you *could* put it like that. I'm Coco Lanyon. I expect
you know me from the Morning Dawn Facial Elixir TV advert.'

'No,' Nancy said simply: I don't suppose she gets a lot of time to watch the telly.

As well as the fur hat, Coco was wearing shocking pink Ugg boots and a long, white quilted coat. Her hair was platinum-pale too, but her face was still almost as pink as her boots.

Her voice, a trifle on the shrill side, must have penetrated Nicholas's ears, because his wizened face suddenly appeared around the side of the chair again and he chipped in, in his own high but sweet, elven tones, 'I'm Auld Man Christmas, you know!'

'We know, Dad,' Nancy said. 'You just sit back and let me see to the customer.'

'I'm not a customer,' Coco snapped. 'I'm merely in search of transport.'

'But why are you going to Old Place?' I asked and she swivelled her ice-blue eyes in my direction and looked down her retroussé nose at me . . . or tried to, because I was inches taller.

'And *you* would be?'

'Holly Brown. I'm looking after Old Place while Jude Martland's away.'

'Oh, right . . . did your husband drive you down? Because if so, you can take me back up with you right now.'

'You're mixing me up with the couple who usually come – I haven't got a husband and I didn't bring my car today, because it would never have got up the hill. In any case, why *do* you want to go there?'

'You mean – Guy hasn't arrived yet?' she demanded, staring at me.

'He hadn't when I left a couple of hours ago and we certainly weren't expecting him – *or* you. Why did you think he might be here?'

'Because this is where he *said* he was going, of course!'

'But . . . surely he wouldn't have come here when he's fallen out with his brother?' I asked, puzzled.

'Oh, but he rang old Noël early last week, so he knew Jude

would be in the States right over Christmas and it would be safe to hole up here. But I'm not letting Guy get away with this – he can't throw me over just because I sent the announcement of our engagement to *The Times* and set a date for the wedding! We're going to Mummy and Daddy's for Christmas, too, and they've invited *all* the family to an engagement party on Boxing Day.'

'You didn't tell Guy any of this beforehand?' asked Nancy, clearly fascinated.

'He's a commitment-phobe, he'd have carried on dithering forever,' Coco said shortly. 'He may have dashed up here in a panic, but he'd better have got over it by now, because he's coming straight back to London with me.'

I wouldn't put it past her, either, because even cross and pink-faced she was stunningly beautiful . . . if you liked chilly blondes with ice-chip pale blue eyes, that is, and presumably, both Guy and Jude did.

Still, I certainly didn't want another unexpected visitor, so she could remove him with my blessing. 'I suppose you'd better come back to the house with me, I don't really see what else you can do. Perhaps he's arrived by now – he probably stopped off for lunch on the way, or something.'

I turned to Nancy. 'Would it be all right if we left the luggage here for a bit? I've got all my shopping and I don't suppose Coco can carry much more than the beauty box up with her. That case is *enormous*!'

'What, this little thing?' Coco said, astonished. 'It's only an overnight bag, in case we decided to go back early tomorrow instead of today. And I'm definitely not carrying anything anywhere, because I'm still exhausted from the walk from the car. *You* can go up to the house and tell Guy to come and fetch me. I'll wait here and—'

George stuck his head through the half-open door just at that moment and, spotting me, said, 'I thought you might be in here,

Holly, Orrie said you headed this way. Did you want a lift back up to Old Place? It's snowing again and I'm on my way home.'

'*I* certainly do!' Coco exclaimed and he raised a flaxen eyebrow at her.

'This is—' I paused. 'I'm so sorry, I've forgotten your second name.'

'Coco Lanyon – the model.'

'She was the one that was engaged to Jude last Christmas, and then took up with Guy instead,' Nancy explained helpfully.

'Only they've had a bust up,' Nicholas piped. He was evidently following the intricate plot without difficulty now he was fully awake. 'She thought he was up at Old Place and she's followed him.'

'Ah, that explains it! I thought I just saw that big black Chelsea tractor of Guy's go up the lane, monster that it is,' George said. 'It's well-gritted and he took a run at it, so he probably made it.'

'There, you see?' said Coco. 'He *is* here.'

'Is that your car in the ditch further down?' asked George. 'Ben from Weasel Pot said some madman had tried to get a sports car up the hill.'

'Mad*woman*,' Nancy suggested and Coco gave her a nasty look.

'Yes, it's mine and I'd like it towed out and brought up to Old Place as soon as possible.'

George removed his cap and scratched his head thoughtfully. 'Them from Weasel's Pot'll tow it out for you all right, but it'll cost you. And there's no point them trying to get it up to the house, so they'll probably leave it here in the village. Those little cars are too low down to be any use in the snow – *or* in the country, come to that,' he added disparagingly.

'Whatever,' she said haughtily. 'Now, please take me up to Old Place.'

'If you don't mind, George,' I said apologetically. 'But just as far as the lodge will do, I don't want to put you out any more

172

and we can drop off the bags there. Perhaps Guy will go down and fetch them.'

'Don't be silly, he must take me right up to the house,' Coco insisted. '*You* can walk if you want to.'

'I'll take *you* home gladly, Holly – but I've two sheep in the back now, and the dog's in the front, so I've no room for another passenger.' He raised a fair eyebrow at Coco. '*You'll* have to wait and see if Guy will fetch you, unless you want to try asking young Ben – he went into the public bar.'

'Young Ben?'

'From Weasel's Pot.'

'What is this weasel's pot you all keep rabbiting on about?' she said irritably.

'The farm you passed after turning off the main road,' I told her. 'They have the council contract to plough the lane up to the village, and George here ploughs the lane down.'

'That's right, and you can ask Ben about towing your car out too, while you're at it,' George suggested.

'Look, I'm in a hurry, so *you* get a lift up with this Ben, and tell him to get my car out for me,' Coco said to me. Then she indicated her case to George, clearly expecting him to pick it up. 'Right, I'm ready – but you'll have to put the dog in the back.'

'Sorry, no can do,' he said, not looking sorry at all. 'And I didn't offer *you* a lift in the first place. I'm none too keen on that perfume you're wearing and if it makes my Land Rover reek of musk, it'll unsettle the dogs. They squeeze it out of weasel glands, you know.'

She stared at him. 'Rubbish! This perfume is very, very expensive and they wouldn't use something like that!'

'Isn't it musk rat glands?' I said. 'That sounds more likely.'

'Happen you're right,' he conceded.

'There's an old Lancashire saying about weasels,' piped Auld Nicholas and then declaimed in a thin, singsong voice: '"*If you*

173

see a weasel, pee in its ear. If you see another, tie its bum up with string."'

'What on earth does that mean?' demanded Coco.

'No idea,' Nicholas said. 'Hee, hee!'

'Senile!' she muttered and, abandoning him, turned a sweetly seductive smile on George. '*Please* do take me up to the house – I'm so cold and tired! I can pay you for your trouble, you know.'

'I've told you already, try your wiles on young Ben, you'll get nowhere with me,' he said shortly and she furiously flounced out in the direction of the public bar.

'Let's hope you get rid of her and Guy tonight,' George said, helping me out to the Land Rover with my million and one purchases. 'If not, she won't be driving that sports car home, because nothing short of a four-wheel drive will make it down to the main road by morning.'

'But Guy's got one of those, you said? So I suppose he'll drive them back tonight and arrange something later about her car,' I suggested hopefully.

The sheepdog obligingly made room for me on the bench seat and we set off, George refusing to stop until he'd taken me right to the front door, where we found a large people-carrier still steaming gently: Guy *had* arrived.

I staggered in with my shopping and found all the family in the sitting room, which someone had now artistically festooned with swags and swathes of artificial greenery, mixed with the real thing that George had brought.

Tilda was sitting in her usual place on the sofa before the fire, Merlin fast asleep on the rug at her feet, while Noël, Becca and Jess were putting final touches to the Christmas tree.

A tall, dark, thin and very handsome man was leaning on the stone mantelpiece watching the proceedings and I would have easily recognised him as Guy from the family photos, even if I hadn't expected to see him.

As I came in and put down the heavy bags I thought the room looked like a stage set, especially the way they all turned to look at me as if they'd been given a cue. Merlin hauled himself to his feet and ambled over, tail wagging furiously.

'Ah, Holly, there you are! We've had an unexpected addition to the family party,' Noël said gaily. 'This is Guy, Jude's younger brother.'

'How do you do?' he said, with a charming smile, shaking hands. 'I've been hearing all about you!'

'That sounds ominous,' I said, bending down to stroke Merlin. 'Actually, I knew you were here because I just ran into your—'

'Have you got anything for *me* in that shopping bag?' interrupted Jess.

'Yes, some chocolate tree decorations.' I rummaged in the hessian bag and found them.

'Oh good, we hadn't got any of those and Uncle Guy didn't think to bring anything at all.'

'I didn't think I'd need to, because I expected to find that couple here Jude usually hires when he's away. And since I knew they'd already invited Tilda, Noël, Becca and Jess for Christmas dinner, I thought one more wouldn't make any difference.'

'And you knew Uncle Jude wasn't here to throw you out on your ear,' Jess said. 'You were sneaky and mean, going off with his girlfriend, even if I didn't like her much!'

'Neither do I now, that's why I'm here,' he drawled, not noticeably put out by this criticism.

'Jess, that was very rude of you,' Tilda said.

'What the child said was true, though: you've always wanted what your brother had, from being a child. Then as soon as you got it, you lost interest,' Becca said bluntly. 'And you had a damned cheek, thinking you could just move in here while he was away and be looked after by the couple house-sitting.'

Guy reddened. 'Part of the reason I came was because I was worried about Noël and Tilda, left to cope on their own. It was thoughtless of old Jude to cancel Christmas and go off in a huff.'

'He was going to New York anyway and we told him not to bother about us – we could manage on our own. In fact, I was quite looking forward to cooking a Christmas dinner again,' said Tilda, 'and I would have done, if I hadn't had that damned fall.'

'I know you would have cooked a wonderful dinner, m'dear,' Noël said soothingly. 'But we're quite happy to be back at the old homestead again now, with Holly in charge, aren't we?'

'I could see that's what everyone wanted and I wouldn't stand in your way,' she said, casting herself into a martyr's role with relish, though she'd clearly been more than relieved to be whisked up here and looked after. 'You behaved very badly, Guy, so we could quite understand why Jude felt like a change this year and wanted to get away – especially when he found out about that engagement announcement.'

'Yes, that's all very well, but Jude is the head of the household now and he has responsibilities, like seeing Old Nan and Richard are looked after,' Becca pointed out, shaking her head. 'He didn't need to invite Guy and that girl, so there would have been no problem.'

'Never mind: thanks to lovely Holly here, it has all worked out well,' Noël said, 'and Jude will be back for Twelfth Night, which is the most important thing.'

'You still haven't told us why you've dashed up here, Guy,' Tilda said. 'Didn't you tell us last week that you were spending Christmas in London with that girl?' She frowned. 'What *was* she called? It was something to do with clowns.'

'Coco,' said Jess. 'Like a bedtime drink. Though it would have been much worse if she'd been called Horlicks, wouldn't it?' she added innocently.

'Different spelling of Coco, I expect, like Coco Chanel,' I said quickly. 'And speaking of Coco—'

'I think Horlicks suits her. I'm going to call her that from now on,' Jess broke in gleefully.

'I would *so* much rather you didn't, darling,' Tilda said.

Guy was grinning. 'Don't be a spoilsport, Tilda! But luckily you won't have to call her anything, Jess, because she isn't here. She never really took to Old Place last Christmas anyway, she's more of a town girl, our Coco.'

'I suppose you got tired of her, like all your other girls?' Tilda said, with a slight note of indulgence. Guy seemed to be a bit of a favourite of hers, though Becca didn't seem too keen. I suppose all that charm can't have the same effect on everybody.

'Let's just say I had a wake-up call,' he admitted. 'Things got a bit rocky when she fired off that engagement announcement to the papers – and then when she told me her parents were organising a big family engagement party on Boxing Day I thought, "no thank you" and bailed out.' He shrugged. 'I'm not ready to tie myself down yet.'

'As I said,' Becca observed dispassionately, 'as soon as you get the prize, you lose interest.'

'Thanks for that quick character analysis, Becca. But actually, she was so easy to poach that I did Jude a favour. If they'd got married, it would never have lasted.'

He gave me a delightful smile – he seemed distinctly profligate with them. 'But I'd *much* rather be here in the bosom of my family instead. You don't mind if I stay, do you, Holly? You wouldn't throw me out into the cold, cold snow?' he wheedled.

He was a bounder, as they would have said in the twenties, as beautiful and untrustworthy as a snake. If he took after his Uncle Ned, then I could understand how poor, innocent, strictly-brought-up Granny had been so quickly swept quite out of her depth!

I looked helplessly at Noël and Tilda. 'I . . . well, everything is snowballing! I only came here to keep an eye on the house and look after the animals – and then suddenly I'm holding a house-party without the owner's permission! And I couldn't get him on the phone either, though I did try.'

'Oh, but Jude won't object, I assure you,' Noël said. 'The dear fellow will understand.'

'I'm not sure he will, Noël, because Mr Martland's girlfriend is—'

'Uncle Jude won't mind in the least about *us*,' Jess interrupted, 'but he will about Uncle Guy!'

'I wish you'd drop the "uncle" bit, sweetheart – it makes me feel terribly old,' he complained.

'You *are* terribly old,' she said witheringly.

'If you think *I'm* old, Mini-Morticia, then your beloved Uncle Jude must be ancient!'

'But I don't think of him as old, because he's fun,' she said, which was a surprise to me, since nothing I'd heard about him so far would have led me to think of him as a fun person. 'You're silly and mean and you're going all wrinkly round the eyes.'

'Laughter lines,' he said, though he turned his head and examined his face anxiously in the cloudy bevelled mirror above the fireplace. 'Yes, laughter lines . . . and is that a car I hear arriving?' he added. 'You're not expecting anyone else, are you?'

'We weren't even expecting *you*,' Becca pointed out.

Jess ran to the window. 'Oh look, it's Ben from Weasel's Pot!'

She went all pink, so clearly she has a crush on the young farmer. But then she wailed, 'Oh no, he's driven off without coming in to say hello! But someone got out first – a woman with an enormous suitcase. Who on earth can it be?'

'I've been trying to warn you,' I said desperately, 'it's—'

Jess turned a startled face towards us. 'It's Horlicks, and she looks *really* mad! Shall I lock the door?'

Chapter 19: I Should Coco

N has been discharged from the army by the medical board and told me he has been offered a job by a friend of his father's as soon as he is fit enough. I thought he might then go on to ask me to marry him, now he will soon be in a situation to support a wife – but he did not . . .

April, 1945

It was too late to follow Jess's suggestion and Coco didn't even knock but simply swept in, looking like a slightly grubby and marked-down ice princess.

I don't suppose she'd realised she'd be finishing her journey in the cab of a tractor, crammed in with her luggage, which she now dropped in the doorway with a loud crash. It appeared to be decidedly the worse for wear, as did Coco: white was not perhaps the most suitable colour for gruelling journeys. She was clearly also in a flaming temper, which wasn't improved by her reception.

'Oh God, what are *you* doing here?' Guy said wearily and Becca, Tilda and Noël all stared at her in astonished unwelcome.

'What do you mean, what am *I* doing here? Don't think you can just dump me like that and get away with it just because you got cold feet at the idea of our wedding. Get over it, because you're coming back to London with me right now!'

'Like hell I will,' he said. 'You might have consulted me before

179

sending off engagement notices and arranging celebration parties.'

'You *agreed* with me when I said May weddings were the best, but you had to pick your date quickly before they got booked up!'

'I might have done, because I don't listen to half the rubbish you talk. But I certainly never said I wanted to get married in May or any other time!'

'Well, that's why we got engaged, wasn't it?'

He shrugged. 'Lots of people get engaged and it doesn't lead to anything, and you were making a fuss about it. I didn't know you would send an announcement to the bloody newspapers! And finding your parents had organised the family round on Boxing Day to give us the seal of approval was the last straw.'

'They didn't invite them specially, it just seemed a good time to toast our engagement, while the family were all together,' she snapped.

'Well, you go and toast it, then, I'm staying right here.'

'Oh, don't be silly! I've driven all the way up here and my car's ended up in a ditch, all because of you. Of course you're coming back with me.'

She gave a distracted look at Jess, who had set up a low chant of 'Hor-licks, Hor-licks, Hor-licks!'

'Does the child have to make so much noise?' she demanded.

'Jess, darling, that will do,' Tilda said mildly.

'She doesn't like you,' Guy said. 'None of us like you.'

'Now, now, Guy,' Noël said. 'Manners! Coco, come to the fire and get warm. I hope you weren't hurt when your car went in the ditch?'

Coco had had a long and wearisome sort of day and she wasn't listening to Noël. Instead she turned on Guy and unsurprisingly lost her temper completely, saying a few choice and very personal things about him in her shrill voice that I could see Jess storing up for future use.

Nettled, he began to fling barbed comments back so, since a battle royal seemed to be starting, I carried my shopping through into the kitchen, followed by Merlin.

I had to switch all the lights on because it was still snowing heavily and didn't look like stopping any time soon, which was a bit worrying from the point of view of getting rid of my two unwanted visitors . . .

I quickly stowed everything away, hiding the presents I'd bought under a pile of tea towels in the cupboard in case Jess took it into her head to rummage about before I'd had a chance to wrap them.

Then I made a cup of coffee while I wondered whether I could stretch the sausage and mash with mustard sauce that I'd planned to serve for dinner to include two other diners, or if I should defrost more sausages. Dessert could be a sort of Eton Mess, with tinned raspberries and yet more squirty cream from the lodge. Or I could do something with the overripe bananas left by the Chirks . . .

I looked at tomorrow's menu, which was to be grilled trout for the adults – there was a plentiful supply in the freezer – and home-made salmon fishcakes for Jess if she didn't fancy that. And dessert would be whichever of the two choices we didn't have tonight.

I'd just put another quick chocolate cake in the oven and whipped up an easy starter of sardine pâté to have with French toast, when Becca and Jess followed me into the kitchen.

'Tilda and Noël have gone into the morning room to watch TV,' Becca said, 'it's all getting a bit shrill in there – tears before bedtime, I reckon. Guy's just told her he can't drive her anywhere tonight, even if he wanted to, because he had a couple of stiff whiskies after he arrived.'

'Oh dear, did he?' I said helplessly. 'I was hoping he might at least take her to the nearest railway station, since he's got that big four-wheel drive – the weather is closing in and even if her car is all right after being in the ditch, I don't think it's up to these kinds of conditions. George certainly didn't think so.'

'Well, I don't suppose there's a police car sitting in the lane in this weather, waiting to catch drunk drivers,' she said. 'He just didn't want to do it.'

'Did you like the Christmas decorations?' asked Jess.

'Yes, they look lovely; I didn't get a chance to say before. Who did the holly, ivy and mistletoe arrangements? So much more swish than sticking stuff in vases, like I did with that first bunch George gave me!'

'Me – one of the useless things I learned at finishing school,' Becca said.

I gave another distracted glance out of the window. 'It's still snowing – do you think we ought to bring the horses in?'

'Yes, that's why we came out, really. I'll do that and get their hot mash early, too. Jess's going to help me.'

'I'm so glad you're here to see to Lady,' I said gratefully. 'I'm going to be so busy with everything else that knowing you're keeping an eye on her and Billy is a weight off my shoulders.'

'Well, I need to see to Nutkin anyway, so another horse is neither here nor there if I have a willing slave like Jess to do the heavy work and keep that damned goat out of the way.'

Jess gave her a pained look: I don't think mucking out and trundling wheelbarrows about is her favourite pastime, even though she is now resigned to her fate.

'That goat is evil,' she said bitterly. 'I've got bruises all up the back of my legs where he keeps butting me.'

'We took Merlin out for a little run before lunch,' Becca said. 'He was missing you – amazing how quickly he's got attached to you, he's like your shadow.'

'I know, I expect he's pining for his master, that's why,' I said. Merlin, hearing his name, half-wagged his tail, looking up at me with warm amber eyes.

'When we've sorted the horses out I'm going to take the sledge up the paddock again – do you want to come, Holly?' invited Jess. 'You can have the other sledge.'

'I would have loved to, but I need to prep the vegetables for dinner and I want to put the jelly layer on the trifle,' I said. 'Tomorrow though, definitely. And we could bake and ice some gingerbread biscuits to hang on the tree, if you like?'

'Oh yes, that would be fun!'

When they'd gone out I could still hear raised voices from the sitting room, despite the closed door at the end of the passage: the acoustics must be jolly good. I could make out melodramatic lines, like:

'I broke off my engagement to Jude for you!'

'I didn't ask you to – it was just a bit of fun on the side until Jude walked in on us.'

'That's not what you said then – I thought you loved me!'

'I'm not responsible for what you think, thank God.'

After that, I shut the kitchen door, too, and put the radio on.

I didn't really need to start on dinner yet, now the pâté starter was in the fridge, but since it looked as though I would be alone for quite a while I took the opportunity to make my presents.

I scalded the empty jam jars from the utility room and dried them thoroughly, before filling them with sweets and covering each with a circle of cellophane topped with one cut from the red and white gingham paper napkins, held down with a red elastic band. They looked really good.

I wrapped them up and labelled them, except for a couple of extra ones I left blank for unforeseen emergencies. Then I stowed them away in the cupboard under the tea towels again, along with the bits and pieces for Jess's stocking – assuming she was going to have one. I made a note to ask Noël or Tilda about that later.

Becca came back in, snow sparkling in her iron-grey curls. 'It's almost dark and still snowing out there . . . and are the lights flickering, or am I imagining it?'

'No, they do keep doing that. I hope the power isn't going to cut off.'

'Oh well, it does from time to time, but the generator will take over if it does. What's happening with those two?' She jerked her head towards the hall. 'Still arguing?'

'As far as I know – unless one of them has murdered the other and is out there burying the body in the snow.'

'Ha!' she said. She looked around her approvingly: 'It looks different in here since you arrived – cleaner, for a start, and it's good to see the Aga being used again.'

'It looked like Mo had made a start on cleaning in here, but Sharon didn't seem to have touched anything in the house at all. I can't imagine what she did when she was here.'

'No, she was worse than useless. I told Jude he should get another couple in to look after the place, but he said he could look after himself.'

'It's not that easy to find live-in staff anyway these days and very expensive if you do.'

'True, and ones that can cook are like hens' teeth. What's that lovely smell?'

'Just another quick chocolate cake – we seem to get through cake at an amazing rate!'

'Wonderful.' Becca cocked her head, listening for any noise from the sitting room, then said doubtfully, 'It's gone ominously quiet in there.'

'I closed the kitchen door so I couldn't hear.'

She got up and opened it again. 'Oh yes – she's crying hysterically now.'

'Just as well I took more sausages out of the freezer, then,' I said gloomily. 'I don't think either of them are going anywhere tonight.'

'No, the weather's worse out there now, so it wouldn't be advisable until the roads are cleared and gritted in the morning.'

'Unless we're totally snowed in overnight, have you thought of that?'

Tilda tottered in, the heels of her velvet mules clicking on the stone floor, and sat in a wheelback chair. 'That imbecile boy has given Coco a snifter of brandy now, to stop her crying, so there's no getting shut of her until tomorrow!'

'We'd just decided we weren't going to get rid of her before morning anyway,' I said. 'But I suppose we're going to need a couple more beds made up.'

Guy appeared, looking harassed, which was hardly surprising since you could hear the sound of loud, angry weeping and the occasional scream of 'Bastard!' all the way from the sitting room.

'She's got a good pair of lungs on her,' Becca commented.

'Things are a just a *little* tricky,' Guy said, with a wry smile. 'Coco wants to go home, only I'm not risking my car taking her down to see if hers has been towed out of the ditch yet, because it's snowing so hard I'd never get back up again – have you looked outside recently? It's a nuisance Jude took the Land Rover, that would have made it.'

'You could run her back to London in your car in the morning,' I suggested.

'No way: I'd already told her it was all off between us, so it's her own fault if she didn't believe me and came up here on a fool's errand,' he said ungallantly.

'So, what's she going to do?'

'She'll have to stay tonight and then perhaps she can get a lift down to the village tomorrow with George when he ploughs our drive, to see if her car still works.' He shrugged. 'If not, perhaps she can bribe one of the boys to run her to the station instead. So,' he said, flashing a smile of outstanding charm in my direction, 'I wondered if you'd be an angel and make another bed up besides mine, which is the one opposite Jude's?'

'I haven't made yours up,' I said shortly, 'nor am I going to! Presumably you know where the linen cupboard is? I've had the fire in the sitting room going since I got here and all the doors upstairs open to air and warm the rooms.'

He looked taken aback. 'Oh . . . right.'

'I think Coco will have to go in the little bedroom on the nursery floor, next to Jess, which I don't suppose she'll be keen on. Otherwise there's only Jude's room, which is locked, and even Noël doesn't have the key to that.'

Becca said, 'It's almost a full house!'

'There's the other servant's room in this wing too, I'd forgotten that, though it's a bit Spartan and unused looking,' I said.

'She wouldn't like that at all,' Guy said.

'Well then, give her your room and you can have one of the others tonight,' Becca suggested.

'Not me! She can put up with the nursemaid's room.' He paused, eyeing me uncertainly, presumably for signs of weakening. 'Well, I suppose I'd better go and do something about the beds, then,' he said finally.

Becca got up. 'I'll find you the clean sheets, or God knows what you'll be putting on them – tablecloths, probably. But after that you're on your own, because I've already seen to the horses and I'm tired.'

'You told him,' Tilda said to me approvingly when they'd gone out. 'He's a good boy really, but he expects other people to carry him round all the time.'

'I just needed to make my situation plain. I'm not a servant and I'm not going to run around after him.'

'Of course not – we consider you as a guest, almost one of the family,' Tilda said graciously. 'And you are quite a good cook, dear – something smells delicious.'

'It's the chocolate cake,' I explained again. 'I'd better take it out. And if you switch the kettle on, I'll make us some tea in a minute. There are cheese scones, too.'

'Shop ones?' sniffed Tilda, as I took the cake out of the oven and turned it out on the cooling rack.

'No, ones I made myself.'

Becca returned and by unspoken agreement we had our tea

at the kitchen table, leaving Coco as sole occupant of the sitting room, though I did offer her a cup of tea and a scone when I took Noël's through to the parlour, which she rejected with evident loathing.

Tilda asked me what we were having for dinner and approved my choice of sausage and mash.

'Good wholesome winter food!'

'I've made sardine pâté for a starter. I thought we could have that in the sitting room on a tray.'

'And what about dessert?'

'It's either a raspberry Eton Mess, or alternatively there are some overripe bananas that the Chirks left, so I could do cold banana custards or bananas in rum, with cream. What do you think?'

'Oh, custards. With just a teeny sprinkle of nutmeg on each one.'

'If you say so,' I agreed. Along with squirty cream, nutmeg and paprika seemed to feature largely in the foodstuffs Tilda had brought from the lodge to add to the catering supplies. 'In fact, I'd better do those now, so they will be chilled by dinner time.'

While I was making the custard, Tilda helpfully sliced up the bananas and put them in the ramekins, talking about her past glories on TV, especially her wonderful series on canapés, on the subject of which she had enlightened the nation.

'You have no need to worry about canapés while *I* am here,' she said generously.

'Well, that's a huge weight off my mind,' I assured her.

'I'd better call Jess in,' Becca said. 'I'd forgotten she was still sledging and it's pitch black out there, though of course the light bounces off the snow. But she must be cold by now.'

While she went to fetch her in, I asked Tilda whether Jess was having a Christmas stocking or not.

'She had one last year,' Tilda said, 'but Roz – my daughter – didn't mention it to me, though she did leave Jess's presents. She

187

might have forgotten about the stocking, because she is the scattiest creature. Or perhaps Jess is too old?'

'Mrs Comfort said they are never too old, so I got a few things from her to make one up, in case.'

'Oh well – you carry on with that, then,' she ordered autocratically, as Jess came in with red cheeks and covered in snow, and was sent straight back out into the passage to remove her coat and wellies.

Chapter 20: Flickering

I begin to wonder if Hilda and Pearl are right about N, because despite the offer of a job he still has not asked me to marry him. Every time we meet he reassures me that we will always be together, but I can't go on in this clandestine way any more and so have told him that I would not meet him again unless we agreed to tell our parents and get engaged.

April, 1945

Luckily Coco retired to her bedroom once it was ready for her, so everyone could go back into the sitting room for a pre-dinner drink and warm-through by the fire, which got them from underfoot while I cleared and laid the kitchen table for dinner.

Now there were so many of us, I suppose it would have made sense to have used the dining room, but I felt too tired to be traipsing to and fro with hot dishes: no, the kitchen would have to do. And with a bit of luck and perhaps an overnight thaw, maybe I could get rid of Guy and Coco in the morning. Getting Coco safely home again was *his* responsibility, after all, and I didn't want him here either, charm though he might.

He was so not *my* type, but if Ned Martland was anything like Guy, then I could see why poor Gran fell for him, and not surprised that he now seemed to be playing fast and loose with her.

I popped upstairs to apply a little makeup, brush my hair and change my jeans for smarter black crepe trousers and a dark red tunic top with a beaded neckline: last night both Becca and Tilda had come down for dinner in long skirts, though since Noël and Jess hadn't changed at all, that might have been more for comfort than anything.

Of course, I don't bother what I wear when cooking for house-parties, because I don't eat with the clients then, but in the kitchen. However, now we were *all* to eat in the kitchen.

The family were gathered together in the sitting room when I went through with the pâté and French toast starter on a tray. Tilda and Becca were in their long skirts again and Noël was now wearing a Tattersall check shirt under a rubbed dark blue velvet smoking jacket, while Guy, in oatmeal cashmere, looked like an advert for upmarket men's clothing. Jess had an endless supply of black jeans and tops, so it was impossible to tell whether she had changed or not. She was sitting at the table by the window, doing something fiddly with scraps of paper.

'Let me take that for you, it looks terribly heavy,' Noël said, starting to get to his feet as if I was some fragile creature, rather than a six-foot Amazon.

'No – do let me,' offered Guy with a ravishing smile, pre-empting him. He put it down on the coffee table and asked me, 'Would you like a drink? Sherry, gin and tonic? Name your poison.'

'No thanks, I'm not much of a drinker, especially when I'm cooking. Is Miss Lanyon coming down for dinner?'

'Coco – and you must call me Guy, because I feel we're on intimate terms already, now all my dirty washing has been dragged out in front of you.'

'I'm sure we all know much more about your private affairs after today than we ever wanted to,' Tilda said severely. 'So, is your young woman going to grace us with her presence this evening?'

'She's not my young woman, Tilda, and I've no idea.'

'I wouldn't put it past her,' Becca said, 'though I'm sure we are all quite sick of the sight of her. I was actually grateful to you when you went off with her last Christmas, Guy – think how awful it would have been if she'd married Jude and settled here!'

'Actually, I think it was the thought of spending most of the year here that put her off Jude before she even set eyes on me,' Guy said dispassionately. 'She's not a country girl and she has her eyes firmly set on her career.'

'If you can call prancing up and down a catwalk half-naked a *career*,' Tilda commented acidly.

'She's trying to break into acting too,' he said and just at that moment the door swung open and Coco stood revealed, a vision of angularly icy beauty. She is so pretty she is unreal and I'm not at all surprised that Guy and Jude fell for her.

She held her catwalk pose long enough for us all to take in the one-shouldered, slinky, nude-silk trousered garment that she was *almost* wearing. I sincerely hoped the slashed top part was held on with boob tape, because otherwise she would be in serious danger of dangling her little dumplings in the dinner.

'Here you all are,' she said gaily, then directed a dazzling smile at Guy. 'Darling, get me a drink, won't you? You know what I like.'

Clearly she'd regrouped and was now changing tactics to one aimed at luring back her errant lover.

'You're going to catch your death in that outfit,' Becca observed. 'Have you got it on the right way round?'

'Of course! It's supposed to look like this,' she said indignantly.

'Then I'd better lend you a cardigan – Tilda's won't be big enough.'

'Oh, I'm quite warm enough, thank you!' Standing close to Guy as she accepted her drink, she laid a hand on his arm and said seductively, 'If not, Guy can warm me up, can't you, darling?'

'Oh yuk! Horlicks is getting soppy,' Jess said disgustedly.

'Do all help yourselves to the starter and I'll call you through into the kitchen when dinner's ready,' I said, making a neat exit.

'Aren't we eating in the dining room?' I heard Coco ask piercingly as I went out again. 'Why do we have to eat in the kitchen, with the help?'

That comment hardly endeared her to me and nor did her announcement, once we were seated at the table, that she didn't eat carbs.

'Or any kind of processed food,' she added, looking at the dish of sausages with something akin to horror.

'These are extremely good sausages I found in the freezer,' I said. 'I'm afraid if you want something else, you'll have to cook it yourself.'

Coco looked at me with dropped jaw. 'Me? Why can't *you* do it? That's what you're here for, isn't it?'

'No, it isn't!' Becca told her.

'That's right, Holly isn't our resident housekeeper and cook, you know, she only came here to look after the house and animals while Jude was away,' Noël said gently. 'She isn't employed to cook or look after his family as well, and is only doing it from the kindness of her heart. And we are all very grateful.' He gave me one of his charming, lopsided smiles.

'Not at all, I'm sure we're going to have a lovely Christmas,' I lied. 'Much more fun than being on my own.'

'And this food is wonderful,' Guy said, tucking into his mustard mash with gusto. 'You can cook as well as look stunning, so you're everything I ever wanted in a woman: will you marry me?'

Jess giggled but Coco shot daggers at both of us, even though he was just playing the fool.

'On your past track record, no.'

'That told him,' Becca said.

'I must say, you have cooked this very nicely,' Tilda said. 'And the pâté was lovely too – simple but good.'

'Hearty plain food is the best,' agreed Becca. 'I'll eat Coco's sausages and mash if she doesn't want them.'

'Not if I get there first,' Guy told her with a grin.

'Or perhaps Jess should have them: she needs to keep her strength up if she's helping me with the horses,' Becca suggested. 'Luckily, she appears to have outgrown her allergy to them.'

Jess gave her a dirty look, but she seemed to be putting away her dinner without any difficulty, even though I'd spotted a crumpled scatter of silvery chocolate tree decoration wrappers on the table where she'd been doing her origami earlier.

'I have to eat *something*,' Coco said sulkily and helped herself to one sausage, a bare teaspoon of mash, and a microscopically small fragment of carrot.

The room went dark again, just for an instant.

'Why do the lights keep doing that? The electricity isn't going to go off, is it?' Coco asked nervously. 'I'd hate that, because I'm sure this house is haunted.'

'Don't worry, if it does the generator will take over,' I said soothingly. 'And if it doesn't, the gardener showed me how to switch it on manually.'

'*Henry* did?' said Noël, opening his eyes wide. 'He has never let me anywhere near it.'

'Or me,' said Guy. 'Not that I want to, I'm not at all mechanically minded, unlike Jude.'

'You're the kiss of death to all machinery,' Tilda told her husband. 'Look what you did to the Magimix.'

'I did fly aeroplanes during the war, m'dear, so you can't say I am hopeless with *all* machinery.'

'That was entirely different,' she snapped and I could see she was tired out and hoped she would go to bed right after dinner. I think the fall must have shaken her up much more than she was letting on, though at least her eye was now only faintly rimmed with a yellow and blue bruise.

Predictably, Coco spurned the banana custards I'd made for

dessert and said she would go and smoke a cigarette in the sitting room until we came through with coffee.

'I'm sorry, I'm afraid this is a no-smoking household: it said so clearly in the owner's information folder,' I said apologetically.

'Oh, don't be silly,' she snapped, 'and anyway, Jude isn't here to see!'

'That's immaterial: I'm responsible for the house until he returns and must follow his instructions.'

'Yes, and we agree with Jude, so you'll have to do it in the porch like last Christmas,' Tilda told her.

'But I'll freeze!'

'You certainly will in that garment,' agreed Becca. 'I'd go and put something more sensible on, first.'

'I haven't got anything sensible,' she said sulkily.

'Well, the coat and hat you arrived in, then.'

'Yes, and that's another thing – my white coat cost me a fortune and after being in that tractor it's never going to come clean again!'

She flounced out and I think we breathed a collective sigh of relief.

'I expect she will just go and smoke in her room instead, she's that kind of person,' Becca said. 'Really, Guy, we could have done without her here, she is *such* a drag. I don't know what you and Jude ever saw in her.'

'Apart from being stunningly beautiful, she can also be fun, believe it or not,' he said dispassionately. 'But she's shallow as a puddle and totally self-centred.'

'You have lots in common then,' Tilda said tartly. 'I can't think why you broke up.'

'I think you are tired, m'dear,' Noël said gently. 'Wouldn't you like to go to bed and I will bring you a hot drink up?'

'Perhaps that would be a good idea,' Tilda conceded. 'The child could do with an early night, too.'

'I'm not a child,' Jess protested, 'and I want to finish making the last present before I go up.'

'Half an hour, then,' Tilda said firmly.

The others went into the sitting room and I took the coffee tray through and then retired to the kitchen to clear away and look over tomorrow's menu, sincerely hoping that I wouldn't have two extra mouths to feed after breakfast!

Guy brought the tray back. 'Still at it? Only everyone else has called it a day and gone to bed. What are you doing?'

'Putting the jelly layer on this trifle and then I'm going to let Merlin out for a last run and check on the horses before I go to bed.'

And I would take the journal back upstairs with me too, because, however weary I felt, I was sure I could manage to read another page or two. It kept drawing me like a moth to the flame – I'd been dipping into it at every opportunity.

The light flickered off and then, with extreme reluctance, back on again.

'The horses will be fine. Put Merlin out and then come and have a nightcap with me,' he suggested.

'No, thank you.'

'Pity. Still, we'll have lots of time to get to know each other so much better over Christmas.'

'I hope not – I'm expecting you and Coco to leave in the morning.'

'Well, Coco's certainly going, even if I have to bribe one of the farmer's boys to take her all the way to London in the tractor. But *I'm* staying.'

'That's very unchivalrous of you!'

'Not entirely: she's such a crap driver I certainly wouldn't let her drive herself back to London in these conditions, even if they do get her car out of the ditch.'

'I still think you should take her yourself,' I said. 'Jude won't want you staying here and I would much prefer it if you left, too.'

'You don't mean that *really*,' he said, but finally, getting no response to his flirting, he took himself and his amazingly effulgent aftershave off to bed.

I put the trifle in the fridge and then, accompanied by Merlin, went through and banked up the fire in the sitting room, set the guard safely round it and tidied up. Apart from the usual creakings and sighing of an old house all was quiet and peaceful.

'Last run, Merlin?' I asked, shrugging into my down-filled jacket and picking up my big, rubber-cased torch, because whatever Guy said, I knew my duty. But we'd only just got to the back door when the lights went out – and this time stayed out.

The generator and I were about to get better acquainted.

Chapter 21: Loathe at First Sight

I have heard nothing from N since my ultimatum and I am missing him dreadfully. The others talk of little except the Victory celebrations tomorrow but though I am so very glad this awful war is over, I cannot wholeheartedly lose myself in the excitement of it all as they do.

May, 1945

When I opened the back door the snow was still falling in big, fluffy flakes, and had banked up so I had to wade through it practically up to the top of my wellingtons.

Merlin turned around almost immediately and asked to go back in, which I couldn't blame him for in the least, even if I would have preferred his company.

I don't think I'd quite appreciated how pitch black it would be out there without the yard lights on and the moon hidden behind clouds. The wind was clanking something against the metal gate, but otherwise the snow seemed to have a deadening effect on the usual country night noises. It's lucky I'm not of a nervous disposition.

I switched on my torch and trudged across to the barn, with its sweet smell of hay and warm horse. Nutkin was hanging his head drowsily and barely flickered his ears at me when I shone the beam at him, but I couldn't see Lady at first. This threw me into a panic until I found her lying down very comfortably in the warm straw, with Billy next to her.

I went quietly out again and bolted the door, then made my way across to the generator room and into the silent darkness. It was just as cold in there as it was outside, since the back wall was slatted for ventilation.

It all looked subtly different in the dim light but, according to Henry, all I had to do was flick a couple of switches to turn the generator on manually – and then, if that had no effect, startle the machine with a quick and underhand thump to a vital bit of its anatomy.

This, he'd assured me, *never* failed.

I'd just pressed down the switches (with no discernible result) when I sensed rather than heard a slight movement in the doorway behind me and knew I was no longer alone.

'What the hell are you doing in here?' demanded a deep, rumbling and ominously familiar voice, which then added more urgently, 'And don't *touch* that—'

But he was too late, because after the first heart-stopping second, logic had told me I was in no danger from that quarter – so I'd ignored him and dealt the generator a sudden blow. This had the desired result: it burst instantly into roaring, throbbing noise.

Then I turned round and said calmly, 'Why don't you put on the light now it's working again, and introduce yourself?'

But unfortunately, when he did, I decided I'd liked him much better in the dark. To say he was a large man was like saying that grizzlies are quite big bears, for he was not only extremely tall, but broad across the shoulders too. A pair of red-rimmed, deep-set dark eyes looked out of a face that only the words 'grim' and 'rugged' seemed to describe, framed by the fur-edged hood of a giant parka.

'My God, it's the abominable snowman!' I heard my voice say rudely, though in my defence it has to be admitted that I'd had a long and very trying day. 'That's *all* we need!'

He covered the expanse of floor between us in two quick strides, pushing back the hood to reveal a lot of short dark hair, all standing on end, and looked down at me (which was not something I was used to) with a heavy frown furrowing his forehead.

Those new theories about us all having a bit of Neanderthal DNA might be true, then.

'Holly Brown, I presume?'

'Yes – and you don't have to tell me who you are, because it's obvious now I can see you better: Jude Martland. I thought you were in America?'

'I was,' he said shortly. 'But the last I heard from Noël was that Tilda had had an accident and been rushed off to hospital, so I didn't know what the hell was happening! I've been travelling ever since.'

Well, that would account for the red-rimmed eyes and the dark stubble, at least, though the bad-tempered expression was probably a permanent feature on a face that could only be described, even by his loved ones, as rugged rather than handsome.

'You were so concerned you came straight back?'

I must have sounded incredulous, because a spark of anger glowed in his eyes and he snapped back, 'Of course I did! With a mercenary witch in charge of my house, I didn't hold out much hope that anyone would be rallying round.'

'Thanks. If I sounded surprised, it's because you didn't strike me as someone who would care enough about any of your family to fly back straight away.'

'I can't imagine where you got that idea . . .' He paused, still glaring at me. 'Do I *know* you from somewhere?'

'No, I'm glad to say I've never met you before in my life.' I rather wished it had stayed that way.

'You look vaguely familiar. But never mind that – where are Noël and Tilda? There was no sign of life at the lodge.'

'Here, of course! They moved in with Jess on the afternoon after the accident, and your Aunt Becca came the next day, so she's here too. I did try and call your mobile to tell you what was happening.'

'I was probably over the Atlantic by then.' He looked at me thoughtfully. 'So, who else had you already invited to stay with you, some friend or other? There were two cars by the gate, though the snow's drifted over them.'

'Of course I didn't invite a visitor!' I snapped. 'I wouldn't *dream* of doing such a thing while looking after a house, unless I had prior permission from the owner.'

'Then whose is the second car?'

'The small one is mine, but the other—'

'A plaintive voice from the cold outer darkness broke in. 'Excuse m-me,' it said through chattering teeth, 'd-do you think you c-could p-possibly c-continue this c-conversation indoors? Only I th-think I've got hypothermia.'

Jude Martland moved to one side, revealing his companion to be a smaller, fair man. He seemed to have several layers of clothes on, though going by the outer one, a light raincoat, none of them was terribly suitable for trekking through snowdrifts in arctic conditions.

'I'd forgotten about you!' Jude said, then turned to me: 'Look, I'm going to bring the Land Rover into the shelter of the yard. You take him into the kitchen and thaw him out.'

'Yeah, and what did your last one die of?' I muttered, but he was running his hands over the gently throbbing generator and didn't hear me. Honestly, men and their toys!

'It's fine,' I assured him. 'Henry showed me what to do if it wouldn't start automatically. There's no mechanical skill involved that I can see.'

'There is if it goes wrong,' he said, then turned and strode off.

'Well, do come into the house,' I invited the shivering stranger and he followed me in gratefully. I made him take his soggy shoes and outer layers off in the passage and put them in the utility room to dry off, along with mine.

Now I could see him better, he was very handsome, in a thin, fair way – chilled but perfectly preserved. 'I'm M-Michael Whiston,' he said, holding out a hand like a frozen blue fish.

'Holly Brown – come on through, it's warmer in the kitchen. And never mind the dog, Merlin is harmless.'

Merlin didn't seem terribly interested in the stranger, except in a polite sort of way, but at the roar of the Land Rover's engine outside and then a pair of heavy thuds – presumably as baggage was tossed through the back door – he uttered a low bark and began to wag his tail.

'Just as well someone's glad to see him,' I muttered. I pulled up a chair next to the Aga for Michael and then fetched a picnic rug from the utility room and draped it around him. He smiled gratefully.

I'd put the kettle on and was making tea by the time Jude came in, in stockinged feet and drying his hair on Merlin's towel. He tossed it aside and bent to fondle the old dog's ears.

'I looked in on Lady – she seems fine,' he said grudgingly.

'Of course she's fine, I kept telling you she was. And Becca's keeping an eye on her now, too.' I handed him a mug. 'Give your friend this, he's got hypothermia. I've put brandy in it.'

'Not the good brandy from the dining room, I trust?'

'No, I used that up in the cake. This is some cheap stuff I got from the pub.'

'You put my Armagnac in the cake?' he asked with disbelief.

'I had to make a Christmas cake in a hurry and I assumed it wasn't much good or you would have locked it in the cellar with the rest of the booze. Mo and Jim wouldn't have touched it anyway and neither would I – all the Homebodies staff are vetted for honesty, soberness and reliability.'

'I forgot about it until too late, but it was Sharon I didn't trust, not Mo and Jim.' He stared at me. 'I'd never have thought of anyone putting the last of my father's good brandy in a cake, though!'

'It's not the last, Noël found another bottle in the cellar. And anyway, the cake is for your family and it smells delicious. Now, for goodness sake, give the tea to your friend before it goes cold!'

'Michael isn't my friend, I'd never met him before tonight. He's just another fool who got his car stuck on the lower road trying to take a shortcut.'

'The SatNav sent me down there,' the man said, gratefully clamping both shaking hands around the mug, though at least his teeth seemed to have stopped chattering. 'But the snow got too bad and I couldn't go any further.'

'I had to bring him with me, I couldn't leave him to freeze to death in his car. I'll be surprised if even the snowplough gets through in the morning, if it carries on like this.'

'*I'm* astonished you got up here at all if it's that bad, because George Froggat said the bottom end of the lane often gets impassable in snow and ice and the weather's much worse now. But I sincerely hope you're wrong, and it thaws out a bit by morning.'

'I had chains for the tyres in the back of the Land Rover, so I stopped and put them on as soon as I left the motorway. But no-one in their right mind would drive up narrow country lanes in this weather without them.' He gave the other man a look of scorn.

'Well, thank you for rescuing me, anyway,' Michael said, with an attempt at a smile. 'And for making me put on half the clothes in my suitcase, too!'

I sat down at the table with my tea and Merlin immediately abandoned his master and came and sat down, leaning against my leg as he usually does, his head on my knees. Jude gave him one of the frowning looks he'd been bestowing on me earlier, though slightly puzzled, too.

Now I'd got over the surprise, I'd started to wonder how Jude's arrival would affect me: after all, I was only here to house-sit and he wouldn't need me now. Still, time to sort that out in the morning. I'd pray for a sudden thaw!

'I'll have to give Michael a bed for the night,' Jude said.

'Then I'm afraid it will either have to be yours or the little servant's room next to mine in this wing.'

He had been pushing back his unruly dark hair, which was trying to curl damply, but now stopped and stared at me with his treacle toffee-coloured eyes. 'Why? What's the matter with the others? I mean, only three of them can be occupied, apart from yours?'

'Actually, no, all the rooms in that wing are in use tonight: your brother Guy arrived earlier and his fiancée – or ex-fiancée I should say, since they've had a falling-out – followed him. I've put her in the nursemaid's room next to Jess, since Guy wouldn't give up his room for her and we couldn't put her in yours, because it was locked and even Noël didn't have the key.'

'What, Guy and Coco are here?' he demanded, missing most of the explanation and going straight to the nub of the matter.

'Yes, Coco managed to run her car off the road and I have no idea where it is now, but the other car outside is your brother's.'

'Guy's got a nerve, coming up here while I'm away!' Anger sparked in his eyes.

'He certainly has: he seemed to think he could simply turn up and the Chirks would feed and look after him!'

'And I suppose you let him bamboozle you into letting him stay?'

'Look,' I said shortly, 'I got back from a shopping trip to the village and he was here already, with your aunt and uncle, in his family home. How do you think I, the house-sitter, was supposed to eject him? Oh, and he'd had a couple of drinks by then, too, so there was no way he could have driven anywhere.'

'I suppose not,' he agreed reluctantly. 'You said Coco had an accident? Is she all right? Where is everyone?'

'Coco's fine, apart from some exhausting hysterics after arguing with your brother when she arrived, but it's been a bit of a day, and they've all gone to bed. I was just about to as well, once I'd checked on Lady and Nutkin, but then the electricity went off and the generator obviously wasn't going to start up on its own.'

'I hope you've been keeping the heating on all the time at a low level, like I said in the instructions?'

'I don't think it has any temperature other than low, does it? But I haven't touched it and I've also kept the fire going in the sitting room day and night and opened all the upstairs bedroom doors to let the warm air circulate and air them, luckily.'

'Except mine, presumably?'

I shrugged. 'Unless any air sneaked in through the key-hole.'

'I don't mind where you put me, I'm just grateful you've taken me in,' Michael offered, sounding much better.

'The only bedroom left used to be a servant's one and is a bit Spartan, but it's warm and comfortable enough and I'll make your bed up and put a hot water bottle in it,' I told him.

'You're very kind: bed with a hot water bottle sounds like bliss.' He gave me that charming smile again and I found myself smiling back.

'That's all right. You'll have to share my bathroom, which is just opposite – in fact, you'd better have a hot bath before you turn in. Come on.'

'What about *my* bed, aren't you going to make that, too?' asked Jude sardonically.

'No – and if your room is chilly and musty, it's your own fault for locking it.'

I led Michael up the backstairs, first collecting his two expensive-looking bags from the hall, where Jude had dumped them in a puddle of melting snow with his own. I put out towels and ran a bath while he unpacked his night gear, then while he was in there I made his bed up.

I heard Jude climb the backstairs and walk along the passage, heading for his own wing, and apart from Merlin the kitchen was deserted when I fetched the hot water bottle.

Hoping Michael wouldn't fall asleep in the bath, I went up to my own bed after washing up the mugs and saying good night to Merlin. Luckily the bathroom was now empty and, in fact, the whole house seemed quiet when I cautiously opened the door to the gallery a crack and listened: a brooding silence reigned.

I had a feeling it wouldn't be quite so tranquil in the morning . . .

By now, I was at that stage beyond exhaustion where you're looking at everything through thick glass, so I climbed into bed and picked up Gran's latest journal, saying aloud, '*Please* let me have jumped to all the wrong conclusions so there's no possibility I'm related to that objectionable man!'

Chapter 22: Outcomes

I have been feeling ill, especially in the mornings, and although it is still early to tell, I am sure I am expecting. I sent a note to N asking him to meet me urgently and intend to slip out very late this evening. Pearl and Hilda, who are in my confidence and very anxious to know the outcome, will wait up to let me back in again.

May, 1945

I woke very early, before it was light, and lay there for a little while thinking about poor Granny, for whom the outcome I had feared seemed to have come about. She didn't marry Ned Martland in the end, but I don't know if this was because he abandoned her (which looks horribly likely) or because he was killed before it could happen.

And here I was, landed in the middle of a Christmas house-party (the very thing I had tried to avoid), for the family of the man who seduced poor Gran – it's bizarre!

But I suppose everything at Old Place might be about to change with the arrival of the master of the house, because presumably I was now redundant – surplus to requirements. Assuming, that was, that Jude knew how to cook?

And it was at that inconvenient moment that I suddenly realised that before the arrival of Guy, Coco and the objectionable Jude, I'd actually begun to *enjoy* all the Christmas preparations and would be sorry to leave!

But if they clear the roads I expect Jude will send Coco and his brother packing back to London, and expect me to leave too. He might want to count the silver first, since he seemed to have a very nasty, suspicious mind.

Up to that point, though, I knew my duty and would carry on as usual, so I got up and showered, then dressed in sensible jeans and jumper and went downstairs to let Merlin out and give the horses a bit of carrot.

It was still pretty dark, but I could see that the snow had drifted up one side of the yard and not the other, where the Land Rover stood. I didn't think it seemed worse than the previous night though, just crunchier underfoot.

I cleaned out the ashes and stoked up the embers of the sitting-room fire, got everything out ready for breakfast and laid Tilda's tray.

While I was busy, the radio kept announcing that it was Christmas Eve, as if I might have the five-minute memory of a goldfish, but somehow these reminders didn't seem to hurt quite so much as they usually did, possibly because I had so much else on my mind at the moment.

Perhaps, at last, I was starting to relinquish the past and move on. A fresh start in the New Year – and maybe a fresh new life to go with it. Thank goodness nowadays having babies out of wedlock was totally acceptable, unlike in Gran's day!

Merlin was eating his breakfast, liberally sprinkled with his medicine, and I had made giblet stock and a bowl of stuffing for tomorrow and was putting a batch of biscuits in the oven, when Michael came diffidently into the kitchen. He looked a different man to the frozen one of the night before – very hand-some in a slightly haggard way, with fine features, light brown hair and hazel eyes. He was wearing a pale cashmere jumper to rival Guy's, over cream chinos, which was about as practical an outfit for the country as any of Coco's.

'Good morning! I heard you moving about down here, so I hoped you wouldn't mind my coming down for a cup of coffee? I'm a bit of an addict – and *something* smells delicious!' he added, sniffing the air appreciatively.

'Spiced biscuits for the tree,' I explained. 'Would you like cereal or a full cooked breakfast?'

'Well, bacon and eggs and toast would be perfect – but I could do it if you're busy?'

'No, that's fine, this is the last batch of biscuits. No-one else seemed awake, so I thought I'd get them done, because I promised Jess – that's Jude's niece – that we could ice them together this morning,' I said, touched by his thoughtfulness. 'But there's a cafetière over there and coffee in the cupboard above it, so you could make us both some while I'm cooking?'

We chatted while he was eating his breakfast and I was washing up those things I'd used for the biscuits that wouldn't go in the dishwasher, like the old metal pastry cutters shaped like Christmas trees, bells, stars and all kinds of other things. I told him how I did cooking and house-sitting for a living and in return he confessed, with a modest air, that he was an actor.

'Oh really? I expect you're terribly distinguished and I should have recognised you, only I rarely have time to watch TV or go to the cinema.'

'Not really famous – I'm mostly stage, except that I had a part in a film last year and made a bit of a success of it – *The Darkling Hours*. Sort of Harry Potter crossed with Tolkien and a dash of C.S. Lewis, but it went down well and I've had a few high-profile cameo roles since.'

'Oh yes, that was a huge success! I haven't seen it, but I've heard about it. You were in that?' I was impressed.

'It certainly put me on the radar.' He smiled rather sadly. 'But while we were filming, my wife had an affair with one of the other actors and we've broken up.'

'Oh, I'm so sorry.'

'We had . . . irreconcilable differences. The marriage hadn't really been working out. Debbie's taken our little girl, Rosie, to spend Christmas with her parents in Liverpool, so I called in to visit her and take some presents on the way up to stay with my Yorkshire friends. But after that, taking the SatNav's short cut led to my downfall.'

'Well, it could be worse – at least you saw your little girl *before* you got stuck. How old is she?'

'Two – and I think she's already forgetting me,' he said sadly. 'At first Debbie said she'd rather I didn't see her at all, but I want to stay in her life if I possibly can and I think we can stay friends if we work at it, for Rosie's sake.'

'Yes, of course you do and I'm sure Debbie will come round.'

He smiled at me. 'I do feel better for talking it through, so getting myself stuck in the snow has had one good result! But my friends are going to be wondering what on earth has happened to me. I tried ringing them from my car last night, but they were out and I had to leave a message. And this morning I can't get a signal at all!'

'No, the phone reception here is lousy. You either have to walk down the drive just past the lodge or up the hill behind the house, before you can get a signal.'

'It doesn't really look like hiking weather out there, does it?' he said, glancing out at the winter wonderland. 'I wonder if it would be all right if I made a brief call from the house phone?'

'I expect it would have been, only the poles have come down, so *that* isn't working either, though there is a call box in the village, about half a mile away.'

'Oh well, that's that. I'm hoping I'll be able to get off a bit later today anyway, if it's stopped snowing and they clear the roads.'

209

'I don't *think* there's been more snow since last night, but it's a bit hard to tell, because it's drifted and there's been a freeze overnight – it's all crunchy underfoot.'

'It'll probably thaw out once the sun comes up properly,' he suggested optimistically.

'A local farmer snowploughs the drive and the road to the village with his tractor, so he'll be up later this morning and can tell us what it's like out there,' I told him. 'If it's passable, then I should think Jude's brother and his girlfriend will be leaving too, so they could probably give you a lift down to your car. Or *I* could, because I'll be leaving myself, though I'll probably have to dig my car out. I hope it starts: I haven't moved it for days.'

He looked up, surprised. 'But – I was a bit too out of it last night, so I might have misunderstood – but aren't you here to look after the house and do the cooking for Jude's elderly relatives?'

'No, actually this was only supposed to be one of my house-sitting jobs, to look after the empty house and the animals over Christmas.'

I'd made some fresh coffee and now sat down with him while he ate toast and marmalade, and explained what had happened. And as I was talking, I began to see everything that had led to this moment as a series of unfortunate events, a bit like the *Lemony Snicket* film, and actually some of it was quite funny. In fact, by the time Guy walked in on us, we were getting along as if we'd known each other for years.

He looked taken aback to see a stranger there and instantly demanded, 'Who the hell is this?'

Coco drifted half-awake through the door after him, ethereally pretty in a diaphanous pink dressing gown and no makeup. Then she too spotted the visitor and jerked wide-awake, exclaiming, 'Michael – *darling*!'

He put down his cup hastily and got up. 'Er . . . Carla?' he ventured uncertainly.

She threw herself at him like a rose-tinted flying squirrel and kissed him with a *mwah! mwah!* noise on both cheeks. 'I haven't seen you for ages! You remember me, don't you – Coco Lanyon?'

'Of course,' he assured her, though I deduced from his expression that he didn't. But he *was* an actor, so he returned the embrace, told her how wonderful she looked, and asked her what she was doing just now, and she told him about her Morning Dawn Facial Elixir TV advert.

'This is Michael Whiston, he's a well-known actor,' I explained to Guy while all this luvviness was taking place.

He helped himself to coffee. 'A friend of yours?'

'No, I never met him before last night. He took a wrong turn when his SatNav told him to and—'

I broke off because Noël, in dressing gown and slippers, and Becca and Jess, who were dressed for mucking out, arrived to find the stranger in their midst and general introductions and explanations ensued.

'Michael and Jude arrived late last night, when I was switching on the generator – the electricity went off and the automatic switchover didn't happen,' I explained succinctly.

'You mean, *Jude* is here?' Guy demanded, getting straight to the crux of the matter.

Coco went white – though actually she was pretty pale to start with, a translucent Nordic fairness. 'Oh God, he's not, is he?'

'Oh, shut up, Horlicks,' Jess said. 'I'm glad Uncle Jude's here! Do you think he's brought me a present, Holly? Can I go and wake him up?'

'The poor boy must have jet lag, to have got here so quickly,' Noël suggested. 'Let him sleep.'

'No, I'm sure he's fine,' I said heartlessly, 'you can wake him in a minute, Jess. But first, could you take this tray up to your granny?'

I'd been buttering toast and soft-boiling an egg while all the explanations were going on and now I added a little pot of tea to the tray. 'There. If you take that, I can get on with everyone else's breakfast.'

'But Guy – Jude is here!' Coco wailed, looking terrified. 'What are we going to do? Oh, I *wish* I'd never come.'

'Don't we all,' muttered Becca.

'Oh, I don't think he'll throw *me* out into the cold, cold snow – not his baby brother,' Guy said easily. 'I can't guarantee he won't throw you out though, Coco.'

'Don't be silly, no-one will be leaving until the roads have been cleared,' I said.

'And of course Jude won't throw you out anyway, m'dear,' Noël reassured her.

'Now, does everyone want a cooked breakfast?' I asked briskly.

Coco shuddered even more. 'An omelette made with egg whites for me,' she ordered. 'Black coffee.'

'You could put the kettle on and make a fresh pot,' I suggested. 'And there are lots of eggs if you want to do your own thing. I'm cooking fried eggs, grilled bacon, tomatoes and toast.'

'And very good it was too,' Michael said, giving me a warm smile and seeming not to notice that Coco was looking outraged. 'I'll make the fresh coffee. Since I'm the unexpected visitor I'd like to make myself useful and you wouldn't let me cook.'

'Well, Noël and I are useless in the kitchen, so *we'll* just keep out of the way,' Becca said.

But to my surprise Guy also made himself useful by buttering the toast, while I fried the eggs and grilled bacon and halved tomatoes brushed with olive oil.

Jess returned, reporting that Jude was now getting up. 'He won't say if he's brought me a present, so he probably has. And I told Granny about Jude being home and *she's* pleased too,' she announced. 'She said she expected he would send you packing,

212

Horlicks, and Guy would have to drive you back in his car, so we could get rid of both of you and have a lovely Christmas.'

'You horrible child,' Guy said dispassionately and then pulled ghastly faces at her until she giggled. Suddenly, despite not wanting to in the least, I found myself liking him a bit, despite his being so horrid to Coco.

'Are those biscuits for the Christmas tree?' Jess asked, spotting them cooling on the rack. 'When did you make them?'

'Early this morning, while most of you were still asleep. I thought we could ice them later, and put ribbon through ready to hang them on the tree. We've got icing sugar and I brought natural food colourings with me.'

'Oh, great.' She slid onto a chair next to Noël and helped herself to toast and jam. 'Horlicks, you shouldn't play with your food,' she said severely.

Coco, who had taken a fried egg and was engaged in cutting out the yolk, looked at her with disfavour. 'I don't know why you keep calling me that, but I wish you'd stop!'

'Yes, it's very rude,' said Becca, but without any great conviction.

Coco ate one mouthful of egg white and then pushed the plate away, though since she had the look of one who retired to sick up her meals immediately after eating them, it probably saved time. Or maybe she was just naturally all bones and angles?

'I need a ciggy.'

'Well, you're not smoking it in *my* house,' Jude's deep voice said from behind her and the huge kitchen seemed to shrink with his entrance. Guy paled slightly for all his bravado and Coco looked frankly petrified.

'Oh, look, it's the Brother Grimm,' I said involuntarily, looking at his set jaw – though to be fair, with one like that it would be hard for him to look soft and pleasant. And I can't imagine why these kind of remarks keep slipping out when he's there, because normally I keep a firm rein on my rebellious tongue with clients!

'Good morning to you, too,' he said to me sarcastically, then took his place in the large wheelback chair at the head of the table as if it was his by right – which, come to think of it, it was. 'I don't suppose there's any breakfast left?'

'Yes, of course, I did extra bacon when I knew you were getting up and I'll fry you a fresh egg. Guy, would you stick a bit more toast in?'

'We seem to have quite the extended family party, don't we?' Jude said, looking round the table. 'Odd, I don't remember inviting any of you – though Noël, Tilda and Becca are always welcome, of course.'

'And me,' said Jess.

'Not when you wake me up at the crack of dawn by hitting me with a pillow,' he said gravely. Then he raised an eyebrow at Coco and Guy. 'Congratulations! I saw the notice in *The Times*. When's the wedding?'

'There isn't a wedding, or even a proper engagement,' Guy said. 'Coco was jumping the gun.' He picked up his piece of toast and added, nonchalantly, 'Come to think of it, there wasn't even a gun – I've been trying to get rid of her for weeks.'

'That's a lie,' Coco exclaimed. 'Everything was fine! I can't think what's got into you suddenly, Guy!'

'Sanity?'

'He's fickle, m'dear – takes after his Uncle Ned,' explained Noël kindly, which was definitely not the sort of thing I wanted to hear about Ned Martland just then!

'Was Ned Martland *really* fickle?' I couldn't resist asking Noël.

'Yes, m'dear, but he genuinely fell in love with them. Heart soft as butter – but he couldn't marry 'em all, could he?'

'There you are, Coco,' Guy said easily. 'I can't help it, it's in my genes. I'm moving on to the next woman already.' He blew me a kiss.

'Oh, rubbish,' she snapped, then with an effort she rallied, got up and kissed Jude's unresponsive (and unshaven) cheek, twining

214

her arms girlishly around his neck. 'Jude, darling, Guy and I had a misunderstanding and he's still cross, so that's why he's being silly, but I know you'll be happy for us, about the engagement.'

'There is no *us*, I kept trying to tell you,' Guy interrupted. 'Sending an engagement notice to *The Times* without telling me doesn't actually constitute one.'

Coco burst into tears. 'You are so cruel to me!' she sobbed. Looking around for sympathy she did the flying squirrel thing at Michael again. 'Please take me away from these horrible people – this terrible, terrible place!'

'That's an awful line and you used it with me last Christmas,' Guy remarked critically, 'right after Jude found us together. And you're never going to make it as an actress because the delivery was terrible.'

Coco's sobs began to verge on the hysterical and Michael patted her gingerly, while making a face at me over her head.

'Poor child,' Noël said. 'I really don't think you've treated her well, Guy.'

'Oh, just fill the big jug with cold water and throw it on her,' suggested Becca, which was probably also something they had taught her at finishing school.

Coco hastily removed herself from Michael's shoulder, to his evident relief, and, declaring that she was going to dress and pack, flounced out of the room. I supposed I ought to do the same really – the packing bit, not the flouncing – though the thought was not terribly inviting. But then, neither was the idea of spending Christmas under the same roof as Jude Martland.

Noël rose from his chair, saying to Jude, 'Glad to have you back, my boy. I'll go and see if Tilda is getting up.'

'How is she doing?'

'Almost herself again,' he assured him. 'You'll see for yourself, shortly.'

'It was kind of you to rescue me,' Michael told Jude, 'but I

215

hope to leave later too, just as soon as we know the roads have been cleared. Perhaps you can give me a lift down to my car?' he suggested to Guy. 'Or Holly says I might be able to get the local farmer to take me on his tractor?'

'Yes, George Froggat, who has the farm up the lane, will clear the road and our drive some time this morning, and he'll tell us what the road's like. I'd certainly love to see Guy and Coco on their way, and I expect you're keen to get off as well, but I can't very well turn you all out if it's impassable,' Jude said, though he looked as if he'd like to.

'Glad to hear it, though a couple more days of Coco's hysterics and we might change our minds about turning *her* out into the snow,' Guy said. 'But I'm prepared to pay George good money to take her away, so all is not yet lost. In fact, I'll take my coffee into the sitting room and watch out for him.'

'So long as he takes *you* away, too,' Jude called after him.

'You wouldn't throw your little brother out into the cold, cold snow, would you?' Guy said plaintively, turning in the doorway and clutching a melodramatic hand to his chest.

'Yes, I would,' Jude said uncompromisingly. 'And Coco's your responsibility now, so it's up to you to see she gets home safely.'

'There's a good fire in the sitting room, if you would like to go through with Guy,' I suggested to Michael.

'And it's time we saw to the horses, Jess,' Becca said. 'It's getting late.'

'Oh, but I'm going to ice the biscuits with Holly!' she protested.

'I need to clear up the kitchen and do one or two other things first,' I told her. 'We'll do it when you come back in. And it's so bitterly cold out there that I'm not sure they should go out today, even double-rugged.'

'So, who made you an equine expert suddenly?' Jude said rudely.

'Oh, you only have to explain something to Holly once, and

she's got it,' Becca said. 'But the horses can probably go out for a couple of hours. They've got the field shelter.'

When they went out Jude got up too, narrowly missing his head on the lamp that hung over the table.

'Could we have a word?' I asked.

'Later. I want to have a look at Lady in the daylight myself without her rug, and make sure she hasn't lost any condition. *And* check on the generator – which, by the way, you needn't go near now I'm back. After that I'll be in my room next to the library, catching up with the mail.'

'Yes, but—'

'Later!' he snapped again and went out before I could point out that there probably wasn't going to be any post for a while and also that, if he meant his email, the phone was off, making a dial-up connection impossible.

And before I could mention my urgent desire to remove myself from under his roof.

Chapter 23: Pieced Together

At my news N went quite pale with shock, though he quickly recovered and took me in his arms, repeatedly reassuring me that everything would be all right. He was so much his old, loving, sweet self that I went back to my lodgings feeling very much better.

May, 1945

A little later the generator stopped roaring suddenly as the mains electricity came back on. According to Noël, in winter it flickers on and off more often than the fairy lights on the tree. Still, at least the generator had switched itself off, as it was supposed to.

By late morning we were all gathered in the sitting room over elevenses of tea, coffee and, by Tilda's request, the Dundee cake that was Old Nan's annual gift to them.

'Then we can say how much we enjoyed it, when we see her,' she pointed out.

'*Are* we seeing her?' asked Guy.

'Oh yes, she and Richard will be here for dinner as usual tomorrow.'

Jess and I had water-iced the biscuits in bright colours and were hanging them on the tree with loops of embroidery silk that she had found in an old Victorian sewing box from the morning room, for want of ribbon. Becca was steadying the ladder while I reached up to do the higher branches.

Tilda was on the sofa in front of the fire, with Merlin on the rug at her feet, and Noël, Michael and Guy were at the table in the window, trying to finish piecing together one edge of the jigsaw that I'd bought at Oriel Comfort's shop, with Coco restlessly watching them from the window seat. There is something very compulsive about a jigsaw puzzle, although it didn't seem to have that effect on Coco; but then, that was probably nicotine deprivation.

Jude had retired to his little studio office next to the library, though he must have heard Coco's screech when she finally saw George's tractor coming up the drive pushing aside the fresh snow like an icebreaker, because he was there when I came back from letting him in.

I expect I must have looked a little bit pink and ruffled, but I regained my composure while George got over his surprise at finding Jude back from America.

'Never mind that,' interrupted Coco from the window seat. 'What I want to know is, has the road been cleared, so we can get away?'

'I hope by "we" you mean you and Michael,' Guy said.

'If you are going to be so mean and I can't get my car out, then I'm sure Michael would drop me at a railway station.'

George took off his battered felt hat and ran his fingers through his thick thatch of silver-fair hair so that it stood on end. 'Hold your horses! Liam had a hell of a job clearing the lane down to the village this morning, the old snow's ridged into ice underneath the fresh stuff. And young Ben from Weasel's Pot was at the pub, and he told him the lane below the farm is impassable and nothing's moving down on the main Great Mumming road either.'

'But that's ridiculous! Surely, if Jude got up here last night, it's possible to drive down again?' Coco exclaimed.

'It hadn't frozen over with all this fresh snow on top last night,' George said, looking her over dispassionately, as if she was a rather poor heifer.

'And I only just made it up the hill to Weasel Pot with chains on the wheels,' Jude put in.

'Yes, and though I don't doubt you could get down to the village and back, it would be pointless going further, you'd just get stuck,' George agreed.

'But you or someone else with a tractor could get me out of here, couldn't you?' wheedled Coco in a little-girl voice. 'Me will pay you wots and wots of money!'

'Excuse me while I throw up,' I muttered.

George shook his head. 'I told you, it's impassable.'

'But presumably the council will be out clearing the main road by now, won't they?' suggested Michael. 'Might it be possible later today?'

'You can't have been listening to the weather forecast or watched the news – the snow's wreaked havoc all over the country. The council won't bother with the little roads either, when it's all they can do to clear the main ones.'

'Guy!' Coco said, turning to him. '*Do* something!'

'Don't look at me, I can't perform miracles,' he said and she gave an angry sob.

'It's your fault I'm here in the first place! Mummy and Daddy will be wondering where on earth I am, and they've invited the whole family round on Boxing Day to meet you because we're engaged *and* bought champagne to toast us. And—'

'Oh God, she's going hysterical again,' Becca said disgustedly. 'Shall I throw some cold water on her? *Please* let me do it this time – I'd feel so much better!'

'Now, Becca,' Noël chided. 'The poor child's just a little overset.'

But Coco was not so far gone that she hadn't heard this implied threat. She retreated to sob quietly on a sofa as far removed from Becca as possible and Michael followed her after a minute and sat next to her, talking quietly and patting her hand.

'I'll be off then,' said George, looking hopefully at me, but I avoided his eye and let Guy see him out this time.

'It looks as if I'm stuck with all of you over Christmas, unless some miraculous thaw takes place, which seems unlikely,' Jude said with resignation when Guy came back.

'We might as well make the most of it, then,' Guy said. 'Coco, do stop making that noise.'

'I c-can't help it – I want to go home!' she wailed.

'It's not looking very likely at the moment.'

'I'm sorry to put you out like this,' Michael apologised to Jude.

'Oh, *you're* the least of my worries. Don't give it a thought.'

'Perhaps someone will help me dig out my car, just in case it does thaw out this afternoon?' I asked. Jude turned and looked at me from his treacle-dark eyes and snapped, 'Why, where the hell do you think *you're* going?'

'Home, if I can get out. But if not, I thought perhaps the pub might do rooms . . . I mean, now you're back, the job I was hired for is finished, isn't it?'

'Not so fast,' he said, 'you invited a houseful of people here and promised to cook for them, so you can't just take off like that.'

'Actually, I only invited half of them.'

'But, Holly, you can't go,' wailed Jess, 'it won't be as much fun without you! And what's more, Uncle Jude can't cook!'

'There is that,' he admitted. 'Though of course, Tilda can.'

'Tilda can't cope with the cooking, not after her fall,' Noël said. 'She's still recovering.'

'Load of old fusspots – I'm fine,' Tilda insisted. 'Though why spoil things when Holly and I have everything organised between us?'

Jude turned his dark eyes forbiddingly in my direction. 'Anyway, when did I say I wanted *you* to leave? And, by the way, the pub *doesn't* let rooms.'

'You *didn't* say you wanted me to. But now you're here, the job I was engaged for is ended and I'm sure you would rather I went, so—'

221

'The job damned-well isn't ended!' he interrupted. 'I'm paying you at great expense to do the cooking for my family over Christmas and you're going to stay and earn your money, every last penny of it!'

'Oh, no, you're quite wrong, Jude,' Noël told him, looking surprised. 'Holly refuses to charge us any extra, though I have told her she should be paid for all her extra trouble, when she was expecting to have a peaceful couple of weeks on her own.'

'I don't find cooking for you any trouble,' I assured him.

'Of course she doesn't,' said Tilda. 'And very good she is, too.'

'Thank you,' I said, touched by this unexpected tribute.

'Not as good as me, obviously, but very good,' she qualified.

'Loth though I am to disillusion you both,' Jude said to them, 'I am in fact going to be paying Homebodies through the nose for Holly's services.'

'No, you're not,' I corrected him. 'It's your own fault if you assumed I would do anything you wanted if you offered me enough money, but I've already told Ellen that I'll only be putting in a bill for house-sitting and any extra groceries I've had to buy.'

I smiled at Tilda and Noël. 'I was enjoying myself, actually.'

'And of course you must stay, Holly, we wouldn't dream of letting you do anything else!' Noël insisted. 'In any case, if she can't get out, what is she supposed to do, camp out alone in the lodge until she can leave?'

'I'd be very happy to stay at the lodge, if you didn't mind?'

'No, no, of course you are staying here, m'dear!'

'Yes, for we've decided the menus right through to Twelfth Night!' said Tilda.

'And Holly's not only a brilliant cook, she's *fun*,' Jess told her uncle. 'Merlin loves her too,' she added as a clincher.

Indeed Merlin, deducing from his master's voice that he was angry with me, now clambered onto my lap and was facing him protectively, all long, dangling limbs and rough fur.

'He does seem to be her shadow, I can't think what's got into him,' Jude said, staring at his dog. 'So, Holly Brown, you've wormed your way into the heart of the family in a very short space of time, haven't you? You seem to be a very dangerous, Becky Sharp sort of woman to me. And I'm *still* positive I know you from somewhere.'

Having read *Vanity Fair*, I wasn't too keen on being likened to Becky Sharp – and I certainly wasn't a fortune hunter out to marry him!

'We all thought she looked familiar too,' Noël said, 'but I expect it's only that she has the Martland look – the dark hair, height and light olive skin. So not only does she feel like a member of the family already, she also looks like one and fits right in!'

'I suppose that could be it,' Jude agreed.

'But I get my light grey eyes and dark hair from my grand-mother,' I put in quickly. 'In fact, apart from being tall and dark, I don't *really* look like any of you.'

'You're much prettier than Jude, that's for sure,' said Guy, eyeing me thoughtfully. 'Though *pretty* isn't really the right word – you're beautiful, in an unusual way.'

'What, me?' I said, astonished. After years of bullying about my height and looks, not to mention Gran's repeated assertion that I had no reason to be vain, I found this hard to believe.

'Yes – even George looked smitten with you – and if he didn't kiss you under that handy bunch of mistletoe in the porch before you brought him in, why were you blushing?'

'It was nothing, he just took me by surprise. I hadn't even noticed the mistletoe hung in the porch until he grabbed me.' I could feel myself going pink again, because there was no mistaking that George fancied me!

'Becca and I hung that up,' Noël explained. 'There's always a bunch of mistletoe there.'

Behind me, Coco's piercing voice could be heard saying to

Michael, 'Guy said that housekeeper woman was beautiful – but she's not, is she? And I mean, she might be tall enough to be a model, but she's *way* too fat!'

I turned round and snapped, 'If you think being a healthy weight is fat, then you're sick! In any case, I'd rather be fat than so skinny I rattled when I walked! Excuse me: if no-one's leaving, I'd better go and do something about lunch.'

I went out to the kitchen since clearly I hadn't got much option but to stay, unless the roads miraculously cleared and this now seemed unlikely. Lunch was only going to be soup and sandwiches and I would lay it in the sitting room. I was getting tired of having so many people underfoot in my kitchen. There were some nice pale blue two-handled soup cups with saucers and stacks of paper napkins. I'd found a stash of real linen ones in the downstairs cupboard, but as far as I was concerned they could stay there until Jude had managed to find a handy skivvy willing to wash and iron them for her lord and master after use.

A few minutes later Jude followed me in and closed the door, then stood there with his arms folded, looking at me in a frowning, puzzled sort of way. I ignored him, as much as you could ignore something that size glowering at you, while I put the soup on the stove and got out some little oval tins of expensive game pâté I'd discovered in one of the cupboards. The use-by date was the end of December, so they needed eating.

'I wish you'd sit down and stop looming about,' I snapped eventually. 'Cooking isn't a spectator sport, you know.'

He pulled out the sturdiest of the wheelback chairs and sat on it and it protested, but weakly: I think it knew its place.

'My mother liked to cook and I loved to watch her,' he said unexpectedly.

'I envy you that, because I never knew mine: she died when I was born. Gran told me lots about her, but it's not the same thing,' I said, softened by this picture of him as a child, hard though it was to imagine now. 'Perhaps some of the cookery books on the shelf are hers?'

'I expect they are, but she was just an amateur, while you, as you told me on the phone, are a highly-paid cook.'

'Chef.'

'Whatever.' He fixed his treacle-dark eyes on me and I noticed for the first time that they had disconcertingly mesmerising flecks of gold in them . . .

I wrenched my gaze away with an effort and carried on with what I was doing and he said, 'Look, Holly, I don't understand what game you're playing, though it's pretty clear you're up to *something*; but since we need your help over Christmas, I'll pay you whatever you want. It seems as if you're going to be stuck here with us, anyway.'

'Unless I go and stay in the lodge? But I'm not *up* to anything and nor did I offer to look after your family for money. I did it because I felt sorry you'd spoilt their Christmas – and also, I *really* like them.'

'So, are you saying you were just winding me up when you told me your charges were astronomical and that I couldn't afford them?' He scowled blackly at me.

'My cooking charges *are* astronomical, but I didn't actually say I was going to bill you for them at any point, did I? I told Ellen not to.'

'You let me assume you were!'

'Only because you annoyed me by assuming I was totally mercenary.'

'I don't know what's the matter with you – I got on fine with Jim and Mo! And surely you can't be this rude to all your clients?'

'I only give back as good as I get! In fact, I'm a perfectly calm, competent and reasonable person.'

'Oh yes, *perfectly* reasonable: after all, you only implied I'd neglected my elderly relatives and then got me so worried that you wouldn't look after them properly that I got on the first

225

plane back from America. *Then* I found you'd filled my house full of people.'

'*I* filled your house? Whose family, ghastly ex-fiancée, free-loading brother and refugee actor are they anyway, may I ask?' I demanded. 'And did anyone ask *me* if I wanted to double the number of people I was cooking for? *Or* offer to help me – apart from Michael, who isn't part of your family at all!'

We glared at each other. He was looking a bit rough, which was probably equal parts bad temper and jet lag . . . or maybe he always looked like that?

'If your uncle and aunt wouldn't mind, perhaps it *would* be best if I removed myself down to the lodge,' I said after a minute. 'I'll leave you detailed instructions for cooking dinner tomorrow and tonight's is really quite simple. I can show you the menu plans and Tilda will tell you—'

'Just stop right there!' he snarled, then wearily rubbed a hand across his tired face and gave a long sigh. 'Look, Holly, I think perhaps we've simply got off on the wrong foot. Couldn't we put the past behind us and start again? If I apologise in fifteen different positions and not mention money, will you *please* stay over Christmas and do the cooking?'

There was a slight element of gritted teeth about this apology and proposal and I said suspiciously, 'What, as general skivvy?'

'As a house guest who has kindly offered to do the cooking.'

'I'll think about it,' I said, 'perhaps you are right, and we should let bygones be bygones and start over again. But meanwhile, if your vacuous ex-fiancée demands another egg-white omelette, I might just oblige and then rub her silly face in it.'

He grinned suddenly with genuine amusement and I blinked at the transformation: he looked younger – perhaps not much older than me – and if he wasn't handsome, he was still interestingly attractive . . . if you liked the strong-featured, hard-jawed type, that is.

'She has elderly parents who've spoiled her rotten, but she's

226

not usually quite this bad.' He paused and added, 'Was it my imagination or was she turning the charm on me at breakfast?'

'Only in a general way, I think,' I said, considering this. 'She's all over Michael like a rash, of course, but then, he's apparently a well-known actor and she's met him before, so it isn't really surprising.'

'I got the impression he was just soothing her down, because it's *you* he seems to be getting on with like a house on fire. In fact, if you've been snogging George as well, you seem to have managed to get off with two total strangers in no time at all.'

'I wasn't snogging George and I haven't "got off", as you put it, with either of them,' I said with dignity. 'They're just both very nice men.'

'Well, my brother isn't and he seemed to be eyeing you up a bit, too.'

'What, saying I was beautiful?' I laughed. 'Oh, that's silly, he was just winding Coco up. I think he's being a bit cruel to her, because he must have led her on to think they were going to get married, or she wouldn't have sent off the announcement and told her parents, would she?'

'You've met her now: *you* tell *me*.' He got up, narrowly missing the lamp suspended over the kitchen table. 'So, do we have an agreement? You'll stay and do the cooking?'

'I suppose so,' I agreed reluctantly. 'But I'm doing it for Jess, Noël, Tilda and Becca – and for Old Nan and Richard.'

'Richard?' He raised a thick dark eyebrow. 'Another man you're on first-name terms with already?'

'Don't be so daft, you great streak of nowt,' I said crisply, which had been one of my grandmother's favourite put-downs to uppity men, and he grinned again and got up, clearly taking my agreement for granted.

But by then I'd realised that flouncing off to the lodge and being a hermit really wasn't an option anyway, not when there was a Christmas dinner to cook, and people I was fond of who would be disappointed if it wasn't right.

'I'll stay until after Boxing Day, at least, then see what the roads are like. But until then, this is *my* kitchen and I won't have any interference with my cooking – is that understood?'

'I can't guarantee that from Tilda,' he said dubiously.

'That's all right, she doesn't interfere, just *suggests*.'

'Then it's a bargain,' he said gravely and offered me a shapely, long-fingered hand the size of a bunch of bananas. At least, unlike Henry, he didn't spit in his palm first.

Chapter 24: Birkin Mad

Hilda and Pearl said N should have asked me to marry him right away, but I am positive he will when we meet again on Thursday and then all will be well.

May, 1945

After lunch it was pretty clear that the weather wasn't going to change: in fact, the sky was ominously pewter-coloured again. Coco still didn't seem to grasp that some way couldn't be found to get her home and in the end said that if no-one would help her, then she was going to walk to the village and possibly even down to the main road, where her phone would work and she could summon help.

'Who from?' asked Guy interestedly.

'The AA? The police? *Someone* to take me back to civilisation!'

'Look, it's not going to happen, much though we wish it would,' Jude said impatiently.

'No, nothing short of a helicopter could do the trick, I'm afraid,' Noël told her. 'But I'm sure we will all have a fun Christmas together,' he added optimistically.

'A helicopter!' She seized on the idea avidly. 'The air-sea rescue people could—'

'Oh, don't be so stupid,' Jude snapped. 'You can't ask the emergency services to helicopter you out, just because you want to go home!'

'I don't think there's really anywhere flat enough for them to land anyway,' Noël said, considering it. 'Only the green, and the houses are all a bit too close to that. Of course, they can winch people up.'

'Well then, Jude could take me down to the main road where there is bound to be somewhere flat enough. I can phone Mummy and Daddy and get them to arrange something. Or you can lend your Land Rover to Guy and we could both—'

'Nothing doing,' said Guy. 'Give it up.'

'You're all so horrible to me, except Noël and Michael! I want to talk to Mummy and Daddy,' she whined.

'If you start that howling again, I'm going to slap you,' Becca said uncompromisingly, which seemed to work just as well as threatening her with a drenching.

'Look, Coco,' said Michael kindly, 'I ought to phone my friends and let them know what's happened to me, so why don't you and I walk down towards the village together until we can get mobile signals? It'll give us a chance to see what conditions are really like, too.'

'All right,' she agreed sulkily, 'but if I can find someone who can get me out of here, I'm not coming back!'

'We'd better find you both something more practical to wear before you set out, then,' Tilda observed. 'You won't get very far dressed like that.'

Becca rooted out old wellingtons and waxed coats that more or less fitted and they set off down the drive, Coco's rather Dr Zhivago white fur hat striking a strange note. They walked through the virgin snow at the side of the drive, so where the tractor had ploughed must have been too slippery.

'I hope they're going to be all right and Coco doesn't do anything stupid,' I said, watching them from the sitting-room window until they disappeared into the pine trees above the lodge.

'Michael seems a sensible chap, so I'll be surprised if they go very far,' Jude said, 'and even Coco will be able to see that it's impossible to get out. Not that I want her or Guy here, of course, but I'm prepared to put up with them under the circumstances.'

'Thanks,' said Guy dryly.

Jude looked measuringly at his brother. 'Don't think I've forgotten how you behaved last Christmas, though, and how much it all upset Father, when he was so ill,' he said evenly.

Guy looked slightly shamefaced. 'No, well – look, I'm really sorry about that! It's just that as soon as I set eyes on Coco I fell madly in love – she's so stunningly pretty.'

'You did? I thought you just took her away because she was my fiancée!'

'No,' Guy said wryly, 'I fell for her, hook, line and sinker. But then I fell out of love with her quite suddenly, just after she sent that engagement notice to the papers. It was quite a wake-up call. What about you?'

'*Me?*' Jude said. 'Oh, the minute I saw her again. In fact, in retrospect, you might have done me a favour by breaking up our engagement, because I don't think I'd grasped before quite how silly she is! I must have been blinded by her looks.'

'Me too,' agreed Guy. 'It's strange how when I thought I was in love with her, everything she said seemed funny and endearing, whereas now it's intensely irritating.'

'Still, that's not her fault – but it *is* yours that we're landed with her for Christmas,' Jude said. 'You'll have to look after her and see she doesn't make a huge nuisance of herself until we can get her out of here – and also has a bit of fun, too.'

'That's a tall order – but Michael might do the trick. He's a good-looking guy and a well-known actor and she seems to be turning her sights on him a bit, did you notice?'

Jude nodded. 'Yes, she was wittering on about acting and some TV commercial she'd been in. Okay, let's foist her onto him, that should keep her happy and occupied.'

'That's so unfair – Michael's way too nice for Coco!' I exclaimed unguardedly and they both looked at me.

'Have *you* got your eye on him too? You'll have to work fast if you don't want Coco to cut you out,' advised Guy. 'You haven't seen her when she swings into action!'

'Don't be silly, I barely know the man,' I snapped. 'But I *can* see he's good-natured and kind, which is more than can be said of you two!'

'Attagirl,' commended Tilda drowsily from the sofa. Then she swung her tiny feet off it and slid them into her marabou and velvet mules. 'Well, I'm glad you two boys are friends again.'

'I wouldn't go quite that far,' Jude said, but when she insisted on them shaking hands he did so and even allowed a relieved Guy to thump him affectionately on the back.

'Pax?' Guy said hopefully.

'Pax,' Jude agreed.

'Have I missed something?' asked Noël, who had been snoring away on his own sofa like a small buzz-saw for the last ten minutes.

'The boys are friends again, Noël, and I think I will go and have a little rest on my bed now,' Tilda said. 'What are the rest of you going to do this afternoon?'

'I'm going down to the studio for an hour or two,' Jude said. 'Make sure everything is all right.'

'You could have walked down there with Michael and Coco,' Noël pointed out.

'I could, but I didn't want to.'

'Can I come with you, Uncle Jude?' asked Jess.

'Yes, if you wrap up warmly.'

'And Holly, too?'

'Oh no,' I said quickly, 'I'll be glad of some time to myself in the kitchen, there's lots to do.'

'You never stop,' Becca commented. 'Cooking seems to me to be very hard work!'

'It is, and especially hard on the feet: that's why I usually have a rest from it over the winter. But I do like cooking and I've never catered for a large Christmas house-party before, so all this is a novelty and a challenge.'

Jess said, 'Holly's writing a cookery book, but she hasn't thought of a good title yet.'

'We could have a brainstorming session later,' suggested Guy.

'Thanks, but I'll storm my own brain in due course,' I replied and retired to the comforting ambience of the kitchen. Merlin went with me, though he did cast a 'my loyalties are divided' look back at Jude. He's so much happier when we're in the same room – and I'm starting to get the feeling that Jess is, too!

I added more vegetables to the soup pot and put it on the Aga, then did a bit of food prepping for later, including bringing the turkey into the kitchen to come to room temperature for tomorrow. But really what I wanted to do was search among the recipe books on the shelf to see if I could find anything like the Revel Cakes that Nancy at the pub had described. And the very first book on the shelf, the big, fat, red hardback copy of *Mrs Beeton*, turned out instead to be a box, full of handwritten recipes and cuttings from magazines and newspapers: quite fascinating! This kind of thing is like treasure trove to a keen cook.

The Revel Cake recipe was in there, written in a faded copper-plate hand on thick cream paper. I copied it out into my own notebook and put the original back into the box. It seemed to be a spicy bun mixture, with one or two additions, like saffron and a sprinkle of chopped candied peel on top, and I expect it evolved into that over centuries from something very much plainer. You pulled the dough into a long roll and then made little concentric coils, like fossil ammonites. If I was here long enough and had the time, I could make and freeze batches to leave for Twelfth Night. I wondered how many would be needed?

The house seemed to have gone pleasantly peaceful and when I put my head through the sitting room door it was empty, apart from Becca, stretched out asleep on the largest of the sofas. There must be something naturally soporific oozing out of the walls.

I could hear the TV from the morning room, some kind of sport, going by the roars, so Guy was probably in there with Noël.

I threw another log on the fire and then retired to the kitchen again, this time to read a bit more of Gran's latest journal. Now I'd met Jude Martland and his attractively untrustworthy brother, I even more urgently wanted to discover if Gran really had been pregnant and, if so, whether Ned was going to offer to do the right thing by her. I can't say it was looking very promising at the moment and if Guy is really like his uncle, then Ned can't have had any staying power whatsoever. And in that case, I really wouldn't want to find I was even *distantly* related to his family!

But if my mother *was* Ned Martland's daughter, then my grandfather was the brother of Jude and Guy's father, which would make us cousins – removed cousins it's true, though not, if Ned abandoned Gran, far enough for my liking!

Then I thought of dear Noël, Becca, Jess and even Tilda, who I am growing fond of despite her being such an old toot, and realised that I wouldn't mind being related to *them* at all.

I restrained the urge to skim forward in the journal, but settled down with my fingers crossed, hoping that maybe Gran wasn't pregnant after all, broke up with the untrustworthy-sounding Ned, and married my grandfather instead.

Unfortunately, everything in the journal pointed to a different conclusion – as did my mother's birth certificate when I went upstairs and had a rummage in the trunk and found it. This was probably why I was a bit short with Jude when he and Jess came back, bringing a breath of chilly air with them.

Jess said she'd made a snowman while Jude had been messing

about in his studio, and that the mill pond was almost completely frozen over.

I shivered: 'You didn't go on the ice, did you?'

'No, I wanted to, but Uncle Jude told me not to.'

'What's the delicious smell? And are those scones?' Jude asked hungrily.

'It's just the soup – I like to keep a big pot going in winter. And the scones are cheese ones for tea. I was just about to take them through to the sitting room. I thought Tilda might be down by now.'

'Whatever I ought to be paying you, you'd be worth it,' he said sincerely, taking the tray I'd set out.

'And as I keep telling you: you couldn't afford me.'

He looked down at me curiously. 'I don't know why you're so convinced I'm penniless.'

'Oh, I'm sure you're not *entirely* penniless, but you're an artist with a neglected house and no live-in staff, so clearly you aren't exactly rolling in it.'

'It's a lifestyle choice.'

'What, the grubby, neglected house?'

'No, I meant not having any staff living in. Actually,' he added, 'I hadn't realised the house *was* getting in a mess until I came back and saw how much better it looked now.'

'You shouldn't have been so stingy and paid Sharon a bit more, then. She wasn't exactly going to bust a gut for half the minimum wage, was she?'

'Is that what she told you I paid her?'

'Yes, and no Christmas bonus either. Do you mean – it wasn't true?'

He laughed. 'No – and so much for trying to do a good turn! When I advertised the job she came to me with a sob story about her husband being unemployed and being so angry he was taking it out on her. I felt so sorry for her I took her on – and paid her double.'

235

'*Double?*'

'Yes, believe it or not. Then I realised how useless she was *and* caught her trying to steal some of my sketches from the wastepaper basket in the study. I really wanted to get rid of her, I just didn't know how.'

'Oh . . . then I'm sorry. I thought you were mean as well as poor,' I apologised.

'Uncle Jude's got lots of money, Holly,' Jess said. 'Mummy says his sculptures sell for ridiculous amounts and he's rolling in it.'

Jude gave me the strangely attractive smile that softened the hard line of his mouth and quirked it up at one corner. 'You didn't think Coco wanted me for my good looks alone, did you? So yes, whatever your charges are, I could pay them. But since you won't accept that, I'm under an obligation to you.'

'You needn't be, because I'm not doing it for you.'

'I know, but I still feel under an obligation. I'll just have to find another way to pay you.'

I discovered I was still staring up (a novelty in itself) into his gold-flecked dark eyes and hastily looked away. 'Did you see Coco and Michael?'

'No, but everyone else is in the sitting room. I thought they'd be back by now, but they must have gone on to the village.'

'I hope Coco doesn't try anything silly.'

'Michael seems the sensible kind, I don't suppose he'd let her.'

'What are we having for dinner tonight?' asked Jess, getting on to something she considered more important.

'Pheasant pie with redcurrant jelly and winter vegetables. I'm making great inroads into the frozen pheasants. And we'll have the trifle for pudding, if you help me whip the cream and sprinkle hundreds and thousands on it later.'

'Or we can use squirty cream, that's my favourite.'

'Yes, I noticed and I got the last of Mrs Comfort's stock, so you can use as much as you want to.'

'Cool! But I don't know if I like pheasant pie.'

'You can try it and see, and if not, I'm bringing the ham through as well so we can take the first cut at that: it's a monster and should last for days.'

Eventually the remains would turn into pea and ham soup, *my* favourite – if I was here long enough to make it.

I slipped out of the back door later and made for the track up the hill to call Laura, but the snow had drifted across it quite deeply in places and the signal was still poor when I had to stop. Then we kept getting cut off, which was frustrating.

I managed to tell her about the ghastly Coco and the handsome love-rat Guy landing on me. 'And if Guy is like Ned Martland, as they keep telling me he is, then I can understand why poor Gran fell for him, though it's looking more and more as though he got her pregnant and then abandoned her, just as I feared.'

I lost the signal then, but when I got her back I dropped the final bombshell: 'But the icing on the cupcake of life is that Jude Martland turned up late last night, too!'

'But he was supposed to be in America, wasn't he?'

'Yes, but he thought I was a cold-hearted, money-grubbing bitch who wouldn't look after his aunt and uncle after Tilda had her accident!' I said indignantly. 'So he just got on the first plane home. *And* I like him even less in person than I did on the phone, if that's possible.'

'Hasn't he got any redeeming features?'

'He might have one or two,' I admitted reluctantly, 'but the annoying parts outweigh them.'

'So, why aren't you on your way home, then?'

'We seem to be snowed in and none of us can escape, unless we get a sudden thaw.'

'Sounds like a fun house-party, then!'

'Yes,' I agreed glumly. 'The only good thing is that Jude brought an actor called Michael Whiston with him.'

'Oh, I've heard of him, he's very attractive!'

'Yes he is, and also a really nice man and – oh, damn!' The connection had cut for the third time, so when I got her back I said, 'This is hopeless, so I'll give up and try again tomorrow. Give my love to the family.'

'And Sam?' she asked hopefully, but then the signal symbol vanished once more and I shoved the phone back into my pocket and trudged back down the hill, where no-one except Merlin had noticed my absence.

The afternoon was beginning to grow dark and I, at least, was getting worried about Michael and Coco, when the familiar tractor appeared up the drive, this time with a gritting trailer behind it and a youth at the wheel who I guessed from his silver-gilt hair to be George's son, Liam.

Crammed into the cab with him were our two missing refugees. By the time I'd opened the door, Liam was helping a drunk, tearstained and dishevelled Coco out of the cab, followed by Michael, who was looking long-suffering and carrying one of Oriel Comfort's inspirational hessian bags: *Raindrops Are God's Tears of Joy*.

Liam gave me a wink and a knowing grin that I found hard to interpret – or perhaps didn't *wish* to interpret – then jumped back into the cab and roared off, spraying a generous flourish of grit as he went.

'I see you found the shop open?' I said to Michael, with a nod at the bag, and he smiled.

'Once I'd seen the state of the roads it occurred to me that since we were clearly going nowhere for Christmas, I ought to contribute a bit to the festivities here. Then once I was in the shop, something came over me.'

'You mean Oriel Comfort came over you: she's *very* persuasive. You should see what I bought last time! But come in, you both look freezing.'

Since Coco seemed likely to remain drooping there like a half-melted candle, Michael took her arm and towed her in after him. 'We're not too cold, actually – we were freezing when we got to the village, of course, but I left Coco in the pub to phone her parents and thaw out while I was in the shop.'

'So I see,' I closed the front door and surveyed her. She swayed slightly and blearily focused her ice-chip eyes on me.

'Mummy said Daddy had the flu, so Christmas and our engagement party were cancelled anyway! She said there was no point in my rushing back, I should stay here – but they never liked Guy anyway.'

'Right . . .' I said soothingly, removing her waxed coat and hanging it up on a peg, then pushing her down and pulling off her wellingtons, while Michael divested himself of his own borrowings.

'And when I said what about my presents, because I was *so* looking forward to finally getting a Birkin bag, she said, "What Birkin bag?" Coco continued in a high-pitched whine. 'Can you believe it? I told her months ago to get on the list for one, because it was what I wanted for Christmas, and the stupid cow forgot!'

'I don't think you should call your mother a stupid cow,' I said, any feelings of faint sympathy vanishing abruptly. Coco had all the warmth and emotional depth of a winter puddle: how on earth could seemingly intelligent men like Jude and Guy ever have fallen for her?

She gave me another bleary look and said rudely, 'Who cares what *you* think?' Then she heaved herself up. 'I'm going to have a hot bath.'

'Let's hope she doesn't fall unconscious and drown in it,' Michael said, though not with any great concern, so she must have tried even his good nature and patience to the limit. 'I think I'll go up and follow suit, if that's all right?'

'Yes, good idea. Come on, I'll make you a hot drink to take with you. Did you have any lunch?'

'Yes, bread and cheese in the pub, though Coco's lunch was entirely liquid, as you see. Her parents should have christened her Vodka, not Coco.'

As his contribution to the festivities, Michael had very thoughtfully bought two large boxes of chocolates and three bottles of the special sherry from the pub that Nancy had told him the older members of the party favoured.

'Oh good,' I said, relieved. 'Becca brought some, but the way they knock it back, it wasn't going to last. And the chocolates will go down well, too.'

'I've also got a small gift for everyone,' he admitted, 'from Mrs Comfort's *Sunbeams are God's Thoughts* range.'

'I bought a few things too, but mine are mostly edible gifts. I'm going to put them under the tree later.'

'I'll do the same, then, and I've bought wrapping paper, but if you have a roll of Sellotape I could borrow, that would be great.'

He's such a nice, kind, thoughtful man and I really like him! I'm going to give him one of the extra jars of sweets I've already wrapped. I suppose I should give one to Coco, too, but she isn't going to want sweets, I wouldn't have thought: too full of sugar.

And nothing, in her eyes, will compare to her longed-for Birkin bag, anyway.

Chapter 25: Christmas Carol

I waited and waited in our usual place and N did not come. What am I to think? Surely something must have happened to prevent him coming and I will get a message soon? Or is this some terrible kind of retribution for my sins?

May, 1945

Jude and Jess did the horses together to give Becca a rest and then Guy, all charm, offered to lay the dining table (we were dining more formally tonight, it being Christmas Eve) and help me in any other way, and I took him up on it. He and Michael (who had come back down with his wrapped gifts and put them under the tree), did all the donkey work and carried things through for me.

When everything was under control in the kitchen and everyone was in the sitting room, including a sullen and still not entirely sober Coco dressed in something scarlet and scanty, I took in a tray of filo pastry savoury starters and stayed for a drink.

Michael had presented his sherry and chocolates to Tilda, presumably as titular presiding lady of the house, the alpha female of our wolf pack. He was now so much in favour that when everyone else had gone through to the dining room and he was helping me to carry through the main course, he told me he felt just like an invited house guest and that he thought

Christmas at Old Place would probably be more fun than with the friends he was intending to stay with.

'It's certainly going to be different to any Christmas *I've* ever had,' I said, and told him a little about my Strange Baptist upbringing and how I had only really celebrated Christmas in a religious way, apart from the all too brief years of my marriage.

'And then my husband died in an accident at this time of year, and my mother too – and now my gran, who brought me up: so you see, celebrating Christmas doesn't come naturally to me!'

'No, I can see why you would much rather have ignored the whole thing,' he agreed, and then gave me a kind hug. 'Poor Holly!'

Jude, who had just come into the kitchen, stopped dead on the threshold. 'I came to see if you wanted me to do anything for you – but Michael seems to have got that covered,' he said rather surlily and went out again, closing the door with a near slam.

'What's biting him?' I exclaimed.

'I expect he thinks we're getting a bit too friendly,' Michael said with a grin. 'He's probably jealous.'

'Don't be daft, he doesn't like me, so why should he be jealous? Maybe he disapproves of the help getting matey with the guests?'

'But Coco seems to be the only one who thinks of you as staff.'

'She appears to be transferring her affections from Guy to you, have you noticed? You'd better watch your step, Michael!'

'I will, but I expect it's only because she thinks I can help her into acting – which I can't, of course, even if she can act, which I doubt very much.'

'No, I should think she can only play one part: Coco,' I agreed.

The dining table looked lovely, with a red damask cloth and red candles in the silver holders.

Coco remained silent and sullen for most of dinner, eating little and drinking too much and Jude had gone quite morose too, though he doesn't appear to be a laugh a minute person anyway. But everyone else seemed in good form even though Jess was clearly over excited about the approach of Christmas Day.

Tilda even complimented me on the pheasant pie and said she couldn't have done it better herself, though I noticed that Coco merely scraped a little of the middle out of her piece and ate it with about a teaspoon of vegetables. Then she reacted with loathing when offered trifle.

'But it's lovely! I did the cream and decorated it, didn't I, Holly?' Jess said.

'Yes, you made it look beautiful. How about an apple or clementine, then, Coco? Or a little cheese?'

'Cheese is full of fat and I hate fruit.'

'So what do you usually eat at home?' I asked curiously.

'If anything,' Jude said, *sotto voce*.

'Steamed fish and edamame beans,' Guy said with a grimace.

'Oh, there's lots of fish in the freezer, Coco – in fact, we're having a whole salmon on Boxing Day. But there aren't any edamame beans.'

'I don't even know what they are,' Jess said.

'They've only really got popular lately – stars seem to eat them a lot. I don't know why, because I don't find them very exciting,' I said.

'I'm sure *Michael* knows what they are,' Coco said, her intimate smile clearly meant to show that they inhabited the same, more sophisticated, world. Now she'd had another glass of wine she'd perked up again, unfortunately, and was turning the full battery of her charm on Michael. He began to look a little nervous.

She said she was sorry she'd been upset earlier, but knew he would understand the artistic temperament. Then she told him all about the facial elixir advert all over again, and how her agent was going to send her for an important role in a new film, and kept on and on, even when Jess sighed loudly and said, 'We know all about that already, Horlicks!'

But this slightly febrile cheerfulness waned a little when we went back into the sitting room and she spotted the heap of gifts under the tree, because they reminded her that she wasn't going to get her Birkin bag.

Jess, who had been lovingly fondling the ones with her name on, said, 'You have got some presents, at least three, Horlicks.'

'I can't imagine why you keep calling me by that silly name,' she said, but looked slightly mollified, though I didn't imagine that she was going to be delirious with pleasure to receive Michael's Oriel Comfort-inspired gift, or the jar of bath scrub I'd hastily whipped up in the kitchen from sea salt, olive oil and essential lavender oil.

I didn't know what the third one was, though going by the rather slapdash wrapping, Jess had put it there. I hoped it wasn't something horrid.

Jude insisted on making the coffee and bringing it through to the sitting room while I relaxed, which was unexpectedly thoughtful of him, though the gesture was spoiled because he also brought the petits fours I'd intended for Boxing Day. Now I'd have to make some more.

The coffee was good, so he's not entirely devoid of kitchen talents. He certainly seemed to like marzipan . . .

'Do you happen to have any more ground almonds at the lodge if I run out?' I asked Tilda.

'Oh yes, I'm sure we have – Edwina uses them a lot. Do go down and rummage in the kitchen and fetch anything you need,' she said graciously.

The men went to play snooker in the library and Coco drifted aimlessly after them.

'Do you think she's anorexic?' Becca said. She was puzzling over the big jigsaw, which hadn't got very far yet. I leaned over her shoulder and moved some pieces of the edge from one side to the other: it was pretty obvious where they went from my angle.

'She does seem to vanish for ages after every meal,' Tilda said. 'Not that she eats much anyway. Maybe she's throwing it back up?'

'She eats loads of laxatives,' Jess said unexpectedly. 'That's weird, isn't it?'

'How do you know?' I asked, surprised.

'I saw her eating what looked like a handful of sweets when she thought she was alone, so I had a look in her handbag and it's stuffed with packets of Fruity-Go. Her bedside table drawer is, too, and she's forever going to the loo.'

'Jess, darling, you really shouldn't root about in other people's rooms,' Tilda said mildly. 'But no wonder she spends ages in the bathroom!'

'That must be how she stays as thin as a tapeworm,' Becca agreed. She and Jess helped carry out the coffee things and then went to play Monopoly with Tilda while I stacked the dishwasher, cleared up the kitchen and fed Merlin.

When I went back into the sitting room, everyone had returned and Guy, Michael and a bored Coco were grouped around the jigsaw puzzle. Jude, Tilda and Jess were finishing a game of Monopoly which Tilda won, a veritable property tycoon.

Noël seemed to be waiting for me. 'Ah, there you are, m'dear – just in time for a Martland family tradition.' He picked up a leather-bound copy of Charles Dickens's *A Christmas Carol*, and began to read aloud, rather beautifully.

Even Coco stopped her restless movements and fixed her eyes on him, though when he reached the part with the ghosts she kept casting nervous glances over her shoulder, as if one might be standing right behind her.

We all applauded at the end and Noël stood up to take a

modest bow. 'Thank you! We used to read a few scenes from *Twelfth Night*, too – but on New Year's Eve.'

Coco came alive and avidly seized on this. '*Twelfth Night*? I know that, we had to do it at school. There are lots of boring bits that are supposed to be funny, but quite a lot of mixed-up love scenes, too.'

'I've played Sebastian in the past, at Stratford,' admitted Michael.

'Then perhaps we should revive the tradition and you could take the part again?' suggested Noël.

'Assuming you're still here by New Year's Eve,' Guy said.

'We could do it earlier if the roads thaw and it looks like we can get away, can't we?' Coco said, and then enthused, 'And why can't we *act* out the parts, not just read them?'

'I suppose we could, if you want to,' Noël said. 'We have several printed copies of the scenes we used to use in the library.'

'You can be Sebastian, Michael, and I will be the fair Olivia,' Coco said, striking a pose. 'Guy, you can be Orsino and I suppose Holly had better be Viola, seeing she's Sebastian's twin and she can look like a man.'

'Thanks,' I said. 'But that doesn't work really, does it? Sebastian and Viola are supposed to be very like each other.'

'The audience will just have to use their imaginations, then,' she snapped, and I could see she was angling to do her love scenes with Michael. However, from what I recalled of the play, that left me to fall for Orsino.

'I hate acting,' Guy said. 'I don't even perform in the Revels, so it'll have to be Jude. Noël will link the scenes as usual and prompt, and I'll be your admiring audience with Tilda, Jess and Becca.'

'I'm not much of an actor either,' Jude said.

'Or me,' I put in hastily.

'Well then, you and Holly can just read the parts, okay?' Coco said impatiently.

She was the only person really keen on doing any acting, presumably to show off her skills to Michael and, perhaps, to get a little closer to him. However, no-one put up much of a protest and Noël said he would find the printed parts the next day.

I expect we were all too relieved that Coco had found something to occupy herself with to object and she became quite animated while talking with Michael about rehearsing.

But still, I thought we would be long gone by New Year's Eve, and she would abandon the play like a shot if she could get away!

Tilda decided to go to bed and ordered Jess upstairs too, though she didn't want to go.

'I'm too excited, I'll never sleep.'

'Then Father Christmas won't come,' Tilda told her.

'Oh, Granny! The presents are all here, and I know it was Mummy who did the stocking last year, because it was so awful. I'm not even hanging one up this time.' But she trailed off after her.

'It's very late, but it's been a pleasant evening,' Becca said and Noël agreed, 'Yes, best get off to bed myself too, I think.'

Even Coco seemed ready to go up – all that emotion and alcohol must have been exhausting, though I noticed she lingered long enough to look at her presents under the tree, which was sort of *slightly* endearing: twenty-four going on five.

Saying good night, the party broke up and vanished one by one, except for Jude, who went to let Merlin out for a last run and check on the horses. I banked the fire up and collected a couple of abandoned sherry glasses and was in the kitchen washing them up when he came back in. Snow flecked his dark hair, so it must have been coming down thick and fast.

Merlin greeted me as if he hadn't seen me for a month instead of a few minutes and Jude regarded him with disfavour. 'That creature must have gone senile in my absence, I think he's forgotten who he belongs to!'

'That reminds me, I must wrap his present up when he's not looking.'

'You got my dog a present?'

'Just a large rawhide bone from Oriel Comfort's shop. She really does stock everything, doesn't she?'

'So much so that I expect her shop to suddenly explode under the strain one day,' he agreed. 'I don't suppose you've some spare Christmas wrapping paper? Only I got a few things in the airport on the way home, when I had time to kill between flights.'

'Yes, Mrs Comfort only had huge rolls of the stuff so there's plenty left, even though Michael's had a bit, too,' I said, getting the paper out of the cupboard.

He muttered something that sounded suspiciously like, 'I bet he has!' then headed out, stopping on the threshold to ask, 'You *are* going to bed now?'

'Yes, I just have one or two last things to do down here first.'

He looked at his watch. 'I almost forgot – it's nearly midnight and, snow or not, Richard will be at the church. Come on!'

Grabbing my hand, he towed me through the silent house to the front door, which he unlocked and threw open. A flurry of snow touched my face and faintly on the breeze I heard the distant, magical sound of church bells in the valley below.

'Merry Christmas!' Jude said as they stopped. Above our heads the bunch of mistletoe revolved in the breeze and he stood very still, looking down into my face. Then, as if driven by some compulsion he would have preferred to have resisted, he bent his head and quickly brushed his lips against mine.

I shivered, but the surprise made me acquiescent, and I was still standing in the open doorway, snow whirling round my head and my face tilted up to his, when he just as suddenly turned on his heel and went off without another word.

Men!

* * *

I transferred the sausage and bacon rolls, stuffing and bread sauce from the freezer to the fridge before I went upstairs to my room.

I'd hidden all the items that were to go into Jess's Christmas stocking in my wardrobe, so when I'd changed into the unexciting long white cotton nightdress and robe that Gran had made for me to the archaic pattern she favoured herself, I laid everything out on the bed next to a large sock. A *very* large sock.

I put a clementine in the toe, since it was a satisfying shape, but had decided against the nuts. Then everything else I'd bought went in, pushed well down, with the yellow-eyed wolf sticking its head out of the top.

After that, I sat reading Gran's journal until I thought Jude would have gone to bed – and *poor* Gran, my guesses had been quite right and her big romance was all going pear-shaped.

Because I'd arrived at that stage of tiredness where you feel spaced-out but entirely awake, I read on for longer than I intended. But at least when I did finally pick up the stocking and tiptoe quietly (apart from some odd rustlings from the stocking) across the gallery and along the west wing passage towards the nursery, the house was silent and everyone was fast asleep . . .

Or so I thought, right up to the moment when Jude's door swung silently open like something from a fairground House of Horrors and he grabbed me and pulled me into his room, closing the door behind us. I gave a strangled yelp and pushed him off, my hands meeting the bare skin of a well-muscled chest . . . an *extremely* well-muscled chest.

'Shhh!' he said, switching the light on, which was possibly even scarier, since he was towering over me wearing only loosely-tied pyjama bottoms. His dark hair was standing on end and I wouldn't be surprised if mine was, too. I dropped my hands as though they'd been burnt and took a step back as he released my arm.

'What on earth were you doing, sneaking round the house at

this time? Where were you going?' he demanded suspiciously in a menacing rumble.

'I *wasn't* sneaking,' I hissed furiously back, 'and you nearly gave me a heart attack, grabbing me like that, you total imbecile! It's just as well I'm not easily frightened.'

His dark eyes wandered down my thin white cotton robe to my bare feet and back again. 'Miss Havisham, I presume?' he said sarcastically. Then he spotted the bulging stocking I was holding. 'Or wait – it must be Mother Christmas! And isn't that one of *my* socks?'

'Yes, if you left it stuffed into a pair of wellies in the garden hall. I washed it yesterday and sewed this bit of ribbon on to hang it from the end of her bed by – it's for Jess.'

'I didn't think you were doing it for me. But isn't Jess too old for that kind of thing?'

'Not according to Mrs Comfort, she says they're never too old. I wouldn't know, I never had one as a child. But Jess did say that last year's was a huge disappointment and she thought her mother only remembered at the last minute.'

'She's a bit scatty, is my cousin Roz. Shoved in a small chocolate selection box and a clementine.' He frowned down at me. 'And what did you mean, you never had a stocking?'

'I was brought up by my grandparents – my gran mostly, because my grandfather was much older than she was. But they were Strange Baptists – he was a minister in the church.'

I waited for him to ask me what was strange about them again, but instead he said, 'Oh yes – I think you mentioned that as the reason you don't usually celebrate Christmas. A bit like the Plymouth Brethren?'

'I suppose so, in some ways: they certainly only celebrated the religious aspects of Christmas.'

I hadn't put my slippers on, because I thought I would be quieter without them and now I realised my feet were blocks of ice and it was more than time to go.

'Fascinating as it is to discuss my childhood and religion with you in the middle of the night, Jude, if you'll excuse me, I'd better get on.'

I tried to push past him, but he was still blocking the way, an inscrutable expression on his face. 'You know, I still find you very hard to read, Holly Brown!'

'Well, don't rack your brains over it,' I said sweetly, 'I'm an open book. Now, I'd like to get this done because I've had to set my alarm *really* early so I can put that enormous turkey in the oven, and if I don't go to bed soon it won't be worth it. What a monster!'

I think he was unsure if I was applying the epithet to him or the turkey, but he finally shifted to one side and I made my escape. But unfortunately, just as I emerged into the passage, I came face to face with Noël, who must have been returning from the bathroom.

However, he merely smiled in an avuncular and unsurprised way and murmured, 'Ah, getting to know each other better, I see? Good, good!' with no apparent innuendo intended, and carried on.

I got a touch of the Cocos and had to clamp my hand across my mouth to keep a hysterical giggle in, while behind me, Jude said, sounding amused, 'We can only hope he was sleepwalking and will have forgotten he saw us in such compromising circumstances by morning.'

I turned to look back coldly at him and in return he gave me an enigmatic smile that I would have quite liked to have smacked off his face. Then he retreated, closing his door silently behind him.

I mouthed a very rude word then tiptoed off up the nursery stairs, turned the handle and crept in. Jess was dimly illuminated by a moon-shaped nightlight, curled up in bed with one arm around her teddy bear, looking angelic and very much younger. I hung the stocking on the end of her bed and sneaked out again.

I only hoped it wasn't a huge disappointment to her, though surely after last year's it had to be an improvement?

This time I walked on the far side of the passage as I passed Jude's room – but my precaution was needless.

Chapter 26: Socked

There is still no word – can he really have abandoned me with so little compunction? I now see how truly I have fallen from grace and I feel the baby is my punishment for it. I do not know what to do . . . where to turn. Hilda and Pearl are my only support – and how I wish now I had heeded their warnings!

May, 1945

I went downstairs very early in jeans and jumper, ready for cooking, not using the backstairs but the dogleg ones from the gallery. Descending slowly into the dark sitting room, I inhaled the strangely exciting mingled scents of woodsmoke and pine needles, which instantly brought to mind past Christmas mornings with Alan, all the more poignant for being happy memories.

I stoked the fire and plumped up the cushions, stuck a few pieces of jigsaw into the last remaining places round the edge (a compulsion too hard to resist), then switched on the tree's fairy lights. They twinkled in the dark corner under the stairs, reflecting off the gift-wrapped pile beneath. It seemed to have grown since I last looked, with an added layer of parcels inexpertly wrapped in the paper I'd bought.

Suddenly I spotted my name on one, written in a bold hand I recognised from all those handwritten additions to the

Homebodies manual. I was just about to pick it up when I firmly stopped myself, because I wasn't a child like Jess, unable to keep from fondling my presents!

I cast the ash from the fire onto the icy patch outside the back door, just as Gran used to, and let Merlin out into the still-dark world. At least it seemed to have stopped snowing, though it had frozen hard again overnight.

In the stable both horses were still half-asleep, but Billy bleated plaintively at me. I gave them all extra Christmas chunks of carrot, then left them for Becca to do later, as she had told me she would. It was bitterly cold out there, the icy wind holding a threat of snow, so perhaps it would be better if they stayed indoors today. I worried even more about Lady now I'd grown to love her, and I was even getting attached to Billy. Still, that was a decision I could safely leave to Becca and Jude now.

Merlin and I were both glad to get back indoors again, though even as I was kicking off the snow from my boots and giving him his breakfast, I was thinking about the day's cooking.

There was breakfast to prepare too and everyone would come down at intervals, getting under my feet if I wasn't careful. I couldn't serve it in the dining room, since I wanted to lay the table for Christmas dinner, so I decided to put a cloth on the small round table in the sitting room and put the toast rack, butter, marmalade and jam on that, then people could collect Holly Muffins like the ones I'd made at Jess's request the other day and take them in there to eat.

But first things first: the monstrous turkey was stuffed, foil-covered and stowed in the biggest of the ovens, with a lordly antique blue and white dish to receive it when it was finally roasted, which had matching gravy boats and lidded vegetable dishes.

The previous night I'd taken the chipolata sausages wrapped in bacon, sage and thyme stuffing, giblet stock for gravy and bread sauce out of the freezer ('here's some I made earlier!'), and now I prepared the sprouts and put them in a plastic bag in the fridge. The parsnips and potatoes were soon peeled and sitting in cold water and the pudding provided by the Chirks could go in Jude's industrial-sized microwave . . .

When that was all done I lifted tomorrow's salmon out of the freezer, along with the last packet of filo pastry I'd brought and a packet of prawns to make today's starter, and left them on a stone shelf in the larder to defrost slowly, the fridge now being a little full.

Once I'd emptied the dishwasher I checked my list and time-table and I seemed to have everything well in hand. As it was *still* extremely early, I sat down with a well-earned cup of coffee for a few quiet minutes before starting breakfast.

A few minutes was literally all I had, because then Jess suddenly appeared, still in her pyjamas and dressing gown, bringing her stocking with her to show me what she'd got. She laid it on the kitchen table and began pulling out the contents.

'I woke Uncle Jude up first and he said it was *his* sock and he'd like it back when I'd finished with it, only without the pink ribbon.'

'It has to be his, really, no-one else has feet that big.'

'He said he wasn't Father Christmas when I asked him and I think I've seen some of the things in Mrs Comfort's shop, so maybe Mummy actually *remembered* this year and asked Granny to make me one?'

'She must have done, there's no other explanation. What did you like best?'

'Oh . . . the wolf, I think. Or maybe the bracelet . . . When do you think I can open the rest of my presents?'

'When everyone else has come downstairs and had breakfast, I expect.'

'Uncle Jude said he was getting up, he might as well, now I'd woken him.'

'You can give Merlin his present now, if you like?' I suggested, as a slight sop.

'Oh yes!' She jumped up eagerly. 'You know, sometimes I think giving presents can be nearly as good as getting them.'

'Definitely!'

Merlin was suitably gratified and, after nosing off the loosely-wrapped paper, retired to his basket by the Aga, where he could be heard chomping away at one end of the rawhide bone while I was cooking bacon and eggs for two sustaining breakfast muffins each. Then I sent Jess upstairs to put some clothes on.

'Granny likes me to wear a dress on Christmas Day,' she said disgustedly.

'Oh, do we dress up a bit?' I asked. 'I don't often wear a dress in winter either, if it makes you feel any better, but perhaps I should go and change later.'

'It would feel fairer if you had to do it, too.'

'Okay, but you'd better put your jeans on now and give Becca a hand with the horses, if you wouldn't mind? That would be a great help.'

'Unless Uncle Jude's down first and does it,' she said hopefully.

'If he is, then perhaps you could help me lay the dining-room table, instead.'

But by the time she reappeared Becca was in the kitchen finishing her breakfast and there was still no sign of Jude. When they'd wrapped up warmly and gone out to the stables, I fetched the last packets of muffins from the freezer: I'd underestimated how hungry everyone would be this morning and we'd already eaten two apiece. There was still plenty of other bread, both loaves and buns and several of those long-life part-baked baguettes so we wouldn't run short. I might make soda bread one day for a change, too.

No-one else appeared, so after pottering round a bit more, ticking things off my list, I went upstairs and changed into a dark-red velvet dress and flat, soft, black leather ballerina slippers. Cooks spend so much time on their feet that they tend to prefer comfort above style – and anyway, killer heels would have made me a giantess. Though here I wouldn't have stood out quite so much, because Coco is only two or three inches shorter than I am and Jude positively *towers* over me.

The colour of the dress flattered my light-olive skin and dark hair, which swung smoothly against my neck. That's the only advantage of having thick, straight hair: it obligingly hangs where you put it, like a heavy curtain. I added a little makeup and then, remembering Sam's comment, a slightly Nefertiti-ish dark line around my eyes and a bit of lippy (I'm not exactly high maintenance). Then I tried looking mysterious in the mirror, but I can't say it really came off.

I put in the garnet earrings that were Alan's last present (I found them hidden, gift-wrapped, weeks after his death), with feelings of sadness and regret, rather than my usual mixture of grief and anger. And I suddenly realised, with a pang of loss, that since I had arrived at Old Place I no longer had the comforting sense that he was walking beside me. I suspected he had gone for good, leaving me to go on entirely alone . . .

It was just as well my eyeliner was waterproof. I dabbed my eyes with a tissue and then ran down to the kitchen and wrapped a big white apron from the drawer over my dress. I cooked lots of bacon and eggs, which I'd just put on a hot, covered dish ready for the next Holly Muffins, when Jude finally arrived, his dark hair still wet and curling slightly from the shower. He was wearing a loose blue chambray shirt with a T-shirt under it and jeans, which was a lot more than he'd been wearing the night before . . . I felt my face going hot, but hoped he didn't notice.

'Sorry I'm so late, but I fell asleep again after Jess woke me up and—' He broke off and examined me critically. 'Have you been crying?'

'No, chopping onions – I wept buckets.'

'Right,' he said uncertainly. 'I meant to be down early to see to the fire and get more wood up from the cellar, as well as do the horses so you and Becca didn't have to, but I'm afraid I dozed off again.'

'I expect you're still jet lagged, but I'd be grateful if you fetched more wood up because I haven't got round to that yet and the log basket's almost empty. Becca and Jess are doing the horses now, so they should be in soon – we've already had our breakfast.'

'I think the smell of the bacon is what finally woke me up and got me down here,' he confessed.

'I'm doing bacon and egg muffins, and toast too if anyone wants it, but they'll have to eat it in the sitting room, because I don't want you all under my feet while I'm cooking the Christmas dinner.' I stood poised over the cooker, spatula and warm plate in hand. 'Do you want one muffin or two?'

'Two, at least. Do you want *me* from under your feet as well? Only you might want some help, even unskilled labour.'

'I have it pretty well in hand, thanks – I'm very organised, you know.'

'Yes, I'd noticed that,' he said gravely, with a glance at the menu charts and timed to-do lists I'd pinned to the kitchen corkboard.

'Michael's also offered his help as skivvy and he's very handy around the kitchen.'

'I'm also handy . . . even if I don't know much about cooking. I'd like to learn some time.'

'What, you'd like to learn to cook?'

'A man gets tired of ready meals,' he admitted.

'Well . . . I suppose you *could* help a bit.'

As the rest of the party straggled down, I ushered them firmly back out of the kitchen while Jude ferried tea, coffee and muffins to the sitting room.

'Noël's the last,' he said, coming back in with a tray, 'he said he just wanted one.'

'Just as well, we're on to the very last muffin after that. I don't suppose Coco ate one?'

He grinned. 'She did, actually, but then she dashed out to the downstairs cloakroom, so I hope she isn't sicking the whole thing back again.'

'I think she uses alternative methods to control her weight,' I said and he looked slightly baffled.

'Laxatives – I don't suppose the muffin will even touch the sides going down. What a waste of good food!'

He looked startled. 'Really? I'd no idea, I just thought she didn't eat enough.'

'She's so painfully thin that maybe we should lock her in the dining room after lunch without her handbag, until she's digested something?' I suggested.

'Is that where she keeps them?'

'It is, according to Jess.' I swiftly assembled the last muffin and put it on a tray with a little pot of tea. 'Could you take Tilda's tray up? Then I expect she'll come down. She'd better, because I can hear Jess and Becca coming back in, and Jess is so desperate to open her presents she'll probably *explode* if she has to wait much longer!'

'She was really excited about that stocking you did,' he said and looked thoughtfully at me. 'She thought her mother had asked Tilda to do it – it was really kind of you to think of it.'

'It was Mrs Comfort's idea really – and don't tell Jess it wasn't her mother,' I warned, just as Jess burst through the door.

'Uncle Jude, Uncle Jude, can I open all my presents now?' she yelled, flinging herself at him.

'By the time you've washed your hands and changed, you'll be able to, because your granny will be down,' I said. 'I've put my dress on, so you need to keep your end of the bargain.'

She pulled a face and rushed out again and off up the back-stairs like a herd of clog-dancing baby elephants.

'You look very nice in your red dress, Holly,' Jude said, as if the compliment had been drawn out of him with hot pincers, and then took himself off.

Since most of me was covered with a Victorian frilled apron, I expect he was just being polite to make up for nearly scaring me to death last night . . . Though come to think of it, he hadn't *seemed* terribly repentant at the time.

Men are so weird.

If you're terribly organised you can easily spare time for other things even while cooking the Christmas dinner, so when I was called into the sitting room for an orgy of present unwrapping everything was fine to be left, though I remembered to take my pinny off first. Merlin, his rawhide chew firmly clenched in his jaws, came with me.

Jess was in charge of ferrying the presents to their recipients and, to my surprise, I ended up with quite a pile, though they included Laura's, which I'd brought down with me when I changed earlier.

'There's another one here for Merlin,' Jess said.

'You'd better unwrap that one for him,' Jude suggested, so I knew the rubber ball inside was from him. Merlin retired under the nearest table with his booty, where the occasional squeak of rubber as he clamped his teeth on his ball, or the squidgy squish of rawhide chewed soft, could be heard during any pause in the conversation.

While Jess ripped the paper off her presents as fast as she could, the rest of us started on ours with a little more restraint. I decided to open Laura's first, which was a lovely emerald green pashmina scarf wrapped around a well-thumbed book that I immediately recognised: her copy of *The Complete Guide to Pregnancy and Childbirth*. Inside she'd written:

Happy Christmas, Holly! I know what you're like once
you've made your mind up so, since I'm calling it a day
after number four, I'm handing this on. But I can't help
hoping that you might just be snowed up with a nice man
– that George sounded as if he had possibilities – and
change your mind about going it alone!
  Love, Laura

I took a quick look round but no-one seemed to be looking in my direction except Jude, who I hoped was too far away to make out what the book was. I quickly wrapped the scarf around it again.

Jude had already sent presents to Tilda, Noël and Jess when he thought he would be away for Christmas, but on some impulse (probably to fill in time between flights, since he can't have known that the family party was about to double in size) he seemed to have bought up half an airport gift shop as well. There were giant foil-wrapped chocolate pennies and those chocolate bars that look like gold ingots, small teddy bears dressed as Beefeaters and London bus keyrings. These items seemed to have been labelled randomly, but we all got at least one. I had a penny and a bear. Coco, who was again inclined to be tearful about the Birkin bag that never was, got an ingot and a keyring.

Unlike Michael, who had thoughtfully bought and wrapped a small article of Comfort for each person present (pens and notebooks inscribed with Oriel's *Sunbeams are God's Thoughts* line) Coco only received, she didn't give – not even thanks.

As well as my booty from Jude's spending spree and Michael's gift, Tilda and Noël gave me a copy of Tilda Thompson's *Party Pieces* recipe book, printed in 1958, all about the art of the canapé. I was delighted and I kissed them both gratefully.

'You didn't kiss me for *my* presents,' observed Jude, and since I wasn't sure if he was serious or not, I did kiss his cheek, though

I had to stand on tiptoe to do it, which was a novelty – as was his very unusual, and extremely masculine, aftershave. Then, in the interests of fairness, I kissed Michael, too.

'Thanks, Michael – I love my *Sunbeams* pen and notebook!'

'Hey, what about me?' asked Guy. 'Where's my kiss?'

'You didn't give me a present,' I pointed out. Guy, who like Jude had already sent presents to the lodge, hadn't felt the need to do anything further.

'*I* didn't give anyone a present,' Becca said. 'I never do. Just money to Jess, so she can get what she likes.'

'You brought us two bottles of very fine sherry, m'dear,' said Noël.

'I thought *you* were going to give me a ring for Christmas, Guy,' Coco said, with an accusing look. 'I thought this Christmas was going to be *really* special!'

'You thought wrong,' he said flippantly. 'But you might find one in your cracker at dinner.'

'Oh yes, they're very good crackers – *we* brought them,' said Noël. 'There's no saying what you might find in them!'

'Why don't you open the rest of your presents, Coco?' I said hastily.

My jars of sweets and chocolates had gone down well, though Coco was unexcited by her homemade bath scrub and Michael's offering, dropping them onto the sofa next to her, half-unwrapped. But then she opened Jess's gift and seemed, at last, to be genuinely pleased with the necklace of origami beads on knotted silk cord inside.

'Yours was my first experiment, Horlicks, and it's a bit wonky so I thought you might as well have it,' Jess said. 'I just had time to make one for Holly, or she would have got it instead.'

Becca, Tilda and I had lovely necklaces, too.

'They're all gorgeous,' I said admiringly. 'You are clever, it must be very fiddly making the little paper beads.'

'It is, a bit, but I'm really good at it now,' she said modestly. 'I get orders for them at school, I've got quite a good thing going. I'm going to branch out into earrings, too.'

'And mine is dark red, just like my dress – how amazing a coincidence is that?' I said, putting it round my neck and squinting down at it.

'It's not: I looked in your wardrobe and there was only one dress in there, so I made it to match.'

'Jess, you really shouldn't snoop in people's bedrooms, we've told you before,' Becca said severely.

'I didn't, I just *looked*. There was a pile of notebooks on the chest of drawers and I accidentally knocked them off . . .' she added innocently, looking at me through her thick black fringe. 'One fell open and it looked like a sort of diary?'

'Yes it is, but not mine, just a journal my gran kept, a very interesting one about nursing during the war. I found it in a box of her papers I'm sorting out.'

Jess lost interest immediately and changed tack. 'Uncle Jude, Holly looks pretty in dark red, doesn't she?'

'Holly looks lovely in everything,' Guy said, with one of his charming smiles, 'Anyone with her looks who can also cook deserves my total adoration.'

'Oh, don't be so daft,' I said uncomfortably, unused to this sort of teasing, though I noticed that Jude hadn't said anything one way or the other this time, even out of politeness – in fact, he seemed to be back to the suspicious stare again. 'I know I'm nothing to write home about.'

'Get on with you, m'dear!' said Noël gallantly.

'Has anyone ever told you you look like that head of Nefertiti?' asked Guy with an air of originality.

'Yes – my best friend's cousin Sam did, though I couldn't see it myself.'

'Who's Nefertiti?' asked Jess.

'An ancient queen of Egypt, noted for her beauty,' Noël said.

'There's a photo in one of the books in the library, I will fetch it later and show you. And speaking of photographs . . .'

He whipped out a little camera and his family all groaned in a resigned sort of way.

'Another Martland Christmas must be recorded for posterity!'

Chapter 27: Knitting

Today one of the nurses showed me an old society magazine that she had been given by a patient, saying that there was a picture in it of N and his fiancée, the daughter of a lord, and asked me hadn't I been sweet on him when he was a patient there? She is a spiteful creature and hoped to hurt me, but she could not have known how this news pierced me to the heart and destroyed all my faith in the man I loved! All the time I thought we were courting, he'd been engaged to another girl – and one of his own social standing.

May, 1945

Noël insisted on taking several pictures for the family album although, as Michael pointed out, some of those present were not actually family.

'But all friends,' he said merrily. I'd already noticed that he, Tilda and Becca could put away a tidy amount of sherry between them, but Christmas Day seemed to have given them licence to start on it right after breakfast.

'I was in last year's photographs,' Coco said sulkily, 'and look where it got me!'

'That was because you dumped Jude and went off with Guy instead,' Tilda said acidly. 'So if you have in turn been dumped by Guy, it serves you right.'

'Yes . . . well, that's all water under the bridge now, m'dear, isn't it?' Noël said hastily and then marshalled us all into various groupings, whether we liked it or not. Coco automatically fell into languid model poses at the click of a camera. She was wearing a tunic like a gold satin flour bag over mustard leggings and clumpy shoe-boots, but it looked quite good on her.

'There, that will do until we can get one with Old Nan and Richard in, too,' Noël said finally. Then he smiled at me and added, 'Now *you* will be in the family albums for posterity, too!'

'Did she want to be?' asked Jude, eyeing me narrowly again.

'We've been looking at the old albums, especially the pictures of past Revels,' Noël explained. 'And very fascinated you were too, m'dear, weren't you?'

'Totally,' I said, seizing the moment to try and find out a little more, 'especially in that lovely one of you with your brothers and Becca at the Revels, taken just before the war.'

Becca said sadly, 'Oh, yes, that was the last one when we were all together. Jacob was killed at Dunkirk and Ned died in that accident not long after the war . . . and now poor Alex is gone, too.'

'Well, there's no need to go all maudlin,' Tilda said crisply.

'No, you're right,' she agreed. 'Better to remember how much fun we had – we were all so young in that picture!'

'Noël said Ned was the black sheep of the family?' I prodded her.

'Yes, though he wasn't really *bad*, poor fellow, just weak-willed where women were concerned. But he was handsome and charming, very charming . . . Poor Ned. Guy is very like him.'

'Thanks,' Guy said dryly.

'You've had more girlfriends than I've had hot dinners,' Becca said forthrightly.

'But at least he never got any of them pregnant,' Tilda pointed out. 'Or not that we know of, anyway.'

'You mean – Ned *did*?' I asked, startled but schooling my face to an expression, I hoped, of polite interest.

Noël, looking troubled, nodded. 'A little mill girl – or at least, I think she was a mill girl, I can't quite remember after this space of time. He came running back home and told our parents and they were horrified – not just because they thought she was unsuitable, but because he was already engaged to the younger daughter of Lord Lennerton and was about to start working for him. They had hoped he was going to settle down at last.'

'Well, you can't say that's like me,' Guy said indignantly. 'I hold down a responsible job and I've never got a girl into trouble. I haven't,' he said with a darkling look at Coco, 'even got *engaged*!'

He'd wandered over to the jigsaw and was now staring down at it. 'Someone has put the missing edge pieces in that we couldn't find last night!'

'That was me early this morning, they just sort of fell into place as I was passing,' I said apologetically, then hauled the conversation back to where I wanted it: 'So what happened after Ned came clean to his parents about . . . the little mill girl?'

'Nothing, because he was killed soon after that,' Becca said.

'He always drove a little too fast and recklessly,' Noël explained. 'He misjudged a bend and that was it. Tragic – very tragic.'

I was just thinking that the whole affair was even more tragic for my grandmother, when Jude suddenly said to me, 'You're very interested in the family, and especially in my Uncle Ned?'

'Not at all, I simply find old family photographs fascinating,' I said lightly, meeting his dark, suspicious gaze with limpid innocence. 'I brought a boxful of my gran's that I'm sifting through at the moment – papers and photographs all mixed up.'

'Ah, yes, didn't you tell us that she was the wife of a Baptist minister?' asked Tilda.

'Strange Baptist,' said Jude, and Coco asked predictably, 'Why, what was strange about them?'

'Nothing, it was just what they were called,' I explained patiently. 'They took their name from a Bible quotation, "Strange are the ways of the Lord", though someone told me once that

that was a mistranslation and it only appeared in one version of the Bible.'

'And is this the same box of papers where you found your gran's wartime nursing journal?' asked Jude acutely.

'Yes,' I said shortly, then got up. 'Excuse me, I need to get back to the kitchen.'

'Can I do anything to help?' asked Michael, Guy and Jude almost simultaneously.

'Yes, lay the dining room table for me. There was a long Christmas runner for down the middle of the table in the linen cupboard – it's on the sideboard with the box of crackers Tilda and Noël brought. And, Jude, could you sort out the drinks? I don't drink much, so I've no idea what you want with it.'

'Jess and I are going to help, too,' announced Tilda, hauling herself upright and inserting her feet into her marabou-edged mules. 'We're going to make a hedgehog.'

'*A hedgehog?*' Maybe that's what had been in those awful pinwheel sandwiches on the day I arrived – roadkill!

'Yes – you know, chunks of cheese and onions on cocktail sticks, stuck into half a grapefruit,' Jess explained, as they followed me into the kitchen. 'Granny gives them little eyes and a nose with cloves.'

'Oh, of course – how lovely!' I said. 'But I'm afraid I haven't any grapefruit. Would half a large potato do, if I scrub it first?'

'Yes, but Jess will scrub it,' Tilda said. 'I'm sure you have lots else to do.'

'I just need to pop these filo pastry spicy prawn parcels in the oven, they won't take long. Those and the hedgehog should be more than enough to hold everyone while I finish off the dinner.'

When the hedgehog was made, Jess, together with Noël, Tilda and Becca, went into the parlour later to watch the Christmas message her parents had recorded on DVD for her. Then she came and insisted I went and watched it too, which luckily was at a moment when I had ten spare minutes between things.

I thought her parents looked quite mad – they were both dressed as Father Christmas, even down to the white cotton-wool beards, for a start – but in a fun way. Roz is another tall, dark-haired Martland.

Liam, George's son, brought Old Nan and Richard up to the house at about one, and by arrangement was to call for them again later. I was busy in the kitchen when they arrived and by the time I carried the tray of starters through they were already drinking sherry before the fire, so it was just as well Michael bought some more!

'Me and Granny made the cheese and pickle hedgehog,' Jess pointed out proudly. 'It's crumbly Lancashire cheese and silver-skin onions, but we had to use half a scrubbed potato to put the sticks in, we haven't got any grapefruit.'

'It looks lovely,' Noël said, as Michael helpfully passed round plates and the red paper napkins covered in reindeer that I'd got from Oriel Comfort's.

'Are there carbs in cocktail onions?' asked Coco doubtfully. She must have spurned the sherry because she was holding a glass of something dark green instead, though I couldn't imagine what *that* was. Crème de menthe, maybe? There were all sorts of odds and ends in the drinks cabinet in the dining room.

'No calories at all, and the cheese is almost fat-free too,' I lied, and she perked up a bit and selected the cocktail stick with the smallest chunk on it.

'More sherry, vicar?' asked Guy, winking at me.

Old Nan, unasked, held out her glass too and smiled at me over the top of it, all blindingly white false teeth and deeply-netted wrinkles. 'Where on the family tree did you say you came in, dear? I've forgotten,' she said amiably. 'One of the distant cousins, of course, but which . . . ?'

'I'm not a member of the family at all, I'm just looking after the house,' I told her and she looked at me severely and declared obstinately, 'Oh yes you are – you can't fool Old Nan!'

'She gets confused,' Becca whispered to me. 'Just agree with her, it will save lots of trouble.'

'I've brought you a present anyway,' Old Nan said and, after a quick scrabble in her oversized knitting bag, she pulled out several small tissue-covered parcels and thrust one of them at me. 'Come and get yours, the rest of you!'

'What a lovely hat,' I said, unwrapping a ribbed and bobbled creation in electric blue and candy-pink stripes. 'Thank you so much!'

Jude unexpectedly plumped down on the sofa next to me, which made a protesting squeak – and *I* probably did too, because the cushions tilted and practically slid me into his lap.

He examined my gift critically. 'Actually, I think yours is a tea cosy, because it has a hole each side. *Mine's* a hat.'

'They might be for my ears?'

'No, because your ears would get frostbite, which would defeat the whole point of wearing a warm hat, wouldn't it?'

'Yours *is* the tea cosy,' Old Nan said to me.

'Thank you, I'll treasure it forever.'

Old Nan liberally distributed her knitted offerings so that everyone, including Michael and Coco, had a hat, scarf or tea cosy – or, in Jess's case, a knitted mouse with a long yarn tail and whiskers.

'Of course, Tilda and Noël have already had their *real* present,' Old Nan said in a pointed sort of way.

'Oh yes, the Dundee cake – and I'm afraid we have already eaten it,' Noël confessed, 'and very delicious it was too.'

Her wrinkled face dropped with disappointment. '*All* of it?'

'Yes, but there is a very fine Christmas cake uncut, that Holly has made for us.'

'Lavishly using the best brandy, the last of the stock my father laid down,' Jude said darkly.

'That's all right, then,' Old Nan said brightly, then gave Coco, who was sitting next to Michael, a hard stare.

Michael had evinced genuine delight with his magenta-and-pink-striped scarf and wound it round his neck, but Coco was still fingering her lime-green bobble hat with a blank expression. Though actually, her complete repertoire of expressions only seemed to encompass blank or sulky, which didn't bode well for her acting aspirations.

'Isn't that the flibbertigibbet Jude was engaged to last Christmas, the one that ran off with Guy, instead?' Old Nan asked Becca in a piercing whisper.

'I didn't run off with anyone,' Coco snapped, overhearing. 'In fact, Guy made all the running!'

Richard smiled benignly around. 'But now the past is forgiven and forgotten and here we all are together again for Christmas. Coco and Guy are engaged to each other, Nan.'

'No-one is engaged to anyone,' Guy said firmly.

'But then, if you're not engaged, what is *she* doing up here?' demanded Old Nan querulously. 'I didn't like her last time!'

'And back at you!' Coco said rudely.

'Old Nan is my invited guest,' Jude pointed out to her, 'while *you* are not, so you'd better mind your manners.'

Jess suddenly jumped up, exclaiming, 'Oh, I nearly forgot – Liam brought a present from his dad for you, Holly! I left it in the hall while I was hanging the coats up.'

She ran to get it and I asked hopefully, 'Did everybody get one?'

'No, just you,' Becca said with a grin.

Jess returned with a long parcel that could only be a stick – and it was, with a beautifully carved ram's head handle.

'You *are* honoured to have one of those,' Jude said, taking it from me and examining the carving. 'He's renowned for them, but he usually sells them and rarely gives one away.'

'He *loves* you, he wants to *marry* you!' chanted Jess, dancing round me like an evil sprite.

'No such thing,' I said with composure, though I might have blushed slightly since they were all staring at me.

'Then why did he give you a special present?'

'Jess, don't tease her,' Tilda said.

'But who can blame old George for being smitten?' asked Guy, raising an eyebrow. 'He's a widower you know, Holly, with his own farm – a bit of a catch. You could do worse.'

'Uncle Jude is a widower, too,' Jess said, 'and he's got Old Place and lots of money because his statues sell for *squillions*.'

'That's a slight exaggeration of my eligibility,' Jude said, unembarrassed.

'I didn't know you'd been married,' I said, turning to him in surprise.

'*We* forget, because it was such a long time ago and she died young, a bit like that film – what was it called?' said Becca. '*Love Story*, that was the one.'

'It was nothing like *Love Story*,' Jude said shortly, his face going all shuttered, so it was still clearly a painful memory even after all this time.

'And he isn't Holly's suitor, either, so it doesn't matter, does it?' said Coco with a brittle laugh. 'I can't see why everyone is getting so excited, just because an old farmer has given the cook a walking stick.'

'He's not actually all that old, just a bit weathered,' Becca pointed out. 'Late forties, at the most.'

'That *is* pretty old,' Jess said. 'Uncle Jude is only thirty-eight.'

She seemed to think this was a matter for congratulation.

'And I'm a mere thirty-six,' Guy said, bestowing one of his ravishing smiles on me, though to no effect: unlike Gran, I wasn't going to be taken in by a handsome, womanising Martland.

I was sure he didn't *really* fancy me, he just probably automatically flirted with any woman around.

'And I'm a very successful investment banker, too,' he added as a clincher.

'Change the B for a W and that's more like it,' Jude muttered rudely next to me, surprising me into a snort of laughter.

'Don't listen to him,' Guy said. 'Anyway, you'll find I'm much more fun than George: he spends most of his days talking to sheep.'

I wasn't used to this kind of flirting, however insincere, and I didn't know how to play the game, so it was a relief to escape back into the kitchen.

And I only hoped Jess hadn't got it into her head to try and matchmake me with her beloved Uncle Jude, because it was an idea doomed by our mutual antipathy from the start!

Noël welcomed us into the dining room with a lively rendering of *The Twelve Days of Christmas*, accompanying himself on the piano and Tilda joined in the last verse with a brittle and slightly wavery soprano.

And the Christmas dinner, if I may say so myself without sounding too immodest, was cooked to a turn.

The golden-roasted turkey and chipolatas wrapped in bacon, the bread sauce, the crispy roast potatoes and parsnips, the firm, small sprouts from Henry's garden and good Lancashire gravy so thick you could almost stand a spoon up in it . . . *all* were perfection.

Once everyone was well lubricated with alcohol to a state of reasonable bonhomie, we pulled crackers, shared the mottos and wore the silver cardboard crowns (which, oddly enough, suited Jude best – with his broad brow, thick straight nose and strong jaw, he looked like a rugged prince fresh off the battlefield). Then we set to, and even Coco, with an air of reckless abandon probably engendered by whatever the green drink was she had had earlier, ate at least a teaspoon of everything.

I only hoped it would stay in her system long enough to do her some good, and although I was considering hiding her supply of laxatives when I had an opportunity, I wasn't sure quite what the effect of going cold turkey on the Fruity-Go would have on her . . .

Finally Jude ignited the brandy over the large, domed pudding and carried it into the specially darkened room, the blue flames dancing. Michael brought up the rear, carrying the brandy butter and white sauce.

At the end of the meal Jude opened champagne and everyone toasted my cooking, which was very gratifying. Then he proposed a second one to Noël's birthday.

'And Holly's, too,' Noël said, raising his glass to me, 'we share the same birthday.'

Then they all retired to the sitting room, totally stuffed, though Jude, Jess and Michael helped me clear the table first.

I loaded as much into the dishwasher as it would take and joined them, after sneaking a bit of turkey into Merlin's bowl and giving him a Christmas kiss on the top of his rough grey head.

Old Nan and Tilda had fallen asleep at either end of the big sofa, their feet up on the cushions, and Noël reclined on the smaller one: but the rest of the party were playing Monopoly at one of the tables, even Coco, though she kept laughing a lot for no particular reason and declaring that she was only going to buy *pink* properties.

I drifted over to the jigsaw (they irritate me until they are finished, because I like everything neat and tidy) and immediately spotted that one piece was upside down. When that was righted, after carefully examining the picture on the box, I completed a whole corner of sky.

But then, I've found in life that it always pays to scrutinise the packaging.

Chapter 28: Christmas Present

In the end I had to face up to the inescapable truth that my lover had abandoned me. There was no help for it: in desperation I went home and told my parents of my plight. The scene that followed was worse by far than ever I could have imagined.

May, 1945

Liam duly appeared in the big farm Land Rover with chains on the wheels, ready to take the guests home. Both were carrying care parcels of cake, sausage rolls and turkey and stuffing sandwiches, to keep them going once the dinner wore off, though personally I felt like a python that had swallowed a goat, and might not have to eat for a month.

I gave Liam another hastily-packed jam jar full of sweets as a reciprocal present for his father, though I'd also done one for him, so the gesture wouldn't seem *too* particular – I was feeling flattered but cautious! I'd now run out of my stockpile of goodies and Liam's were the Jelly Babies (my particular weakness) that I'd bought for myself.

'Could I hitch a ride with you as far as the lodge?' I asked. 'I can get a mobile signal there and I want to phone my friend to wish her Happy Christmas. But I'll walk back, I need the exercise.'

'It's going to be dark soon,' Guy pointed out.

'I can hardly miss my way back though, can I? And I'll take

Merlin with me for company, if that's all right with you, Liam? I won't be long.'

'We'll see to the horses while you're out,' Becca said, 'won't we, Jess?'

'Or I can do it, Becca, if you'd like a rest?' Jude offered.

'No, that's all right – you can do it in the morning and give us both a lie-in!'

'I'll give you the key to the lodge, if you wouldn't mind just checking that everything is fine again?' asked Noël.

'Of course, and perhaps I could collect one or two things that we've nearly run out of from the kitchen while I'm there?' I wasn't quite sure what he thought might go wrong at the lodge, apart from a burst pipe or the abominable snowman taking up residence . . . which he wouldn't be doing, because he was already living here, at Old Place!

And as that thought crossed my mind, my eyes met Jude's dark ones, disconcertingly and broodingly fixed on me again with his brow furrowed. Perhaps he thought I might ransack the lodge for family silver while there?

I had to wear my long winter coat instead of the warm hooded anorak I would have preferred: one of the penalties of putting on a dress in winter. But it was that or risk frostbite in my extremities.

Richard and Old Nan were temporarily revived by air so cold that you could feel it penetrating right into all the little branchy bits of your lungs, like extreme Mentholyptus inhalation, but they'd dozed off again by the time Liam dropped me and Merlin at the lodge.

Everything was fine and I ransacked the kitchen cupboards and filled my rucksack with more ground almonds, dried fruit and other odds and ends that I might need if the Big Freeze continued. Then I locked up carefully and walked a few yards down the side of the road, my feet scrunching on virgin snow, until the signal showed strongly on my mobile.

It took quite a while for Laura to answer, probably because the noisy family party going on in the background made it hard for her to hear her phone, but when she did, she said she was fine.

'Stone cold sober, of course – oh, the joys of pregnancy! Just you wait.'

'Yes – speaking of pregnancy, I unwrapped that book you gave me right in front of everyone else this morning!'

She laughed. 'Sorry about that, but I forgot you wouldn't be alone. Did they see it? They'll think you've got a bun in your oven if they did!'

'I hid it quickly and only Jude seemed to be looking at me at the time. He was right the other side of the room, though, so he'd need eyes like a hawk to read the title. He *has* been giving me some funny looks ever since but that's nothing new: a brooding stare seems to be his natural fall-back expression.'

'Ah yes, how is the lord and master, apart from the brooding, Heathcliff stare and deep, sexy voice?'

'We've sort of come to a bit of a truce, but he's still wary and he seemed very suspicious when I was asking Noël a few questions about Ned Martland earlier. Just because I'm tall and dark, like most of the Martlands, I think he might have started to worry that I'm a family by-blow, wanting a share of the inheritance. And come to that, I might *be* a family by-blow, or the daughter of one, but I don't *want* to be.'

'I take it you haven't got far enough in the journals to find out for sure, yet?'

'No, though it's not exactly looking promising.'

'Well, let me know. And I *hoped* Jude would turn out to be nicer than you thought and you'd get to really like each other,' she said optimistically. 'Is he good-looking?'

I considered this. 'He's dark, but not handsome like his brother Guy, because his face is too rugged and he has a square jaw that makes him look a bit grim. But he does have a very attractive smile, when he bothers to use it.'

'He must have used it, or you wouldn't know! And isn't he tall as well as dark? Handsome isn't everything!'

'Yes, he must be a good six-foot-six tall and very broad across the shoulders, though he tapers right down to really slim hips – in fact, he's pretty fit without his clothes on!' I added teasingly.

'Holly!'

'Don't get excited, I just ran into him on my way to hang up Jess's stocking last night and he was only wearing pyjama bottoms.'

'He sounds to me as if he has a lot going for him, if you can get past your first dislike. I mean, if he's way taller than you are, that has to be good, right?'

'But I'm not used to a man towering over me and making me feel small, so I'm finding it a bit disconcerting, to be honest. He kissed me under the mistletoe too, even though he doesn't like me – but it was something and nothing, so I don't know why he bothered. Men are so odd!'

'Hmmm . . .' she said thoughtfully. 'How about the other men?'

'I'm getting to really like Michael Whiston, he's such a nice man and he also likes to cook, but I'm not attracted to Guy the love-rat in the least, because apparently he bears a huge resemblance to his Uncle Ned.'

'And also, presumably, because you know he's a love-rat?'

'There is that, though I do find myself quite liking him sometimes against my better judgement: he has a lot of charm. He and Jude have made up their argument, but he's still clearly jealous of his brother, which isn't a nice trait, and he's been totally fickle and heartless with Coco. I'm starting to feel a bit sorry for her, actually,' I added.

'But I thought you loathed her at first sight?'

'I did. But the thing is, she's twenty-four going on five years old and has clearly been Mummy and Daddy's little princess all her life, so she can't seem to cope with not getting her way in everything. She bursts into tears, or sulks. Michael and Noël are the only ones who've been really kind to her, because they're both very soft-hearted. But now she's showing signs of setting her sights on Michael, so he probably wishes he hadn't been so nice!'

'Oh?' she said interestedly. 'Does he fancy you instead, then?'

I laughed. 'No, not at all – and I'm sure Guy doesn't either, though he tries to flirt with me. But Michael and I are getting to be good friends.'

She sighed. 'All these men and you don't fancy a single one of them, not even a *tiny* bit?'

'Don't forget my *real* admirer, George.'

'George?'

'The slightly-weatherbeaten blond hunk of a farmer. He sent me a present today, a beautifully carved walking stick. Apparently it's a great honour to be given one, though I suspect from something Liam let slip while driving me down to the lodge that he also hedged his bets by giving one to Oriel Comfort at the village shop, too.'

'Do you *really* fancy him, then, Holly?'

'A bit . . . he's very attractive in his way, but I can't see myself as a farmer's wife. Or *anyone's* wife – not again. Been there, done that, and I'm not looking to find another husband, I'm just going to go it alone, as planned.'

'You won't *be* alone if you go ahead with the AI and it works,' she pointed out. 'Look, why not give it six months first, Holly? Go out with a few men and —'

'I went out with Sam, and that didn't work.'

She sighed again. 'Once, which is hardly giving it a chance, and you haven't been out with anyone else, have you? If men show any interest, you back off.'

'But not many of them do, or they're not serious, like Guy, so you might as well give me up as a lost cause. I met my soulmate and losing him hurt too much to want to try again, even if I believed there was another Mr Right out there, which I don't.'

'You're hopeless!' she said, but affectionately. 'The children loved their presents, by the way.'

'So they should, when you told me exactly what they wanted!'

'But I didn't tell you what *I* wanted, and *that* was lovely too.'

'Easy! I remembered when the saleswoman in Debenhams sprayed that perfume on your wrist and I thought you were never going to wash your arm again! And I adore my scarf, by the way – I'm wearing it now. Light but very warm.'

'The family send their love and wish you were here with us.'

'It's probably better that I'm not, I'd only be a reminder that Alan wasn't there.'

'Don't be daft, you know he's always in our thoughts anyway, especially around this time of year. But we've accepted what happened and moved on with our lives, even though we miss him terribly – and since your gran died, I'm getting the feeling that you're finally beginning to do the same.'

'Yes, I realised I'd dealt with Alan's death by closing the door on it, rather than properly grieving. But now I keep thinking of him and remembering the happy times we had, especially at Christmas.'

'You were twice as brisk and bossy once you'd moved to the country and started working for Ellen, but now you sound much more like the old Holly, though with a bit of extra bite.'

'Thanks.'

'I expect being pitchforked into having to cope with Christmas has done you a power of good.'

'You're probably right, but I still feel guilty about forgetting the anniversary of Alan's death.'

'No, that was a very healthy sign and you shouldn't feel guilty in the least.'

'There's so much to do every day at Old Place that I hardly have a minute to myself and certainly no time to brood over the past – or if I do, it's over Gran's past, because I'm dying to find out what happened.'

'But if there's loads to do, then even if the roads thaw, Jude might want you to stay on?' she suggested.

'Actually, I *have* agreed to stay and cook right over Christmas – there weren't really a lot of alternatives. After that, we'll see. At least there are other people now to look after the horses and sort out the generator if our electricity goes off again.'

'That "*our*" sounds very proprietary!'

'I've put in so much hard work on Old Place, I feel I have an interest in it,' I said. 'I've got really attached to Merlin, too – and Lady is a sweetie. She makes this blowing noise down her nose whenever she sees me, but that might be because I keep giving her chunks of carrot. Actually, I'm rather missing helping to look after her now that Becca has taken over,' I admitted. 'She used to shove her nose down the back of my neck when I was mucking her out and it was all velvety.'

'What, Becca?'

'No, you imbecile, Lady!'

By now it was quite dark and really too bitterly cold to stand there much longer. My feet seemed to have turned to ice despite having Merlin sitting on them (he's not daft), so I said my goodbyes and headed for home.

Chapter 29: Abominable

My father sat there as if poleaxed for several minutes, then told me very coldly that I was no daughter of his and I was to leave his house and never return. My mother, though she cried, did not go against him. He told her to pack the rest of my things and send them on to me.

May, 1945

I was just trudging back up the drive through the dark stand of trees above the lodge when a huge menacing figure suddenly stepped right out in front of me.

The adrenaline was pumping and I had my heavy, rubber-coated torch raised ready in my hand to defend myself with, by the time it occurred to me that Merlin wasn't in the least alarmed. I upended it and clicked on the beam, following him as he bounded forward and greeted Jude, who must have been lurking at the end of the path that led to his studio.

'Hello, you fickle old fool,' he said, fondling Merlin's ears, then he looked up apologetically, squinting into the light in a way that did little to aid his beauty. 'Sorry, did I startle you? I felt like some fresh air and thought I might as well go down to the mill and maybe walk back with you. I didn't like the idea of you wandering about alone in the dark and snow.'

'Actually, I wasn't at all nervous until you suddenly loomed up. I have a perfectly good torch, as you see.'

'Yes, I've noticed – and taking the beam out of my eyes would be a kindness,' he said acidly.

I lowered it slightly.

'Thanks, it felt like I was being interrogated under a searchlight. It must be a *big* torch?'

'All the better to hit you with, if you'd turned out to be an assailant,' I explained. 'Rubber casing, though, so it would only have concussed you, at worst. Or best.'

'No chance, you couldn't have reached up that far!'

'I might have had to go for a different, softer target,' I admitted and he winced. 'Generally, though, most muggers wouldn't be much taller than me.'

'I suppose not,' he said, falling into step beside me as I headed past him up the drive. Merlin took up his position with his nose pressed to the back of my leg – or rather, the back of my long winter coat.

There was no snow under the thick stand of pines, though it glimmered ahead where the wood opened up to the snowy turf in front of the house. Somewhere away to the left was the faint rushing noise of the stream, mingling with the sound of the bitter wind stirring the treetops.

'Christmas dinner was wonderful,' he said finally, breaking the silence. 'Did I tell you?'

'Yes, you even proposed a toast to my cooking. And I loved my presents – thank you. They were a surprise, because I wasn't expecting any except Jess's necklace, which she'd been hinting about.'

'That's okay, I'm just glad I had that mad moment in the airport shop and bought the place up. But you must be tired – you've barely stopped since early morning.'

'No, not really, I'm used to cooking for house-parties, though I don't usually do anything else *but* prep, cook and clear. Tonight we're only having sandwiches, sausage rolls, cake, mince pies and trifle for supper, which I'll put out in the sitting room – that should do it. Or people can take a tray into the morning room if they want to eat and watch TV.'

'You know, I really am grateful that you took Tilda and Noël up to Old Place after Tilda's accident,' he said. 'It's made me realise just how frail they are – I think seeing them every day must have blinded me to it. I just took everything Tilda said about doing the cooking at face value.'

'In her head, Tilda is still capable of doing everything she used to and she seems to have deluded herself and Noël that she still does most of the cooking at home, though according to Jess it's their housekeeper that actually does it.'

'I think Noël knows, but he always goes along with whatever she says for a peaceful life. She tries to boss you about, too, I've noticed.'

'I don't mind, it's a head-chef sort of bossing – I had to take a lot of that when I first started my career in a restaurant in Merchester. I ended up being head-chef there myself before . . . well, before I left and joined Homebodies instead.'

'Was that after your husband died?'

We were now out of the trees and crunching through the crusty snow up the side of the drive, where it was less slippery. 'Yes, I wanted a complete change.'

If he was asking personal questions, then I didn't see why I shouldn't, too, so I said, 'I hadn't realised until today that you were a widower?'

'Yes, I met Kate at art college, we married while still students and then, as you probably gathered, she died of leukaemia a few months later.'

'That was tragically young. What was she like?'

'Sweet, talented, funny . . . brave, especially towards the end,' he said, remembered pain in his voice. 'I felt guilty just for being healthy when she was literally fading away before my eyes. Coco looks a bit like her – I think that must have been what attracted me to her, though she's nothing like Kate in character.'

'I'm *so* sorry: I shouldn't have reminded you of her.'

'It doesn't matter – it's better to face your demons, isn't it?'

'That's the conclusion I've come to,' I agreed, 'but it's taken me some time.'

'But your loss is much more recent than mine: I lost Kate such a long time ago that mostly she's just a sad, distant memory . . . though I knew I never wanted to feel pain again like I did when I lost her,' he added in a low voice, more to himself, it seemed to me, than for my ears.

'I was married for eight years and my best friend is my husband's sister, so I'd known Alan most of my life. We were *very* happy.'

'I expect he liked being bossed about, then,' he suggested outrageously; back to normal Jude mode, just as I was feeling much more in sympathy with him.

I was about to vehemently deny this suggestion when the words stuck to my tongue, because it was perfectly true, even if Alan didn't actually mind. 'It wasn't like that,' I explained. 'He was easy-going, but stubborn, too – if he made up his mind to something, I couldn't change it.'

Like taking up jogging, for instance, which led to his death . . .

'He was killed in an accident, Jess said?'

'Yes, just before Christmas – another reason why I've never celebrated it since. In fact, I usually spend the anniversary of his death somewhere quiet, where no-one knows me.'

'Then—' he stopped. 'Oh, *now* I see what made you so reluctant to do what I wanted at first! I'm sorry if you were forced into a celebration you didn't want!'

'That's okay, I've started to think all this enforced festivity is actually good for me. And Alan was a sensitive, quiet man with a strong sense of humour – he wouldn't have wanted me to become a hermit on his account, even once a year.'

'No, not if he loved you, he wouldn't,' he agreed. 'Have you been out with anyone since . . . ?'

'His cousin, Sam.' I didn't say that it wasn't a real date at all, since I didn't want to sound totally unsought after. 'What about you?' I didn't see why he should ask all the intimate questions!

'Oh, loads of girls, but nothing serious until Coco: there was something . . . vulnerable about her. I thought she needed looking after. And she's stunningly pretty too, of course.'

'True,' I said, feeling oversized, ugly and capable, none of them terribly attractive traits. 'There is something of the little girl lost about her, isn't there? But it would be like living with a petulant toddler forever.'

I hoped that didn't sound sour-grapes.

We crunched on a bit towards the house and then out of the blue he asked, 'The grandmother who brought you up – is that the same one whose diaries you're reading?'

'Yes,' I admitted reluctantly, 'though it's not so much a diary as jottings about her nursing career during the war. My mother died giving birth to me, which sounds a bit Dickensian, but she had acute liver failure. And my grandfather was much older than my gran, so I only just remember him.'

'Your life seems to have been a succession of tragedies!'

'Not really, not much more than most people's are. And yours doesn't sound much better either, when you think about it, because you lost first your wife, then your mother and father.'

'Well, let's not wallow in it,' he said more briskly. 'At least, thanks to Noël, Christmas at Old Place has always been a high spot of the year, whatever happens – he does love the whole thing. And so do I, really – deciding to stay away this year was a stupid idea. I feel guilty for forgetting that Jess's parents weren't going to be at the lodge for the holidays, too.'

'You do seem to be her favourite uncle.'

'She's taken a shine to you, too,' he said and added pointedly, 'like Merlin. Have you been putting something in their food?'

'Only goodness,' I said. 'Noël seems to have unlimited enthusiasm for the Revels too, doesn't he?'

'Local people appear to have been telling you an awful lot about them, which we don't do usually,' he said thoughtfully. 'They must forget you're a stranger, probably because, as Noël said, you're tall and dark like the Martlands.'

There seemed to be a slight questioning note in his voice, so I thought I would get things straight (or as straight as I was absolutely certain of, to date!): 'Until a couple of weeks ago, I hadn't even heard of you,' I said, which was true enough. 'I take after my gran's side of the family, who came from Liverpool originally. Gran always thought there was a foreign sailor ancestor in the mix somewhere.'

'Oh? Well, the Martland colouring dates back to a long-ago Spanish bride and the darkness genes seem to win out, more often than not, over centuries of fair brides. Becca's hair was dark before she went grey, too, though her skin was always peaches and cream, not sallow like mine and Guy's. She was quite a beauty in her day, was Becca.'

'Since first Alan's cousin and then Guy thought I looked like Nefertiti, maybe I have Egyptian blood and should get regressed and find out?' I said dryly.

'I wouldn't take anything my brother says too seriously.'

'I think I'm quite smart enough to work that out for myself, thanks, and anyway, he isn't my type.'

'What exactly *is* your type?' he asked curiously. 'What was your husband like?'

'Same height as me but slim, fair, blue eyes . . .'

'Sounds like Michael.'

'I suppose it does, really. *He's* a really nice man too, like Alan, very kind and thoughtful,' I said warmly and we were silent after that until we reached the house.

We went round through the courtyard so Jude could go and have a look at Lady and I could go and towel-dry Merlin before letting him loose in the house. His shaggy coat was hung with icy droplets, so that he looked as if he was covered in Swarovski crystals: but he was already a precious object to me.

At Coco's insistence, Noël had found the printed excerpts from *Twelfth Night*, so she could practise her scenes with Michael. This seemed to me more of a ruse to retire with him to a dark corner, though he firmly declined to go into a quieter room where they could be on their own.

Noël said the rest of us could read through our parts tomorrow, which would be soon enough, since we were not going to act them out.

'Though I daresay you could all perform, even if you don't memorise the words and have to *read* your parts,' he said, 'it would make a pleasant change?'

It all seemed to me, as the Bard would have put it, much ado about nothing, but if it kept Coco relatively quiet and occupied I was prepared to put up with almost anything!

'Do you like Uncle Jude now?' asked Jess when, at her insistence, I went up to say goodnight.

'Well, I—'

'Only he keeps looking at you, so I think *he* likes *you*.'

'I think he's just still sizing me up, that's all.'

'He's much younger and richer than George.'

'That's very true, but I'm not actually searching for a rich, young, new husband, Jess, so—'

'I think he really *does* like you,' she insisted.

'You're wrong, Jess – I'm not his type, or he mine,' I assured her, though I did feel a bit more sympathetic towards him since our conversation on the walk back earlier. 'Funnily enough, he asked me what my husband was like earlier and I told him fair and blue-eyed.'

'Uncle Jude's wife was blonde too, I've seen her picture.'

'Yes, like Coco: opposites often do attract.'

'But not always?'

'No, not always.' I looked down at her, tucked into the little white-painted bed, along with her worn teddy bear, the wolf and a Beefeater bear and said, 'But in the case of your Uncle Jude and me, it ain't gonna happen, baby!'

She looked disbelieving, but let it drop . . . for the present, though she did seem horribly taken with the idea.

'I'll tell you a secret,' she said, 'Horlicks snores!'

Back in my room, I picked up Gran's journal, which earlier I'd been dying to get back to, only now the words seemed to be dancing about on the page so I didn't get very far.

But my heart was absolutely wrung for her and I positively *hated* Ned Martland!

Chapter 30: A Bit of a Poser

When I left my parents' house my eyes were blinded with tears so that I could hardly see where I was going. I made my way to an old weir, deep in dark woodland, and I admit that it was in the back of my mind to end it all. However, as I stood there, a single beam of sunlight pierced the trees and I seemed to hear a gentle voice telling me that I must go on. I had transgressed, it was true, but it appeared that God still had a purpose for me.

May, 1945

Waking early as usual on Boxing Day, I reread the entry in Gran's journal and cried over it, despite knowing that she really wouldn't drown herself like the heroine of a Victorian melodrama, but in the end marry and keep the child – my mother.

Poor Gran sounded *so* racked with guilt and desperation!

I still can't help but feel fond of Noël, Tilda and Becca, but their acceptance of Noël's casual dismissal of Gran as 'a little mill girl in trouble' does not reflect well on them. Evidently none of them ever wondered what had happened to her after Ned abandoned her!

But I'll have to accept that I'm part of this family, whether I want to be or not, though at least now there's a rational explanation for the pull of attraction to both the people (or some of them) and Old Place that I've felt since I arrived here.

The house was still totally silent when I got up and let Merlin out into the darkness of the courtyard, then cleaned out the grate in the sitting room and scattered the ashes outside the back door as usual – in fact, by now I had gritted quite a decent path halfway to the stables!

Merlin followed me back in, shaking off flecks of snow from his wiry dark grey coat, and ate his arthritis-pill-laced breakfast with gusto, while I slipped back out to Lady's stall with a morning gift of Henry's home-grown carrots for her, Nutkin and Billy.

I clipped back the top of the stable door to the courtyard and I was in the stall, standing with one arm across Lady's warm back while she nuzzled carrot chunks from my hand, when Jude looked in. I knew who it was, because his enormous frame eclipsed all the light from the courtyard, until he shifted slightly to one side.

'Hello – did you forget that I said I'd come down early and do the horses instead of Becca and Jess this morning?'

'No, but I only came out to give Lady a bit of carrot, that's all. I haven't got time to see to her and everything else!' I snapped. It might be totally irrational, but I felt angry with him because it was his uncle who had put poor Gran in such a harrowing plight!

'That's okay, I'll do it,' he said, sounding mildly surprised – but then, we had seemed to have come to a better understanding of each other yesterday so I don't suppose he expected to have his head bitten off.

'And I was going to clean out the fireplace in the sitting room, too. Just leave all that for me, now I'm back.'

'I like to get things sorted early – but someone should run the vacuum cleaner over the sitting-room floor later, if you *really* want to be helpful,' I said and he gave me a puzzled look from his deep-set dark eyes.

Lady, having eaten her carrot, turned her head and vigorously rubbed her nose up and down my arm, the muscles of her neck rippling and Jude suddenly said urgently, 'Stay *exactly* like that!'

I had no time to wonder if the command was meant for me or Lady before he'd whipped out a small camera and flashed it right in my eyes.

'What on earth . . . ?' I began indignantly, but he ignored me and kept snapping away. Lady seemed quite blasé about it: if anything, she held the pose better than I did.

Nutkin, who had closed his eyes and dozed off after his share of the carrot, opened them and stared at us with mild astonishment through the barred partition dividing the boxes.

'Right, now stay like that while I fetch a sketch pad,' Jude said, putting the camera back in his pocket.

'I can't, I've things to do in the kitchen. And why do you need *me*? I thought you were only interested in horses.'

'They *are* my main subject, but I sculpt all kinds of other things and I often include a human form with my animal sculptures. The way you were standing with one arm across Lady's back while she turned her head towards you was full of lovely, flowing lines,' he said regretfully, as I gave Lady a last pat and unbolted the door to come out past him. 'Oh, well, I suppose it doesn't matter – I have the pictures on film and in my head,' he said, though he still seemed a bit reluctant to move out of my way right until the last minute, looking down at me with those deep-set eyes like dark, peaty, dangerous pools . . .

But right then, that just reminded me of poor Gran again.

Back in the warmth of the kitchen I said to Merlin, 'Your boss is a great, big, surly, autocratic bear!' Though in fact *I'd* been the surly one this time: he had just been bossy. Merlin wagged his tail politely.

I prepped everything ready for lunch, which was actually going to be another early cooked dinner, but dead easy: the whole salmon I'd taken from the freezer the previous morning, Duchesse potatoes, petits pois and a piquant sauce.

Jude stayed outside so long I'd forgotten about him. By the time he came back in, Michael had also come downstairs and we were laughing together over something silly as I cooked bacon for breakfast and he laid the table.

Jude, who I could now see in the clearer light of the kitchen, was sporting so much black stubble along his formidable jawline that he looked like an overgrown Mexican bandit, glowered darkly at us and went on through without a word. Perhaps he's not really a morning person? Or *any* time of day person?

He did reappear later, washed, shaved and smelling faintly of the wholesomely attractive aftershave that was presumably designed for rugged men, and put away an impressive amount of breakfast. But he didn't really join in the conversation with the others, though he probably wouldn't have got much out of Coco, anyway. She drifted silently in, wearing her diaphanous pink negligee, like some species of attenuated jellyfish, and then communed silently with a cup of black coffee until I cut the yolk out of a fried egg and plonked the remains down in front of her. She shuddered.

'Eat it!' I ordered and she gave me a slightly alarmed look and picked up her knife and fork.

Jude seemed increasingly abstracted and soon disappeared into his little study/studio next to the library. Perhaps a lot of his taciturnity is actually artistic temperament and he simply vanishes into a new idea? I get a bit withdrawn when I'm working out a new recipe, only without the rattiness, of course . . . or usually without the rattiness. I did feel I had been a bit mean to him earlier, taking something out on him that wasn't his fault.

Everyone else (except Coco) had talked around him as they ate, as though he were the elephant – or Yeti – in the room that all saw but no-one mentioned, so presumably they are quite used to his moods.

Jess made me promise I'd go out as soon as I'd finished clearing up in the kitchen and join her in sledging down the sloping paddock with Guy and Michael – and even Coco ventured out eventually, in borrowed wellingtons and her grubby once-white quilted coat.

I'd been sledging before of course, though using a flattened cardboard carton to sit on, but I'd never made snow angels until Jess and Guy showed me how, by falling backwards into the virgin whiteness and waving my arms up and down to make wing shapes. The horses and Billy were astonished.

It was great fun and so was the snowballing . . . until I got one down the back of my neck. I wasn't so keen on the icy trickle down the spine as it melted.

We were all freezing and wet by the time we went in to dry off and change, but healthily glowing too. And everyone glowed even more when Guy concocted mulled wine in a jam pan on the small electric stove, demanding cinnamon sticks and other ingredients while I was busy putting the salmon in the larger Aga oven, wrapped in a loose parcel of foil with butter and bay leaves.

He left the pan and all the mess for me to clear, of course – but then, that's typical of most men when they cook anything, isn't it?

I didn't drink the small glass of wine he gave me, beyond a token sip to see what it tasted like (surprisingly nice).

Michael came back long after everyone else, because he'd trudged up the hill in the snow to phone his little girl, but this time his ex-wife wouldn't let him speak to her.

'Debbie said it would just upset her, because since my last call she keeps asking for Da-da and she's been unsettled.'

He was so upset that I gave him a comforting hug – and just at that moment Jude wandered in, cast us a look that was hard to read, silently poured himself some coffee from the freshly-made pot, and went out again.

He does choose his moments to appear! And I expect he's drawn *entirely* the wrong conclusions – if he noticed at all, that is, because he did look *very* abstracted.

I gave Michael the remains of my mulled wine: that seemed to cheer him up a bit.

We had a starter of little savoury tomato and cheese tartlets I'd made and frozen a couple of days ago. Becca took a plate of the tartlets to Jude in his study and said he was working, but he still hadn't emerged by the time we were in the dining room, sitting down to the perfectly-cooked salmon (adorned with the very last bit of cucumber, sliced to transparency), so I went to call him.

He was leaning back in his chair, his long legs in old denim jeans stretched out, and the crumb-strewn plate by his elbow. The desk and the corkboard behind it were covered with line drawings and photographs of me and Lady, so he must have one of those instant digital printer things and possibly an instant digital memory, too.

'Dinner – it's on the table,' I announced loudly, but when he finally looked up at me it took his eyes a couple of minutes to focus. Then he smiled seemingly involuntarily – and with such unexpected charm and sweetness that I found myself responding. Then the smile vanished as suddenly as if it had never been, leaving only the memory of it hanging in the air like the Cheshire Cat's grin.

'Dinner?' I repeated, and finally he got up and followed me obediently to the dining room, though he didn't seem to notice what he was eating, even when Tilda pointed out that the capers in the piquant sauce had been her idea. It was sheer luck he didn't choke on a salmon bone, really. (But I can do the Heimlich manoeuvre, I would have saved him.)

Before dessert, which was a choice between the very last scrapings of the trifle and Christmas cake, he abruptly got up, declaring that he was going down to work in the mill studio for a couple of hours.

'Can I go with you again, Uncle Jude?' asked Jess eagerly. 'You promised to show me how to weld.'

'Not today – another time,' he told her and her face fell. 'Holly – you come down to the studio in about half an hour or so, I want you to pose for me.'

'Me? Not *nude*?' I blurted, horrified, then felt myself go pink as they all looked at me.

'Not if you don't want to, though I'll have had the big Calor heaters on for a bit by then, so the place will have warmed up,' he said, his mouth quirking slightly at one side. I *thought* he was joking, but I wasn't quite sure.

'Absolutely not,' I said firmly. 'I've got some black velvet leggings and a fairly clinging tunic jumper I can change into, if you like, but that's as figure-revealing as I'm prepared to go.'

'I'll settle for that,' he said gravely.

'*I* certainly like the sound of it! Can I come and watch?' asked Guy cheekily.

'Or maybe *I* should go, as chaperone?' Michael suggested, twinkling at me.

Jude scowled at them both, his sudden burst of good humour vanishing. 'Unnecessary!' he snapped and went out. We heard the front door slam a few minutes later.

'The dear boy does spend most days down at the studio when he is at home,' Noël said. 'He works very hard.'

'Edwina usually takes him a flask of coffee and sandwiches for lunch,' Tilda said, 'she dotes on him and I am sure he would starve if she didn't, because he forgets the time when he is down there.'

'Does jolly good sculptures, especially the horses,' Becca said. 'Look like mangled metal up close, then step away – and there they are! Seems like you're going to *be* in one, Holly.'

'I don't know why he wants *you* as a model when he could have had *me*,' Coco said, inclined to be even sulkier than Jess.

'Oh, but anyone can have you,' Guy said ambiguously, though luckily Coco didn't seem to have caught the double meaning.

'It's because you'd be two-dimensional, Horlicks,' Jess said.

'That was quite good, Jess,' Tilda said impartially, 'if a trifle rude.'

'It was only that he saw me with Lady this morning and liked the way I was standing with my arm across her,' I explained. 'I expect if it had been Becca he'd seen, he'd have asked her instead.'

'Oh, I don't think so!' Becca said, with one of her deep barks of laughter. 'Face that sank a thousand ships.'

'It seemed to be lines rather than features he was interested in.'

'Well, I've certainly got a lot more of those than you have.'

'I still think he's really mean,' Jess complained. 'He promised to teach me how to weld and there's lots of modelling clay in the studio, too. I'm *bored*.'

'I don't see how you can possibly be bored, with the amount of presents you got yesterday, young lady,' Tilda observed. 'Go and play with that wee-wee thing your poor, misguided parents bought you.'

'Wii, Granny!' Jess said.

'I hope you and Jude aren't going to be down there long, because I thought we could all read through our parts in the play later this afternoon, now we've had a look at them,' Coco said, which was optimistic as far as Jude and I were concerned at least, since we both had other interests to keep us occupied already.

'I'll be busy when I get back, it might have to be after supper,' I said and her face fell.

'I'm not sure that Viola isn't a better part for me, with Michael as Orsino, now I've read it,' she said. 'We might have to re-cast.'

'Oh? I thought Olivia was the big romantic lead?' I said.

'Viola seems to get the better lines and I have to pretend to fall in love with her for most of it!'

'Do you?' I said, surprised. I really would have to find time to read it!

'It's a comedy of errors, with two entwined romances,' Michael explained. 'But I see myself more as a Sebastian than an Orsino, and I already know the part.'

'I suppose I'd better stick with Olivia then,' she said reluctantly. 'We could practise our scenes on our own somewhere, Michael, if the others are busy?'

She bestowed on him an intimately promising smile and a fleeting expression of horror crossed his mobile face. Then, with huge aplomb inspired by the instinct of self-preservation, he tossed a big fat truffle of a diversion in front of her: 'Noël, didn't you mention that there were costumes somewhere in the attic we might use, if we really wanted to get into our parts?'

'Oh – *costumes*!' breathed Coco, avidly taking the bait.

'I know where they are – the dressing-up box!' Jess said, brightening up instantly too. 'I could show you!'

'Perhaps I'd better go with you,' Noël said anxiously. 'It's not the big chest at the front – that has the Twelfth Night Revels costumes in it, though of course the heads are stored with the swords in the barn behind the pub. No, it's the cabin trunk further back.'

Actually, I'd much rather have explored the dressing-up box with them than trudge down through the snow to pose for Mr Bossy-Boots Martland, but I had a feeling that if I didn't show up he would come back and carry me off by brute force anyway: he was quite capable of it.

'I think you should *all* dress up for your parts,' Jess said. 'Don't worry, Holly, I'll find something nice for your big love scene with Uncle Jude.'

'*Which* big love scene?'

'Haven't you read the play yet?' asked Coco.

'Yes, at school, but I've forgotten about it; it was a long time ago. And I haven't even had time to read through those printed scenes you gave us all. But I thought the central love affair was between Sebastian and Olivia?'

'There's a sort of double love tangle going on,' Noël explained. 'The play has its roots in mumming, with lots of cross-dressing and characters not really being who they appear to be – a bit like the Revels!'

I really *must* try and glance through my helpfully-highlighted printout and find out *exactly* what I've let myself in for!

Chapter 31: Fool's Gold

I felt guided by this voice to visit the father of my childhood sweetheart, the Strange Baptist minister of the chapel in Ormskirk. I had been avoiding Mr Bowman ever since my fall from grace, which must have both puzzled and hurt him.

May, 1945

I changed into my black velvet leggings and dark green tunic jumper, which is an outfit I usually only wear for relaxing in when I am on my own, since it's all very clingy, especially in the bum and twin peaks areas.

When I knocked on the studio door there was no reply, but I went in anyway: it was too cold to hang about outside like an unwanted carol singer.

Jude barely looked up from what he was doing, which was hauling out thick metal rods and wire from a large plastic bin, and grunted at me, but I don't speak pig, so I left my snowy wellies just inside the door and had a wander around in my socks until he became a little less *Animal Farm*.

The building had once had two floors, though now the upper one had been removed and skylights set into the roof to make a large, well-lit space. The walls were painted a creamy white and it smelt of a complicated, but not unpleasant, mingling of Calor gas heater, damp sacking and hot metal. Jude's aftershave might have been based on it.

There were enormous double doors let into one wall, presumably for the removal of finished sculptures . . . and come to think of it, that must be why the path up from the drive was wide and rutted, because they probably had to reverse large vehicles right up it to the studio.

It was furnished with a large, raised wooden model's dais, like a mini-stage, a smaller door that presumably gave on to a storage area for materials, a small furnace of some kind, easels, tables, large metal and wooden stands, a tilting draughtsman's desk and workbenches covered in a clutter of sketches, tubs of brushes, modelling tools and pencils, bits of clay, little models of sculptures and fragments of twisted metal. It all looked in need of a good sort and dust to me, but I expect he preferred it like that.

Dotted about on what remained of the floor space were finished sculptures in various mediums, most mounted on bases, plinths or stands of one kind or another. The biggest – life-size, in fact – was unmistakably Lady, even if it *was* composed of metal triangles, but Becca was right and from close to it looked like a heap of junk. Another was just a series of fluid lines in bent tubular metal that were equally unmistakably the Celtic red horse up on the hill.

He'd been telling the truth about it being reasonably warm down there once the heaters got going, but nothing would have induced me to strip down to the buff, though I did finally take my anorak off and hang it up. That was as far as I was prepared to go.

When I turned round, I found Jude was looking at me assessingly, one corner of his straight mouth quirking up in a way that seemed to denote private amusement.

'*Very* dryad.'

I am a little on the large side for ditsy dancing in the woods, so I ignored this as sarcasm and asked, 'What did you want me for?'

'To try and capture the way you were standing this morning,

with your arm across Lady's back and her head turned towards you. The whole thing looked as if you were fused into one . . . though it would have been better if she hadn't been wearing her rug. Still, I've got loads of photographs, sketches and models of her already, like this one.' He indicated the finished life-sized sculpture. 'If you stand next to it, in the same pose, I could get some ideas down of the scale and how it will go, even if the horse isn't in the right position.'

He seemed serious, so I climbed onto the rectangular block the sculpture was sitting on and draped an arm across it as directed, while he pulled an easel up at an angle and stuck a large sketchbook on it.

'Is this one sold somewhere?' I asked. 'Don't you always work to commission?'

'Only sometimes, I generally just do what I feel like and then sell it – or not, if I don't want to. I decided to keep that one. Turn slightly to face her head . . . No, just *your* head, not your whole body!' he exclaimed, then with two impatient strides he seized me and actually *manhandled* me into the position he wanted, which felt *really* weird.

Then he went back to his easel and studied me minutely, as if I was a slightly dodgy car he was thinking of buying, for want of anything better, before swiftly making sketch after sketch, using big sticks of charcoal. These he then simply dropped on the floor around his feet.

At first I was disconcerted by the way he barely took his brooding, deep-set dark eyes off me, his brow furrowed with concentration, but I slowly relaxed as I realised it was an impartial and remote scrutiny: it wasn't me as a *person* he was seeing at all!

From time to time he dragged the easel into a different position, so he could draw me from all angles and presumably get some concept of me in the round. It seemed to take him ages – but then, I do have a *lot* of round.

'I wish I had Lady here,' he said at one point, and then later murmured, as if to himself, 'and I *wish* you would take your clothes off!'

'I bet you do, but it ain't gonna happen! Look, Jude, I've gone numb down one side, so can I move now? I must have been standing here for hours.'

'Oh . . . yes, I suppose you have,' he said, blinking at me as if he'd forgotten I was an animate object, with a voice and a lot of opinions. 'I think I've got enough to make a start.'

'On a sculpture?' I climbed down slightly stiffly and fetched the flask of coffee I'd had the foresight to bring with me.

'Yes, but I'll make a maquette or two, first.'

'Maquette?'

'A small three-dimensional study, exploring ideas.'

'Right.'

'We'll see if Lady will oblige with the same pose without the rug when she comes in later and then I can take a few more pictures. And I'll need you down here again tomorrow.'

He came and sat next to me on the wooden edge of the model's dais and I handed him a plastic mug of coffee and a mince pie from a plastic box.

'I can hardly wait,' I said politely.

'It wasn't so bad, was it?' he asked, sounding surprised. He was close enough so I could see all the fascinating little specks of gold – probably fool's gold – suspended in his molasses-dark eyes.

'Well, no . . .' I admitted, 'though I thought you were only going to do one or two quick sketches, not dozens.'

'You're going to be immortalised in brazed and welded steel for posterity,' he promised, which has to be the best offer of any kind I've had for a long, long time – and certainly one up on the popcorn and Coke Sam bought me the time we went to the pictures.

'Where's Merlin?' he asked.

'I left him up at the house. I wasn't sure if he was allowed in the studio or not.'

'Yes, he always comes with me, unless lured away by visiting dryads,' he said wryly and then we sat there silently, but fairly companionably, drinking our coffee and eating mince pies.

'Sorry I bit your head off earlier, I was upset about something,' I said eventually.

'That's okay – anything you want to share?'

I looked away from his enquiring eyes and shook my head firmly. 'The others have gone into the attic to look for costumes for the play,' I said, changing the subject. 'The way Coco's carrying on, we'll end up having to act out *our* parts too, though in my case I'll have to read the lines, because I won't have time to learn them by heart.'

'I don't know them by heart either: it used to be Becca, Tilda and Noël who did most of the reading. At least it doesn't take long, because not only is it quite a short play, but Noël's edited out all the slapstick and Malvolio stuff and filled in with a brief linking summary,' he said, then glanced at me from under his heavy dark brows and added, his already thrillingly deep voice going even lower, 'But if we act them out, then I expect I can manage a few *appropriate* actions.'

The corner of his straight mouth quirked up again, but I wasn't quite sure what he meant by that, since most of his actions towards me so far have been highly *inappropriate*, like dragging me into his bedroom on Christmas Eve!

Jude came back to the house with me and we went round through the stableyard, where we found that Becca had just brought the horses in and started grooming Nutkin.

'I was playing hide and seek with the others, but me and Tilda got spotted first, behind the sitting-room curtains,' she said. 'One of my feet was sticking out. They'd found everyone except Coco when I thought I'd better do the horses, so I left them to it. She's so skinny, she probably slipped between a crack in the floorboards.'

'That's a slight exaggeration, but she is worryingly thin now,' Jude said.

'I'm thinking about confiscating her laxatives,' I confessed. 'I don't want her to waste away while I'm doing the cooking and have her on my conscience.'

'Even if you do, she'll probably just go back to them when she leaves,' he pointed out.

'Perhaps, but at least I'll have tried.'

Jude removed Lady's rug and took some more pictures of me standing with her, though I declined to take my wellies off this time, even if I did reluctantly part with my anorak. He even drew a couple of quick sketches, though the light wasn't exactly brilliant in there and Lady kept trying to nibble the edges of the paper.

'You're a muse now,' Becca said, pausing in her steady brush-strokes. 'I've read about artists and their muses, you need to watch yourself!' And she laughed heartily.

Luckily I don't think Jude took in what she'd said, because he seemed to have mentally retired to his own little Planet Zog again, closing his sketchbook and walking off to the house without another word to either of us.

We exchanged a look and then I put my anorak back on and started to groom Lady, which has to be one of the best arm-toning exercises going.

When I went into the house a little while later, Coco was still missing and they were getting anxious about her.

'I can't think where she's got to,' Guy said. 'We've even looked in the attic, which was supposed to be out of bounds, but there's no sign of her anywhere.'

'Did you check to see if her coat and hat were missing? She might have gone outside,' I suggested.

'Yes, I thought of that,' Michael said, 'but they're still there. I don't think she'd have stayed out very long anyway, it's too cold. And she's not exactly the hillwalking type, so she won't have got lost.'

'No, I just thought she might have had a sudden impulse to set out for the village, but obviously not.'

'Did you look in all the chests and trunks?' asked Tilda from the sofa, where she was comfortably reclining while watching the hunt. 'Only I suddenly remembered that story about the bride playing hide and seek on her wedding day and vanishing, only for them to find her skeleton in a chest years later.'

Noël looked very struck by this. 'Of course! It's just the sort of silly thing she would do – and there are two or three in the attic, as well as the sandalwood chest on the landing.'

Guy, Jude and Michael dashed upstairs, but I couldn't myself see Coco squeezing herself into a trunk. 'Did you check the cellars?' I asked Jess.

'Yes, and the utility room and everywhere else I could think of. Come on, let's go up the backstairs and see if they've found her yet.'

I followed her upstairs, stopping to check the wardrobe in my room and Michael's and the linen cupboard between them. And then suddenly I remembered Noël telling me there was another door at the top of the staircase, leading to a stairway to the unused servants' rooms in the smaller attic over this wing. It was in a dark corner, easy to miss, but from behind it came a faint scrabbling and a wavering cry of, 'Help! Heeelp!'

'Coco? It's all right, we'll have you out of there in a minute,' I called, tugging at the handle, which wouldn't budge. 'Quick, Jess, go and get your Uncle Jude and the others, I can't shift this.'

Jude could, though, and with one mighty wrench it creaked open, revealing a tearstained, pallid figure huddled on the bottom stairs.

He picked her up as if she weighed nothing and she clung to

him whimpering, 'I thought no-one would ever find me and I was going to be there forever! And I went upstairs to see if there was another way out and something big and white flapped at me!'

Shuddering she turned her face into his shoulder as he stroked her hair and said gently, 'It's all right, Coco, I've got you now.'

At that moment I felt a sudden pang of something that I feared might be jealousy: *I* had never been held so tenderly in someone's arms as if I was feather-light and fragile! (Alan would have fallen over, had he tried.)

'You'd better put her on her bed,' Guy suggested. 'Come on, Coco, you're safe now and we would have found you eventually.'

'I hadn't even noticed that door was there,' Michael said.

'Noël told me about it and I suddenly remembered. But Guy's right and she ought to go and lie down for a bit. Someone make her a hot drink and I'll sit with her.'

'Guy can do that while I check for the mysterious ghostly thing,' Michael said. 'If I vanish, you know where I am!'

I followed after Jude, who had laid Coco down on her bed and was now attempting to detach her arms from their death grip around his neck.

'Oh, there you are,' he said to me with some relief.

'Guy's making her a hot drink and Michael's gone to see what frightened her in the attic.'

'Oh, it was horrible, swooping at me out of the darkness!' Coco shuddered, reaching for Jude again, though he was now out of reach.

Guy brought a mug of tea and said, 'I've told the others we've found her and Michael says there was a pigeon up there – one of the windows is broken – so that must be what flew at you.'

Coco sat up and took the mug, pleased if anything with all the attention she was getting and starting to look a lot better. 'Is there sugar in this?' she asked after a sip.

'Sweetener,' Guy said, though I was sure he was lying. He exchanged a look with Jude and they both made their escape, while I seized the moment to give Coco a good lecture on the danger to her health from guzzling laxatives like sweets. She took it like a chided little girl and I felt about a century older and quite mean by the time I'd finished.

Then I removed her stash of Fruity-Go from the bedside table. 'I know you've got more in your handbag, but I suggest you ration yourself to a normal dose every day until you run out, then stop them altogether. If you eat small, sensible meals, you'll be fine, you really don't need them.'

'And you won't tell Mummy, will you?' she asked, since I had used this as a threat, without any intention of carrying it out. 'Only she'll have me locked up in some ghastly addiction clinic!'

I agreed that no, I wouldn't do that, before carrying away my spoils and flushing them straight down the nearest loo. It took several flushes before they all vanished.

Coco came down later in a slightly chastened and quiet frame of mind, but soon showed signs of reviving since everyone was being nice to her, in their own way. She'd brought her handbag with her and kept a firm grip on it at all times, so she was obviously afraid I would change my mind and empty that of laxatives, too!

After supper, Jess showed me the long satin dress she'd picked out for me, which was not only a fairly sickly shade of salmon pink, but about twelve inches too short, though apparently for most of the play I would be disguised as a man anyway.

Coco had appropriated a white dress in which she looked like an emaciated bride and Jess herself wore a crown made of papier-mâché and glass jewels. She'd been wearing it to supper, too.

'I just like it,' she explained. 'I don't have to have a real costume since I'm only Props, though Michael said that's one of the most important jobs in the theatre. I have to make sure everyone is dressed for their parts at the right time, with all the things they need.'

'I think *you'd* better wear a man's overcoat until the end of the play, where you're revealed as Sebastian's sister – there's one hanging up in the hall. Your boobs are *way* too big,' Coco said to me, making me immediately sorry I'd been kind to her earlier – but I expect now she was feeling better she was getting a bit of her own back about the Fruity-Go.

'I find myself unable to second that opinion,' Guy said and I gave him a cold look.

'Holly's in perfect proportion,' Jude said. 'I should know, because I've spent most of the afternoon drawing her.'

I wasn't sure whether to be embarrassed about having my figure discussed in this way, or take this remark as a compliment.

'She's too tall though, even for a model,' Coco objected.

Jude looked slightly surprised. 'Do you think so? She seems about the right height to me.'

'*I* am perfect, all the top designers say so,' Coco said.

'Well, it's a strange world and it takes all sorts!' Noël said cheerfully. 'Now, what did we find for Jude to wear in the play?'

'Just this dark blue velvet cloak,' Jess said. 'And a sword and moustache.'

'I don't mind wearing the cloak, but I draw the line at stick-on moustaches,' Jude said firmly.

'I daresay he could grow one by tomorrow if you insisted on it,' Tilda remarked from the sofa in front of the fire. I think that might have been a *slight* exaggeration . . . maybe *two* days.

Guy went back to the half-finished jigsaw, though going by his expression, it annoyed him that I had stuck a couple more pieces in earlier. He gave me a suspicious stare that reminded me strongly of his brother.

We pulled chairs into a half-circle near the Christmas tree, ready to read through our parts for the first time, but first Noël gave us a brief run-down of the plot and the characters we would be playing.

'Orsino, Duke of Illyria – that's you, Jude – is in love with Olivia, played by Coco.'

'"If music be the food of love, play on. Give me excess of it; that, surfeiting, the appetite may sicken and so die,"' declaimed Tilda thrillingly from the sofa.

'Precisely, m'dear,' Noël said. 'Now, Sebastian and his twin sister Viola – you and Michael, Holly – are shipwrecked. Viola thinks her brother is dead, so she disguises herself as a man, and takes service with Orsino, as Cesario.'

'All this cross-dressing must have been even stranger in Shakespeare's time, when Viola would have been played by a young boy, playing a woman, disguised as a man,' Michael said, with a grin.

'I'm glad *I* don't have to pretend to be a man, I'd never pull it off,' Coco said. 'Olivia is a ravishingly beautiful countess, but she doesn't fancy Orsino.'

'That's one interpretation,' Jude said. 'But she's certainly not very bright, because when Orsino sends Viola/Cesario to woo her, dressed as a man, she falls in love with her.'

I was feeling confused already and Coco frowned, 'I'm not too keen on that bit, can't we change it?'

'I think we ought to leave it as the Bard put it, m'dear,' Noël said, 'it's integral to the plot. So basically,' he continued, 'Viola falls in love with Orsino, who thinks she is a boy. Olivia falls in love with Viola, ditto, Orsino thinks he loves Olivia, and Sebastian isn't really dead, he's on his way there with his friend Antonio.'

'Then it all comes to a head with lots of misunderstandings and mistaken identities, until finally Sebastian is married to Olivia and Orsino decides he'll settle for Viola.'

'But only if she looks good in a dress,' Jude remarked, with a sideways look at me, but I didn't rise to the bait.

We read it through aloud, with a bit of good-natured heckling by Becca and Tilda. Luckily, I didn't seem to have too many soppy things to say to or about Jude/Orsino, since he doesn't know Viola isn't a boy until right near the end. It was a bit embarrassing when Coco had to pretend she was in love with me as Cesario, though . . .

Michael's scenes with Olivia were also towards the end, when all the tangles get cut, but she still seemed dead set on getting him alone on the pretext of rehearsing them, a move he was clearly determined to resist to the death! I couldn't work out if Coco had fallen for Michael (which wouldn't be a surprise, since he's very handsome, in a slightly drawn and haggard way), or simply saw him as a stepping stone to an acting career; but she'd certainly abandoned any claim on Guy and was going all out on a charm offensive.

Meanwhile Guy still persisted in trying to flirt with me and the fact that he wasn't getting anywhere increasingly appeared to puzzle him. He followed me into the kitchen later when I went to make cocoa for those who wanted it, which was just me, Jude and Jess, because the rest of the party were hitting the sherry or the hard stuff again.

'You know, I really like you, Holly,' he said, 'and I want to get to know you better. But let's face it, I'm getting nowhere, am I? Why is that – am I too shallow, or don't you like the colour of my socks?'

'You simply aren't my type.' I was clattering pans and cutlery into the dishwasher for one final go of the day.

'No? That's strange, because I've always considered myself a universally appealing one-size-fits-all type,' he said modestly.

'Not as far as *I'm* concerned: and my gran would have said you were all mouth and trousers.'

'Is that good?'

'No. Don't forget that I've seen first-hand that you're a total love-rat, too – *and* everyone says you're just like your Uncle Ned, who abandoned one poor girl when she was pregnant because he was already engaged to another at the time,' I said acidly. 'So no, I don't think you'd be much of a proposition, even if I believed you were serious and not just being daft.'

He sighed. 'You've got me all wrong . . . but I'll change your mind. Till then, couldn't you *try* and like me?'

'I do a bit, sometimes,' I admitted. 'You can be quite funny.'

'I'm not sure if that's good or not. But the right woman would be the making of me, Tilda says so – and *you* look a bit of all right to me.'

'I wouldn't have thought anything short of a frontal lobotomy would change you,' I said dubiously, 'but then, she knows you better than I do.'

He laughed. 'I wish now I hadn't let Jude take my place as Orsino. He's going to get all the hands-on action.'

'There won't *be* any hands-on action and I only agreed to do this stupid play to keep your wretched girlfriend in good humour, so she didn't ruin Christmas for everyone else . . . and to cheer her up a bit, because I felt sorry for her.'

'She's not my girlfriend anymore and she's already got her sights on Michael to fill the vacancy. He's proving surprisingly resistant to her charms, though, just as you are to mine.'

'Yes, that's because *he's* not daft, either.'

'Or perhaps because he's got other interests?'

I looked at him with surprise and then laughed. 'Do you mean me? Michael and I are becoming good friends, but there's no attraction between us of any other kind. Strange as it may seem to you, I'm perfectly happy single.'

'Me too,' Michael said, coming in just in time to overhear the last sentence. 'I wish someone would tell Coco that!'

Guy grinned and went back to the others and I said to Michael, 'I think it's mean how Jude and Guy keep throwing you and Coco together, just because they're tired of her. They hope chasing you will keep her amused.'

He shrugged. 'I've been pursued before, not to sound too

immodest – and she's not my type. But I'm looking on it as a sort of price to be paid for being made so welcome here over Christmas, the unexpected guest.'

'I wouldn't say *Jude* seems to be making you very welcome!'

'I think he has his reasons,' Michael said with a smile. 'Just as I suspect Guy is flirting with you partly to wind his brother up – though that's not to say that he doesn't find you attractive, too, because I can tell he does.'

'I can't see why Jude would care if Guy *did* get off with me. But it isn't going to happen, even if Guy is under the delusion he can twist me round his little finger if he turns on the charm enough.'

'We'll just have to keep rescuing each other if we get cornered,' suggested Michael.

'Aren't you two ever coming back into the sitting room?' Jess asked, appearing in the doorway still wearing her jewelled crown. 'I'm bored again!'

'Just finished,' I said, putting the mugs on the tray to carry through, along with some Parmesan twists and little bowls of nuts and olives.

Jess came right into the kitchen and directed an interrogative stare at Michael. 'Michael, do *you* fancy Holly? Only Guy and George and Uncle Jude do.'

'Jess!' I exclaimed.

'No,' he answered gravely, 'I think she's a really nice person and I hope we'll always be good friends, but I don't fancy her in the least.'

'Oh good, that's *exactly* what I thought,' she said, her brow clearing. 'She doesn't really like Uncle Guy that much, I can tell, and George is way, way, too old. So that just leaves Uncle Jude, doesn't it?'

'To do what?' asked Jude, bringing in a tray full of dirty glasses – all lovely old lead crystal ones that would need hand-washing.

'Oh, we were only discussing who's got a sweet tooth,' I said quickly. 'Jess, do you want me to show you how to make instant microwave meringues and chocolate cake in a mug?'

'What, *now*?' she asked. 'Isn't it too late?'

'Not really – it only takes a few minutes. Then you can eat them before you go to bed.'

'Great,' she said. 'I wish you were *always* here, Holly – don't you, Uncle Jude?'

'I don't know,' he said, sombrely regarding me. 'She's a bit like an irritating speck of grit in an oyster, and I'm not sure if she's going to turn into a pearl or not.'

If Michael and Jess are right, and Jude *is* a little bit attracted to me, it sounds as if he really doesn't want to be – and I feel exactly the same way about him!

Chapter 32: Puzzle Pieces

Mr Bowman is a sweet, kindly man and, though I knew he would be deeply grieved by my story, I hoped he might also find it in his heart to give me some measure of forgiveness and understanding.

June, 1945

Gran's story has turned terribly sad, but of course I now see where it's all heading and feel so glad that someone as nice as my grandfather rescued her! But no wonder she was so reserved and totally buttoned up after that!

However, though I can guess the outcome, I'm determined not to jump ahead to the last entries, but read it in order, even though after her decision to go and see the minister she spent three more whole pages in examining the state of her conscience and the depth of her guilt in such exhaustive depth it eventually sent me to sleep.

This morning, after I'd let Merlin out and given the horses a bit of carrot each, I came back in to put the kettle on, only to find Jude already in the kitchen dressed in old jeans and a navy sweater ready for action, sitting by the table putting on his socks.

'Do you think you could rescue my other wellie sock from Jess some time and remove the pink ribbon?' he asked, looking up. 'This is my only other pair and they're going through at the heels.'

'Okay, unless you'd prefer me to sew matching ribbon to the other, instead?'

'Perhaps not,' he said and then went off saying he was going to replenish the logs in the cellar from the ones in the wood store outside, because we'd got through an awful lot and the next ones could be drying out.

Later he cleaned the ashes from the sitting-room fire before going back out to see to the horse: these were all the sort of jobs I was only too happy to relinquish to him. Well, except looking after Lady: I enjoy spending time with her now.

When I'd fed Merlin I consulted my menus and schedule for the day, so that by the time he returned from the stables, I was well on the way to getting some turkey and ham pies in the oven.

He proved useful for making cups of tea while I was working and then he sat in a chair by the Aga out of the way with a sketchbook, his eyes following me around the room as I made a tray of mincemeat flapjacks and then cast a few fresh additions into the bubbling soup pot.

Now that I knew the way Jude's eyes followed me round the room was just an impersonal artistic scrutiny, it didn't really bother me at all. In fact, I kept forgetting he was there and carrying on like I always did when alone – talking to Merlin as I tossed him the odd scrap and, I expect, occasionally singing. I suppose I get almost as engrossed in my work as he does in his.

'There we are,' I said eventually, ticking a couple more things off the day's schedule, 'just breakfast to get ready now.'

'Do you get up and go on like this early every morning?' he asked curiously.

'I do when I've got a house-party job. When it's house-sitting, of course, I just see to the pets, or plants, or whatever I'm keeping an eye on, then the day is my own,' I said pointedly. 'When I'm cooking, though, I find it best to plan the menus and schedule in advance to make it all so much easier later.'

'I feel *really* guilty now, especially since you keep saying you won't accept any extra money. I'll have to think of some other way of thanking you for all this hard work.'

'So you said. But don't bother, because I volunteered to do it – though of course, I didn't know it would be double the number of people I originally invited.'

He put his sketchbook away and helped me to cook the breakfast which, as I said to him, seemed to be the one meal he *could* put together without a microwave.

'You obviously haven't found my secret cache of microwave all-in-one all-day frozen breakfasts yet, then,' he said sardonically. 'Though *you* can talk, after teaching Jess how to make microwave desserts last night!'

'I'm not against microwaves, it's just what you do with them. The meringues and cake are a short cut, but also fun. And now they have the Tilda seal of approval.'

'They have my seal of approval too, come to that and, by the way, I expect you down at the studio again after lunch.'

'I thought you'd finished with me yesterday?'

'No, don't you remember? I said I wanted to make a maquette or two next.'

'Yes, but I didn't think you'd need me for that. And it's Sunday, so another early cooked dinner – cold cuts, roast potatoes and vegetables. I must raid Henry's carrot store, I gave the last to the horses. Oh, and pudding will be frozen Arctic Roll, specially requested by Noël. It has to be one of *your* favourites, too, because there are *six* in the freezer.'

'It is,' he admitted, 'but strange as it may seem, I like it with lots of hot custard poured over it.'

'Well, that can be arranged, even if it does seem weird. But then, I suppose Baked Alaska is a bit odd, too.'

'I expect Richard will hold a short church service today, seeing the regular vicar won't be able to get through,' he said thoughtfully. 'Guy can take Becca, Noël and Tilda down in my Land

317

Rover if they want to go, which they probably will, and stay in the pub until he brings them back. Coco and Michael could go with him, so long as he doesn't let Coco get drunk again.'

'*I'd* quite like to go to the pub,' I said wistfully, 'but I'd better stay here and get dinner ready instead.'

'I'm afraid they're bound to bring Old Nan and Richard back with them,' he said apologetically. 'And did anyone tell you that they always come on New Year's Eve for dinner too? They can be more audience for the revived *Twelfth Night* readings.'

'No-one tells the cook anything. But two more won't put me out unduly. There's soup to start with, loads of turkey and ham, and I'll do a few extra vegetables.'

'I think there's still a jar or two of Mrs Jackson's fruit chutney in the larder,' he said.

'There is and I brought some of my own apricot chutney, too.'

I could hear people stirring in the house now – the clank of the water pipes, the creaking of old floorboards and, not least, the unmistakable thump of Jess's feet as she ran across the landing and galloped down the wooden stairs.

'Everyone's about to appear – and these sausages are done, so I'm off to the studio,' Jude said, handing the tongs to me. 'Tell Guy about church and the Land Rover. I'll see you later – and *I'm* not coming back for lunch so bring me something to eat.'

'Yes, boss,' I said sarcastically, and that totally transforming smile lit his face again for an instant: then one blink and it was gone – and so was he.

Later Guy, Coco and Michael all managed to squeeze into Jude's Land Rover along with the church party, including a mutinous Jess who would rather have gone to the pub. Noël said they would come back up with George, who he was sure wouldn't mind giving them a lift in his larger vehicle, along with Old Nan and the Vicar.

It looked a bit uncomfortably sardine-like, even though Jess and Coco didn't take up much room and Tilda is the size of your average fairy. Becca *is* pretty substantial in the beam end, though. Once they were in, the windows immediately fogged up and Guy leaned across Coco and cranked down the passenger side.

'You can phone your mum and see if your father is feeling better yet, Coco,' I suggested and she looked at me blankly.

'Why? It doesn't matter if he is, because it's too late. My engagement is *totally* over.'

'And not even a Birkin bag to go back to,' Guy commiserated and she flushed angrily.

'I hate you, Guy Martland!'

He ignored her and instead said invitingly to me, 'Sure you won't come? You can sit on my lap.'

'No thanks, I need to sort out early dinner,' I said, though actually, now it came to it, I rather fancied a bit of time to myself, too.

And it was *bliss*. I had a quick tidy through the house, plumping up the cushions in the sitting room and pausing to put a few more pieces in the jigsaw puzzle. I can't imagine why it was taking everyone so long to finish, and I know it annoys Guy when he finds I've had a go, but there's something quite irresistible about a large jigsaw, isn't there? Oriel was right.

After that I retired to the kitchen with my laptop and updated the notes for my cookbook with things that I'd tried and tested over Christmas, talked to Merlin and then went out with him for a little walk up the track.

A skin of ice had formed on the water trough in the paddock, and I broke that into jagged pieces like clear toffee and hooked them out onto the ground, before we left. Lady was pawing the snow to expose the grass beneath, ignoring the haynet, but Billy was up on his hind legs against the fence having a good go at the bottom of it and Nutkin was thoughtfully chewing a mouthful from further up.

There hadn't been any fresh snow for ages, so perhaps the

worst was over and soon it would start to thaw? Then I, and the rest of the uninvited and unwanted members of the party, could leave . . .

Somehow, that was no longer quite such an enticing thought.

The Little Mumming expedition returned in two Land Rovers, the pub party fairly merry, especially Coco. Still, Michael had at least remembered my request to bring back yet more sherry supplies for the elder members of the party, who were getting through it at a surprising rate.

George helped Tilda, Noël and Old Nan out of his Land Rover, though Richard and Becca jumped down unassisted from Guy's, being still pretty spry. Then he rounded them all up and drove them into the house, a bit like a friendly but worried sheepdog.

I took the chance to thank him for his lovely present and he beamed and in turn thanked me for mine.

'Won't you come in?' I asked.

'Only as far as the mistletoe – if you insist!' he said meaningfully, and winked at me – and for a minute, I admit I was quite tempted!

'Oh, it fell down, so we had to put it in a vase,' Jess said very quickly, appearing suddenly by my side like a sombre Jack-in-the-box. Tilda had dragooned her into a short black dress over tights for church, though she'd completed the outfit with big black lace-up boots and a long coat. 'You can't stand under it any more,' she added, 'so it doesn't count.'

'Pity,' he said good-humouredly, though now he was close enough I'd spotted the faint imprint of a perfect lipstick bow on one of his lean, pink cheeks in an odd raspberry shade that reminded me of Oriel, so he'd obviously been spreading his net wide again.

But he didn't go away *totally* disappointed, because I fetched one of the turkey and ham pies from the kitchen wrapped in tinfoil to take home for him and Liam. He opened the corner of the foil to look at it, and I thought he was going to go down on his knees in the snow and propose right there and then.

'What's he got that I haven't?' demanded Guy as he drove off.

'Sincerity?' I suggested.

I'd laid the table for Sunday dinner in the dining room, which was easier than the kitchen for such a large party, and then afterwards I cleared up and left them in the sitting room with coffee, sherry, mincemeat flapjacks and the last remnants of the Christmas cake, while I changed into leggings and tunic jumper and took a Red Riding Hood basket of lunch down to the studio, accompanied by Merlin this time.

I didn't go straight there, though: first I walked on a bit past the lodge so I could update Laura on my suddenly becoming an artist's model.

'It's weird, because he stares at me while he's drawing, but it's sort of impersonal. Not that he doesn't keep looking at me at other times too – Michael and Jess are convinced he fancies me.'

'How do you know he's staring, unless *you* keep looking at *him*?' she asked astutely.

'He *is* a bit hard to ignore when he's in the same room,' I admitted. 'In fact, he's a bit hard to ignore when he's in the same house: the atmosphere sort of changes.'

'Hmmm . . .' she said thoughtfully. 'Perhaps he does fancy you?'

'He might a bit, but having been widowed and then jilted, I don't actually think he wants to – and anyway, he still thinks I'm up to something.'

'You are, in a way – trying to find out the truth about your gran,' she said. 'And I think you're more attracted by Jude than you're admitting, because you're afraid of falling in love again, too!'

'A bit of physical attraction is neither here nor there! He's not my type and, going by Coco, I'm not his! It's really embarrassing playing Viola to Jude's Orsino, though,' I said, and gave her a graphic description of our play-acting.

'Michael is Sebastian, my twin brother, so he gets off with Coco as Olivia in the end, but desperately wishes he didn't, poor man. He'd feel *much* safer with me. But at least the play's keeping Coco fairly amused. She managed to lock herself in an attic earlier today and had a panic attack, and I seized the moment to give her a talking to about her laxative consumption and confiscated most of them.'

'Wasn't that a bit high-handed?'

'It was for her own good. If the snow doesn't thaw soon, I might even get a bit of meat on her bones and colour in her cheeks before she goes home.'

'So I take it there's still no chance of escape yet?'

'No, but in any case, I don't think Jude would let me go until he's finished with me.'

'That sounds . . . dodgy. But interesting.'

'As a model in the studio, idiot!'

I'd made Jude a sort of hot chopped-up version of the roast turkey dinner, like giant toddler food, and put it in one of the wide-mouthed Thermos flasks from the kitchen to keep it hot.

One good thing about him is that even with half his mind on his work, he still appreciates my cooking. I shared the flask of coffee, sitting next to him with a certain quiet companionship on the wooden model's dais while he ate it.

Merlin sat between us, alternately leaning first against me, then Jude, then back again, and sighing a lot.

'What's the matter with this stupid dog?' Jude asked eventually, puzzled.

'Conflict of loyalties, I think. He feels he should be with you, but he doesn't really want to leave me. Ideally, he'd like us both to stay in the same place all the time.'

'But I notice when it comes to the crunch, he more often follows *you* than *me*.'

'Yes,' I admitted, 'but he'll forget all about me when I'm gone. I *am* going to really miss him, though!'

I put one arm around Merlin and gave him a hug.

Jude watched me with an absent expression I was becoming familiar with and said, 'Hmmm . . . must do some sketches of you two later. But first, back to work again – I'm making an armature to support the sculpture. The maquettes are on that table over there, if you want to see.'

He got up and went back to constructing something substantial and vaguely horse- and human-shaped in bent metal rods, pushed into a large hollow support on a fixed base.

There were three small models on the bench, one in clay, one seemingly twisted from wire, and one constructed with snippets of tin stuck together with blobs of wax.

Weird.

I went back to sitting on the edge of the dais and watched him for a bit to see if he might want me for anything, since he'd been so insistent I go down; but I think he'd forgotten me again. Maybe he'd just wanted his lunch brought?

He didn't seem to feel the cold at all. Although it wasn't that hot in the studio he'd stripped off his jumper and the thin T-shirt beneath was stretched across an impressive array of muscles I remembered all too clearly from my private viewing of them on Christmas Eve, tapering down to a slim waist and hips . . .

I was just thinking that although he was a giant, he was a very well-proportioned and fit-looking one, when he looked up and gave me one of those dramatically sudden, heart-stoppingly sweet smiles, before going back to work again.

I don't think he realises he's doing it! But I expect it's only an expression of sublime happiness, blissed out in the act of creation.

Now *that feeling* rang a bell in the distant recesses of my memory . . .

From time to time he made a random comment, evidently

thinking aloud. Once he said, 'I must arrange a way for Jess to speak to her parents, when we can get out of Little Mumming,' and later he told me my lines were nearly as beautiful as Lady's. I took that as a compliment.

Eventually, when I could see the light outside was starting to go, I got up, and Merlin uncoiled himself to come with me. 'Jude, I'm going now. You won't forget to come back for supper, will you?'

He looked up absently. 'No, okay,' he said, but I wouldn't put money on him remembering, unless his stomach insisted.

When I got back Becca and Jess had long since brought the horses in and Guy had driven Old Nan and Richard home in Jude's Land Rover.

The kitchen was in a bit of a mess because Jess had been showing Tilda how to make microwave meringues and chocolate cake in a mug. I promised to write the meringue recipe down for Tilda. I could imagine endless plates of them appearing at the lodge, garnished with the ubiquitous squirty cream and, perhaps, sliced strawberries in summer.

'We found Coco in your room earlier,' Jess said, 'searching for her Fruity-Go.'

'That's because there are hardly any left in my handbag,' Coco said sulkily. 'I only wanted a few more.'

'I'm afraid I flushed them all away – cutting out the middle woman, as it were,' I confessed and then she slightly hysterically accused me of wanting to ruin her figure, her career and her entire life.

Tilda told her she should be grateful someone cared about her health, but if she found herself constipated she would brew her up a nice dose of senna pods.

That seemed to have a remarkably calming effect.

Jude did remember to come back for supper, which was just sausage rolls, tomatoes (the very last of the salad), smoked salmon sandwiches and more microwave cake and meringues (with swirls of squirty cream, of course). We'll all be as fat as pigs by New Year.

Guy had noticed some additions to the jigsaw and accused me of putting them there, as if it was a crime. When I admitted my guilt, he said pettishly that since I was so good at it I might as well finish the whole thing.

He and Coco have so much in common, it's a pity they didn't make a go of it!

I told him I'd got it for everyone to share and we'd *all* done a bit of it, even Coco (probably the upside-down bits in the wrong place), so he could stop throwing his rattle out of the pram.

'Hear, hear!' said Becca.

Honestly, hurt male pride over something as trivial as a jigsaw? And okay, beating him at snooker and then Scrabble first probably didn't help . . .

I would quite happily have continued playing Monopoly, Scrabble or Cluedo with the others all evening, but no, Coco had us all practising our scenes in the play again, though mainly she just wanted an audience to watch her unintentionally hamming it up with poor Michael. I think it's called overacting.

However, I caught the bug and started hamming it up a bit myself – and then, to my surprise, Jude began playing up to me, so it was not such a drag as it might have been.

Chapter 33: Turning Turkey

Mr Bowman was extremely shocked and grieved by my story, but said though I had done wrong, the fault was not all mine. He offered to seek out N to try and make him see where his duty lay, but I refused, because clearly N has abandoned me and could never have been serious in the first place, since he was already engaged to marry someone else. But then we prayed together for guidance . . .

June, 1945

I fell asleep last night on another of those long, moralising passages from Gran's journal, this time describing what Mr Bowman said in his prayers (which obviously he must have said aloud, since she wasn't telepathic) and how grateful she was that he hadn't turned her away like her parents had.

Then she compared her lot at length to some scene in *The Pilgrim's Progress*, which apparently had a Slough of Despond, though that does seem a *bit* harsh on Slough.

Times were so different then: I still couldn't understand how Ned could have been so heartless as to abandon her.

When I let Merlin out, I saw that it hadn't snowed any more, but nor did the winter wonderland show signs of going away any time soon: it was all deep and crisp and even, as the carol says.

Jude was downstairs again soon after I was, but I don't mind if it becomes a habit, since he doesn't get in my way while I'm making my preparations for the day. In fact, it's handy having someone to ply me with cups of tea or coffee while I'm working, tend the fire and do other odd jobs around the house, though so far he's shown no sign of taking me up on the vacuuming.

Becca was down quite early too, but Jess has now been let off morning horse mucking-out duties, to her huge relief. I expect she's already in training to become nocturnal when she's a teenager.

This morning's first task had been to remove the remaining meat from the turkey carcass and put the bones on the stove to simmer for stock. Then I turned what was left – which was a surprising amount, really – into a good spicy curry to go into the freezer. A few bits of turkey found their way into Merlin, too.

I'd finished this and the kitchen was filled with the aroma of gently simmering stock and rich spices by the time Becca and Jude came back in from the stables, adding a not-unpleasant hint of warm horse and hay to the mix.

'Something smells good,' Jude said appreciatively.

'It's just stock and turkey curry for the freezer.'

'What are you doing now?' asked Becca. 'Isn't that the old mincing machine?'

'Yes, I found it in one of the drawers.' I finished screwing it down firmly on the edge of the kitchen table. 'I'm making mince for burgers – that's what we're having for dinner tonight.'

'What, you're turning my best steaks from the freezer into burgers?' demanded Jude predictably, spotting them on a plate.

'There aren't enough steaks for everyone, but minced up there *is* enough to make burgers – and they'll be delicious, you'll see,' I promised, turning the handle briskly.

'I have to believe you,' he said, watching me with that now-familiar quirk of the lips, 'everything else you've cooked so far has been!'

'It certainly has and Jude should offer you a permanent job,' Becca suggested with a grin.

'He couldn't afford me.'

'Yes I could, I can't imagine why you persist in assuming I'm on my uppers.' He paused on his way out, presumably to change and shave, since he was back to the Mexican bandit look. 'Can we have chips with the burgers?'

'You can have my version of them, done in a baking tin in the oven with a little olive oil and a few herbs.'

When he came back, looking about as civilised as a Yeti can get, he helped me to cook breakfast for everyone again before he went off to the studio, reminding me to come down after lunch and bring him something to eat, so clearly the pattern of our days is now going to be like this. Perhaps he just wants me on tap, in case of a sudden urge to check the pose, or something? Or then again, it may be just a cunning ruse to get his lunch delivered daily until Edwina returns to the lodge.

After breakfast Tilda got up and she, Noël and Becca decided to watch an old film on video – they seem to especially love musicals.

Jess and Guy were all for going out with the sledges again, but I think Michael would have been quite happy to carry on sitting at the kitchen table, drinking coffee and discussing recipes with me; except that Coco said that if he wasn't going out they could practise their love scenes together, and he changed his mind. In the end we all went out, though I came in earlier than the rest to make another chocolate blancmange rabbit for later, seeing as the first one hadn't just gone down well with Jess, but had also been a surprise hit with everyone else. Then I set out a nice lunch of turkey and ham pie, warm garlic bread (garlic paste and ready-to-bake baguettes from the larder) and the last of the tinned pâté.

When lunch was cleared I left for the studio with Jude's substantial picnic and the big flask of coffee.

By then Coco had got her way and she and Michael were to practise their parts for the play this afternoon – only not alone, but with Noël helpfully reading mine and Jude's parts and Jess in attendance as Props, wearing her crown.

Jude had finished making the armature and was welding bits of leaf-shaped metal together around it when I went into the studio, though he stopped and gave me a protective visor like the one he was wearing.

'Sparks aren't going to fly as far as the dais, are they?' I asked, though I noticed Merlin had taken one look at his master and retired underneath it.

'No, but the light from the torch is very bright, better to be safe than sorry,' he said, and then went back to work. As yesterday, he just seemed to want to have me around, without actually needing me.

The torch was fuelled by two different sorts of gas cylinders and I thought it all looked a bit dangerous, though he seemed to know exactly what he was doing.

'Are you *really* going to teach Jess to do that?' I asked, pouring him a cup of coffee when he finally stopped to eat his late lunch.

'Yes, why not?' He sat down on the edge of the dais next to me. 'It's safe enough if I watch her all the time – I know what I'm doing. I'd like to leave it until she comes for part of the summer holidays, though, when she'll be thirteen.'

'Does she spend most of the school holidays with Noël and Tilda?'

'It depends – her parents are away a lot. You'll have gathered that Roz and her husband Nick study wildlife and make documentaries, so Jess does end up here with Noël and Tilda quite a bit. But sometimes she gets to fly out to exotic locations, too.'

'You're her favourite uncle, she cheered up no end once you came back.'

'She's seems to have taken a shine to you, too – like Merlin, she's happiest if we are both in the same room!'

'I'm sure I was just your stand-in and you're her real security figure,' I said. 'She does seem surprisingly accepting about her parents being away so much and having to go to boarding school.'

'Actually, she loves it. It's a surprisingly old-fashioned and Enid-Blyton sort of school, where the girls can go riding and keep pets, but after thirteen they have to leave, so that will be difficult for her. It's not how I'd want to bring up *my* children if I had any, would you?' he said, and gave me a swift, sideways glance that I found impossible to interpret. 'I'd want them around, not packed off somewhere away from home.'

'Me too, I can't see the point in having children otherwise,' I agreed and we were silent for a minute. I was thinking about single motherhood, and how different it would be for me, compared to how it would have been for poor Granny – but it was still quite a daunting proposition. Good forward planning is obviously required in that situation, just as in cooking.

Goodness knows what Jude was thinking about.

When he went back to work we exchanged a few sporadic (and sometimes illuminating!) remarks, and then after a bit Merlin and I slipped out and walked home . . . Or back to Old Place, which is somehow starting to *feel* like home.

I beat Guy three times at snooker, and what with that and my having finished a whole section of the jigsaw in an absent moment earlier, when I had gone in to put more logs on the fire, he was a bit huffy.

Oddly, it didn't seem to put him off flirting with me after we'd had yet another read-through of the play scenes. And, do you know, I think Michael was right because Guy only *really* flirts with me when Jude's there! So he must think he's making Jude jealous . . . unless he's misinterpreting Jude's interest in me?

Jude had so far performed no suitable *or* unsuitable actions, apart from twirling an imaginary moustache in a faintly lascivious way at me and tossing his blue velvet cloak over one shoulder. We were getting hammier and hammier in our scenes and it was driving Coco mad, especially when Michael joined in.

'You're not taking it seriously!' she practically screamed when Jude and I were overacting the scene where Orsino says he quite fancies Viola, now he knows she's a woman, only he'd like to see her in a dress. (And I'd thought Jude had been joking about that bit.)

'It's only a family entertainment, after all,' Noël said. 'Why not have fun? I expect that's what Shakespeare intended when he wrote the play.'

'I'm sure Michael would rather we did it seriously,' Coco said.

'No, I do enough serious acting the rest of the time – and really, I'd have preferred a *complete* rest from it.'

She pouted, which is not a good look on someone of four, never mind twenty-four.

'Can she act?' I asked him later, when no-one could overhear. Michael is forever taking refuge from Coco with me in the kitchen, and he's proving very helpful at peeling vegetables and hand-washing anything that won't go in the machine, though he borrows my long rubber gloves to do it. I suppose actors can't really afford to have dishpan hands.

'No, she's as wooden as a log,' he said, with an attractive grin.

'Yes, that's what I thought. Poor Coco!'

'Poor nothing! Her parents are super-rich and have spoilt her rotten, so it's about time she learnt that money can't buy you everything.'

'It's certainly not going to buy her way into acting if she's useless, is it?'

331

'It isn't going to buy her *me*, either,' he said grimly and I laughed.

'You'll be so glad to get away from here.'

'No, actually, apart from Coco this has been one of the best times of my life! I'm really enjoying it. What about you?'

'Me? Well, it's just work really – another busman's holiday like yours, but . . . well yes, I suppose I *am* enjoying it. Or most of it. It's strange, because I've always felt miserable at Christmas before.'

'That's not surprising, considering how many sad things have happened to you around this time of year,' he said sympathetically.

'Yes, but in retrospect, I can see hiding myself away and going into mourning at the first sound of a Christmas song and a bit of tinsel wasn't the *best* way to go about dealing with it,' I admitted. 'But I think I've now been immunised against fear of Christmas forever.'

'Or immunised *with* it, so you now *have* to celebrate it?' he suggested.

He might just have a point.

Tuesday followed much the same pattern as the preceding days, except that as soon as the sun came out you could see a thaw starting on the courtyard cobbles and the part of the drive where George and Liam had ploughed it clear.

I went down to the village with Guy, Coco and Michael mid-morning, in order to stock up on my depleted food supplies at Oriel's shop, though of course there would be no fresh fruit, bread or vegetables yet, let alone a new consignment of the squirty cream so beloved of Tilda and Jess!

We all went into the shop – I think we felt that we hadn't seen one for months.

'I hear George gave you one of his sticks for a present?' Oriel asked me, stacking up flour, baking powder and tinfoil in front of me on the counter.

'That's right and it's beautifully carved. It was very kind of him,' I replied cautiously.

'Oh yes . . . he's *kind* all right, is George,' she said jealously and I felt a sudden pang of sympathy: I found George very attractive, but I wasn't seriously interested in him and until my advent Mrs Comfort had been without a rival. What if she was in love with him?

'Yes, he's such a nice man that I wish I had a father just like him,' I said firmly and she looked pleased. A broad smile crossed her face.

'A *father*? Would you now? I suppose he *is* a lot older than you.'

He was . . . though not that old! But anyway, it had the desired result and in a flood of bonhomie she presented me with a paper bag of Jelly Babies, free.

I slipped off while the others were still debating their purchases, leaving Oriel telling Coco firmly that no, she couldn't sell her all her remaining stock of laxatives: she was rationing them to one box per customer until new deliveries arrived.

I went to check that Old Nan and Richard were all right and gave them the last slices of the turkey and ham pie and some cake I'd brought with me. Then I rang Laura from the church porch, where it was a little sheltered.

She said Ellen had called her, complaining that she couldn't get hold of me to tell me about the wonderful job she had lined up for me, starting the weekend after Twelfth Night, and how she was sure I wouldn't mind cooking for a Middle Eastern client's huge house-party at a swish London address, now I'd had a nice rest from it.

'I hope you put her right!' I said indignantly. 'I've done nothing but prepare and cook meals since I got here. And she knows I only do home-sitting until Easter.'

'I wound her up by telling her you'd settled in so well that they'd probably pay you a fabulous sum to keep you as permanent cook.'

'Funnily enough, Jude said much the same . . . and *I* said he couldn't afford me. But apparently he really is quite well off, you were right.'

'Of course he is, dimwit! His sculptures go for megabucks, I Googled him!'

'Well, I'm not going to take a permanent position here anyway. I'll just slip quietly out of their lives as soon as it thaws. And providing Jude has stopped needing me to hang around being a muse, too.'

'I think you quite like it!'

'It is sort of thrilling watching him with the torch thing welding metal together,' I admitted. 'He seems to like to have me there, though he's so absorbed he forgets he isn't alone for long stretches. Then he sort of comes to and spots me and smiles and says something.'

'Like what?'

'Oh, all kinds of things: sometimes he asks me about myself, but usually it's whatever's going through his head right at that moment. He likes his food, too, and I take him lunch down in the early afternoon, after we've had ours up at the house.'

'This all sounds as if it's becoming very intimate and cosy!' she teased me. 'Weren't a lot of artists' muses also their mistresses?'

'Maybe, but I'm hardly likely to go that route after Gran's example and with a member of the same family who let her down, am I?' I reminded her. 'I mean, even if I found big, bossy, taciturn men attractive, Jude is almost certainly my cousin.'

'But not even a *first* cousin.'

'No, his father was my grandfather's brother . . . I think,' I said, trying to work it out.

'That's not *terribly* close,' she said encouragingly. 'They can't touch you for it.'

'Oh, *Laura*! You're as bad as Jess.'

'The little girl? Is she matchmaking?'

'She's not actually that little – she's nearly thirteen and she's

334

going to be another tall Martland. But yes, she's trying to push me and Jude together at every opportunity. She adores Jude and we seem to have been cast in the role of surrogate parents, since her parents have to be away. I think she'd like it to be a permanent arrangement, but I've told her it ain't gonna happen!'

'Famous last words,' she said, and I told her she was a hopeless romantic but in this case she might as well give up.

Over at the pub I found Coco drinking vodka and soda and Guy and Michael with pints of beer, talking about football, which is not something I find of any interest. So I had coffee and chatted to Nancy instead, until eventually I had to chivvy the others out, or there would have been no lunch on the table that day.

This made it much later than usual when I took Jude's lunch down to the studio and he was inclined to be a bit narky when I told him why, but I expect hunger pains had stopped the flow of his inspiration, or something.

However, he cheered up once he'd eaten, and while he was working we had quite a few exchanges of companionable conversation – and also several equally companionable silences. I am finding the time spent in the studio strangely relaxing . . .

Jude's good mood lasted for the rest of the day, until just after our next totally unnecessary play rehearsal, when he went all morose and Neanderthal again. I think it was because he came into the kitchen when Michael and I were having a slightly cruel giggle about Coco's acting.

I'd just spoken Olivia's line, in a simpering falsetto, '"Nay come, I prithee: would'st be ruled by me?"' and Michael, as Sebastian, snatched me into his arms, crying passionately, '"Madam, I will!"'

'Excuse *me*!' Jude said and then dropped the tray of glasses down on the table so that one fell over and broke, before going back out and slamming the kitchen door, for good measure.

Michael gave me a knowing look, and I threw the oven glove

at him. Okay, I now admit Jude's jealous: but that still doesn't mean he intends making any move on me which – now I'm pretty sure he's my cousin – is just as well!

When I was cosily tucked up in bed that night and flicking through Gran's last journal to find my place, a tiny black and white photo fluttered out onto the duvet.

It was unmistakably Ned Martland – I knew those features so well now, from the family album. But he looked very young and handsome, standing by a prewar motorbike. On the back he'd written, 'All my love, your Ned.'

Obviously, he hadn't seen fit to mention that she'd only had all his love on a *temporary* basis.

I propped the picture up against my alarm clock so I could study it better, trying to puzzle out his character from his features. And that's how I fell asleep – and plummeted right into a tangle of dreams in which Jude was welding bits of old motorbike together, wearing little more than his protective visor . . .

It was pretty disturbing stuff, I can tell you. I woke up in a muck sweat.

Chapter 34: Slightly Thawed

Mr Bowman said that had Tom not lost his life in the war we would have been married with a family by this time and he felt Tom would want him to help me. There was only one way that he could think of to do that, which was to give me the protection of his name, so he asked me to marry him right away. He is the kindest and most generous person in the world and, since I could see no alternative, I gratefully accepted.

June, 1945

Jude came down early again next day, still in a deeply morose and taciturn mood, which probably wasn't helped by my inability to look him straight in the eye after last night's red-hot dreams.

Then he vanished back upstairs as soon as he'd seen to the horses with Becca, so there was no-one to ply me with tea while I worked, or help cook the breakfast while passing the odd, quiet remark . . . and somehow, I missed the companionable silences, too. It's strange how quickly you get used to something . . . or some*one*.

Becca asked me on her way through the kitchen if we'd had a falling out. 'I don't know what's got into the boy this morning!'

'Not that I know of, though he's hardly spoken to me since last night,' I told her, though I didn't add that I thought he might have misinterpreted finding me in Michael's arms again, since that might lead to a whole lot of other questions I didn't even want to think about.

He didn't come back down until Jess and everyone else apart from Tilda were eating breakfast, and even then he didn't sit down, just made himself a thick bacon sandwich and wrapped it in foil to take with him.

'I won't need you today,' he said to me curtly.

'Can I come then, Uncle Jude?' asked Jess eagerly.

'No,' he said and went out and Merlin, for once, followed him – though with a troubled look back at me. Perhaps he was reattaching himself to his master?

'I hate Uncle Jude!' Jess said bitterly.

'I thought it was me you hated, Mini-Morticia?' Guy said.

'Only when you call me Mini-Morticia, *Uncle* Guy,' she said and he winced.

'Never mind Jude, he seems a bit grumpy today for some reason,' I said. 'I don't suppose he was thinking what he was saying. Why don't you start making a snowman out at the front now the thaw seems to be starting, while there's still lots of snow? Then, when I've cleared breakfast away, I'll come and help.'

'I suppose I *could*,' she said sulkily. I hoped some of the others might offer to go with her, but Michael had decided to walk up the track and phone his ex-wife, in the hope she might have relented about letting him speak to his daughter, and no-one else seemed to be terribly keen, though Noël said he would look out later, to see how the snowman was coming along.

But when I went out after about twenty minutes, Jess was nowhere to be seen, and there was no sign of activity other than a shovel stuck upright in a patch of virgin snow and a trail of footprints leading off towards the drive.

Her wellingtons and coat were missing, so I checked the yard and paddock first, and then the house, without result. Michael had come back and he and Guy were playing snooker in the library, but when I asked they said they hadn't seen her.

'I entirely forgot to go and see how the snowman was doing,' Noël confessed guiltily when I went back to the sitting room to report her disappearance.

'I bet she's gone down to the studio to plague Jude into letting her mess about with the modelling clay, or something,' Becca suggested.

'Oh yes, that will be it,' Noël said, 'though of course she should have told one of us where she was going first.'

'But then we would have stopped her from disturbing Jude,' Tilda pointed out. 'You know he can be such a bear when an idea strikes him.'

'He can be a bear anyway,' Coco said. She was sitting by the jigsaw puzzle, so I expect she'd rammed a few more pieces into the wrong places. Then she drifted out, probably to feast on the last fluff-covered Fruity-Go from the bottom of her handbag, or to have an illicit cigarette in her room with the window open.

'That girl's a waste of space,' Becca said, then added that someone should go down to the studio and bring Jess back. 'But don't look at me, I think I ate too much breakfast and I want to have a doze in front of the telly. *White Christmas* is on again.'

'Oh, is it? I might join you,' Noël said.

'And I will too, if Holly doesn't need me,' Tilda agreed, though I wasn't about to suggest *she* trekked off down the drive in her high-heeled marabou and velvet slippers to look for Jess.

'I'll walk down and bring her back with me. I can give my friend another ring while I'm down there.'

'Oh, good! Tell Jess she's very naughty and bring her straight back,' Tilda said.

I set off down the snow at the edge of the drive, which was definitely not as crisp as it was yesterday. It didn't seem quite as deep, either, so perhaps was starting to subside from underneath in the way drifts sometimes do, leaving a crystal shell of harder snow on top.

It was more than possible that Jude had sent Jess straight home again, so at any minute I expected to find her dejectedly trudging towards me. And I decided I didn't really need to call Laura again either, since nothing much had happened to report since yesterday, apart from Jude's suspiciously jealous-looking hissy fit.

It occurred to me that there was no-one else in the whole world *except* Laura who genuinely cared about me any more: no family or other friends close enough. Yes, there was a circle of people I'd known from school who all met up occasionally, including Laura and my erstwhile Homebodies boss, Ellen, but that was not the same at all . . .

Laura's family were always kind, but I had distanced myself too much after Alan died and now the breach is unbridgeable. We grieved in different ways – they celebrated his life and I pretended it had never happened. But I'd changed so much in the last couple of weeks . . .

And here at Old Place I was suddenly surrounded by long-lost relatives, even though none of them realised the connection and would probably be highly embarrassed if they did ever know! Jude would immediately believe the worst, that I was out for what I could get, and think he'd been right to be suspicious all along!

Still, since I wasn't going to tell them, it didn't matter.

There was still no sign of Jess when I turned off the drive up the track through the dark pine trees, so I thought Jude must have relented and let her stay. But then, as the trees opened out onto the banks of the stream below the studio, I suddenly spotted her black-clad figure – right in the middle of the frozen mill pond, testing the ice by stamping on it with one booted foot.

It made an odd, high-pitched, singing sound and my blood ran cold: I raced for the bank, calling urgently, 'Jess! Jess! Stop that and come back here this minute!'

She half-turned, startled by my voice – and then there was a horribly loud cracking noise like a small explosion and down she plummeted with a scream and a splash. For a heart-stopping moment she vanished completely . . . and then her head popped up and she was floundering among bobbing shards of ice in the bitterly cold black water.

I didn't stop to think, just ran out onto the frozen pond and flung myself face down, reaching out to her. I managed to grab first one of her cold little hands in a firm grip, and then the other, soaking myself in freezing water to the shoulders in the process.

'It's all r-right,' she said through chattering teeth, though her face looked blue-white, 'I can s-swim.'

But how long would she last in water at that temperature? And the ice beneath *me* was starting to crack too, I could hear it; but I didn't know if I was capable of sliding backwards and pulling her with me – and I certainly wasn't letting go of her.

It was just looking as if I would be joining her – though in that case I thought perhaps I would be able to boost her out onto the ice to go and fetch help – when I heard the slam of the studio door and Jude's deep voice exclaiming, 'What the *hell*?'

Perhaps my shouts had alerted Merlin: I could hear frantic muffled barking.

'I think the ice underneath me is breaking,' I called, as calmly as I could. 'But if it does, I have a plan to get Jess out and you can go for help.'

'I have a better plan: can you keep hold of her if I pull you *both* out?'

'Yes, of course, if you're quick. My hands are starting to go numb.'

He *was* quick: my ankles were seized in a grip like iron and, with a mighty heave, I was sliding back across the ice like a walrus in reverse gear, bringing the sodden dead weight of Jess with me.

'Oh God, Holly, I could have lost you both!' he said, scooping me up into a suffocating bear hug as soon as he'd landed us safely, and then just as suddenly sitting me down in the snow while he did the same to Jess. Then he said grimly, 'Jess, you know you shouldn't mess about by the water on your own, let alone go on the ice!'

'You *w-were* here, I w-wasn't on my own,' she said through chattering teeth.

'But I didn't *know* you were here – and Holly didn't know how deep the water was when she came to your rescue,' he said, pulling off her wellies and tipping out the water. 'You would have frozen to death if you hadn't got out. What if I hadn't heard you, or Holly hadn't come just when she did? How long do you think you would have lasted?'

'You w-would have heard me shouting,' Jess said. 'Or maybe I c-could have climbed back onto the ice.'

'No chance – and Holly would have been in there with you in another few minutes, freezing to death.'

'Never mind all that now, she's going to get pneumonia if she carries on sitting there, soaked to the skin,' I told him.

'*You're* pretty wet and cold too,' he said, frowning at me. 'I'll just switch off things in the studio and get Merlin, then we'll have to run all the way up to the house, there's nothing else for it.'

'*Run?*' I repeated incredulously, because I was starting to feel limp and shaky and as if I'd like a nice lie down in the soft snow.

'It'll warm you up,' he said, then vanished into the studio and came back a minute later with Merlin, who washed our faces with a warm tongue in an excess of relief.

Jude rammed Jess's wellies back on, hauled us both to our feet, and forcibly propelled us back towards the house at a shambling run, slipping and sliding through the snow, only his firm grip on our arms keeping us upright.

I expect it looked quite comic, even if it didn't feel like it.

Luckily Becca saw us coming from the morning-room window and deduced that something was wrong. She capably took charge of Jess, whisking her off for a hot bath.

'And you too,' Jude said to me, divesting me of my boots and wet anorak in the warm kitchen as if I was a helpless toddler . . . which was actually about what I felt like.

'Oh, I'm all right,' I protested, though I was shaking with cold and shock. 'I'll just go and change.'

'No, you won't – you'll have a hot bath too, I'll go and run it for you now,' he insisted. 'Come on, you can get the rest of your things off while I'm running it.'

My fingers were so frozen I had trouble getting out of my jeans, but I managed it and then when I got in the hot bath I got pins and needles as the circulation returned, which was *agony*.

Once that wore off my body felt heavy and limp, even though my mind was churning with painful thoughts: the whole experience had shocked me to the core in more ways than one. Not only might Jess and I have died (though I was still pretty sure I could have got Jess out, if I'd fallen in the water), but it had brought back all the trauma of Alan's death, too.

But I couldn't stay in there forever and Jude must have heard the water running out, because there was a cup of hot, sweet tea laced with whisky on my bedside table when I emerged . . . right next to the photo of Ned I'd left propped up there, though since it seemed to have fallen on its face, I hoped he hadn't noticed.

The tea was disgusting but I drank it anyway, in case he took it into his head to check, which would be just like him. I could feel the unaccustomed whisky thawing some of the internal chill.

When I finally went back down to the kitchen, in one of my warm, comfortable tunic jumpers and dry jeans, Jude was there waiting for me and made me more tea, insisting I sit down next to the Aga.

'But not six spoons of sugar in it this time, or whisky!' I protested weakly.

'Sugar's good for shock and I was worried it might have caused you some lasting harm . . . but maybe I *shouldn't* have put whisky in it?' he added, sounding worried.

'No, I – I think in a way it might have done me good.'

'What is it?' he asked, turning with the mug in his hand and getting a good look at my face. 'You're not feeling *ill*, are you?'

'N-no, I'm fine. It's not that – it's just that my husband, Alan . . . that's how *he* was killed, running onto a frozen lake to save a dog that had fallen through the ice . . . Only it was really deep and he wasn't much of a swimmer, so he died and . . . well, I've only just realised that he couldn't help it!'

The words poured unstoppably out of me and a rush of tears filled my eyes, blinding me. 'I've been so angry with him all these years for being such a fool – leaving me alone the way he did, just to rescue a d-dog – and I would have done exactly the same for Merlin, or any other living creature, let alone Jess!'

And then I was crying in earnest and Jude put down the mug and came and pulled me up into a warm, comforting, enveloping embrace against his broad chest, patting my back with a large and surprisingly gentle hand as I cried.

'He couldn't *help* it!' I sobbed into his shoulder, in a wimpy way I would normally deplore. 'He *couldn't* help it!'

'No, he'd have had an adrenaline rush and his impulses would have taken over on the spur of the moment, just as yours did – and thank goodness you were there, because I might not have heard Jess and I don't think she could have got out alone – she'd have died. And you risked your own life to save her, so I could have lost you *both*.'

I could have pointed out that he'd never had me in the first place, but I was feeling too limply acquiescent and in need of comfort. I fished out my handkerchief, mopped my eyes and blew my nose.

'Feeling better now?' he asked, then as I looked up to reply, that wonderful fleeting smile of his suddenly appeared . . .

And then, I'm not sure how, my arms were around him, too,

and we were kissing as if we would never stop . . . Until he suddenly wrenched his mouth from mine and held me at arm's length.

'I'm so sorry, Holly! I shouldn't have taken advantage of you, when you were so shocked . . . but that took me by surprise too – I really didn't intend to kiss you.'

'It's all right, it doesn't matter – forget it,' I said shakily, recalling all the reasons why that very passionate kiss shouldn't have happened between us. 'I think it must have been the whisky – I'm not used to it.'

'Was it just the whisky, though? I got the feeling you wanted to kiss me as much as I wanted to kiss you,' he said and our eyes, inches apart, met and held for a long moment.

I looked away first. 'Perhaps . . . but it was just a physical thing.'

'Was it, Holly?' he said quietly. 'I think we need to talk when you're feeling better . . . but first, there's something I really need to ask you right now—' he began.

But whatever it was, it would have to wait, because just at that moment Becca popped her head through the door to tell us that Jess seemed to be no worse for her icy plunge and was tucked up under a blanket in front of the sitting-room fire with Tilda, reading a book.

'Feeling okay now?' Becca asked me kindly. 'Jude looking after you?'

'Yes, I'm fine, thank you,' I said, though I knew my eyes must be red, a dead giveaway. 'I'd better do something about lunch, because it's practically dinner time and everyone must be starving.'

'I'll do that,' Jude said.

'No, I can manage.'

'Then manage *me*: you sit next to the Aga and boss me about – you're good at that.'

'It takes one to know one,' I snapped back and he grinned.

'There you are, you're feeling better already!'

I gave in and sat down – by now the whisky seemed to have gone to my legs anyway. 'It was only going to be Gentleman's Relish sandwiches and cups of soup, followed by mincemeat flapjacks or the last of the mince pies – I took those out of the freezer earlier.'

'I think even *I* can manage that. And actually, I'm not a *totally* hopeless cook, whatever you might think.'

'Don't forget that I've seen the extent of your ready meal supplies in the freezer.'

We were surprisingly amicable in our bickering, now that the awkwardness of an embrace which had taken both of us by surprise had worn off. But though we might have acknowledged a mutual physical attraction, I expect he was now remembering all the reasons why taking it any further would be a really bad idea, just as I was.

I wondered what on earth he had been going to ask me when Becca came in: maybe if I was a secret pretender to the throne of Old Place?

I felt absolutely fine later and insisted on cooking dinner myself, though I ended up with Michael and Jude, in slightly wary alliance, as assistants. Tilda and Jess made another potato-hedgehog starter with cheese and small pickled onions on cocktail sticks.

But at least Jess and I were excused the final play rehearsal and could loll about watching the others, until ordered off early to bed with hot water bottles by Jude. When I protested that I had things to do in the kitchen first, he said there was nothing that couldn't keep until the morning and also that he was perfectly capable of locking up and all the rest of it himself, pointing out that he had managed to survive perfectly well before my arrival, so I gave in.

He'd been giving me very searching looks all evening, but since they weren't dissimilar to the ones he sent my way when he was drawing me, he was probably just sizing me up for another sculpture: given my watery performance, a Little Mermaid, perhaps?

I was quite happy to go off to bed, really, because I was starting to feel exhausted and strangely light-headed, though calm in an odd sort of way: I suppose the whole experience on the ice had been a very cathartic one, when I came to think about it.

Now I'd accepted that Alan couldn't help the actions that had led to his death, I could finally forgive him, letting go of the anger that had burdened me for the last eight years and enabling me to remember him, quite simply, with love.

And Gran? According to her journal, she seemed to have determined to do much the same:

Yesterday I packed my bags and departed from my lodgings without fuss, and was married that afternoon by special licence, a friend of my husband's in a nearby town officiating. It all seemed like a strange dream, but I now mean to put out of my head all memories of what went before, and make Joseph the best possible wife, even though our relationship will always be only that of loving friends.

June, 1945

Chapter 35: Acted Out

Joseph put a newspaper into my hand this morning, pointing to the report of the death of my lover in a motorbike accident. Then he left me. Later, we prayed together for N. I am so sorry for his family and for his fiancée, if she truly loved him. That chapter of my life is now closed . . . apart from the child I carry.

June, 1945

Jude was downstairs early and back to being quietly helpful, though there was still some awkwardness between us – in my case largely because that passionate kiss had featured largely and rather feverishly in my dreams last night. I knew *he* was thinking about it too – our eyes kept meeting and then we'd both immediately look away.

I felt absolutely fine, with no ill after-effects, as I assured him when he asked, accompanying the question with one of those searching stares from his deep-set dark eyes.

I was glad that we seemed to be friends again and he seemed cheerful enough (probably, in the light of day, deeply relieved that I hadn't taken the kiss seriously!).

He even fell in with Coco's suggestion that we have a quick run-through of our play scenes after breakfast, before he went to the studio, since it was New Year's Eve (which, what with everything else happening, I had managed to forget!) and the final performance was to be later today, in front of an invited audience of Old Nan and Richard.

We played our *Twelfth Night* roles straight and serious, no hamming this time, and then off Jude went, commanding me to bring his lunch to the studio later, so we were back to normal again – or what passed for it.

'Okay,' I agreed, 'but I won't be able to stay long because I've got way too much to do. I want to turn the ham bone into pea and ham soup for tomorrow, for a start, and then I thought I might make some soda bread.'

'Sounds good to me,' he said. 'By the way, Guy, one of us will need to drive down and pick up Old Nan and Richard this afternoon.'

'I'll do that if you like, then,' he offered and then gave me a glinting, flirtatious smile. 'Holly can come with me.'

'Holly will be too busy cooking dinner for eleven people,' I replied pointedly.

'We've discussed the menu: it's all very straightforward,' Tilda said. 'Smoked mackerel mousse on toast triangles – my very own recipe – roast lamb with rosemary and then treacle tart and custard.'

'Lovely,' Becca said. 'I'm not going to want to go home when the roads have thawed. Maybe I could ask Richard to pray for more snow?'

Merlin had stayed with me this morning, but accompanied me down to the studio when I took Jude's lunch.

He was welding, totally absorbed in his work, so I put on the spare visor and sat in my usual place on the dais to watch him until he finally switched off the torch.

'It's coming along, don't you think?' he asked, examining his handiwork critically. Already, what had started out looking like a few linked metal leaves had begun to elongate and swirl into the interlinked forms of horse and woman. It was turning out a bit like one of the maquettes he'd made, so I could see roughly where it was heading.

'Yes, and I believe you now when you say you get paid good money for your sculptures,' I teased him and he grinned.

'You're very good at dampening my pretensions, but my work is much in demand, I'll have you know! "Some are born great, some achieve greatness and some have greatness thrust upon them."'

'Is that from the play? I don't remember that bit.'

'It's in one of the scenes we're not doing,' he said, sitting down next to me. Merlin came out from under the dais and nudged his way between us, leaning his weight affectionately against Jude's shoulder; though that might have been just a keen interest in the sandwiches.

Jude was silent while he ate, his mind clearly on his work rather than anything else, but when he'd finished and I was packing the remains back into the basket, he suddenly said, 'Holly, we need to talk about yesterday, when I—'

'Oh, let's forget all that,' I said brightly. 'We'd both had a shock and it makes you do the strangest things. I feel *much* better now.'

'Yes, but Holly, you—'

I picked up the basket and headed for the door. 'I must go – see you later. I'll be so glad to get this wretched play over with!'

The New Year's Eve audience, well primed by a good roast lamb dinner and a drop or two of sherry, were prepared to watch three rank amateurs and one professional actor massacre scenes from the Bard with equanimity.

In fact, *I* wished I could have watched it instead of acted in it, because it must have been hilariously funny, what with me spending most of the time looking like a waif in Jude's enormous greatcoat, Coco a skeletal Bride of Frankenstein and Jude, resigned but unable to resist slightly hamming it up, in his blue velvet cloak and imaginary moustache.

Michael played it straight, but gave a muted performance, probably to stop the rest of us looking quite so awful: but if so, it didn't really work, especially in the parts that hinged on Sebastian and Viola looking identical: 'An apple, cleft in two, is not more twin than these two creatures: which is Sebastian?'

You couldn't have found two people more *unlike* than Michael and me if you tried, so I couldn't blame the snort of laughter that came from Guy's corner of the room at that point.

However, the rest of the audience applauded each scene enthusiastically, though that might have had something to do with the sherry.

Michael spoke his final lines very well, considering he had the distraction of Coco draped adoringly around him by this point, and then it was Jude's turn to declare his love for me – such as it was:

'Cesario, come – for so you shall be, while you are a man; but, when in other habits you are seen, Orsino's mistress and his fancy's queen.'

To my mind, that line's about as romantic as Prince Charles saying, when asked if he was in love with Diana, 'Yes – whatever *love* means,' even if Jude did accompany the words with a look of smouldering promise. I think I may have underestimated his acting abilities as well as his artistic ones.

There was another round of applause and Old Nan dabbed her eyes with a pink tissue and said sentimentally that it was terribly moving and she loved a happy ending. 'And I'll knit you and Jude a nice Afghan for your wedding present,' she declared, beaming at us.

'We're not really getting married, it was just in the play, Nan,' I explained.

'I don't hold with all this living together out of wedlock,' she said severely. 'Don't think you're getting my Afghan until you tie the knot with this poor lass, Jude Martland!'

'All right, Nan,' he said. 'I'll bear that in mind.'

'Interesting play, isn't it?' the vicar said, allowing Guy to refill his sherry glass. 'Nothing is what it seems right until the end and it must have been even more confusing in Shakespeare's day, when the female parts were played by boys.'

'Yes, so a boy was playing a girl, pretending to be a boy!'

'That's right. It all harks back to mumming and ancient pagan cross-dressing fertility rituals, like the Man-Woman character at the Revels, as you will see.'

'If I'm still here,' I said. 'It does seem to be slowly thawing, so I might have left.'

'Of course you'll be here,' Old Nan snapped tetchily, waking suddenly from a half-doze in time to catch this. 'Where else would you be?'

Quite possibly in a smart house in London cooking falafels, if Ellen got her way, I thought!

Guy ran Old Nan and Richard home again soon after that. To my surprise, no-one seemed interested in staying up until midnight to see the New Year in since, as Noël explained when I asked, Twelfth Night had always been Little Mumming's night of transition from the old year to the new, and that was not likely ever to change.

Everyone went to bed except Jude, who followed me into the kitchen where I was about to wash the sherry glasses.

I thought he was going to let Merlin out and take a last look at the horses, but instead he came and turned me round by the shoulders, staring down at me as if my face was a slightly untrustworthy map he was trying to read, to find a destination he was not sure he wanted to reach.

'What's the matter?' I asked uneasily.

'It's what Richard was saying: because *you're* not really who you say you are either, are you, Holly?'

'What do you mean? Of course I'm Holly Brown!' I hedged.

'Oh, I'm sure that's your *name*, but I've suspected practically

352

from the first moment I set eyes on you that you were related to us, probably on the wrong side of the blanket. Given Ned's nature and the way you seemed to steer the conversation onto him at every opportunity, he seemed the likeliest candidate. Then when I saw that photograph of him on your bedside table, it all clicked into place and I realised that your grandmother must have been the—'

'"Little mill girl" Noël told us about, that Ned got into trouble?' I finished bitterly. 'Yes, she was, but she wasn't a mill girl, she was a nurse.'

'I'm *so* sorry,' he apologised, though it was hardly *his* fault. 'What happened to her?'

'It's all in her diaries, the ones I've been reading since I got here – how he seduced her and then, when she got pregnant, dumped her and ran off home. She found out he'd been engaged to someone else all the time,' I told him, 'and then her parents disowned her too, and she was so desperate she even thought about taking her own life.'

'Oh, God, that's terrible!' he said.

'Yes, but then the local Strange Baptist minister came to her rescue and married her – my grandfather.'

He ran a distracted hand through his dark hair, so that it stood on end. 'I had no idea! It doesn't reflect very well on my Uncle Ned – or my family – does it?'

'No, nobody seemed to care what happened to her.'

'Did she ever know he'd been killed?'

'Yes, but only because she saw it in the local newspaper. It must have been a horrible way to find out.'

'The family really forgot about her and the baby, they never offered her any money for support? I find that so hard to believe!'

'So far as I've got in the journal, she'd heard nothing from them – and anyway, she wouldn't have wanted their money even if she hadn't married my grandfather. And if you think *I* came here hoping to ingratiate myself with the family to get some

353

kind of financial gain out of the connection, then you're *quite* wrong!' I added indignantly.

'The thought *did* cross my mind at first,' he admitted, 'but not for long. I mean, half the time you didn't even seem to like us, especially Guy – which was when I twigged that he was supposed to be just like Ned and started to put two and two together.'

'Believe it or not, I had no idea I was related to you, until I started to read Gran's diaries.'

'You mean, you'd never even heard of the Martlands before?'

'Not until a couple of weeks before I came here.' I described Gran's last words. 'Then Ellen told me the name of the family she wanted me to house-sit for and I thought it was just one of those strange coincidences: there seemed little chance your Martlands could have any connection to my gran. In fact, I was more than half-expecting the lost love of her life to have been one of the doctors at the hospital!'

'I can see why you feel bitter about what happened, but Ned always sounded weak rather than bad, so perhaps if he hadn't been killed, he *would* have supported her?' he suggested.

'I don't think so and nor did Gran, or she wouldn't have felt so abandoned that she thought of killing herself.'

'Well, thank God she didn't,' he said and then added, frowning, 'and I suppose this makes us cousins of a kind, though *not* first cousins, which is probably just as well . . .'

His hands on my shoulders tightened their grip and, seeing his intent, I said hastily, 'Too close for kissing.'

'Have you never heard of kissing cousins?' he said, raising one eyebrow and giving me that brief, intimate and spine-sapping smile.

'I don't think the saying means *that* kind of kissing,' I said, resolutely releasing myself and stepping back. 'We're still too close for that, even if our connection is illegitimate – and anyway, I'm not going to go the way of my grandmother, falling for a Martland!'

'But I'm not remotely like my Uncle Ned!' he said, looking slightly hurt. 'And I don't think the relationship is close enough to matter – if we don't want it to.'

'Look, Jude, there may be a bit of physical attraction between us, but you're really not my type, and I'm *certainly* not yours, so how closely related we are isn't ever going to be an issue. And no-one else needs to know about this: in a couple of days I'll be gone as if I was never here.'

'Yes they do – Noël needs to know,' he said stubbornly. 'He'll be delighted and so will Tilda and Becca, not to mention Jess, because they're fond of you already. I don't think you'll manage to escape us so easily, after that.'

'You're not really going to tell him!'

'Just watch me!' he said, then looked down at me thoughtfully and asked quietly: 'Is there anything else you'd like to tell me about, Holly . . . in confidence?'

'No, nothing at all!' I snapped and he seemed strangely disappointed.

What on earth else can he have expected me to confess to? Being the lost heir of the Romanovs, perhaps?

I escaped to bed after that, where I tried to distract myself from the scene in the kitchen by reading a bit more of the journal, though I wasn't expecting any more revelations: I knew the outcome.

Granny seemed to have stoically thrown herself into the role of minister's wife and if there was some talk in the congregation about the sudden wedding and the disparity in their ages, they seemed to have accepted it.

I was just nodding over another long, long passage about Gran's undeserved good fortune and the mercy of God when I heard a loud yell from Michael's room next door, followed by a loud crash and a more feminine scream and exclamations.

I leapt out of bed and rushed onto the landing and then

355

paused with my hand on the doorknob to his room, suddenly wondering if I was interrupting something I shouldn't be!

Jude, who was closest, arrived from the other direction and I could see from his expression he'd got the same idea – and that he thought I was coming *out* of Michael's room, not going in!

'Sorry,' he said abruptly. 'I thought I heard a scream.'

'You did, but it wasn't me.'

Michael's door swung open and Coco stormed out, the near-transparent folds of her negligee clutched around her.

'Forget it!' she said viciously over one shoulder.

'Coco?' I heard Michael say, before she slammed the door behind her, cutting him off.

'What?' she said, catching sight of us. 'Look, I was sleepwalking, all right?' And she brushed past Jude and vanished.

He gave me one of his more unfathomable looks and followed her.

Chapter 36: Piked

Joseph asked that he might be moved to a different chapel, since Ormskirk had so many sad memories now and it would give us a chance to start afresh. At my request, he is reading The Pilgrim's Progress *to me in the evenings while I am knitting or sewing, so that my head, heart and hands are all occupied.*

June, 1945

When Jude came down this morning he didn't mention the Coco episode – and neither did I. I was hoping that, on reflection, he would keep his discovery about who I really was to himself, too.

When he came back in from the stables I was just making a stuffing for the pike, to an old English recipe I'd found in one of my books. I'd never cooked one before, but waste not, want not. I'd run out of sausage meat for the stuffing, but had defrosted some of the last of the excellent pork sausages from the freezer and removed the contents, which would do just as well.

Jude must have been warm from mucking out, because he pulled his jumper off and the T-shirt underneath came with it . . . I was still staring at him, slightly mesmerised by the play of muscles across his broad back, when he turned and caught me.

'The thaw seems to have well and truly set in,' I said quickly, concentrating my attention back on what I was doing, though when I risked another glance up he was giving me that intent

357

look from his deep-set eyes under a furrowed brow again, the slightly suspicious one that should have been dispelled now he knew about Gran.

'Holly, I hope you'll remember what I said last night: if you want to confide in someone, you can trust me.'

'Mmm . . .' I said, totally puzzled. Confide *what*, exactly? He already knew all my secrets – even, now, that I fancied him!

'What on earth *is* that you're stuffing?' he asked in a totally different voice.

'It's a pike Becca caught last year and shoved into the bottom of your freezer. I strongly believe that if you kill living creatures, then you should eat them. So we are.'

'I didn't even know it was in there!'

'That's because you never delve deeper than the surface layer of convenience foods.'

'True. By the way, I'll be back for lunch today,' he said, which was a surprise. Perhaps inspiration had flagged?

After breakfast I went out in the snow again with Guy, Jess and Michael, because as Jess pointed out, it might not be around much longer. She was right, too, because it was now subsiding faster than an exuberant soufflé that had overreached itself.

Coco had come down late and in a mood of silent sulkiness, which I put down to a combination of post-performance boredom and the result of whatever happened – or didn't happen – between her and Michael last night. She was certainly giving him the cold shoulder.

Michael snatched a moment to unburden himself while we were climbing to the top of the paddock with the sledges. 'Coco came to my room last night!'

'Yes, I know – and so does Jude. We both heard the screams and yells and came out onto the landing. She said she was sleepwalking!'

'Sleepwalking nothing!' he replied. 'One minute I was fast

asleep, and the next she'd tossed the duvet off and jumped on me, stark naked!'

'No!' I gasped. 'That was pretty brazen.'

'So I yelled – as you do, if someone jumps on you when you're asleep – and automatically threw her off. She landed on the floor and screamed . . . and that really woke me up so I realised what was happening and tried to calm her down.'

'I don't think it worked, Michael!'

'No, especially when she came on to me again and I made it clear I didn't fancy her in the least,' he said ruefully.

'I expect that would make her angry,' I agreed. 'Not many men would have turned her down!'

'Perhaps not . . .' He paused and glanced at me, 'but the thing is, Holly – well, I'm gay,' he confessed. 'That's really why my marriage broke up.'

'Really? Yes, I suppose that would make a bit of an irreconcilable difficulty,' I said, surprised, and he laughed.

We'd reached the top of the paddock now and I put down my sledge. 'But if you don't mind my asking, Michael, why did you get married in the first place?'

'Debbie knew I was gay because she was my best friend and we shared a flat – but then she suddenly changed and thought she could change me, too. I wanted a family, so I think I let her persuade me it would work and we got married and had our little girl.' He smiled sadly. 'For a while I thought we might be able to make a go of it. But then she fell for someone else – and so did I. And I don't know why I'm telling you all this,' he added, sounding surprised. 'My being gay is still a bit of a secret.'

'I expect you haven't really talked it over with anyone before, that's why. And of course I won't mention it to anyone else, but why does your being gay have to be a secret?'

'I usually get the romantic lead roles and I just don't feel audiences would take me seriously if they knew I was openly gay, even though I'm sure most people in the business have a good idea.' He ran a hand through his light brown hair, which ruffled attractively, and smiled ruefully. 'I don't know! I'm just certain that I'm not ready to step *right* out of the closet yet.'

'I understand – and anyway, your private life should be just that. But poor Coco!'

'Poor me, you mean!'

'She's mad with you, though I'd have thought she'd still want to keep on your right side, because of getting into acting.'

'Yes, but she isn't very bright, is she?' He sighed. 'I think she's going to be a real pain now that the play's done and I've turned her down – but maybe with this thaw they'll clear the roads soon?'

'And then we can *all* go home,' I agreed briskly and he gave me a look.

'Not quite *all* of us, I don't think, if Jude has anything to do with it!'

I felt my face going slightly pink. 'If you mean you think there's something going on between Jude and me, then you are quite wrong!'

'No, I'm not: the way you keep catching each other's eye is a dead giveaway, not to mention all those cosy hours alone in his studio, when he made it quite plain he didn't want any other visitors. I can't imagine why you're both in denial.'

'Don't be silly!'

'I'm serious! In fact, I think I'm in imminent danger of having my nose punched if he catches me in anything even *remotely* resembling a compromising situation with you again.'

I remembered Jude's expression of black rage when he'd briefly thought I was coming out of Michael's room last night and shivered. 'There may be a little physical attraction between us—'

'Like the way the air crackles between you whenever you're together?' he said helpfully.

'—but that's all,' I finished. 'In fact, he more or less told me the other day that losing his wife made him never want to fall in love again – and I feel exactly the same way. It hurts too much when you lose them.'

'Aren't you two ever coming down?' called Guy from the bottom of the hill and I climbed onto the red sledge and pushed myself off with such force that I shot down past the astonished horses and nearly went into the fence at the bottom.

I'd made the pea and ham soup and fresh soda bread, so we had that for lunch along with cheese, pickles and chutney. My stocks of staples like cheese and butter were dwindling rapidly, so really it was just as well that the thaw *had* set in.

Despite my coaxing, Coco refused to come into the kitchen with us and eat anything, saying she must have put on pounds over Christmas because of my meanness and she needed to get back in shape for her next modelling assignment, so apart from Michael it was just family . . . of which I was a member, even if it appeared that Jude had thought better of telling the others.

But, hard on the heels of that thought, he suddenly looked around the kitchen table and announced, 'There's something I feel it's important you all know, though Holly doesn't want me to tell you.'

'You're getting married – hurray!' cried Jess and his sallow skin flushed a bit.

'No, it's not that sort of thing, Jess,' he said. 'I'm not starting to announce my engagement on an annual basis. In fact, perhaps you should go somewhere else while we discuss this – it's very personal to Holly.'

'Oh no – I'll be quiet, I promise!'

'If you're going to tell everyone, you might as well include Jess,' I said resignedly.

'Okay,' he agreed. 'Well, Holly's been reading through her gran's diaries while she's been here and discovered that she's the granddaughter of Ned Martland.'

'What, Holly's grandmother is the mill girl Ned—' began Noël, astounded, then stopped suddenly.

'Seduced and abandoned, yes,' I agreed, 'though actually, she nursed him back to health, she wasn't a mill girl.'

'Oh dear,' Tilda said, rather inadequately.

'Understatement of the year, Tilda,' said Becca.

'So you can see why she was a bit reluctant to mention it and claim relationship with a family like ours,' Jude said.

'Not that I blame you for what Ned Martland did,' I said quickly, though of course sometimes I *had* a bit . . .

'I certainly didn't intend to sound disparaging about your grandmother,' Noël apologised. 'And in fact, I am extremely happy to meet you at last, m'dear!' He exchanged a meaningful look with Tilda and continued, 'Many's the time I've said to Tilda that I wished I could have found Ned's girl after he was killed.'

'Then why didn't you?' I asked bluntly.

'Well, the thing is, there was a dreadful fuss when he told my parents about her and the baby, especially since he was engaged to the daughter of Lord Lennerton at the time, who was going to give him a job so he could work his way up to the board. It looked like he was finally about to settle down, so our parents were pleased – which made finding out about your grandmother even more of a blow.'

'But he knuckled down and did what they wanted?'

'Not exactly. We didn't know much about his girl, except that she was from a working-class background – not even her name. But the thing is, my brother Alex and I could see Ned had genuinely fallen in love with her, and we thought he should marry her anyway, not pay her off like our parents wanted him to do.'

'Did he *really* love her?'

'Oh yes, I'm sure he did, though he didn't realise it until he came home and began to miss her. But he was weak-willed so it took him weeks of dithering before he made his mind up and wrote to his fiancée to break it off. Then he went to tell your grandmother that he wanted to marry her.'

'He actually *did*? But he can't have seen her, because she would have said so! She did see the notice of his death in the paper, but she was married to my grandfather by then.'

'He probably found out that she had married someone else, then, and was killed on the way back home. I suppose we will never know precisely what happened. But after that, there seemed no way of finding her.'

'I think we all expected her to turn up,' Becca said. 'Our parents would have felt duty-bound to support her and her child, if she had.'

'I've felt so guilty all these years that she didn't ask for help – and also that it was my doing in persuading him to go back to her, that made Ned take the road that day and led to his death,' Noël said sadly.

'But you didn't know that would be the outcome, and at least he was doing the right thing,' Becca pointed out.

'If he'd discovered she'd married someone else, perhaps he was too upset to concentrate on the way back and that might have caused the accident?' I suggested, softening towards Ned a fraction.

'But he was fast and reckless on that motorbike anyway, wasn't he?' Jude said. 'You've always told me that.'

'And *this* is the uncle you all keep telling me *I'm* like!' said Guy rather bitterly. 'Weak, vacillating . . .'

'Actually, you aren't quite *that* bad, dear,' Tilda allowed.

'Thanks!'

'Well, the past is all water under the bridge now,' Noël said. 'I hope your grandmother was happy in her marriage?'

'Grandpa was the father of her childhood sweetheart, a Strange Baptist minister. I only just remember him, but he was a lovely, sweet-natured man – everyone loved him.'

'Thank God,' Noël said sincerely. He did look as if a burden had been lifted from his shoulders and Tilda, next to him, patted his hand. 'You feel things too much, Noël.'

'Thank you for telling me all that, though,' I said. 'I do feel so much better about Ned now I understand that he did really love her, in his way. And she never forgot him, you know: just before she died she said his name and smiled, and I'm sure she could see him in the room.'

Jess, who'd been obediently silent throughout, now piped up, 'Does that make you my auntie, even if you *don't* marry Uncle Jude, Holly?'

'I suppose I am, in a distant sort of way,' I agreed. 'But there'd be no question of me marrying Jude even if we weren't cousins, so it's all academic.'

'But people do marry their cousins, don't they?' she insisted, but fortunately by then Noël, Becca, Tilda and even Guy had gathered around me to warmly welcome me into the family, the missing Martland come home: a bit like the one ewe-lamb that was lost in the parable Gran used to tell me when I was little.

Jude went off down to the studio and took Jess with him, though she had to promise not to go anywhere near him while he was welding. I hoped he would tell her to drop the whole matchmaking idea, because if he did have any designs on me, they were not likely to be marital but more of the quick-fling variety. He'd made it clear he was not looking for anything more . . . and so had I, come to that.

Still, feeling a flush of sudden warmth towards the world, I made Coco an egg white omelette, which looked vile, and took it through to her with a glass of fizzy water. She was in the morning room huddled miserably in front of the TV, though due to a burst of snowy interference it was hard to tell what she was watching. She actually thanked me for the omelette, though she did say that fizzy mineral water made you fat.

'Spoil yourself,' I said encouragingly, leaving her to it while I went back to the kitchen to study my recipes and whip up a dessert to follow tonight's fatted calf – or fatted pike, in this case.

Chapter 37: Bumps

We have moved to Merchester and today Hilda visited us here for the first time and confessed that N came to look for me on the day of his accident, meaning to ask me to marry him, but she and Pearl told him I had already married someone else . . . They had not wanted to cause me further pain but, after discussing it, thought now that it was important that I knew this.

August, 1945

The drive is now clear of snow, even if it is still banked up on either side of it, and right after breakfast there was a loud tooting of horns and we all poured out to see that Liam and Ben had towed Coco's sports car up to the door.

It was distinctly battered around the rear bumper and they'd gaffer-taped one end of the registration plate to the back to stop it completely falling off.

'Oh my God,' Coco exclaimed, clutching a hastily-snatched waxed coat (how the mighty are fallen!) around her thin shoulders. 'My poor car!'

'Better have it looked at by the garage in Great Mumming, before trying to drive it anywhere very far,' advised Liam.

'Yes, these low sports cars are useless on snow anyway and even if you made it to the motorway, you'd be blinded by spray from other vehicles,' Ben said critically. Then he spotted a bashful Jess and said kindly, 'Hello, we've heard you've taken to swimming in ice holes like they do in Sweden and places!'

She blushed. 'I just fell in. I thought it was completely frozen, but the bit right in the middle wasn't.'

'Done it myself years ago, when we were skating on it,' Ben admitted. 'Do you remember, Liam? Soaked me to the skin and I went home freezing.'

Jess brightened. 'Oh, did you?'

'She still wasn't supposed to be down near the river on her own,' Jude pointed out.

'Well, I don't expect she'll do it again – I didn't,' Ben said.

'How are the roads doing?' asked Jude.

'I don't expect there's any sign of the main one being cleared and my car dug out?' Michael asked hopefully. 'Not that I'm in a hurry to get away, but I don't want to be a burden on you for longer than I can help it, Jude – you've been very kind.'

'*I'm* in a hurry,' Coco said. 'I'm *desperate* to get out of here!'

'We saw the snowplough go through on the Great Mumming road earlier, but no traffic's been through yet. Maybe later today,' Liam said. 'But you can't get down to it anyway yet, because the hill below Weasel Pot is too bad. It might be all right tomorrow, if it keeps thawing like this.'

'Me and Dad walked down first thing and the end of Weasel Pot Lane is one big snowdrift, though it's sinking. You can see the red roof of your car,' Ben added consolingly to Michael, 'so the snowplough didn't run into it by mistake. Often happens, that does.'

'Oh . . . that's good,' Michael said nervously. 'Thank goodness I didn't buy a white car – and I'll certainly never follow SatNav again!'

367

'If the Three Wise Men had had SatNav, goodness knows where they would have ended up,' agreed Noël, who had delayed coming out long enough to wrap himself in his overcoat, deerstalker hat with flaps and scarf.

'If there's a bit more of a thaw tomorrow, we could go down and dig your car right out,' suggested Guy. 'Then it'll be even easier to spot. It's pulled off the road, isn't it?'

'Yes, Jude helped me push it onto the verge . . . or where we thought the verge was, because it was a bit hard to tell at the time.'

'I could come back to London in your car with you when it's clear, couldn't I?' Coco suggested, fluttering her false eyelashes at Michael hopefully, his rebuff clearly forgotten in her eagerness to get away. 'The AA can rescue mine later.'

'I'm going to see the friends I was to visit first – and actually, I'd thought of finding somewhere local to stay so I could watch the Twelfth Night Revels: I've heard so much about them now that I can't bear to leave without being there. Though I won't mention it when I leave, of course.'

'Good man!' Noël said.

'You're one of us,' Becca agreed.

'And naturally you're welcome to stay here for it,' Jude said, though not altogether enthusiastically.

Coco was pouting. '*I* don't want to stay for some stupid Morris dancing that no-one cares about anyway. Guy, you'll just have to drive me home, that's all there is to it. Then I never want to see you ever again.'

'*I'm* not leaving before Twelfth Night either,' Guy said.

'But last year we did!'

'Yes, but that was because I'd just had a punch-up with Jude. I don't have to get back to work until afterwards, so I might as well stay.'

'I think you're all mad – I just want to get home!' she wailed.

'I do think that the least you can do is take Coco back home,

Guy,' Jude said. 'It's your fault she got stuck here after all, and anyway, you never take part in the Revels.'

Guy raised a quizzical dark eyebrow at his brother. 'Are you trying to get rid of me?'

'I certainly feel my days have been enlivened by your company for long enough.'

'We could dig *my* car out tomorrow too, it's sitting in a snowdrift behind the house,' I suggested.

'Why? *You're* not going anywhere yet,' Jude snapped at me rudely, then brushed past into the house, only to reappear a few minutes later ready to go down to the studio. 'I'll expect you after lunch,' he tossed at me in passing.

'Holly is Jude's muse,' Becca explained to the boys, who looked blank.

'*And* she's a distant cousin,' added Noël. 'Isn't that lovely? One of the family.'

'Everyone'd guessed that already,' Liam said.

I did go down to the studio as ordered, but diverted long enough to give Laura a quick update on what had been happening, mostly the edited lowlights, like being outed to the entire family as an illegitimate relative, until I told her about the accident.

'But you could both easily have died!' she exclaimed, horrified. 'Thank goodness Jude heard you! Are you really all right?'

'Fine – but afterwards I fell to pieces, because it made me realise that Alan couldn't have stopped himself running onto the ice to rescue that dog – sheer instinct takes over in that sort of situation and I'd have done just the same for Merlin. It was . . . cathartic. I cried buckets over Jude Martland and he was very comforting.'

'So there you are, he has a kind heart!'

'And then he kissed me. Or I kissed him – he'd put a lot of

whisky in my tea for the shock and I wasn't myself. He could give George lessons,' I added thoughtfully.

'*Holly!*'

'Don't get excited: he was the one who stopped. He said he hadn't meant to take advantage of me when I was upset . . . but he'd probably just thought better of it. I told him it didn't matter, it was just shock and whisky, and we'd forget it.'

'Is that possible?'

'Yes,' I said firmly. 'Apart from him being my cousin, he's already made it plain he's not looking for any long-term commitment and I'm not about to repeat Gran's mistakes with another Martland male, either.'

I didn't dwell on my increasingly confused feelings about Jude, but I'm sure she read between the lines because she knows me too well.

Jude stopped working straight away when I went into the studio and wolfed down his lunch, so he must have been hungry. After that, he feverishly drew sketch after sketch of me with Merlin, almost as if he suspected I might suddenly vanish into thin air, before going back to his welding.

He was stripped to his T-shirt again . . . and it's no use: I may know he's not my type and he's out of bounds because he's my cousin – but my God, I have to admit there's something terribly sexy about him when he's welding!

I was so hot, if I'd gone out and rolled in the snow, it would have hissed.

Maybe I just have cabin fever, after being cooped up here so long? The sooner I get away, the better!

In Gran's journal that night she rambled off into another long soliloquy on the subject of God's plans for her and about loving forgiveness, though not everyone shared her views:

My parents have still not forgiven me, despite my marriage: perhaps they think I tricked Joseph into it. We have arranged that I will go to Joseph's sister in Cornwall well before the baby is expected, which will seem natural enough: Joseph has told her the truth and she wrote a wonderfully kind letter to me . . .

I couldn't believe that it was already Sunday again! Where has the time flown to?

Richard had sent word that he was holding another church service, since clearly the official vicar would not be making an appearance. According to Becca he only held services in the village twice a month anyway.

'It's not what it was when Richard was the vicar here, before they joined the two parishes together. He's not part of the community,' she grumbled. 'Though of course, Richard holds a service on the Sundays when he doesn't come, so we don't feel the loss.'

Guy and Michael were to drop them off at the church on their way to dig out Michael's car, but I declined to go with them since I wanted to have a trial run with the Revel Cakes and had steeped some saffron overnight ready. Jude decided to help them instead of going straight to the studio, but Coco, who was hideously bored, elected to give herself some kind of super-duper beauty treatment upstairs.

I didn't tell her I'd put her designer padded coat in the washing machine on hand wash. It looked so filthy, there didn't seem to be anything else to do with it and I thought it would come out okay if I tumbled it on low heat afterwards . . . But then, even if it didn't, she would probably have binned it once she got home, anyway.

'You don't know how to clean a fur hat?' I asked Tilda a couple of hours later when the church party had returned, dropped off by George, and a batch of delicious Revel Cakes were sitting on the wire rack, golden yellow with saffron and crusty with candied peel and sugar.

'Talcum powder and a good brushing might help?' she suggested.

'I thought it would be nice to send Coco off tomorrow looking less like a tramp,' I explained. 'I washed her coat and it's come up quite well. It's in the tumble drier now.'

'It'll be so lovely if we can get rid of her,' she agreed. 'What *is* that delicious smell?'

'Revel Cakes, though really they're more of a fruit-topped bun, aren't they? I found the recipe in a box in the kitchen, but I thought I'd better have a trial run before baking lots of them, because I only had dried yeast and not fresh. Would you like one?'

'I think we'd *all* like one,' Becca said. 'I'm going to miss your cooking when I've gone home – and now the lane down to the village is thawing out, I haven't really got much excuse to stay on, have I?'

'None of us want to outstay our welcome,' Noël said, 'and we've had a truly wonderful Christmas, thanks to you, Holly! But if Edwina manages to get here tomorrow, as she originally planned, *we* will be able to leave, too.'

'Edwina does my shopping with theirs and fills my freezer up with ready meals,' Becca said. 'She's a little powerhouse! Even Jude gives her his shopping list sometimes, too.'

The car-excavation party were late getting back for lunch, but eventually drove up in Michael's red car, though they'd had to jump-start it.

'Ben managed to plough down to the lower road, and there's traffic along it now,' Guy said. 'I wasn't sure Michael's car would get up the hill, but it made it once Ben had spread some grit and put a spare set of chains on the wheels.'

From the way they all talked about it, you'd think they'd just returned from some perilous Arctic expedition, mugged by polar bears at every turn!

Coco had come down to lunch (or not to lunch), looking much as she did before her beauty treatment, and was told that she could probably leave tomorrow.

'With me driving you – under *extreme* protest,' Guy explained.

'And wearing your lovely white coat,' I said. 'I've washed it and it's come up just like new!'

'You *washed* it?' she exclaimed, staring at me with wide, ice-chip blue eyes.

'It's surprising what will wash on a gentle cycle, and there didn't seem to be anything to be lost. I gave your hat a brush too, but really you need a specialist cleaner for that one.'

Typically, Coco didn't thank me for my efforts, but examined her coat as if incredulous it should have survived my cavalier treatment of it.

Tilda had said she had a packet of saffron at the lodge and I could see I'd need more for the Revel Cakes if I was to do a very big batch. So after lunch was cleared away, Jude and I walked down the drive together, though this was not by any intent on my part: he just happened to be setting off for the studio at the same time.

He was pretty quiet – but then, he often was.

'How many Revel Cakes do you think I'll need to make?' I asked him as we walked down through the pine trees to the lodge, passing the track up to the mill – he'd decided to go to the lodge with me first, for the exercise, though I would have thought digging Michael's car out was enough of that for one day.

He thought about it. 'About forty or fifty? Everyone in the village and from the farms comes and they'll eat at least two of them each, I would have thought. Mrs Jackson used to take a big, flat wicker basket of them down – I think it's still hanging up in the scullery.'

'Well, baking those should take up quite a big chunk of

tomorrow,' I commented, as we got to the lodge and he turned to leave me. It was quite dark in the last shadows cast by the pine trees, and the sun hadn't finished thawing the crazy-paving path to the front door. This was a fact I only *truly* appreciated when I skidded on the half-frozen slush and came crashing down hard on my derrière. After the first moment of shock, it was *really* painful and brought a rush of tears to my eyes.

Jude scooped me up as if I weighed nothing and, taking the key from my hand, carried me into the lodge and deposited me on the sofa.

'My bum's soggy, I'll make the sofa wet,' I protested, getting straight back up again. 'Ouch, that really jarred me all the way up my back!'

'I hope you're going to be all right,' he said, looking at me with surprising anxiety. 'I mean, you should be more careful in your condition and think about the baby, even if it *is* early days yet.'

'Baby, what baby?' I demanded blankly, staring at him wide-eyed and thinking he'd run mad. 'What on earth are you talking about, Jude?'

'Look, Holly, I saw that pregnancy and childcare book you got on Christmas Day, so I know you're expecting.'

'Oh – *that*!'

'I suppose the father's that Sam character you've mentioned a couple of times? And I expect it was another reason why you were so interested in finding out about your real grandfather – it takes a lot of pregnant women that way, I think. Does Michael know?'

'Hello – did I hear my name?' said Michael, putting his head round the door at this inauspicious moment. Then he saw us, inches apart and staring inimically at each other, and looked embarrassed.

'How did *you* get here?' I exclaimed.

'I thought I ought to drive my car up and down the drive

for ten minutes to charge the battery up,' he explained, 'and then the door of the lodge was wide open, which seemed a bit weird.'

'Come right in,' invited Jude, looking particularly grim, rather than his everyday version. 'I was just asking Holly if you knew she was pregnant?'

'I beg your pardon?' Michael said.

'Of course he doesn't know, you halfwit – because there *is* no pregnancy,' I snapped.

'You're *not* pregnant?' Jude gave me a searching look. 'But – why the book then?'

'If it's any of your business, which it isn't, I've decided that this spring I'm going to try for a baby, using AI.'

'AI?'

'Artificial insemination.'

'You couldn't do it any other way?' he asked incredulously. 'What's the matter with the men where you live?'

'Of course I could, but I didn't *want* to do it any other way!'

'Won't Michael oblige? After all, you two seem to be thick as thieves – that's why I asked if you'd told him when I thought you were pregnant.'

'Look, Jude,' said Michael patiently. 'Holly and I have become good friends, but that's all there is to it – and all there ever will be. And I'll tell you why: it's because I'm gay. Holly already knows.'

'You're *gay*?'

'Yes, but I'm not officially out,' he qualified, 'only to close friends.'

'But – you were married. You've got a little girl!'

'That was a mistake.'

'Right . . . But then, why the secrecy?'

'I've already explained to Holly: I'd feel weird doing male romantic leads with everyone knowing. I'll come out officially when I'm past it.'

'You're *gay*,' Jude repeated . . . And then one of those sudden smiles transformed his face. 'That's *wonderful*.'

'Thank you for your support,' Michael said dryly.

Jude's smile turned into a wicked grin. 'But poor Coco! Flogging a dead horse.'

'Poor *Michael*, you mean!' I said indignantly. 'You and Guy threw him to the wolves all right.'

'Sorry,' he apologised, not sounding very.

'That's all right,' said Michael. 'Well, I'll leave you two to it and go back to the car – I left the engine running. I can probably get out tomorrow,' he added awkwardly.

'Oh, stay as long as you like,' Jude said expansively, his good humour restored.

'I'll hitch a lift back up to the house with you,' I said quickly. 'I just slipped on the ice and it's painful. I'll probably have some impressive bruises on my backside by morning.'

'Okay,' he said and Jude went off to the studio while I fetched the saffron and then carefully locked the door.

'Phew, I feel so much safer now Jude knows my little secret,' Michael admitted, turning the car and heading for home. 'I thought he was going to spoil my good looks one of these days. Are you *really* going to try AI, Holly?'

'Yes, I made up my mind to go it alone, before I came here,' I explained. 'I knew I wouldn't ever find another man like Alan.'

'Perhaps not, but you might find someone very different, if you looked . . . like Jude,' he suggested.

'He's certainly *different* all right, and he brings out the worst in me.'

'You're attracted to each other, that's a start.'

'That's just a physical thing . . . and anyway, even if it wasn't, I think our family relationship is too close for anything else.'

'Right . . . well.' He gave me another charming sideways smile. 'In that case, there's always me if you want a volunteer donor that you actually know – and I can tell you from my daughter, I make *very* nice babies! Only for God's sake don't tell Jude I volunteered!'

'That's really sweet of you,' I said, touched. 'I'll bear it in mind.'

Chapter 38: Photo-Finish

The baby arrived, thankfully late and quite small, but healthy.
It is a girl and we have called her Anne. She is very precious
to both of us and Joseph dotes on her as if she were his own.
He says she is a gift from God.

January, 1945

Gran's journal slowly peters out soon after the baby – my mother
– arrived, but I expect she found other things to occupy her time
with and was too busy. I knew she'd been a very active minister's
wife.

I was still quite stiff and sore from my fall and my bum
was probably black and blue – but also maybe green, from
the liniment Becca gave me to put on after a long, hot soak in the
bath. She said she swore by it, so I gave it a go even though it
smelt very odd and I suspected it was designed for horses.
It certainly seemed to take a lot of the soreness out. I ought to
try it on my fetlocks after a hard day in the kitchen!

I wasn't quite so quick off the mark as usual going downstairs
and I knew Jude had beaten me to it, because I heard him down
in the courtyard as I was getting dressed. He'd cleaned out the
sitting-room fire, too, when I checked . . . and there was just one
small, tantalising corner of the jigsaw left to do. Before I knew
it, the pieces were snapped into place, and the Victorian Christmas
scene complete.

I'd put saffron in water to steep overnight for the Revel Cakes, and the liquid was a beautiful golden yellow. When I'd made myself a cup of coffee, I got out the biggest mixing bowl, a vast affair with a blue-glazed inside, and made the dough. Kneading it energetically for ten minutes released quite a bit of bottled-up emotion and was probably very therapeutic. Jude came back in while I was pummelling and looked at me with some surprise.

'Revel Cakes,' I explained, 'They're a sort of lightly-fruited spiced bread, really, so the yeast needs to work for two or three hours at least, before I make them.'

I dropped the yeasty yellow mass into the bowl, covered it in cling film and set it near the Aga to rise.

'Sorry I got the wrong end of the stick yesterday,' he apologised, putting the kettle on and making more coffee without being asked, one of his main early morning assets, while I started on my next task, a hearty winter casserole of venison for dinner tonight, which we would have with jacket potatoes from Henry's store, followed by a baked custard. This was apparently Noël's favourite dessert, just as it had been my Gran's.

'You certainly jumped to some strange conclusions about me – but then, you're always doing that!'

'You're right,' he admitted. 'I've misjudged you all along. But this time the truth is even weirder! Holly, I can't believe you're *seriously* going to go it alone and have a baby by AI! You can't have thought—'

'I've thought of *everything*,' I interrupted. 'I have it all planned – and it's none of your business anyway, is it?'

He sighed and ran his fingers through his dark hair, which was starting to curl, being in need of cutting. 'It feels like it is – but we can discuss it later.'

'No, we can't: I'm going to be busy all day and then I'll have to pack.'

'But, Holly, you don't really intend to dash off tomorrow morning if the roads are cleared, do you? Why not stay for the

Revels? It seems silly to miss them now and the family will be *really* disappointed if you aren't there. You could stay one extra night, couldn't you?'

I looked at him and weakened slightly, because I so desperately wanted to see them now I'd heard so much about them . . . especially Jude as Saint George!

'I suppose I *could* . . . But I don't have to stay on, I can pack my car and leave right after it's over, like Michael's doing.'

'But he's only driving as far as his friend's place near Leeds tomorrow night, and you'll have a much longer drive. Anyway, if you leave immediately, you'll miss all the fun.'

'What kind of fun?' I asked suspiciously, remembering Sharon's hints of some kind of Wicker Woman sacrifice.

'Well, the wassail, for a start.'

'Wassail?'

'A sort of hot apple and ale punch that Nancy brews up.'

'Oh yes, I think she did mention that.'

'And Old Nan, Richard and Henry will all expect you to be there too, right to the end with the rest of the family. So you see, you might as well stay over that night.'

That brief but wonderful smile flashed across his face like a rare comet and I felt my willpower dissolving faster than sugar in hot water . . .

One more night couldn't hurt, could it?

'Okay,' I heard myself say.

'Good.' He looked pleased, but that was possibly because he knew he was going to get one extra well-cooked dinner before he was forced back onto his usual diet of convenience foods.

He started off cooking bacon for breakfast while I finished the casserole and put it in the slow oven. The pot custard could go in later, when I baked the Revel Cakes, and possibly a carrot cake – goodness knows, we had enough of those, since Henry was clearly the Carrot King.

For once, everyone else came down for breakfast at more or

less the same time, except Coco, who arrived late demanding black coffee – though I made her eat an omelette too – and then went back up to finish her packing. You'd have thought she'd already have done it, if she was so desperate to leave!

Guy set off in his big Chelsea tractor right after breakfast with Coco, her white coat a testament to my laundering skills, but her hat still a trifle manky. She'd made it so unendearingly plain that she couldn't wait to shake the dust of the place off her stilettos that we all gathered outside, prepared to wave her off with *huge* enthusiasm.

'Goodbye, Horlicks!' Jess called gaily, but she pretended she hadn't heard.

Guy kissed everyone goodbye before he got in, including me, and wished me good luck, though I don't know why he thought I would need it more than anyone else.

'And by the way, I forgive you for doing the last bit of jigsaw!' he added.

'It was too tempting and I didn't think you'd have time this morning. But now Jude can take it back to Oriel's shop and get half the price refunded.'

'Thrift is clearly your middle name,' Jude said to me with amusement as we waved goodbye to the vanishing people-carrier. 'Are you going to come down to the studio later?'

'I could walk down with your lunch early, but I won't be able to stop – I'll need to get back and start making fifty fiddly little spiral Revel Cakes. The dough will have risen by then.'

Or at least, I *hoped* it would.

I made my pot custards and the carrot cake, went out to have a long talk over the fence with Lady, then gave Merlin a good brushing in the tackroom, which would be his last before I left.

That thought made me feel sad: I'd become so attached to

381

him that I would be lost without my faithful shadow following me about. I'd miss Lady, too, and even Billy . . .

We had an early lunch, which Jess didn't eat a lot of, due to her having searched out and devoured every last remaining chocolate decoration on the tree while everyone else was occupied. The older members of the party had been closeted in the morning room with *Road to Rio* and Michael, who is house-trained, had washed, dried and pressed his laundry in the utility room.

I was so busy I should have asked Jess or Michael to take Jude's lunch down to the studio for me, but instead found myself drawn down there one last time, like iron filings to a magnet.

And I was glad I had, because the sculpture was really taking shape! It looked a bit as though a tornado had whirled huge metal leaves into the semblance of a horse and woman, rather than having been purposely constructed: I suppose that was what Jude intended?

He was deeply absorbed in what he was doing and I put the basket down where he would spot it when he returned to Earth and tiptoed away – or as much as you *can* tiptoe when wearing wellies.

Rolling dough into fifty small sausages, winding them into tight spirals and sprinkling them with chopped candied peel and sugar took *forever*.

Just as I was transferring the last lot from an oiled muffin tin to the cooling rack, Noël popped in to tell me that their housekeeper, Edwina, had managed to get through in her small estate car, bringing fresh groceries for both them and Becca, so I made a tray of tea and some of the carrot cake and took it through to the sitting room.

Edwina was a spare, middle-aged woman with severely scraped-back sandy hair and the expression of a martial marmoset. She seemed to have them all organised for their own good, even Tilda, and I could see she was very efficient.

'I found Jude in his studio and he told me what happened and that you were all up here,' she said. 'I've filled your fridge and freezer, Becca, and you owe me fifty-seven pounds and eighty-five pence – the receipt's on the worktop by the microwave.'

'Oh, thank you, Edwina,' Becca said gratefully. 'I'll ride Nutkin home after breakfast tomorrow, and then perhaps someone could drop my bags off later?'

'I expect Jude will,' Noël said.

'Jude suggested you and Tilda stay here tonight and come home in the morning and I said it was a good idea,' Edwina said. 'It'll give me a chance to take down the decorations and have a good clean through.'

'Oh, good,' Noël said. 'Holly's made a custard tart for tonight and I was looking forward to it.'

Dinner being sorted, apart from popping the ready-scrubbed jacket potatoes in the oven, I went up early to change into my red velvet dress: this was, after all, the last family dinner I would have here. I thought I might as well make a bit of effort.

And, hot on the heels of that thought, it suddenly dawned on me that I would be alone at Old Place with Jude tomorrow night – apart from Merlin and Lady and Billy, of course . . . I can't think why I hadn't realised that before! But still, he would be in one wing, and I the other . . .

There was still lots of time, so I started packing a few things together, like my laptop and cookbook notes, and bundling Gran's journals back into the trunk again . . . though first I reread the last entry. And then, for some reason, it occurred to me to turn the page and there I found another tiny black and white photo, fixed in with a sort of gummed paper hinge.

N with his parents, she'd written underneath. *He showed it to me, then must have dropped it, for I found it one day after he had gone then slipped it into my bag and forgot about it.*

On succeeding pages she'd later added one or two more random entries, mainly to mark tragic events – and hadn't she already had enough to bear? The one about my mother made me cry:

> *It was very hard to lose my only child and a cruel blow to Joseph. But he said we must accept God's will and not see it as a punishment for any wrongdoing, for he firmly believed that the Almighty was not a vengeful God.*
>
> *December 1972*

'Holly's staying until the day after tomorrow,' Jude told everyone at dinner.

'Oh, good. And then you will be back again soon, now you have found us, won't you, m'dear?' asked Noël.

'Of course, I'll miss you all,' I said, though there was little likelihood I would ever see them again . . .

'Easter,' he suggested, 'if not before.'

'There isn't an Easter Revel too, is there?'

'No, only a little pace egging, that kind of thing,' he said vaguely. 'But you're one of the family now, you should be here.'

'That reminds me,' I said, picking up the photo, which I'd put inside a folded bit of card next to my plate. 'I found another picture stuck into the last of Gran's journals – it's Ned again, with your parents.'

I handed the photograph to Noël and he nodded. 'Oh, yes – I remember this picture of Ned being taken. It was just after he came to live with us.'

'What do you mean, "live with us"?' asked Jude puzzled. 'Where else would he live?'

'He means after Ned was orphaned,' Becca said helpfully.

'No, I don't know,' Jude exclaimed. 'What on earth are you all talking about?'

'I thought you knew – my parents adopted Ned, who was a

second cousin. He'd have been two or three years younger than Jess at the time,' Noël said.

'So . . . Holly is only the granddaughter of a *connection* of the Martlands?' Jude said, astounded.

'Well, he *was* a Martland all right, anyone could see that, though through the distaff line, and we always thought of him as our brother. But yes – and actually, I suppose that accounts for why Holly looks like him more than anyone else in the family.'

'Seems like it,' said Jude. 'Well, well!'

Jess asked, puzzled, 'So is Holly still my auntie, then?'

'Nominally, but the family connection by blood is so diluted it's transparent,' Jude said cheerfully.

'But she still is, and always will be, a member of this family,' Noël said and then, while I slowly digested the implications of his revelation, he meandered on about the Revels and how my arrival had been the end of one thing and the beginning of something new, just as the Revels symbolised the end of the old year and the start of the next.

'And then next Christmas, we'll all be together again, a new cycle completed,' he said.

'Except Coco, I hope,' Tilda put in acerbically.

'She wasn't so bad in the end, m'dear.'

'Huh!' Tilda said inelegantly.

'And me,' said Michael, who had been interestedly listening, 'I won't be here.'

'Oh, you'll always be welcome, too,' Jude told him, 'I feel you're quite one of the family,' and Michael grinned at him.

'Uncle Jude, if you and Holly aren't really cousins, does that mean—' began Jess, but I hastily diverted her by appealing to her greed.

'Jess, why don't you go and fetch that box of Chocolate Wishes that the Chirks left? I'd forgotten all about them. They're sort of a chocolate fortune cookie.'

'Oh *yes*!' she squealed, running out of the room.

The wish inside mine said, *Follow your heart: you are already in the place you were meant to be.*

If the chocolate hadn't already been moulded together, I would have suspected Jess of writing it herself and putting it in there.

'So we're not even kissing cousins any more – or perhaps this means that we *are*?' Jude said, following me into the kitchen later while I was stashing a load of dirty crockery in the dishwasher.

I turned to find him standing too close for comfort and looking down at me very seriously.

'It's good news anyway, because ever since we kissed, I can't stop thinking about you and you're driving me mad!'

'You're driving me mad too, Jude Martland, but *not* in a good way!' I snapped, on the defensive as usual. But this time I knew it was because I didn't want my heart breaking again – and Jude could do just that, if I let him.

That sudden smile appeared. 'Couldn't we try that kiss again? You might change your mind!'

'No! I've had such a rollercoaster of a journey finding out about Gran – and now this, to end it all! I don't know what I think any more about *anything*: I'm *totally* confused.'

'Poor Holly,' he said sympathetically – and just then Jess burst in to ask if either of us wanted the last Chocolate Wish.

'No, I think I just got the answer I wanted from mine,' Jude told her.

Chapter 39: Signs and Portents

Right at the end of her journal, in an entry dated simply 'Christmas 2001', Gran had written very poignantly:

It is poor Holly's turn to suffer a great loss – that of her husband. But she is still young and I pray that one day she will find long and lasting happiness with someone else.

Just as I once knew, without the shadow of a doubt, that God still had a purpose for me, I am certain that my prayers for Holly will be answered, like a True Cross on the sampler of my life.

I don't think having my heart broken by another Martland is quite what Gran was praying for and Jude certainly didn't fit into the pattern of *my* life sampler. In fact, he was more in the nature of a huge, tangled knot, rather than a True Cross, and I'm sure she herself would have described him as a great streak of nowt – I could hear her saying it now.

What on earth was I thinking of, agreeing to stay on tomorrow, for Twelfth Night?

Becca got up early this morning, which I was grateful for, since it meant I wasn't left alone with Jude. After a largely sleepless night I still felt just as confused about my feelings for him – and about *his* intentions.

When they came back in from the stables, bringing that now-familiar sweet smell of horses with them, Jude didn't linger helpfully in the kitchen, but went off to shower and change and by the time he'd come down again the rest of the party had started to appear, too.

There was that strange last-day-of-the-house-party feel about things that I was familiar with at second-hand: a reluctance to leave, mingled with looking forward to being home. But since I shared it for once, I found it unsettling . . .

'We didn't put the horses out first thing, since Becca and Nutkin are off after breakfast,' Jude said, constructing a giant egg and bacon sandwich using a large, floury bap.

'We thought they might as well spend a little time together in the stable before we go, then Jude can put Lady and Billy out in the paddock,' Becca said. 'I mucked out yesterday, so a bit of a clean-up should do the trick.'

'Yes, I'll do that, then drop your bags off afterwards,' Jude agreed.

'And Edwina will come to fetch us shortly, too,' Noël said.

Tilda had actually come down for breakfast, and I thought that now Edwina was back to look after them, they were quite happy to go home – even if Jess would clearly rather have stayed at Old Place!

'I could stay tonight, at least, couldn't I?' she wheedled. 'It's Holly's *last* night!'

'Of course, if your Uncle Jude agrees,' I said quickly and he gave me one of his more unreadable stares.

'Your Uncle Jude is entitled to a bit of peace occasionally!' he told her.

'Ooh! You want to be alone with Holly!' Jess exclaimed with an air of discovery and I felt myself go pink.

'I do, but I can't imagine how you guessed,' he said sardonically.

'Jess; don't tease,' Tilda said. 'Of course you are coming back to the lodge with us.'

'We'll all be meeting up at the Revels later in the day, anyway,' Noël pointed out. 'I can hardly wait!'

Once they had gone, the house felt strangely empty. I expect Lady and Billy were already missing Nutkin, too.

Jude was busy helping to ferry luggage about and then cleaning out Nutkin's empty loosebox and Michael, who had already packed, kept me company in the kitchen while I was doing a few last-minute jobs.

I decided on some of the turkey curry as an easy dinner for tonight and took that out to defrost, then froze lots of single portions of leftover venison casserole (I'd made a double quantity, especially), with easy heating instructions written on the lids: Jude's diet before I came was *dreadful* and I didn't want him to lapse entirely as soon as I'd gone . . .

It was odd with just the three of us eating lunch in the kitchen at the big table and I think Michael felt a bit of a gooseberry, even though I was glad he was there – and Jude didn't seem to mind at all! In fact, he seemed amazingly cheerful, so perhaps he actually preferred being alone and now couldn't wait to have the place to himself?

'Could you take Holly down to the Revels with you this afternoon, Michael?' Jude asked. 'Only I have to go early to get ready and Edwina will drive Noël, Tilda and Jess there.'

'If you've got room for that enormous basket of Revel Cakes, too?' I said. 'Otherwise I'll take my car.'

'No problem: they can go on the back seat,' he said. 'My bags all fit in the boot.'

'What about Merlin? I presume he stays here?' I asked Jude.

'Yes, he wouldn't like all the noise.'

He vanished after lunch, but came downstairs later with an armful of mumming costumes from the attic, which he stowed carefully in his Land Rover before driving off with a casual, 'See you both later!'

His mind seemed to be elsewhere: but then, with Jude, I have learned that this is *not* unusual.

I changed into my red dress, boots and long winter coat for the occasion, with the bright green scarf Laura had given me . . . in fact, if we got down to the village early enough, I hoped to get a chance to slip away and ring her, because I really *needed* to talk to her!

When I carried the huge basket of Revel Cakes into the snug of the Auld Christmas, Tilda, Noël, Becca and Old Nan were already there in front of the fire, but there was no sign of the usual inhabitant. He was probably off donning his costume.

'Where's Jess?' I asked.

'Gone to fetch Nan's distance glasses, she left them behind,' Tilda explained. 'And Edwina's gone to see Oriel – they are old friends, but she will be back in good time for the start. We old things sit outside, well wrapped up, you know.'

'I wondered who the chairs were for,' Michael said.

'I don't want to sit out: I wish I could still take part,' Noël said wistfully.

'I feel a bit left out, too,' Michael agreed, 'but I expect that's the actor in me!'

Nancy was gathering ingredients by the vast vat in which she intended mixing the wassail and I went to see what she was putting into it.

'I've another panful mixed ready in the kitchen,' she told me. 'It's best to be prepared early.'

'Yes, I've always found that a good plan in life, too,' I said, though the more I thought about it, the less prepared I felt to spend a night alone at Old Place with Jude Martland!

'This thing is insulated,' she said, banging the side of the vast tub with a wooden spoon the size of a small paddle. 'They used to keep the wassail hot by sticking red-hot pokers into it, but times have changed and this is much easier.'

'It smells like a fairly heady mix – what's in it?'

'Ale, cloudy apple juice and a roasted apple or two, cinnamon and nutmeg . . . A baby could drink it,' she assured me. 'But it keeps everyone warm and gives them stamina.'

'Stamina?'

'Yes, for the dancing.'

'Right . . .' I said, thinking that that sounded pretty harmless. 'Well, I'm just slipping across to the church for a few minutes – I want to ring a friend and there's a good signal in the porch.'

'I'd have suggested the barn, you get a pretty good signal there, too, but that's where they're all getting their costumes on. I hope they've remembered to make the circlets: I wonder if *you* will get one this year?' She eyed me thoughtfully.

What circlets? I wondered, as I dashed across to the little church and called Laura's number, hoping desperately that she would answer. When she did, I barely let her get a word in before pouring out the news of my latest discovery.

'Laura, I'm *not* Jude's cousin after all! Well, actually, I suppose I am, but so many times removed I'm probably just as much cousin to half of Little Mumming!'

'What do you mean?'

I explained about Ned, my grandfather, having been adopted by the Martlands and she said, 'Great! So now your little Puritan soul has been satisfied, you're free to lust after Jude?'

'And vice versa – not that the thought that we were related seemed to be holding him back from making a move on me before.'

'There you are then, go for it,' she encouraged me. 'I can tell you want to.'

'Yes,' I admitted, 'only I don't know what he wants!'

'I think I could make a guess,' she said dryly.

'Yes, but he's already made it plain he doesn't want to fall in love again and neither do I. But on the other hand, I'm not a light-affair sort of person, am I, let alone a one-night-stand person? And . . . well, he's *difficult*. There's an attraction between us, there's no denying that, but we argue and snap at each other all the time and although he did say once he'd like me to stay on, I don't know if he wanted me as cook, bottle washer and unpaid artist's model, or *what*!'

'*What*, I should think, by the sound of it,' she said, amused. 'Why not just go with the flow tonight and see what happens? Put your Strange Baptist upbringing and all those carefully-worked-out life plans to one side, and go off-piste.'

'You're advising me to have a night of mad passion?'

'If it pans out that way and you want to. Then you can just walk away tomorrow . . . or not. Go for it!' she encouraged.

'I'm afraid, if I do, I might get hurt,' I confessed.

'That's better than keeping your heart in a block of ice for the rest of your life, isn't it?'

'I think you're quite mad!' I said, though I could feel a bit of a smile trying to drag up the corners of my mouth. 'You know, Gran said she hoped I'd meet another nice man and settle down, it was at the back of her last journal.'

'There you are, then.'

'I'm sure Jude Martland isn't thinking about settling down and anyway, he's not really nice, he's surly and bossy most of the time.'

'Artistic temperament?' she suggested. 'And he sounds as if he has lots of good things going for him too. He loves his animals, for a start.'

'I suppose so,' I conceded reluctantly, and sighed. 'Not only the circumstances but the signs and portents seem to be conspiring against me, too: we had some Chocolate Wishes after dinner last night, and the message in mine implied I'd found what I was looking for.'

'So, what are you waiting for?'

'Ah, but I don't believe in signs and portents.'

'Then perhaps you ought to start!' she told me. 'Where's Jude now?'

'I haven't seen him since after lunch and he was a bit distant: but then, he was probably psyching himself up for his performance later.'

'Sounds promising!'

'His performance in the Revels, I meant, idiot,' I said. 'He's Saint George . . . and speaking of the Revels, I'd better get back: it must be about to start soon.'

'Call me tomorrow, let me know you're okay,' she said more seriously.

'I'll be back tomorrow, so you will be able to see for yourself,' I reminded her.

By now it was mid-afternoon and the light was just starting to fade. People had begun to gather around the green and in front of the pub, where the vat of wassail had been carried out and set on a sturdy table, together with my huge basket of Revel Cakes.

Tilda, Noël and Old Nan were enthroned nearby, wrapped in tartan travelling rugs and fussed over by Edwina, but I went with Becca, Nancy, Jess and Michael to stand on the grass with the other spectators after we'd had a warming beaker of wassail, though by then Jess was sulking because Nancy wouldn't let her have any.

The crowd murmured and then hushed as a torch was put to the big bonfire and carried round to light the circle of twelve braziers spiked into the ground. Now I noticed for the first time that there was also an inner ring of strangely-wrought metal horses' heads, unmistakably Jude's work, to which had been attached bunches of holly, ivy and mistletoe and red bits of cloth that stirred in the breeze: the whole green looked like a barbaric henge of fire.

Then, approaching from the direction of the barn behind the

pub, I heard the sound of a fiddle and Richard appeared, playing a lively air as he walked and dressed in a long green fur-edged velvet robe over (I hoped) lots of warm clothes.

Following him into the circle of light from the braziers jogged six Morris Men dressed in traditional white, with bells jingling and red ribbons flying, but carrying long swords and with painted black masks across their faces, which gave them a strange, slightly sinister look.

'Those are the Rappers,' Becca whispered.

I recognised George Froggat and Nancy's husband, Will, but not the rest. They formed a set and danced, using their swords a bit like staves (so I hoped they were blunt!), and then fell back into two rows, leaving the centre free for the strange figures who now came forward in procession, each introducing himself to the spectators with a short, rhyming couplet.

There was Auld Man Christmas, the diminutive Nicholas Dagger, in a blue velvet robe, an evergreen crown, and carrying a club almost as large as he was; a scary Red Hoss, painted scarlet and with jaws that could open and close with a loud snap; the Dragon, green and leathery, with a fearsome head and long tail that dragged on the ground and the strange Man-Woman figure. From the front he – or perhaps that should be *it* – looked just like the Rappers in white shirt and trousers and straw hat; but then he turned around, revealing a woman's mask over the back of his head and a long skirt.

'That's Liam as the Man-Woman,' giggled Jess, as he began to circle round, handing out circlets of ivy and mistletoe to any woman who seemed to catch his fancy, which included an excited Jess, Nancy and Oriel Comfort. But he didn't give *me* one and I felt quite left out!

Richard stopped playing for long enough to bow and introduce himself to the crowd as the Doctor. And then, finally, Jude in his guise as Saint George walked out of the darkness to large cheers: a huge and strangely fearsome figure, wearing a white surcoat with a red cross and a helmet with a nosepiece. He was carrying an even bigger sword than the Rappers . . . and in his other hand, a gilded, sparkling circlet of ivy and mistletoe. He strode over and placed the circlet on my head, and I was so surprised by this that I expect my jaw fell lower than Red Hoss's (who was Henry, by the way – I'd spotted him inside when he snapped his jaws in my face).

Then Jude walked back to the middle of the circle while Nancy, who was standing nearby, giggled. 'He used to give that to me, not having a lady of his own!'

'*I am St George*,' boomed Jude, '*a bold and brave knight. In Egypt with a dragon, I did fight.*'

'Why Egypt?' I whispered to Becca.

'The Crusades made some of the elements change: other places have Saint George kill a Turkish knight, but we carried on with the Dragon – and here it comes.'

From somewhere inside the great, leathery beast a voice that was unmistakably young Ben's from Weasel Pot shouted, after a couple of opening roars:

'*I am the Dragon*
With a roar I'll slay
And yon bold knight
With his life will pay!'

Then he and Jude rushed at each other and a mock fight ensued – only for the Dragon to kill Saint George. The crowd gave a united groan.

'That shouldn't happen, should it?' I asked Becca worriedly, looking at Jude stretched out on the grass.

'It's all right,' whispered Jess, who had edged up beside me. 'Wait and see!'

Auld Man Christmas, Red Hoss and the Man-Woman, whose roles had so far consisted of working the crowds and scaring small children into fits, now turned inwards to face the tragic scene and said as one:

'Alas, poor Saint George!'

The Dragon moved into the middle of the circle, leaving poor Jude lying on the cold half-thawed turf, though fairly near the bonfire, so I hoped he wouldn't entirely freeze to death.

Richard struck up another air on the fiddle and the six Rappers began to dance again, this time their swords weaving together, to form a series of intricate patterns that culminated in a sort of knot with a hole in its centre. The Dragon approached – and then suddenly they lowered the knot of swords over its head, tightened it with a scraping clash of metal – and the Dragon's head flew off, to land with a soggy thump near my feet.

I nearly had a heart attack and it was a huge relief when I realised it was hollow!

The dancers fell back into two rows again, revealing the headless Dragon lying on the ground, and there was a round of applause and some cheers.

Richard swung round on his heel and pointed his violin at the lifeless Saint George, declaiming loudly:

'I am the Doctor
Be not affright
With my trusty potion
I'll put all right!'

Then he took a small bottle out of his pocket and pretended to sprinkle something over the recumbent knight. I watched, riveted, as Jude slowly stirred, sat up and then got to his feet and bowed, to more rapturous applause.

'That's it – come on!' Becca said, and she and Jess and everyone else rushed into the circle and joined hands, dragging me with them. Somehow in the crush I found myself with Jude on my left and the Dragon, without his head but with his tail looped over his arm, on my right, as we all joined hands and danced round. I could see Michael, Jess and Becca among the circle of dancers – and George, holding Oriel's hand. She looked flushed and happy, her ivy and mistletoe circlet tipped over one eye.

No-one else seemed to have a gilded one . . . and it was just as well that Jude had pushed it down firmly onto my head, because he suddenly whirled me round and round until I was too breathless to go on.

'It's no use, I'll have to have a rest!' I begged, panting, and he laughed and walked with me over to the pub, his arm still around my waist, though he took his rather scary helmet off first: that was a bit of a relief. We stood talking to Noël, Tilda and Old Nan and I accepted a beaker of the warming punch . . . and then possibly another. In fact, I lost count of how much I'd had, but it tasted innocuously of warm apples and Nancy *had* said you could give it to a baby . . .

My foot started to tap in time to the music and Jude's arm tightened around me a little as Nancy took the beaker from my hand and replaced it with a fresh one.

'Nancy,' I said suspiciously, focusing on her cheerful, flushed face with an effort, 'when you said you could give this to a baby, were you serious?'

'Yes, if you wanted it to go to sleep for a couple of hours. Maybe not, these days though, when they've even taken the alcohol out of gripewater.'

Richard played the music for what looked like a final mad bout of strip-the-willow, then handed his fiddle on to someone else and joined us.

Michael, who'd followed him, said, 'It's been really fascinating to watch. It's such an interesting mixture of pagan fertility ceremony and miracle play.'

'That's very astute of you,' said Richard. 'The red ribbons, holly, ivy and especially the mistletoe wreaths the women are given *are* all to do with rebirth and fertility.'

'And the triumph of good over evil, that's what the Saint George and the dragon part signifies,' Noël put in.

'Doesn't the pagan element bother you, Vicar?' Michael asked.

'Oh no,' he said cheerfully, his white hair blowing in the breeze.

It was certainly now starting to unsettle *me*, despite the soothing effects of large quantities of punch!

We waved Michael off, and then the actors in the Revels went to the barn to remove their costumes, reappearing in normal guise. By then, the last of the wassail and the Revel Cakes had been consumed and people started to disperse: some home, and some into the Auld Christmas. Edwina dragooned Tilda, Jess and Noël into the car and drove them back to the lodge, but Becca walked off home, a Revel Cake wrapped in a paper napkin in her pocket for later.

'They're supposed to be a lucky talisman if you keep it for the year,' she'd told me, 'but I think I'd rather eat it.' Then she'd looked at me and added, 'And perhaps you'd better eat something as soon as Jude gets you home, too: that wassail packs a lot more punch than you think.'

'That's because it *is* punch,' I said, and giggled.

'I'll look after her,' Jude promised, putting his arm around me again, probably because I was swaying slightly.

'Yes, *that's* what's worrying me,' Becca said grimly, and he laughed.

Chapter 40: Twelfth Night

Driving back with Jude I felt warm and cosy, but also strangely limp and boneless too.

'That was lovely,' I said dreamily.

Then the phone in my pocket rang, waking me slightly. 'Can you stop here? Only I'll lose the signal if you go past the lodge and it must be Laura.'

'Or Sam?' he snapped suspiciously, pulling in to the side of the lane.

'Why on earth would it be Sam?' I blinked at him, trying to focus. 'He doesn't even have my number.' I'd managed to dig out the phone by now and said, 'Hello?'

'Holly, are you there?' demanded a strident voice.

'Oh, it's you,' I sighed. 'Yes, I'm here, Ellen . . . but I'm not *entirely* with it.'

'Why, you're not ill, are you? Did Laura tell you about the London job? Only it's next week and I have to know now if you'll do it. You will, won't you?'

'Next week?' I murmured, drifting back off into a warm and sleepy haze.

Jude removed the phone from my limp grasp and demanded rudely, 'What do you want?'

I could hear Ellen quacking loudly.

'No,' he growled, 'she *can't* go and cook anywhere – she's

staying here.' And he clicked the phone off, shoved it back into my pocket, and started the engine again.

'That was a bit cavalier,' I protested, reviving slightly, 'and I'm *not* staying.'

'You can phone her back tomorrow if you want to, when you're fit to make decisions.'

Back at the house we went straight through to the kitchen, where Merlin was delighted to see us. Under the bright lights, Jude took me by the shoulders and stared worriedly down at me.

'I think I should sober you up with coffee, you're not used to our wassail. Or maybe you should just go to bed?'

'Yes, that's exactly what Laura said we should do,' I agreed dreamily.

'I'm getting to like the sound of this friend of yours more and more.' The corner of his mouth quirked up slightly.

'Are you? She's prettier than I am – small and blonde.'

'She might be pretty, but you're *beautiful* – and you're just the right height.'

'Only to a giant.'

'Lucky you've got one to hand then, isn't it?'

'And I don't need sobering, because I'm not drunk,' I told him. 'I just feel . . . good. Relaxed.' In fact, I relaxed right there and then against his broad chest and he sighed deeply and put his arms around me, leaning his cheek against my hair.

'That's nice,' I said, snuggling in a bit closer. 'Jude, when you keep saying you don't want me to go . . . are we talking permanent employment here? Or a quick fling? Only I don't—'

He gave me a slight shake and my mouth snapped shut. 'I'm talking marriage, you idiot! You, me – and children, too, if we're lucky. Which we *should* be after tonight.' The corner of his mouth quirked up with amusement. 'Saint George's wreath never fails – ask Nancy! She's had three of them, nine months to the day after a Revels.'

This dispelled the clouds of wassail slightly and I indignantly tried to push him away. 'You mean you and *Nancy*—'

'No, you idiot, Nancy and her *husband*.'

'Oh.' I relaxed against him again and he wrapped his arms closely around me. 'Did you mean that, about getting married?'

'Old Nan had another word with me about that Afghan she's knitting for us tonight – but anyway, I'm a marrying man and I fell in love with you the minute I set eyes on you. Only I didn't want to admit it, especially when I thought you were up to no good!'

'Well, I wasn't.'

'I know now, but I loved you anyway, though it might have made me a bit bad-tempered.'

'Just a bit – but perhaps trying to pretend to myself that I wasn't falling in love with you made *me* a little grumpy, too! But if we married, we'd fight all the time, wouldn't we?'

'Yes, I'm looking forward to it.'

'I haven't said yes, yet,' I pointed out. 'But I might, if only because I can't bear to be parted from Lady and Merlin.'

'You'd better,' he muttered, kissing me, and it quickly became clear that our last scorching kiss had been little more than a preliminary warm-up.

But when I came up for air, I tried to release myself. 'I'd better put the dinner in the oven, Jude: it's all ready, apart from cooking the rice and—'

'Forget it, you're not putting anything in the oven tonight,' he said, not letting go of me. 'But *I* might, if you tempt me too much.'

'That was *very* rude!' I told him seriously and he grinned.

'I only really want you for your cooking – and your lovely, poseable body,' he said, running his hands over it appreciatively. Then he kissed me again and I completely lost any interest in anything else, even food.

*   *   *

Later – much later, cosily snuggled up against him in his four-poster bed, I said severely, 'I can't think what I'm doing here! Falling for you was definitely *not* in my life-plan.'

'Then plan me into your schedule and write yourself a recipe with me as the main course,' he suggested.

'Just don't think I'll always play a meek Viola to your Orsino!' I warned him.

'You never did do that. But okay – I think our play is done.'

'Or maybe only the first act?' I said seriously. 'I'm starting to see a pattern here, with the end of one thing becoming the beginning of the next, just like Richard was saying earlier . . . Do you think that's mad?'

'No, but it might be the aftereffects of the wassail.'

He pulled me back into a crushing embrace and asked, hopefully, 'Time for a bit more Revelling?'

Read on for some delicious
recipes from Trisha

Recipes

Wassail

A very old punch of ale, apples and spices. It was popular throughout Christmas, especially on Twelfth Night. This will make about six small glasses: increase quantities as desired.

Ingredients:

1 pint of ale (500ml)
⅓ pint of apple juice
Juice and zest of an unwaxed lemon
1 tablespoon honey
¼ teaspoon each of ground ginger, nutmeg, cloves and cinnamon

Method:

Simmer the lemon juice and zest, apple juice and spices gently in a pan for about ten minutes, without letting it boil.

Add the ale and honey, stirring to dissolve, and heat through: again, be careful not to let it boil.

This is drunk warm and you can add a lemon slice to each glass/cup.

Ginger and Spice Christmas Tree Biscuits

These make a thin biscuit that will retain its crispness for quite a while on the tree; though if you make a double batch, you can keep some to nibble at in the biscuit tin, too!

Ingredients:

4oz (100g) butter
8oz (225g) plain flour
6oz (175g) soft brown sugar
1 small egg, beaten
1 level teaspoon of ground ginger
½ level teaspoon ground cinnamon
¼ teaspoon ground cloves (optional)

Method:

Sieve the flour and spices into a bowl and then add the butter, chopped into bits. Rub it into the flour between your thumb and fingers (as you do with shortcrust pastry).

When you have a mix like fine breadcrumbs, add the sugar and most of the egg, then knead lightly into a firm dough. Add the rest of the egg if necessary.

Put the dough in a bowl, cover with cling film and place in the fridge for at least half an hour. (This makes it easier to roll out and cut.)

Heat the oven to 190°C, 375°F, gas mark 5. Grease a couple of baking trays.

Roll the dough out fairly thinly on a lightly floured board, then cut out shapes as desired: you can get Christmas cutters, but gingerbread men also look good on the tree. If you just want round biscuits, then roll the dough into a long cylinder shape and slice thinly.

Pierce each biscuit so it can be hung from a thread or ribbon (I use a chopstick), then place on the baking tray, well spaced.

Bake for about ten minutes, until light golden brown at the edges – but keep an eye on them!

Remove and place on wire racks to cool.

I ice mine by mixing a little icing sugar and water with natural food colouring in egg cups (add water in drips, it needs to be quite thick) and then I use a small nylon paintbrush I keep just for this purpose (wash new ones before use) to blob, trickle and write on the biscuits. This is the fun bit . . . Allow to go hard.

Revel Cakes

Despite the name, these are actually a lightly fruited and spiced little bread roll. Holly soaked saffron in some of the water overnight to give them a yellow colour, though this is not vital. (But if you do, you will need to warm the water again next day before using.) She also added some chopped mixed peel to the dough.

Ingredients (for about twelve small buns – it can be doubled for a larger quantity):
13oz (375g) strong white flour
1 teaspoon caster sugar
7½ fl oz warm water (soak a couple of good pinches of saffron in 5 fl oz of it overnight if using)
1 teaspoon salt
¾ oz butter
½ teaspoon mixed spice
¾ sachet of fast dried yeast
3 oz (75g) chopped mixed peel

Method:
In a bowl or jug, mix the sugar, 2½ fl oz warm water and the yeast and allow to stand for five minutes or until frothy.

Sift the flour and salt into a large mixing bowl together with the spice. Rub in the butter, then make a well in the middle of the flour and pour in the yeast mixture and most of the rest of the warm water. Mix to a dough, using more water if needed.

Knead for ten minutes, then put the dough in a large oiled bowl, cover with cling film, and leave somewhere warm for approximately two hours, until it has at least doubled in size.

Put on a floured board and give it a quick thump or two to let out trapped air, then knead for two or three minutes. If using chopped peel, at this stage stretch the dough gently into a thick square and sprinkle the fruit into the middle. Fold the dough in over it, then knead as before for a couple of minutes.

Put it back in the bowl for ten minutes. Meanwhile, preheat the oven to 220°C, 425°F, gas mark 7. Grease baking trays or muffin tins.

On a floured surface, roll the dough into cylinders about six inches long and wind them round in spirals to make buns the way Holly did, then bake in muffin tins. Alternatively, form into small balls for ordinary rolls and place on a baking tray.

Cover trays with a tea towel and put in a warm place for half an hour, or until they have doubled in size. Bake for about fifteen minutes. When cooked they will be pale golden brown, feel lighter and sound slightly hollow when tapped underneath.

Transfer to a wire rack to cool.